Not taking his ey—
wine, sipping th—
gown. Unfasten—
arouses me."

Not accustomed—
ingly, then submitted, fussing with the first closure, ultimately
freeing it, then she froze, unsure of how to proceed.

"The next, if you please."

The second one fell away.

"You're not wearing a corset, are you?"

She shook her head, but he hadn't needed to ask. The flow and
sway of her breasts jolted him . . .

"Finish with the buttons."

She swallowed, vacillated, then carried on with her task as he
avidly observed.

"Sit for me." He urged her backwards toward the sofa.

"Are we going to—"

"Not yet. I simply want to draw you."

They had all day, and he planned to prolong the pleasure . . . so
that when he actually progressed, they would both be burning
with unfulfilled passion . . .

ABSOLUTE PLEASURE

Cheryl Holt

St. Martin's Paperbacks

ABSOLUTE PLEASURE

Copyright © 2003 by Cheryl Holt.

ISBN: 0-312-98459-6

Printed in the United States of America

St. Martin's Paperbacks edition / February 2003

St. Martin's Paperbacks are published by St. Martin's Press, 175 Fifth Avenue, New York, NY 10010.

10 9 8 7 6 5 4 3 2

CHAPTER ONE

London, England, 1812

"EXQUISITE. Positively exquisite . . ."

Elizabeth stilled and cocked her head to the side, listening intently. The man's whispered adulation was murmured from nearby, and fondly pronounced, as though he was wooing a lady right in the middle of the crowded theater foyer. His diction was unusual, imbued with a hint of the exotic. Perhaps he was Italian or French.

"*Splendida.* Ravishing."

The male voice came again, closer this time and—if she didn't know better—had been uttered from directly behind her. She was dying to turn around, to probe the swarm of faces, in order to discover which pair of lovebirds had the audacity to carry on so affectionately in such a public place.

"Your skin is like silk. So smooth, so soft."

Her brows rose in amazement. No doubt about it, he was hovering immediately to her left. Why, she could feel his warm breath gliding across her nape! Her gown was stylishly designed, trimmed low across bosom and back, revealing a broad expanse of shoulder, arm, and chest, and the fiery puff of his exhalation shimmered over her collarbone and slithered down into her cleavage, settling on her breasts in a manner that was disconcerting and discomfiting.

Though the cramped entrance was stifling, the air hot

and stale with the crush of bodies proceeding toward the stairs and the box seats above, she shivered.

Who was he? And who was the woman with whom he was so enamored that he would risk an improper verbal display where anyone might hear?

Cautiously, she glanced over, not rotating in the slightest, but shifting only her eyes, eager to make out form and substance. When . . . there he was! A stranger, tall and indistinct, a lanky torso dressed in formal black. It was the second week of February, yet he was bronzed as though he'd tarried too long in the sun.

She wrenched her gaze to the stalled line before her, concentrating on putting one foot in front of the other.

But he'd seen her peeking! He laughed, a seductive chuckle that rumbled across her nerve endings and tickled her stomach, filling it with dancing butterflies. Embarrassed at being caught, she stoically stared toward the stairs, which now appeared miles distant and unattainable. An unwelcome flush reddened her cheeks.

"My glorious beauty"—his legs were brushing her skirts!—"please tell me your name so that if I perish in the next instant, I might die a happy man."

That foreign lilt, that fanciful flair in his enunciation, sent a chill down her spine. Was he talking to her?

Frantically, she searched the area around her, vainly hunting for his companion, but perceiving no one. There were dozens of women scattered across the bustling lobby but, at that very moment, she was surrounded by men. Her eyes widened with the stunning realization that she was the sole female he could possibly be addressing.

The bounder! What was he up to, accosting her? She cast about, seeking a familiar face—her father or some acquaintance—who would rescue her from the interloper's inappropriate advance, but there was nary a friend in sight.

Hoping she wouldn't be observed chatting with him, she nevertheless whipped around to confront him, to scare him off with a fierce look or, if necessary, to give him a thorough dressing-down that would make him desist and depart. Yet to her dismay, once she made the move, she couldn't express a single reprimand.

He was so beautiful—if such a term could be used to describe a man. His hair shone in the glittering candlelight. It was swept off his strong forehead, highlighting his aristocratic nose, his full mouth, his immaculate, tanned skin. He was resplendent, his features perfectly assembled, and he had the sort of countenance an artist might paint on the ceiling of a cathedral or carve into a block of swirled marble.

People pushed past, jostling them until he was bumped against her, and for some idiotic reason, her heart fluttered. His fabulous eyes, blue and keen and shrewd, were focused on her mouth, evaluating every nuance in painstaking detail. Leisurely, he examined her pursed lips, then slowly, methodically, he lifted his calculating gaze to hers.

"Gad, but even the blush on your cheeks is becoming."

Her color deepened, and the indecorous comment provided the fortitude she required to retort. "Are you speaking to me, sir?"

"*Assolutamente,*" he admitted without an ounce of repentance. "How could I resist?"

Elizabeth frowned and whipped away, trying to gain insight into the scoundrel's impertinent overture. Men never dared to waylay her. Her exalted station, as the only child of the Earl of Norwich, meant she was protected from unsuitable encounters. In fact, with the exception of a newly hired servant, she couldn't recall when she'd last conversed with someone to whom she hadn't been introduced.

The rogue next to her was impeccably dressed for the event, his clothes excellently tailored, his shirt starched and blindingly whitened, his cravat expertly tied. He seemed to be the finest gentleman, out on the town for an evening of entertainment, yet his conduct was far out of bounds, and he didn't grasp that he was acting in an uncouth fashion.

By her attire alone, he should have recognized that she

was inaccessible. From the expensive fabric of her gown, to the adroit coif of her auburn hair, to the priceless string of emeralds circling her neck, she was the very picture of an affluent, titled English lady, and therefore ruled by society's strict standards for interaction with the opposite sex.

Still, from his choice of words and the slight inflection in his voice, it was obvious that he was a foreigner, so in all fairness, maybe he didn't understand the serious breach he was committing. As she'd had scant occasion to prattle with unknown men, she wasn't certain how to go about educating him as to his lapse, and she decided not to try. The best resolution was to reach the stairs and, ultimately, the safety of her father's box.

"Don't glower so, milady," he urged gently, the fluid flow of his accented speech washing over her. "I mean you no harm. I'm merely enchanted by how lovely you are."

They were packed in with the other theatergoers like fish in a bucket, and each of his avowals was quietly declared, so no one else could hear him; she was sure of it. Another passerby jostled him, and through her ample layers of undergarments, petticoats, and skirts, she could feel his lean frame flattening the length of her backside.

Never before had she been wedged up against a man, and his adjacency instigated a curious medley of previously unexperienced sensations: of sentimental longing, but also a peculiar impression of physical yearning. Her body was attuned to his, as if it was extending out, craving to be merged with his more tightly.

Their odd arrangement instituted an informality that suggested a bond and partiality that was out of proportion to their actual circumstances. Puzzled by the stimulation his proximity invoked, she scooted away as much as she was able.

He countered by resting his fingers on the small of her back. The gesture was outlandish and totally indecent, but she didn't shake him off. It felt good. Shockingly, she couldn't remember when another person had held her hand or hugged her. Her sterile, barren environment was one of polite discourse and tepid exchanges, and nobody possessed an ounce of the zeal essential for tangible contact.

When had that happened? How had she grown so disconnected from others that the simple caress of a man's hand could burn through dress, corset, and chemise?

"Please go away," she decreed through clenched teeth.

"I've been watching you," he said. "From the instant you alighted from your carriage."

He'd been watching her? Was he insane?

Overt curiosity had her spinning in his direction. And conversing with him even though she'd rather have bitten off her tongue.

"To what end?" she couldn't preclude herself from inquiring.

"So that I might learn who you are," he unabashedly replied. "I had to find out."

His divine lips were only an inch from her own, and he was analyzing her, cataloging each trait, and missing no characteristic. His azure eyes bored into hers, then dropped to her mouth, once more, and she couldn't get past the perception that he was dying to kiss her, which was absurd.

As she'd never been kissed in her life, and had never had a man ogling her with anything vaguely resembling ardor, she couldn't deduce why such an astounding prospect might be conceivable, but in an internal, isolated, feminine part of her, she discerned his male intent: He wanted to kiss her, and bizarrely, she was wondering what it would be like.

What if he closed the gap that separated them? Remarkably, the brief fantasy did amazing things to her anatomy. Her pulse raced, her palms itched, and her breasts . . .

They swelled and expanded, the nipples instantly emphasized and erect. They rubbed against the confines of her corset; the lacing was too constricting, and she could barely inhale.

With a practiced flick of her wrist, she opened her fan

and whisked it back and forth, cooling her exposed surfaces, and giving her unruly hands something to do. Of a sudden, they were dangerously inclined to caress the nap of his debonair evening jacket, or mayhap to rest against the center of his chest.

Her inexplicable weakness was appalling, and she couldn't prevent herself from gaping at him in alarm. She was not a spontaneous person; she didn't pine away or fantasize over handsome dandies. Not even as an adolescent, when marriage and family were still a nebulous, oft-contemplated option. The corporeal cravings that induced others to ludicrous episodes of amorousness had never plagued her.

She was too sensible, too discriminating and rational, to be swayed by a comely appearance or masculine physique. Yet, in a matter of seconds, she was all but smitten by an attractive knave who'd done scarcely more than say hello.

Though she was loath to admit it, his whispered compliments were excessively gratifying. Sweet, endearing balms. It had been a long while since anyone had examined her and appreciated the woman lurking beneath the prudently poised exterior.

For years, she'd dawdled in her widowed father's shadow—as his hostess, his companion, his secretarial attendant—until she'd become a master at the art of blending in and never garnering attention for herself. She'd stooped so low in ceding to her father's wishes, needs, and commands, that she was little more than an extension of his illustrious self. Not a woman in her own right, but merely the earl's rather plain, unmarried, boring but efficient daughter.

How marvelous to have her eccentric swain behold another aspect of herself, someone better and more grand. She was secretly flattered, even though he was too bold by half; no sense in encouraging him.

"You're angry with me," he murmured, just when she would have turned away.

Indeed, she was piqued, but how had he guessed?

"As I don't know you, sir," she was compelled to mention, "how could I possibly feel anger or anything else toward you? Now, if you'll excuse me—"

"Gabriel," he interrupted.

The man's breeding was atrocious. Had he no discretion at all? He simply blurted out his identity like a common ruffian.

"Pardon?"

"My name is Gabriel Cristofore."

Italian. Of course, he would be.

The appellation rolled off his tongue, conjuring images of sun-drenched hills and turquoise oceans. Temperate, lazy days and fine red wine. Soft music and romantic suppers.

She'd always dreamed of visiting Italy, but she'd dutifully passed up the lone chance she'd once had to travel to the charming country. Shortly after she'd finished her formal education at age sixteen, her favorite teacher and several students had planned a scholarly tour, but she'd declined to go, succumbing to pressure from her father as he'd insisted that he couldn't manage without her for the six months she'd have been gone.

It still rankled that she hadn't taken that trip. There had been many opportunities lost due to her father's maneuvering and coercion. In many ways, he was like a spoiled, demanding infant, wanting her at his beck and call, with her entire energies devoted exclusively to his happiness.

At his behest, she'd abandoned numerous adventures, staying at home to supervise the mundane trivialities of his day-to-day affairs, until it seemed that all she ever did was tally her regrets.

As she stood there in that heated foyer, an ancient twenty-seven years old, and with nothing to show for her interval on earth but a decade of serving as a combination nanny and governess for her spoiled, overbearing tyrant of a father, she was swamped with a thriving discontentment she'd never previously noticed. She was chafing against restriction and constraint.

What she wouldn't give to throw off the shackles that fettered her, to live as she pleased, to be free of her father and the injunctions he imposed upon her?

The turbulence bubbling just below the surface baffled her. From where did this resentment emanate? Why hadn't she noted it before? Why was it abruptly pleading for acknowledgment?

Yes, she'd been disgruntled recently. With her father's unanticipated, hasty marriage to his seventeen-year-old child bride, Charlotte, everything had changed. The horrid, immature girl had inflicted herself into their once-peaceful residence. Who wouldn't be put out by the transformations? But apparently, Elizabeth's umbrage was more grievous than she'd suspected, and it played a much bigger role in her current condition than she'd ever supposed.

"Well, then—" She composed herself, swallowing down a wave of dissatisfaction that was not befitting and would get her nowhere, and she forced herself to the task at hand: ridding herself of her dapper nuisance. "Good-bye, *Mister* Cristofore."

"You're upset that I approached you." Not chastened in the least by her rudeness, he flashed a smile that lit up the room, blanking out all others who were present.

No one had ever looked at her like that before, as if she was alluring and desirable.

Against all volition and sanity, she reveled in that smile. The brilliance of it made her knees weak, and had her body slanting toward him with an impulsive aspiration to be nearer. She caught herself, but not before pondering why she was so eager to fall recklessly into his arms. The man exuded a wicked spell that was capturing her in its web.

Either that, or she was going mad.

"You're correct. I don't approve." She sounded snobbish and patronizing. "Your behavior is quite scandalous, and I can't fathom why you're so determined to harass me."

"Can't you?" He gawked at her as though she should have readily grasped his motives. "Your hair . . . the shading is so rich, so abundant. And your face . . . so impeccable. Your shape . . . so rounded, so generous, so womanly."

With each indiscreet reference, he waved his hand before her body, indicating the exact feature to which he referred, and she was positive that if they'd been alone, he'd have handled the places he'd mentioned. The inkling made her stir uncomfortably.

What would it be like to be touched intimately by him? She'd never previously contemplated such a drastic happenstance, and doing so produced a surge of uncontrollable fleshly excitement.

The red on her cheeks intensified to a striking crimson, and she furiously fanned herself. Striving for calm, she attempted to ignore his brazen assertions but, try as she might, she couldn't avoid ruminating on his description of her, which didn't fit with her own.

She regarded herself as average, as too full-figured and too dark-haired. In a culture where young misses were lauded for being blond and petite, she'd continually stuck out. At age thirteen, she had started to develop her amply endowed figure, and she'd felt gauche and inept. Her sensitivity over her shape had never abated. As a girl in the initial stages of courting, the oafish boys of high society had been hurtful and crude, and she'd braved her share of offense and discourtesy.

Her father had been the first to subtly suggest that, with her mediocre bearing, she might be better off eschewing marriage altogether. When he'd encouraged her to forgo the marriage market and the family it would have brought, she'd seized the chance.

The few instances when she'd actually voiced doubts as to her decision, her father had habitually contended that her resolution was for the best and, without a thought, she'd agreed. She'd clung to the solitude and beneficial routine that spinsterhood rendered.

In the humdrum monotony that constituted her life, she'd never questioned his conviction that she was ordinary. How oddly refreshing to be apprised of another point of view, even though the man's opinion as to her attributes was ludicrous. Was he blind?

"Every time you open your mouth," she said, "your remarks become more outrageous."

"I can't help but be drawn to those captivating souls who cross my path," he righteously claimed. "I am an artist."

"An artist?" she scoffed.

"Yes. My portraiture work is exceptional. Perhaps you've heard of me?"

"No, sorry." She shook her head, but he wasn't deterred by her inability to confirm his fame.

"Let me paint you. With these talented hands"—he held them up—"we could reveal the goddess hidden within."

"Honestly," she sputtered, stifling a laugh, "what nonsense."

"The endeavor would bring me such joy."

She gazed into his spectacular blue eyes, and they were shining down on her with what appeared to be genuine affection, and it occurred to her that she'd like nothing more than to make him happy.

What was wrong with her?

She was out of her element where he was concerned, because there was something about the cad, an indefinable demeanor, that sucked her in, that made her relish his company. If posing for a portrait would gladden him, then she was enthusiastic to comply.

Craziness, she chastised. Perhaps the domestic troubles with her father and Charlotte were causing her more stress than she'd imagined, and she was gradually growing un-balanced.

"Thank you for your offer, Mr. Cristofore, but I couldn't—"

She stopped in mid-refusal when she realized that he wasn't concentrating on her, but on a spot somewhere across the room. To her consternation, she hated that his attentiveness had been so easily diverted. Wanting to discover what held him rapt, she glanced over, but all she could behold were capes and lapels. He was a head taller than she, so whatever the sight, it was a mystery.

"I must go." He was thoroughly distracted.

Ridiculously, she suffered a pang of remorse. His arrival had been a thrilling escapade, and she could hardly restrain herself from mewling, *So soon?*

With some effort, he refocused his intense consideration on her. "I must see you again. Let me paint you," he hurriedly repeated. "Say yes."

As she vacillated, struggling for a polite way to say no, he slipped a note into her hand and wrapped her fingers around it.

"Arrivederci a presto!"

Then, in a blink, he vanished into the crowd, and she couldn't believe the letdown she endured. It was as though he'd briefly filled her world with cheery colors and had taken them with him when he'd walked away, leaving her with tiresome grays and browns.

Desperate for a last glimpse of him, she tried to dawdle, but the throng behind was driving her forward, and she was finally at the stairs and ascending. She thought to hunt for him from the higher vantage point, but she trudged on, declining to further foster the inane flight of fancy he'd initiated.

A few more steps, and she was at her father's box and slipping inside, only to be interrogated by Charlotte, who'd manipulated the gathering with more finesse and was enthroned and impatient for Elizabeth to attend her.

"It's about time," Charlotte grumbled, petulant as ever. "I've been waiting an eternity. Where have you been?"

Regally, Charlotte glared as though she'd been stranded for hours in some godforsaken locale when, in actuality, she was established in the center of the most lavish box in the balcony and surrounded by a half-dozen youthful associates packed in on either side. As Elizabeth was well aware, Charlotte didn't really care about Elizabeth's tardiness; she just liked to complain.

"Ah . . . reality returns." Elizabeth muttered under her breath, carefully shielding her aversion to the dreadful shrew, and relieved that Charlotte's horde of companions ensured that Elizabeth could sit in the back row rather than next to her unpalatable stepmother.

"What was that?" Charlotte asked, suspicious.

"It was really difficult to make the stairs," Elizabeth blithely replied. "The crush was hideous."

For once, the obtuse carper wasn't in the mood for controversy. She let Elizabeth's explanation slide without further discussion, for which Elizabeth was grateful. Usually, it was impossible to spend five minutes in the girl's company without a quarrel ensuing.

Doing her best to discount Charlotte, she adjusted her skirts and arranged herself in her chair, while trying not to brood over the miniature beauty as the girl chatted inanely with her gaggle of puerile colleagues.

When Elizabeth's fifty-year-old father had decided to marry Charlotte, Elizabeth had been convinced that he had suffered a fit of temporary insanity. One day, they were plodding along in the ho-hum, sedate fashion to which they were accustomed, and the next, he was spouting about how he'd never sired an heir, about his rapid and frantic compulsion to wed again.

As he'd unquestionably needed a son, Elizabeth hadn't argued with his determination or motives for matrimony, but never in her wildest dreams had she envisioned that he would seek out the likes of Charlotte as his bride. Without fail, the spoiled termagant was either whining or throwing temper tantrums. She thrived on berating the staff—once she'd even struck the butler!—and turning their placid household upside down with her foolish demands and antics.

She was a menace, but she was solidly ensconced in her position as countess, holding court like a queen, which meant that, unfortunately, Elizabeth was the one paying the price for her father's impetuous decision. Daily, she struggled to keep the peace.

With his club, business affairs, and obligations in Parliament, the earl was seldom available to witness the havoc the girl wrought. And, of course, whenever the earl deigned to grace them with his exalted presence, Charlotte exhibited exemplary comportment. Elizabeth had spoken to him about the incessant discord, but he wouldn't intervene.

"Women troubles," the earl would grouse. "Can't you just get along with her? Why must I be expected to act as arbiter?"

So Elizabeth had stopped supplicating for his assistance, and persevered as best she could. Yet, it galled, having Charlotte serve as hostess, superintend the house, and assume the duties—and execute them badly—that Elizabeth had once handled so well. Elizabeth was bored out of her mind, having had her responsibilities usurped by a newcomer who had no understanding of administration.

However, she did not want to be perceived as petty or jealous of Charlotte. She was just tired of having nothing to do. More and more, she wished that something—anything—would transpire to jolt her out of the predicament into which her father's precipitous action had landed her.

The ushers rushed down the aisles, deftly dousing the candles with their long sticks, and the audience noise hushed as the orchestra began the overture. The curtains opened, and Elizabeth settled in, hoping she might lose herself in the theater's operatic contribution, but within minutes, the stage couldn't hold her interest. The actors were atrocious, and the singing even worse.

Craving distraction, she peered down at Mr. Cristofore's note, which was still clutched in her fist. She tipped it toward the light and scanned the ornate lettering. It was a calling card.

Artista Straordinario.

"Extraordinary Artist." She harrumphed. The presumptuous title was listed under his name, and she rolled her eyes at his cheeky nature. The rascal was so full of himself!

Irritated, she started to toss the offending message on the floor then, almost as an afterthought, she slipped it into her reticule. Why throw it away? If nothing else, it would be an amusing reminder of their meeting.

Gradually, her attention wandered—to the other boxes, to the pit—and she clasped her opera glass to her eye, investigating nobles and commoners alike, for any trifle that might occupy her until the intermission.

Directly across was an empty box, which was partly sealed off by a curtain. A hint of candlelight glowed from behind it, and she paused, mildly curious as to whether anyone was in the secluded room. She looked . . . then looked again . . . only to determine that a man and a woman were huddled together in the shadows and—she tilted forward to the edge of her seat—they were kissing animatedly!

Furtively, she glanced at those around her, wondering if others in the distracted audience were watching, as well, but no one else seemed to have noticed the ardent couple. Apparently, Elizabeth was the only one who had the exact angle that allowed her to peek through the narrow slit in the curtain.

Transfixed, she clandestinely evaluated them. She'd never seen the likes! People in her world simply did not kiss. Not like this, anyway! The infrequent embraces she'd observed had been nothing but polite pecks, a curt brushing of dry lip to dry lip. Hands and bodies were never involved.

This was . . . was . . . indescribable, and definitely not the sort of behavior in which she'd ever imagined two adults might engage.

The couple's torsos were melded, and the man's hands were—Elizabeth focused in, struggling to see—on the woman's bottom! He was massaging her buttocks, pulling her pelvis into his own, flexing in a deliberate rhythm.

They were straining, reaching, and the longer Elizabeth stared, the more she was drawn in. She couldn't distinguish their faces, so she was surveying an anonymous episode of covert passion. Proper etiquette dictated that, at the least, she lay her glass aside, but the pair's activity was so riveting, so absorbing, that she couldn't.

The man's hand left its perch on the woman's behind, roving a slow, languid path up her hip, her waist, to stroke across breast, bosom, neck, and Elizabeth gaped in aghast fascination. With each area stroked, she tingled with a bizarre excitement that was disturbing and inexplicable.

Tenderly, he caressed his fingertips across the woman's cheek, then broke off the kiss, whispering something into her ear that had her vehemently shaking her head.

The man pulled away, and the candlelight that had protected his identity fell on him, clearly delineating him.

Gabriel Cristofore!

Elizabeth gasped so loudly that Charlotte spun around, scowling over her shoulder.

"Do you mind?" she sharply intoned. "I'm trying to watch the play."

"Sorry."

Elizabeth was so disconcerted that, in an attempt to cover up her surprise, she intentionally dropped her purse onto the carpeting. Pretending to search the floor, she bent over, steadying herself and regrouping, her thoughts tumultuously jumbled.

Who was he, this Italian lothario? He was brash enough to prey on one unsuspecting woman in a bustling theater lobby, then mere minutes later, make passionate love to another nearly in plain view of an entire audience!

She returned to an upright position, centering herself on her chair, while checking to see if anyone else had yet discovered the torrid duo, but they were concealed from all but herself. Like the worst voyeur, she raised her glass to her eye.

Mr. Cristofore was kissing the woman once again. Elizabeth scrutinized angle and intensity, intrigued as he relinquished the woman's mouth to blaze a trail down her chin, her neck, her bust, coming to nestle betwixt her breasts. The bodice of her gown was nipped extremely low, much of her breasts protruding, and he nuzzled across the creamy swell of skin.

The woman gripped the back of his head, urging him on. He acquiesced, tugging at the rim of her dress and pushing at the fabric. Before Elizabeth had any notion of what to expect, the woman's breast was bared.

Mesmerized, Elizabeth evaluated every detail of the mound of flesh, its rounded profile, its jutting nipple. Mr. Cristofore gazed adoringly at the naked orb, kneading, pinching, and tweaking the nipple then—shocking Elizabeth to her very core—he leaned down and licked across it.

In visible ecstasy, the woman shoved her chest forward, offering more of herself for his spirited application, and he readily submitted, flicking at the peak, then sucking it into his mouth.

"Oh, my Lord!"

The immoderately loud remark garnered another frown from Charlotte. "Be silent!"

"Yes . . . yes . . ."

Elizabeth rammed a knuckle between her teeth and bit down hard, effectively averting another verbal blunder.

For an untold interval, she contemplated them. Mr. Cristofore suckled against his lover, much as a hungry babe might; he yanked and tugged, teased and toyed. Unable to restrain herself, Elizabeth dissected every aspect of the lurid scene. When Mr. Cristofore broke the contact, she was so distraught that she wasn't sure how she could remain in her seat, yet the performance wasn't even half finished.

Amazed, undone, she could have observed them all night.

Mr. Cristofore murmured a farewell to the woman, stole a fleeting kiss, then exited the box. The woman waited a few minutes, then she departed, too.

Long after they'd gone, Elizabeth was glued to her spot, staring across at where they'd been.

CHAPTER TWO

GABRIEL Cristofore Preston slipped into the town house he shared with his father, John. Due to the lateness of the hour, the servants were abed, but he wasn't perturbed by their absence. With the schedule he kept, one that entailed chasing after the lonesome women of the aristocracy, he never had the slightest idea when he'd be home, so he could hardly expect his retainers to tarry, waiting for the moment he deigned to return.

Sometimes, when the right opportunity presented itself, he disappeared for days.

He lit the candle that had been conveniently left for him next to the door, hung his cloak, then climbed the stairs to the library where he could enjoy a libation before retiring.

The February night was chilly; he shivered in the dark hallway, and as he stepped into the comfortable room, he was glad to see that the remnants of an earlier fire glowed in the grate. He closed the door to hold in the warmth, added a scoop of coals, then went to the sideboard and poured himself a glass of his favorite Scotch whisky.

When he turned toward the hearth, the ring Helen had slipped on his finger at the theater shimmered in the firelight.

Always remember me, she'd begged.

I will, he'd lied.

The ring was a glaring reminder of how he'd spent the evening—of how he spent many of his evenings. Refusing to let his conscience tug too long or too forcefully at his better sense, he grabbed for a chair and tried to relax, but neither the chafing presence of the glimmering gold band nor its red gemstone bestowed any peace.

He toyed with the ornate clump of jewelry, rolling it around, then removing it and holding it up to the candle, visually appraising it with the flame as a backdrop. Assessing its authenticity, its purity, he tossed it up and caught it in his palm, judging its weight, wondering whether he should extract the stone from its setting, if the ruby would fetch a greater sum individually, or if he should sell the bauble as a whole.

Unconcerned, and not yet ready to seriously reflect on the matter, he flipped it into a bowl on a nearby table, just as the floor in the corridor creaked, and his father entered. His graying hair was askew, his robe crookedly tied. Floppy woolen socks covered his feet.

"I'd given up on you and went to bed," he mentioned gruffly as he strode in, his voice husky from sleep, his eyes drooping.

As he scratched his chest, and made for the sideboard and his own drink, Gabriel stifled a chuckle. During the day, his father was the ultimate fop, never a hair out of place, never a wrinkle in his clothing, or a thread hanging loose. Though he'd been estranged from his family for nearly three decades, he'd been born the fourth son of an earl, and he'd never shed the foundations that were the bedrock of his intrepid, dashing temperament. He was a man of refined, expensive tastes and extravagent, cultivated predilections.

Fastidious, in his carriage, in his behavior, those with whom he regularly interacted would be shocked to view this homey, familiar side of him, the one he reserved solely for his cherished and only son.

"Sorry for the delay."

He pulled up a second chair. "Why aren't you snuggled between a pair of silk sheets with your delightful countess?"

"She had to break it off." Gabriel pressed the back of his hand to his brow in a mimicking imitation of the woman's earlier upset. "She couldn't bear to say adieu, but there was no other course of action she could realistically take."

"Well, you saw that coming."

"No surprise at all," Gabriel concurred.

"When is her husband due in London?"

"Tomorrow," he replied with no small measure of relief.

"Excellent timing."

"Sì."

As his father contemplated his glass, Gabriel surreptitiously spied on him. Presumably he was mentally scrolling through the list of reasons he was mollified that Gabriel's most recent intrigue had been ended so painlessly, but blessedly, John would keep his thoughts to himself. Considering John's amorous past, and his diverse romantic foibles, he was hardly in any position to lecture Gabriel, and they both knew it.

Besides, their disagreement over Gabriel's earning of their living had been settled long ago. John had no penchant for work, and even if he'd possessed a recognizable calling, he'd never lower himself to engage in commerce. Amazingly, he'd stooped to acting as Gabriel's secretary, but he didn't view his post as a *job*; he saw himself as supporting an artist, which he considered a valid hobby for a man of his status.

He was an elegant, courtly soul who relished the finer things in life, but who had no notion of how one located the funds to pay for them. John had been in his twenties when he'd been disinherited, and he'd gotten by on his looks and charm, borrowing from friends, or freeloading off paramours, who couldn't bear to refuse him any request.

As a youngster, Gabriel had deduced that John would

never be capable of providing them with any stability—he didn't have the slightest idea how to go about it other than the acceptable gentlemanly pursuits of turning cards or tossing dice—so they would never have any money but what Gabriel generated. Gabriel loved his flamboyant, extravagant father and was willing to employ any method necessary to support him.

After years of honing his talents, he excelled at painting and at seduction, and he used his combined abilities for financial gain—much to John's unceasing chagrin.

His expertise as an artist helped him to initially entice his female clients into an innocuous business relationship, and their patronage supplied the meager remuneration he procured through portraiture. But it was what transpired after the painting sessions commenced that brought in the true bulk of his income. He painted women who were lonely, who were searching for love and respect, and they just happened to be the sort who were generous not only with their affection but also with the contents of their pocketbooks.

For Gabriel, seducement was a game that offered substantial prospects for fiscal enrichment, as well as copious interludes of passionate trysting.

John could scarcely condemn Gabriel for his libidinous proclivities when, as a younger man, John had been a philandering bounder. Age and wisdom had calmed much of his carnal disposition, but Gabriel had grown up observing and learning from the master.

Like father, like son.

John had provided Gabriel with his first lover. His second. His third. John was the one who'd continually extolled the joys of women, the mysteries to be unraveled, the bliss to be had in their arms. Using his own paramours, father had initiated son in the benefits of erotic rapture and, being a dutiful child, Gabriel had toiled strenuously to acquire the skills his father had sought to teach. In the process, he'd developed an affinity for the fairer sex that matched—and perhaps surpassed—his father's.

Following directly in John's footsteps, he loved women. All types, styles, and kinds. He loved them tall or short, thin or rounded, comely or plain, rich or poor—although in his weaker moments, he could be forced to admit that he definitely preferred them beautiful and wealthy.

Early on, he'd been smitten, mesmerized by their personalities, their quirks, their constitutions. Women were an enigma, a perpetual fascination. His infatuation nearly an obsession, he observed them, he sketched, he painted. Easily, he was charmed by an expanse of soft skin, or the waft of an enchanting perfume, the turn of a head, the lilt of a voice, the sway in a walk. He treasured the lure and the chase, the temptation and the capitulation, the catch and the final fall from grace.

There was nothing quite so rewarding as stumbling upon an affluent, attractive, forlorn female who desperately needed a boost in her self-esteem, or an energizing shot to her flagging pride. Naught restored a woman's confidence and dignity more rapidly than a brief, profound *amore* from which she could walk away at the conclusion having felt valued and cherished.

The women with whom he dallied were miserable, forsaken, badly used by their husbands or others. Victims of their arranged marriages and suffocating environments, they'd never understood or tapped into their base appetites, so they were effortlessly led astray. For years, they suffered silently, dutiful matrons, as their spouses trifled and played with one mistress after the next. They were disgruntled, confused, and discontented with life and their general place in it.

Sadly, they were all seeking reciprocated ardor, tenderness and devotion, that was never received. In their bleak circumstances, they slowly deteriorated, pining away for some scant display of attention and approval, but also for validation that they were mature women with wants, needs, and unfulfilled desires.

With great relish, Gabriel showered them with what they longed for and so much more. He bent over backward to make them feel special, revered, feminine, and rare, and his fondness was never feigned. He thrived on teaching them to trust their sensual inclinations, to revel in their repressed, wanton natures, to indulge their lustful impulses.

In exchange, he gained ample gratification, and not just physically. The monetary rewards could be significant, the dividends of which he was explicitly reminded when John reached over and picked up the ring Gabriel had previously discarded.

"What a gaudy eyesore," he submitted as his opinion. "Her parting *gift*?"

"She insisted that I have something to remember her by." Magnanimously, sarcastically, he queried, "Who am I to deprive her when the gesture obviously conferred such immense joy?"

" 'Joy,' indeed!" John huffed, clearly put out by Gabriel's attitude. He examined the ring by the light, much as Gabriel had done when he'd first arrived. "Superb quality," he grumbled. "It will fetch a pretty penny."

"That it will."

John pitched it to Gabriel, and he snared it and stuck it in his pocket, out of sight. Shortly, he'd peddle it, but not before having a duplicate created with an imitation stone and *falso* gold, so that if he ever crossed paths with the exalted Helen again, she would see the piece of jewelry firmly planted on his hand.

"I can't believe you spent so much time with her, and she'd assume that you'd wear such an ostentatious trinket."

"But she didn't really *know* me, now did she?"

He was proficient at inferring what his paramours yearned for in a man, and he could transform himself into whoever they needed him to be. Kind, compassionate, altruistic, firm, fierce, hot-blooded, potent, his ability to adopt different mannerisms was so effective that he might have had a career on the stage if he hadn't been so adept at dabbling with oils.

The effect was that the women grew attached to the man they supposed him to be, rather than the man he actually was. When their liaisons terminated—which he carefully strove to ensure from the inception—they went on their way, presuming him to have been a dream come true when, in reality, he was usually vastly distinct from the person they'd built him up to be in their minds.

But he had no complaints. He brought them gaiety and excitement. In return, they generously gave him things with which they could readily afford to part. Valuables, *oggetti d'arte*, cash, gems, he never refused any of it, because he deemed their largesse as the completion of a simple business transaction: goods tendered for services rendered.

"Is she still interested in having you complete the portrait you started?" John inquired, always the pragmatist.

"Absolutely."

Gabriel didn't add that she'd vowed to hang it where she could constantly gaze upon it, where it would always provoke memories of him. If informed of the depth of the countess's misplaced fondness, his father would fume and fret but, at the same juncture, he would be elated by the news that she was ecstatic over the final product. John was faithfully hoping to augment Gabriel's customer base through referrals by prosperous patrons such as Helen.

On the few occasions when they'd had a capital row on the subject, John contended that Gabriel's compensation should derive exclusively from the paltry amounts produced by the portraiture contracts John negotiated. But what fun would that be?

Gabriel quickly tired of painting the ill-behaved sons and spoiled daughters of the nobility. It was so much more appealing to paint the wives. He became intimately involved with a woman, discovering her fears and inhibitions, the pressures and burdens that ruled her. Long before brush was ever touched to canvas, he passed innumerable hours talking and sketching, establishing an acquaintanceship, and thus attempting to capture the woman's essence.

Meticulously, he peeled away the layers, searching for the person who was hiding beneath the fancy gown, the expensive cologne, and elaborate coiffure. And of course, as he rolled back the emotional mantle, he also stripped away the clothes.

How could he be expected to resist? He was only a mortal man, after all, and he was invariably eager to accept that which was freely and willingly offered.

He adored naked women, how their hips curved, their thighs molded, their breasts shifted. His notion of heaven would be to sit throughout eternity, a sketch pad in hand, a nude model posed before him, as he struggled to exactly record a fleeting look, a subtle glance, a sudden mood.

Ever the realist, John yanked him out of his reverie. "So, you're ready to begin again. Did you have a chance to review the list of names I prepared?"

He and John had lived on the Continent for nearly all of Gabriel's twenty-seven years, having returned to London only two years earlier. They'd spent most of their time in southern Italy, with brief stays in Paris, Vienna, Madrid, and other exotic cities. Gabriel considered Italy to be home, but despite the mishaps that had originally sent John fleeing into exile, he hadn't ever had the heart to sever the strong ties that bound him to England.

He still harbored an intense, incomprehensible interest in the affairs of the British aristocracy, and he carefully followed their machinations. With the dedication of a mother guiding a daughter into the marriage market, he was acutely aware of the current position of every member of high society.

"Yes."

"Have you settled on your next mark?"

"*Mark* is such a harsh term, Father, don't you agree? I wish you wouldn't use it." He only took what a woman voluntarily proposed, and he would never accept more than she could afford to give.

"Well, I wouldn't be foolish enough to refer to her as a *client*."

"I guess that wouldn't be apropos, either."

"Tell me, who's the lucky girl?"

Gabriel twirled his liquor, vividly recalling the fabulous brunette he'd accosted in the theater lobby. "I shall follow your recommendation. Lady Elizabeth Harcourt."

"Norwich's daughter," John remarked pensively, the very name inducing a swirl of reminiscence. He tipped his drink in a mock toast. "An excellent choice."

"With your stellar endorsement, how could I have selected anyone else?"

"If she's anything like her mother, you'll have a delightful experience."

"I imagine so."

John and the Earl of Norwich had a sordid history that John had never deigned to relate. Gabriel wasn't cognizant of the gory details but, as with most of his father's peccadilloes, their feud had something to do with the earl's long-deceased first wife. Most likely, they'd had an abbreviated affair that the earl had exposed but, in his odd fashion, John had his standards. He would only have engaged in such a relationship for what he would have viewed as lofty motives—that being the woman's wretched unhappiness.

For all John's boasting as to how, as a youth, he'd enthusiastically abandoned his elite familial position, at heart he was the consummate gentleman. He never could countenance the tiniest slight, which repeatedly pushed him into all sorts of unsavory predicaments. He cared about women and couldn't stand to see them disconsolate or tormented, and if the earl had abused his wife, John would have interceded, and though it was three decades later, he would still enjoy the chance to extract some petty revenge.

"You saw her?" John was much more curious than he should have been.

"*Sì*. And spoke with her at length."

"Is she a beauty?"

"Exquisite." Gabriel recalled how he'd whispered the observation in her ear, and how fervently he'd meant it.

A classic female, she'd had a heart-shaped face, dainty chin, high cheekbones, curved brows, and pert nose. Her bounteous, pouting lips were her best feature. She had a mouth that instantly drew a man beyond the notion of kissing, one that made him remember why he paid for costly mistresses or visited high-priced whores. Hers was a mouth that oughtn't be wasted on talking, not when there were so many more delicious pursuits to which it could be put.

Her hair was also particularly outstanding. Those luxurious auburn locks had been swept up in the modern style, but the ringlets dangling across her shoulder had provided abundant evidence of the thickness, of the various hues. To describe her hair as brown was inaccurate; it was brown, with red and gold highlights sprinkled throughout.

The English women he seduced were boring, ordinary, fair, and pale, their traits washed out by generations of immaculate breeding until there was little that was unique. Oh, to stumble upon such a stunning original! He was eager to commence. With painting and more!

Her incredible body, so well developed and lush, was precisely the type he favored. The fabric of her gown had shielded much of her form, but he had a vivid imagination, and he could graphically picture long, sexy legs, curvaceous thighs, perfectly developed breasts.

The lacing of her corset had answered any questions as to whether or not she was liberally endowed. No padding or false weights had been implanted to increase apparent size. The two spectacular mounds had been firmly lifted, granting him an unrestricted vista of their munificence, and leaving no dispute as to the womanly contours of her figure.

He was impatient to see her in her full, naked glory. She would be a feast for the eyes—and hopefully for the hands and the mouth.

At the contemplation of her delectable charms, he felt the giddy rush that persistently overwhelmed him when he was about to initiate a new conquest. There was no finer pleasure to be had—not even from his painting—than the exhilaration he endured during those fantastic days of a burgeoning affair.

"You said she has twenty-seven years," he mentioned.

"By my calculations, yes."

"Why do you suppose her father never married her off?"

"Because he's an ass."

For John, that was sufficient explanation, but Gabriel probed anyway. "Might you expound a bit?"

"No, but once you're acquainted with her, you'll see what I mean." John rose and meandered to the sideboard, depositing his dirtied glass for the maid to deal with in the morning. "When would you predict she'll arrive to make inquiries about an appointment?"

Gabriel recalled the blush on her cheeks, her initial caution, then the unfolding curiosity. With delight and candor, she'd assessed his every move, until by the conclusion, they'd established an affinity, a bond. When he'd espied Helen in the crowd and departed from Lady Elizabeth's presence, he'd sensed that he could have brazenly kissed her without much opposition.

Her defenses were low; her melancholy high. She was so ready for a change!

"I imagine she'll be around in two or three days."

"That soon?"

"Without a doubt," Gabriel answered confidently, and where women were concerned, he was rarely wrong.

Elizabeth sat at her vanity, staring at her reflection in the mirror. She couldn't have said how long she'd dawdled, studying her features, checking for perfection and flaws, and finding mostly the latter.

With a resigned sigh, she shook her head at her whimsicality, marveling at her sudden engrossment with her looks. Not since she'd been an adolescent, and such frivolous things had mattered, had she tried so hard to impartially judge her characteristics: winsome face, clear skin, bright eyes. Her hair was too dark, though, an oddity she'd hated when she was young and striving not to stick out while drowning in a swarm of blond girls.

While she was customarily meticulous as to her daily appearance, she never bothered over the assemblage of her physical traits, but since her encounter with Gabriel Cristofore, she'd developed a heightened interest in elusive detail.

What specifically had he seen that had spurred him to her side with words of flattery and adulation?

A secret thrill coursed through her. The flood of compliments he'd bestowed had given her enormous pleasure. She was allowed a small speck of vanity, wasn't she? She had never been courted, had seldom been noticed by members of the opposite sex, so there was something absurdly phenomenal about being singled out by such a handsome man.

His breathtaking approach had stirred her in more ways than she cared to acknowledge. The twisted covers on her bed provided significant evidence of how she'd tossed and turned throughout the night, reviewing every comment he'd expressed, every response she'd uttered.

Naturally, she hadn't been able to stop thinking about the woman to whom he'd been making love. Though it was improper for her to have watched, she wasn't sorry that she had. Her indiscretion had opened up an entirely new world. She felt as if she'd peeked behind a forbidden curtain—which, in effect, she had—and that, as a result, she would never be the same.

She couldn't prevent herself from ruminating over Mr. Cristofore and what it would be like to be the object of his amatory attention. Previously, she'd never wasted time brooding on the more private side of male-female relations, but now, having been totally immersed in the erotic scene, she couldn't reflect upon anything else.

Clearly, there was a lusty facet to her disposition, because she'd become integrally absorbed by lewd deliberation. Her body was aching and restless, while her mind was preoccupied with indecency. She kept reliving—over and over and over again!—that moment when Mr. Cristofore had huddled before his paramour and suckled at her breast.

The recollection caused a whoosh of heat to sweep up her front. Her nipples extended, her breathing became labored, her cheeks burned, and she lingered there, alone in her dressing room, fanning herself against the abrupt elevation in temperature.

What if she had been the woman with Gabriel Cristofore? After witnessing his ribald antics, she was obsessed with knowing more, and she liberally fantasized over the possibilities, and she couldn't cease her musings.

You could call on him to set up a portrait interview, a tiny voice urged, and she blushed just from pondering the wicked idea. The card he'd pressed into her hand was balanced against the mirror, and she evaluated it intently, searching for any clue it might furnish about the man and his motives.

Unfortunately, she gleaned no clues, and the longer she dwelled upon him, the more she realized that such an insolent libertine was out of her league. She'd never have the courage to visit his studio. And as for requesting that he paint her! The concept was preposterous! Such forward conduct was the epitome of faulty moral comportment.

Yet, it was amusing to conjecture and fantasize. No one was hurt by her wayward meditation, and she thoroughly enjoyed daydreaming about being adventurous and bold. In her current state of doldrums, any diversion was welcome—even a far-fetched, romantic reverie.

A clock chimed down the hall, compelling her to heed that afternoon was upon her, but she was loitering in her room. She'd been up for hours, but she couldn't force herself to go downstairs. A strange lethargy had recently overtaken her, and nothing seemed important, especially not her mundane schedule.

Normally, she'd have risen with the servants, would have been dressed and ready for a busy day when her father appeared at the breakfast table. They had habitually begun their mornings in conference, confirming plans, comparing engagements and calendars, before the earl departed, but now, she couldn't constrain herself to face him, and there was no reason to, really. She had no duties to discuss with him and, she had to admit, he was not the most affable mealtime companion.

Since his marriage to Charlotte, he was surly and cantankerous and, of course, breakfast was generally a disaster, due to Charlotte's histrionics that had her steadily firing the kitchen help. They'd had such a turnover in employees that Elizabeth didn't know the names of many of their retainers, but then—as Charlotte faithfully reminded her—the composition of the staff was no longer her problem.

She was tired of fashioning excuses meant to explain to the earl why the food was horrendous, the service poor, so she'd stopped trying. With his usual disinterest in household proceedings, he refused to listen regardless, so justifications were a waste of energy.

Commotion issued from down the hall, and she hesitated, homing in on the direction from which it was emanating. Charlotte's screeching was definitely evident, but the other person was retorting quietly, so Elizabeth couldn't distinguish who was suffering the lash of Charlotte's sharp tongue. A platter crashed to the floor with a loud bang, and Elizabeth wearily rose to her feet, cursing the fact that her only enduring domestic role was to act as referee between her caustic stepmother and those retainers who had been loyal enough to stay on despite the chaos.

A second thunderous explosion had her scurrying to the location of the discord. She glided to the door of Charlotte's suite just as a spoon flew out, bounced off the far

wall, and clattered onto the carpet. Pausing, she eavesdropped and assessed the volatile situation, as Charlotte
scolded someone.

"I've told you a hundred times how I want my eggs
cooked!"

"Aye, you have, milady," Mary Smith, head housekeeper and Elizabeth's good friend, replied evenly, "but as
we are on our third cook in as many months—"

"Shut up!" Charlotte shouted. "I've given you sufficient warning. You're fired."

The announcement flowed out so often and so
smoothly that Elizabeth was beginning to suspect the vicious girl stood in front of the mirror and practiced it.

"As you wish."

Mary's inflection showed no inkling of emotion at
having been discharged from a position she'd held for
twenty years, and Elizabeth was livid as she stormed into
the room.

"She's not fired!"

"Don't interfere, Elizabeth!" Charlotte warned.

"I am!" Elizabeth countered just as harshly as she advanced on the bed where Charlotte lounged like a pampered
queen with piles of pillows fluffed behind her back.
"You've gone too far."

Swathed in an expensive robe, Charlotte trembled with
affront, her hair hilariously flopping from side to side,
wrapped as it was in curling rags. The tray that had been
poised on her lap was on the floor, the utensils, plates, and
glassware scattered about, the spoiled food soaking into and
staining a priceless rug.

Several maids cowered in the corner, while Mary faced
the little despot, shoulders squared, pride intact. Elizabeth
kept her indignant gaze locked on Charlotte's, not glancing
in Mary's direction. "Mary, you're excused."

"I don't give her leave to—"

"Go, Mary," Elizabeth instructed. "The rest of you are
dismissed, as well."

Their relief palpable, Mary and the other women slipped away. Elizabeth and Charlotte glared at one another, silent and unmoving, until the door clicked shut, then Charlotte leapt out from under the blankets.

"How dare you countermand me to the servants!" she hissed.

"How dare you treat Mary so despicably in front of them!"

The girl pointed an angry finger at Elizabeth's chest. "I've apprised that woman of her failings on countless occasions. She'll not continue in my employ."

"We'll see, won't we?"

"I intend to speak with the earl. She'll be terminated like that." Charlotte snapped her fingers dramatically.

"Be sure to let me know how it goes."

The juvenile woman's threats were tiresome, particularly when they were both aware that she couldn't discuss the incident with the earl. Even if she had the nerve—which she didn't—he would neither attend her nor care, and she'd look incompetent for broaching what he would deem to be a petty household affair.

"When I'm through," Charlotte blustered, "you'll be sorry."

"I can't wait to discover my fate," Elizabeth said sarcastically, as she turned to go, refusing to demean herself by fighting. Charlotte thrived on turmoil, so withdrawal was Elizabeth's foremost weapon. "In the meantime, if you expect your breakfast to be fixed correctly, perhaps you should drag your lazy behind out of bed and eat it before one in the afternoon."

"You will not disparage me in my own home!" Charlotte roared.

"Pull yourself together!" Elizabeth scolded. "You're making a spectacle of yourself. Even now, the servants are probably spreading the latest gossip about your uncontrollable temper. You'll be the talk of the neighborhood within the hour."

"They wouldn't dare!"

"Wouldn't they?"

As a parting remark, it wasn't bad. Appearances carried tremendous import for Charlotte. The notion that the servants weren't discreet, that they'd tattle and broadcast the family's ongoing strife, was one of the few methods Elizabeth had found that worked. Charlotte usually backed down when confronted with the prospect of public exposure.

She stepped into the corridor, firmly closed the door, then she sped up the stairs to Mary's room where she had to stave off further disaster. If Mary threw up her hands in defeat and left, who could predict what would happen? Mary's stabilizing influence was the sole factor that had averted absolute catastrophe thus far.

After this current debacle, Elizabeth couldn't blame her if she quit as she'd been intimating. Charlotte's abhorrent display had been one in an endless line that had persistently erupted during the six conflict-ridden months since she'd wed the earl. Mary had stoically braved every blasted episode, deflecting Charlotte's fury, intervening when she could, or accepting the culpability for many lapses that weren't her fault.

Elizabeth peeked in without knocking and, as she'd surmised, Mary was perched rigidly on the edge of her bed, engrossed in her knitting. The needles clicked in a quick rhythm that indicated her level of agitation. While outwardly she appeared cool and composed, there was a tense set to her chin, rage in her gaze, resignation in her demeanor.

"May I come in?"

Mary glowered but said nothing, so Elizabeth entered and shut the door. Leaning against it, she inspected her friend, wondering how she could ever make this right.

She'd known Mary her whole life. The woman had been a combination mother, sister, and companion. Her wise counsel had guided Elizabeth from the nursery onward. Elizabeth's mother had died when she was just three, so Mary had become a surrogate parent even though she'd also just assumed the strenuous duties of head housekeeper.

Over the centuries, the job of housekeeper was inherited as systematically by the women of Mary's family as the rank of earl was inherited by the male heirs of Elizabeth's. Mary had practically been born to the position, no more capable of declining the dubious post than Elizabeth's father had been of being named Earl of Norwich when he'd turned sixteen.

At age forty-five, her blond hair had faded to silver, there were lines around her mouth, and her figure had filled out, but she wasn't happy anymore. Her blue eyes no longer glimmered with joy or surprise, her laughter no longer rang through the halls, and Elizabeth hated the changes her father's marriage had wrought.

"You can't let her get to you," Elizabeth gently asserted.

"Too late, me darlin' Beth." While Mary was a full-fledged English woman, she infrequently evinced the Irish brogue she'd acquired from her father, who'd been the stable master at Norwich. Only when she was most piqued did the slight accent emerge, and the fact that it was detectable now underscored the magnitude of her vexation.

"You know how obstinate Charlotte is."

"This was more than a tantrum. This was personal." After a disconcerting delay, she added, "Maybe she suspects."

Elizabeth nudged, "Suspects what?"

"Nothing." She sighed ponderously. " 'Tis nothing a'tall." Setting her knitting aside, she stood. "I've decided to tender my resignation. I'll seek your father's permission tonight."

"Don't be absurd." Elizabeth was frightened that Mary might actually follow through. "We could never get along without you. Especially with her acting so horridly."

"I can't take the strain or the incessant upheaval."

"I'll talk to Father."

"You've tried before; it won't help." She laughed half-heartedly. "He's made his bed, as they say. There's naught for him to do but lie in it."

"There's got to be a better resolution than your quitting."

"I can't think of a single one."

"But where would you go? How would you support yourself?" Mary had never resided anywhere but with the Harcourt family, she'd never held any other employment. The notion of her departure was ludicrous. Elizabeth put an arm around her. "You're upset, so you're spewing rubbish."

"I *am* upset, but I know what I must do."

Belowstairs, there was another crash, and even from their secluded spot on the fourth floor, they could hear a quarrel ensuing. Needing to arbitrate, Mary started toward the door, but Elizabeth stopped her. "You've been through enough for one afternoon. You stay here. I'll deal with her."

Mary looked relieved, as Elizabeth hurried out. She ran down, only to encounter Charlotte berating a servant in the foyer. After tolerating a bout of vitriolic antagonism, Elizabeth soothed the situation, sent the flustered maid on her way, then threatened Charlotte anew.

Morose, discouraged, she trudged up to her bedchamber, mulling over just how much more conflict she could withstand. With no funds of her own, and no ability to provide for herself, she was as much at the earl's mercy as Mary. The immediate future was so bleak! If only she could change her life! But the choices were limited, the acceptable opportunities obscure.

How long could she persevere in such wretched conditions? If only there was some mode of delivering an illusion of sunshine into her otherwise dreary existence!

She sat at her vanity, once again. Across from her was the card she'd received from Gabriel Cristofore. Overly despondent, she picked it up and rubbed her thumb along the black ink.

CHAPTER THREE

GABRIEL silently stepped to the door of his parlor, which was slightly ajar. He peeked through the crack and couldn't help but gloat. He'd known she'd come! And so quickly, too. How he relished a victory—even a small one!

Lady Elizabeth Harcourt was perched on one of the sofas, accompanied by a memorable silver-haired woman in her mid-forties who, from her conservative dress and deportment, was likely a lady's maid or chaperone.

His father was present, chatting amiably and, with Lady Elizabeth's exalted status in mind, he'd outdone himself. A handsome fellow at age fifty, he'd primped and preened. His suit was vigilantly brushed, his cravat starched white and intricately tied, his shoes buffed to a brilliant shine.

He wore several tasteful rings and, with his manicured nails neatly trimmed, his expressive fingers were notably seductive as he motioned to the tea tray. As he talked, he gestured flamboyantly, and the ladies couldn't stop watching his fluid movements.

Gabriel had inherited his artistic talent from his long-deceased Italian mother. He'd received her astute appreciation for coloration, substance, and form, but he was convinced that the grace in his father's hands had liberally contributed to his remarkable ability. The man's flair was a joy to behold.

Lady Elizabeth's concentration flitted from John to her surroundings, and Gabriel focused on her. The single ladies who came for a session were always apprehensive, and Lady Elizabeth was no exception. Furtively, she glanced about, checking the décor, as if trying to deduce whether Gabriel's request to paint her was real or part of some depraved scheme.

There *was* a definite licentious bent to his plans, so she was wise to be wary, but he'd been through this exercise on dozens of occasions. If he manipulated her with his usual skill, at the juncture where she realized she'd been ensnared in more than a simple portraiture contract, she wouldn't be overly concerned by any ulterior motives he might have possessed at the outset.

On nimble feet, he strolled into the room, and simultaneously, the two women started to rise in welcome, but he waved them to their seats as he moved across the floor to stand in front of Lady Elizabeth.

In his eagerness, he'd forgotten how pretty she was, and surprisingly, he was tongue-tied, incompetent to do anything but stare like a dumbfounded, lovestruck boy.

"Ah," his father interjected, "here's Mr. Cristofore now."

He and John never introduced themselves as father and son. In honor of his mother, Gabriel used his Italian surname, and they both believed it enhanced his mystery and allure with the ladies. An added benefit, with John portraying himself as a secretary, it precluded questions about Gabriel's background or birth status.

John was positive that Gabriel's chances in England would be wrecked if those from John's past learned he'd traveled home with an adult, illegitimate son in tow. John's contention—that his reputation still hounded him after thirty years—was funny but true. In his day, he'd been an absolute terror.

"Lady Elizabeth," John said, gracefully smoothing over the awkward moment, "you met Mr. Cristofore the other night."

"So I did," she answered, an engaging blush reddening

her glossy cheeks. "It's very nice to see you again."

"The pleasure is all mine."

Apparently, she was unaware of the staggering effect her proximity had on him. When he was within ten feet of her, his body surged to a state of profound alacrity. His pulse increased, his skin heated, his senses soared. He could hear the slightest noise, smell the faintest odor. The afternoon seemed brighter, the air fresher, just from being in her company.

He took her hand in his, but touching her was a mistake. Even though she was wearing a glove, the scanty connection jolted him, originating at his fingertips, then rushing up his arm and down his chest, to lodge in the vicinity of his loins, making him hot and uncomfortable, his trousers suddenly too tight.

Kissing her hand, he lingered, inhaling her unique scent. The particular aroma was matchless, mesmerizing. If he'd been blindfolded in a crowded room, he could have picked her out by the distinctive fragrance. It tickled his fancy, reinforcing his certitude that they were entirely in accord, and meant to be together in a physical way.

As he straightened, he was unnerved to discover Lady Elizabeth intently assessing him. Obviously, she'd also been stung by the transitory impact, but there was something more in her gaze, something challenging and inquisitive, as though she knew more about him than she suitably ought. He suffered a pang of cognizance—as well as an unwonted tug at his conscience—that she understood exactly the sort of bounder he was and that she'd visited him anyway.

Could it be? Could she have heard rumors or, God forbid, have talked to one of his prior paramours?

Rigorously, he shook off the nightmarish notion. The women with whom he dallied were selected because they could never tell anyone what they'd been about. As for himself, he was exceptionally discreet. There was no one who could have informed her as to his aberrant nature. Still . . .

John cleared his throat, jerking him to his senses. He persisted in holding the lady's hand, while peering at her like an entranced dolt, so he stepped away, putting a polite distance between them and covering his gaffe by studying her associate.

Most of his female clients brought a colleague along for an appointment or two, and it paid to reassure the lady's companion. The more comfortable the partner felt about the situation, the more expeditiously the client grew at ease, and the sooner she would decide to attend by herself.

With an amicable smile firmly affixed, he converged on the other woman. "And who is your charming friend?"

"Miss Mary Smith," Lady Elizabeth advised.

"Delighted, Miss Smith." He made an impressive bow, just as he'd done with Lady Elizabeth, though he decorously retreated. "Will we be painting you, as well?"

"Heavens, no." She was blushing, too. "I'm simply here to accompany Lady Elizabeth."

"My great loss, then." He meant it. She had a fine, absorbing face, the path of years scrupulously imprinted.

Miss Smith turned to John and said, "You mentioned that he was awfully good at portraiture, but you didn't say that he was an unmitigated flatterer."

"It's the Italian in him," John stated affably, and both women laughed.

"Are the two of you related?"

"Why, no." It was John's chance to be flustered. "What makes you ask?"

"You look so much alike, I just assumed——" She halted, embarrassed by the personal tenor of her inquiry. "My apologies."

"None necessary," John hastily chimed in. In the two years they'd been back on British soil, the astute Miss Smith was the first to notice a resemblance, one they constantly sought to hide, and her perspicaciousness was disturbing. "I'm merely his man of affairs," John insisted, and he pointedly glared at Gabriel. "As a matter of fact, I was just discussing the contracts, explaining the prices you charge and—"

As they'd practiced, Gabriel cut him off. "You know how I hate being burdened with the business side of the arrangement." His adept attention centered on Lady Elizabeth. "Especially when there are so many other intriguing subjects to consider."

With rehearsed dexterity, John tried again. "But we do need to decide on—"

"No, no. I'm sure that whatever Lady Elizabeth consents to pay will be more than fair."

"What can I say?" John shrugged, pretending magnanimous defeat. "He possesses the soul of an artist. He's never been interested in finance."

"I'm fortunate I have you to watch over me."

"Yes, you are," John concurred. As though tendering a precious secret, he leaned toward the ladies. "Painting is his passion. Some days, he's so immersed in his work that I have to remind him to eat and sleep."

As Gabriel had anticipated, the women chuckled. He proceeded to appraise Lady Elizabeth, as if transfixed, which wasn't too far from the truth. "There's nothing quite so rewarding as creating great art."

Lady Elizabeth shamelessly met his bold stare, and he was overcome, once again, by the discomfiting impression that she knew exactly what he was up to and was prepared to beat him at his own game.

"I've often been apprised"—she ran the pink tip of her dainty tongue across her full bottom lip, delicately wetting it so that it glistened—"that intense dedication is essential in order to garner a reputation as an artisan of merit."

"Precisely."

Gabriel wondered if that bit of lip-moistening hadn't been calculated to incite his masculine sensibilities. The ostensibly innocent act was what a trained coquette might do, and it had drawn his unwavering focus to her mouth. He couldn't concentrate on anything else.

Her mouth was impeccable. It hinted at wickedness and provoked a man to carnal ruination. With extraordinary relish, he could visualize her kneeling down, unfastening his pants, baring him. She'd reach inside to find him erect and ready, her fingers would stroke him, then her adorable tongue would flick against the crown. He'd tremble and moan as she sucked at him and . . .

Gabriel wrenched upright, sternly plucking himself out of his libidinous reverie. Disconcerted by the potent effect she had on his person, he couldn't remember ever being so thoroughly titillated merely from being in a woman's presence. Gad, but he was in deep, and he hadn't yet had the opportunity to be sequestered with her! What would his condition be after a few hours? After a few days?

He shuddered to think!

Composing himself, he compelled himself to stick with the routine he and John had established. If they'd been reading from a script, it couldn't have been simpler.

"You'll be a impressive model, milady. I'm terribly anxious to get started." Impudently, he balanced a finger on her chin, raising her face so that he could better examine her. With slight pressure, he rotated her head back and forth as if hunting for incomparability, and she didn't flinch. "What a portrait we'll produce! Such flawless skin. Such marvelous eyes. Such striking bone structure."

"Honestly, Mr. Cristofore," she scolded. "You do go on about nonsense."

"You have a distinct beauty, and it will shine through on the canvas. With such magnificent features, perfection is the only possible result."

She gazed up at him, beseeching with those stunning green eyes, and her thoughts seemed to connect with his. Oddly—for just the briefest instant—he could peer to the spot where her loneliness and despair quietly rested.

Her isolation called out to him, appealing for recognition and empathy from his conniving, corrupt black heart, and he was annoyed. He'd erected a shell around his battered sense of right and wrong. It was the exclusive method by which he could persevere through those occasions when his battle-scarred conscience endeavored to swim to the surface.

He couldn't let her get to him. If he wasn't prudent, he'd start to feel sorry for her, and he'd end up acting chivalrously. He'd paint her for the joy of it, instead of for the enhanced wealth it would inevitably convey.

How ridiculous! She was a woman to whom he'd only spoken a sparse number of words, yet she was causing his protective instincts to blossom. He couldn't permit her personal problems to affect his behavior!

Obviously, she wished his compliments to be genuine— for doubtless they'd been seldom offered in her life even though she'd deserved many—and he felt like the consummate scoundrel he really was. She desperately needed authentic friendship, and it would be wrong to take advantage of her, but his pattern of trickery and deception was so entrenched that he couldn't fathom proceeding in any other fashion.

His finger was still on her chin, and she pulled away, severing the fragile contact. Immediately, their intense link vanished, and he speculated as to why he'd been foolish enough to infer it existed.

Her emotions shuttered, she glanced over at John. "I agree with Mary: he's an incurable flatterer."

"That he is," John good-naturedly acceded.

Gabriel struggled to restore his equilibrium, to carry on with the ruse. "Would you ladies like to view some samples of my work?"

"Actually"—Lady Elizabeth stood—"I'm curious about your studio, and I was hoping we could begin our project today."

He was flummoxed by her pronouncement. His female clients never wished to commence at once! They required crucial wooing until they were more relaxed. A good deal of his initial energy was spent on allaying their misgivings.

"Today?" he queried, baffled.

"Yes." She dazzled him with a frightening smile that had him rapidly reviewing the reasons he'd thought he should enter into an affair with her. "If your calendar is free, that is. I wouldn't want to be an imposition."

"You could never be an imposition."

In consternation, he shook his head. This wasn't proceeding according to plan, at all. She was supposed to be apprehensive, ambivalent, undetermined. Her reticence would let him be covertly persuasive, credibly irresistible, while he gradually wore down her control and vanquished her inhibitions.

"Why delay?" she asked.

"Why, indeed?" He scowled at his father, but John merely cocked a brow, as perplexed as he about her impatience. With women, what man was ever on stable ground? "How is my schedule this afternoon, John?"

"It's open."

"Excellent." Gabriel hadn't intended on hosting a guest, but he faked enthusiasm. He was scarcely equipped, so he'd have to improvise. "My studio is in a cottage in the backyard, where the light is better. Shall we go out?"

"I'd like that." Audaciously, she sauntered over to him and slipped her arm into his. "How long will we be?"

"I'll be doing some detailed sketching. Perhaps two or three hours?"

"Three hours will be splendid." She glowered at Miss Smith who had also risen. "Mary, why don't you finish your errands, then meet me here at four o'clock?"

Miss Smith hesitated, plainly wanting to object or complain that Lady Elizabeth would be unsupervised and at his mercy, but a telling visual communication passed between them, and Miss Smith—evidently acquiescing to the lady's higher rank—backed down without comment.

"If you're sure," she broached suspiciously.

"I'll be fine. Don't worry." Sensing her companion's desire for further persuasion, Lady Elizabeth turned toward Gabriel. "I'm in good hands, aren't I?"

"The best," he could only concede.

"There, see?" She bestowed another penetrating look on Miss Smith, this one a tad more pleading.

"I'll return at four," Mary Smith ultimately said.

Gabriel embraced his unforeseen triumph and whisked Lady Elizabeth out of the room before she could change her mind.

Behind him, John's voice was discernible as he set about smoothing any ruffled feathers, while efficiently assisting Miss Smith in an expeditious departure. Within seconds, his father would have her wrapped in her cloak and deposited in the Norwich carriage.

Quickly, Gabriel ushered Lady Elizabeth out the door at the rear of the house. Anticipation induced him to race, and he practically flew down the three steps and onto the garden walk until he realized that Lady Elizabeth was nearly running to keep up with his lengthy strides.

"Where are my manners?" he murmured sheepishly, halting while she steadied herself. "I didn't mean to rush you."

"No harm done." She confidently matched his keen gaze. "I find myself to be rather in a hurry, as well."

They tarried, face-to-face, probing for hidden insight or nuance. Damn, but if he didn't notice it, once again: an irrepressible perception that he comprehended more about her than he should. They had an unusual affinity that made them closer than the circumstances warranted, that allowed him to distinguish her aims and objectives.

She was as ardent for the pending encounter as he was, and the comprehension gave him pause.

Am I doing the right thing? he caught himself thinking.

As swiftly as the absurd caprice entered his mind, he tossed it away. Of course, instigating a clandestine relationship with her was the *right* thing! Seducement was how he earned his living, how he garnered economic security for his father. She wouldn't be hurt; in fact, she'd likely get much more out of their illicit liaison than he would.

Still, she stirred him, had him doubting his incentives for subterfuge. Veracity had never been high on his list of admirable personal characteristics, and previously, he'd never suffered any qualms about bending the truth or stretching a falsehood—so long as it served his purpose—but the idea of scheming against her, of conspiring to win her affection, left a sour taste in his mouth.

With hardly any circumspection, she was geared to join him in his warren of sin and decadence so that she could voluntarily offer herself up to his indecent intrigues, and he sustained an unfamiliar, piercing twinge of guilt, which threw him totally off guard.

The woman inspired such foreign, outlandish sentiments! The effect she incited was confusing yet exciting, and only bolstered his resolve that he'd selected the appropriate course by setting his sights on her. Their affair would be out of the ordinary, would titillate and inflame beyond his wildest imaginings, so he would let his scheme play out, would enjoy the ride while it lasted, for once unsure of what his condition would be at the conclusion.

CHAPTER FOUR

MR. Cristofore was determinedly staring at her, assessing her motives or, perhaps, guessing at her intent. There was no question but that she'd shocked him with her forward conduct. And Mary, too. The poor woman had to be aghast and bewildered by Elizabeth's demand for solitude.

Previously, Elizabeth would never have dared pass time with a gentleman in his private quarters, be it his work establishment or no. Mary was the only person before whom she'd have risked such scandalous comportment; Mary could be trusted with secrets.

Elizabeth had been raised on formality and proper etiquette, yet suddenly, she was tired of the strictures by which she'd constantly lived. She craved a taste of freedom from convention, a sampling of independence. In twenty-seven years, she'd never acted extravagantly, had never broken a rule or violated a tenet of the numerous silly and frivolous codes that regulated her world.

She couldn't abide that she'd been so virtuous, so obedient, so tractable. For once, she wanted to be a tad mischievous, to savor some of the zest and animation that other—less restrained—women presumably experienced on a daily basis.

The past forty-eight hours had been an ordeal, as she'd chafed and stewed over Mr. Cristofore. She could reflect upon no other topic. She hadn't been able to eat, had scarcely slept.

With an almost insane burst of gladness, she'd penned

the note requesting an audience, and when his reply had come, recommending an immediate appointment, she'd been weak with relief. If he'd changed his mind about painting her, or had had to postpone because of prior engagements, she truly couldn't have survived a delay.

For a long while, her life had been stifling, her days too tedious to be borne. Why, she might just go mad if there weren't significant modifications! Unexpectedly, she was searching for some method of assuaging the monotony, and she was hoping against hope that Mr. Cristofore would be the cure for what seemed to be ailing her.

She'd never had an overly active imagination, steeped as she'd been in ritual and routine but, with no difficulty, she'd fantasized about Mr. Cristofore. While she couldn't picture herself as brash enough to display any body parts for his appreciation, she could certainly envision being kissed by him.

The notion was outrageous, but as she'd never been kissed before, it was also downright tantalizing. Late at night, lying in her cold, lonely bed, she would glare at the ceiling, dissecting the subtleties involved. It was so rousing, so extreme, so . . . so uncivilized.

Her nocturnal recollections provoked intense sensations of longing, and she'd jump out of bed and pace her bedchamber. Overcome by odd bursts of energy, she'd be hot and disturbed, tingly and stimulated, her heart racing for no apparent reason.

Her nipples would peak into painfully tight buds that consistently prodded against her nightdress. She ached and throbbed in numerous locations that demanded a type of attention she didn't understand, making her crave things she couldn't begin to name.

Mr. Cristofore would grasp why she was so tormented, just as he would discern the remedy, so she was eager for the chance to enjoy his uninterrupted fellowship. Not that she believed anything would actually happen. Or that she would accede should he recklessly initiate familiar behavior.

While he zealously acted as though he was smitten with her, she was convinced that his interest was feigned. After all, she'd observed him in action, so she was cognizant of the dubious state of his character. She recognized her limitations and wasn't hurt by stark reality: She was not the sort of woman who could attract a man such as Mr. Cristofore, just as he was not the kind of man to whom a woman of her stoic nature would ever succumb. They were oil and water.

Still, she could dream, couldn't she? Of fiery, capricious kisses? Where was the harm in a little wishful thinking, in some fun and frolic? And if a kiss or two transpired, so much the better! If she let herself be showered with his affable male personality, mayhap after their sessions ended and the blasted painting was completed, this infernal yearning would wane.

With a jolt, she realized that she was loitering at the base of the steps, clutching his arm, and gazing at him like an infatuated girl. Droplets of an icy winter rain drifted down, wetting their hair and shoulders. They'd exited the main house so quickly that they'd left their outergarments behind, and their clothes were speedily moistening.

What an inexperienced ninny he must find her to be! Embarrassed, she turned away, striving to appear as unflustered as possible and, as she took in the walled yard that was shielded from the street by his three-story house, she had to stifle a sigh of delight.

In the center was a cozy cottage, constructed of gray stone with white shutters and trim. Large glass windows, which had to cost him a fortune in taxes, lined the front. A fire burned inside, and smoke curled enticingly out of the chimney. Vines and rose arbors adorned the surface, the leaves absent, the branches withered with the season, but the barren stalks gave ample evidence of the riot of color that would decorate the perimeter come the spring.

It was a storybook place, an abode one might discover tucked away in a shady rural glen on a summer afternoon.

"How positively lovely," she murmured. "An enchanted bower."

"That's how I've always conceived of it."

"Whatever is it doing in the middle of London?"

"The house's former owner built it for his mother-in-law." He shrugged. "The instant I saw it, I fell in love. I simply *had* to have it."

"I can certainly comprehend why." Oh, how marvelous it would be to own such a sanctuary. To have serenity and quiet, no conflict or strife with which to deal. She was unaccountably jealous. "This is where you work?"

"For lengthy hours every day." He studied it then, too, as though having just detected its rarity. "The interior is even more wonderful. Shall we go in?"

"Yes!" She could hardly wait to see the rest.

They started down the walk, and she was damp and chilled. The temperature was frigid, the precipitation bracing, and guiltily, she pondered how long they'd tarried on the stairs. When she was with Mr. Cristofore, her discretion and prudence fled.

Buck up! she warned herself. *Before you step over the threshold and the door shuts behind you.*

While she planned to relish their rendezvous, she wasn't about to do anything foolish. He might make her feel like a giggling, swooning juvenile, but she was an adult, who'd already beheld his capacity for seduction. She wasn't about to be another conquest in what she was sure was an attenuated string of amorous pursuits.

Yet, as the door swung back, and she entered, she could barely keep from clucking her tongue in dismay. The main salon was a veritable sinner's paradise, a sanctuary of iniquity, a lavish, lewd celebration for the eyes, the nose, the skin.

Yes, it was unmistakably an artist's studio. There were easels and shelves covered with haphazard collections of paints, brushes, and other accouterments. Evidently, he had frantic spurts of inspiration that he couldn't contain for there were half-finished oil paintings—portraits, animals, pastoral countrysides, busy city avenues—leaned and piled in the corners. All were in vibrant, intense hues, rich in detail and emotion, and they offered exuberant confirmation of his talent.

However, the room was also a visual feast, meant to sensually invigorate the painter as well as the painted.

Potted plants, many with festive flowers, hung from the ceiling and sat on the floor. Drapes and rugs, in varying hues of blue and green, were scattered about. Exquisite light filtered in, making it difficult to recall the dismal weather outside. She felt as though she'd been transported onto an Italian portico.

There was an older style marble fireplace, and a stove. Both blazed with cheery fires, and the dual heating converted the ambiance to humid and tropical. She longed to shed her heavy clothing, to lounge and pretend she was on a secluded, equatorial island.

A plush fainting couch was positioned in the center. It was covered with cushy pillows that fell to the floor in casual disarray. The material was soft and inviting, imploring her to recline upon it, to sprawl and grow more comfortable than she ought.

How would she keep her wits about her in such an indecent environment? Why would she want to?

Mr. Cristofore's hand was at the small of her back, urging her inside. While any sane woman would have run in the opposite direction, she was excited, in awe, ready for whatever might happen in the risqué atmosphere. She'd come craving amusement and, apparently, she'd found it in spades.

"What do you think?" he asked from behind her. His voice was low and intimate, and it slithered across her nerves, inducing her to prickle and tremble. Crazily, she was wild to acquiesce in any unnatural deed he might suggest.

He stepped nearer, his legs pushing against her dress, so that the toes of his boots dipped under the hem of her skirt. She inhaled vigorously, cherishing his smell, his warmth.

"It's remarkable." She peered at him over her shoulder, and the side of her arm brushed his chest, her hip embedded in the cradle of his thighs. "How lucky you are."

"I agree."

Their gazes met and held, and Elizabeth was stunned by the forceful response that his adjacency produced. A tangible energy flared between them, inducing an invisible field of animation, and she'd never endured anything remotely similar.

Stimulated and enlivened, the hairs on her neck and arms stood up. The air crackled with a peculiar intensity, much as it might with the approach of a lightning storm. If she'd pointed at him, she wouldn't have been surprised to see sparks shooting from her fingertip.

He felt it, too. His anatomy was thoroughly attuned to hers, his torso reaching out, seeking a connection she couldn't define, but even in her naive condition she recognized it as the link that drew lovers together.

Languidly, his fervid appraisal drifted to her mouth, and his keen evaluation ignited a fire in her belly. His lips were just a few inches from her own. Imperceptibly, he shifted nearer, hovering, and for the briefest second, she truly supposed he was about to kiss her—an absurd assumption! She jerked away, her heart literally skipping a beat, and her startled reaction kept him from proceeding with whatever he'd proposed to do.

He increased the distance between them, and his brow creased with concern, as though demanding an explanation for their extraordinary corporeal responses. She had the distinct impression that he wasn't happy; he was confounded and baffled and—she was convinced—more than a bit annoyed.

She might have laughed at his consternation, so plainly was it written on his face, but she decided to take pity on him instead. They enjoyed a perplexing, significant, mutual affinity, when he had calculated for none to exist at all. He was less than ecstatic.

How splendid to bedevil such a magnetic, sophisticated lady's man!

Still, she could never forget that he was a bounder of the first water. Shady incentives had driven him to invite her to a painting session. In all likelihood, he had calculated a scheme that involved a scenario that would have her pining away and incessantly brooding over him and their relationship. The ultimate objective of his plot eluded her, but her inability to grasp his exact aims didn't make his machinations any less real.

While such an intrigue could presumably succeed on a less astute woman, Elizabeth hadn't been called sensible all her life for nothing. She had a good head on her shoulders, and she meant to use it. Two could play at the game of fictitious enamoration, though on her part, at least, the engrossment was genuine. Perhaps Mr. Cristofore had finally met his female match!

"What is it, Mr. Cristofore? Of a sudden, you look . . . pained."

"Me?"

"Is everything all right?"

"Sì."

The introspection that had overtaken him vanished. The puzzlement and irritation that had been so transparent were masked, replaced by his engaging smile, and the fervor and focus of it scalded her.

How absolutely phenomenal to have his undivided attention! Her feminine confidence soared. After a few hours in his company, she'd be a new woman!

"I was merely staring," he explained, "in order to catalog your facial attributes. I do it often. Does it bother you?"

As if she'd mind being scrutinized by Gabriel Cristofore! "No, it doesn't. It's just different. I'm not accustomed to such thorough assessment."

"No one is."

"It's unnerving."

"Don't worry; you'll get used to it."

"I'm sure I will."

"Would you sit?" He motioned toward the decadent, inviting sofa.

"Certainly."

In for a penny, in for a pound, she told herself.

With aplomb, she strolled to the sofa, determined to perch on the edge and to sit as ladylike as she was able. Back straight, hands folded demurely in her lap, she eased down, but as her rear landed on the cushion, poise could not be achieved.

The design encouraged slouching, compelling her to snuggle so that she wouldn't slide off onto the floor. Then, of course, once she'd sunk in fully, she was enveloped by opulence, buffered by sumptuous fabric, and she couldn't see any reason to straighten.

Rashly adapting to the luxury, she abandoned any attempt at composure and leaned to the side, balancing an elbow on one of the pillows. Wanton comportment seemed to come naturally. A few more minutes and she'd be taking down her hair!

"Might I offer you a glass of wine?"

How utterly romantic, to be sequestered with him and sipping intoxicating beverages in the middle of the afternoon! Caution was definitely called for. "Will you be having any?"

"No. It dulls my senses when I need them to be sharp."

"I believe I'll pass, then."

"Are you sure?"

"Positive."

His gaze held hers, once again, then plunged lower, across her chest, pelvis, and legs. When he arrived at her feet, he started up, his perusal meandering, tarrying in spots, and so tangible that it seemed he was really touching her.

He dallied overly long on her hips, then deliberately worked his way higher. Brazenly, he lingered at her bosom, judging her breasts, her cleavage.

Determined not to be timid or abashed, she bravely endured his silent inspection, declining to flinch or hide herself. He could look his fill, and she wouldn't object.

With fastidious informality, he studied the size and shape of her breasts, plainly taking inventory of their weight and girth as though assaying them for future handling. Her loins stirred and she writhed against the sofa, trying to allay some of the intense perturbation occurring inside her torso.

"Does it disturb you when I evaluate you so precisely?" His scorching analysis left her breasts and swung to her face.

"No." Refusing to have him see her as fainthearted, she deliberately surveyed him. She was resolved that he would compare her to his other adept lovers—of whom she was persuaded he'd had many—and that he would perceive her to be mature and worldly.

"You have a fabulous body," he mentioned irreverently.

"Thank you." She replied casually, affecting indifference, as though receiving such compliments was customary.

"You'll be beautiful on the canvas."

"I'm glad you think so."

"I *know* so."

At his vehement affirmation, she nodded. "I bow to your superior artistic estimation."

He chuckled, the sound charming and captivating, and she nestled further into the fainting couch, deciding that she could sit there forever, watching him and hearing him laugh.

"We'll begin with my sketching you." He was deluged by a potent energy, and he grabbed a stool and placed it directly in front of her. "Top to bottom. Head to toe. Back, front, sides. I must capture every aspect that makes you unique."

Without giving her a chance to demur or reflect, he hurried to a shelf, rustled through his supplies, and retrieved a portfolio packed with blank sheets and a thick charcoal pencil. He returned to the stool, scooting it nearer to the sofa's frame, moving in so that his legs tangled with hers, their feet intertwined.

His behavior was shameless, intrepid, but then, from their first encounter, he'd acted unconventionally, and she was swiftly acclimating to his impertinent ways. He was unlike any person she'd encountered before, and she was enchanted by his audacity.

However, while she'd accepted his precipitous proximity with more ease than she'd ever imagined she could, she wasn't mentally prepared to have him progress.

With his materials at the ready, he placed the black tip of his pencil against the creamy page, and she oozed trepidation. While she'd dreamed of being alone with him, had vigorously fantasized about watching him draw and paint and work, now that they were about to embark on their endeavor, her courage lagged.

She didn't dispute his ability. He'd unerringly reproduce every trait, every feature, every flaw. The man had a critical eye; nothing escaped his scrutiny. How would she appear? Did she really want to know?

Her smile faded, and he immediately noticed.

"What's wrong?"

"Nothing," she lied.

"Not true, milady." He could discern her emotional state as no one ever had, and he pondered her exhaustively, as if he could deduce the problem just from staring.

Unfortunately, being in his presence stirred sentiments she'd previously neither perceived nor heeded. Since stumbling upon him at the theater, she was a spontaneously erupting jumble of hankering and regret, and she couldn't bury the feelings she'd habitually striven so hard to suppress.

He leaned in, adding a familiarity to the situation that she couldn't ignore. His demeanor was amiable, accepting, his mannerisms sincere and sympathetic. He inspired trust, and his frankness made her anxious to unburden her troubles.

"You can confide in me," he said. "I'll never tell another soul. I swear it."

"It's so difficult." She was disgusted to note that she was stammering and blushing as though she was an insecure adolescent, once more, and confused by her maturing figure. Her assertive disposition deflated, and she glared at her lap.

He reached out, laying a calming hand on top of her own. "Are you afraid of how I will portray you?"

"Yes." She hated that he could deduce her dilemma. "I've never cared much for my appearance."

With the admission, she peeked up, only to catch him contemplating her with what seemed to be earnest understanding and authentic fondness.

Oh, he's good, she thought petulantly. *He's very, very good.*

But even though she suspected that his expression was practiced, her heart fluttered at the prospect that she might be winning his regard—even if it was slightly falsified. If she wasn't cautious, what an easy mark she'd be!

"I want you to remember something," he said.

He was soothing, cajoling, and she was desperate to credit any outrageous comment he might utter. "I'll try."

"Our time together will create a special bond. We're going to be friends. More than friends. We'll be confidants, companions; it's the way of these sessions. A personal attachment will thrive and flourish. There's no reason to fight it." He gently squeezed her fingers, his unguarded demeanor encouraging confessions. "Why are you apprehensive? Haven't I told you—over and over again!—that you are very beautiful?"

Yes, but I don't believe you! As she could hardly verbalize the opinion, she admitted, "It's just that this is so different. Being alone with you. Posing. I'm a tad unsettled."

"That's normal, but tell me the truth: Do you question my talent?"

"No." His genius was the one factor of which she had no doubt. She had only to glance around the room to see it abundantly displayed.

"Then depend on me to depict you as you are. We'll get through this, and I promise you'll be thrilled with the result." He turned their hands so that hers was lying atop his, the white of her glove pristine and chaste when contrasted with his darker skin. "Let me show you how we'll commence. You'll be more comfortable."

His thumb traced slow circles across her palm. Though no skin was touching, the thin fabric rendered scant protection, and he generated a heat that seared up her arm. The glove was held together by a small row of buttons along the edge and, steadying her wrist, he unfastened the first one.

"May I?" He advanced to the next before she could formulate a response and, in a matter of seconds, the glove was gone.

She couldn't recall when a man had last seen her uncovered hands. Exposing them was a societal prohibition she'd invariably deemed ridiculous but with which she repeatedly complied.

How exciting to have him unveil what was forbidden! The titillation was extreme!

Meticulously, he scrutinized the extremity, tracing the bone structure, the lines, bumps, and nubs. Rubbing and petting, he persisted until the appendage tingled and burned. Just from his palpation! The remainder of her arm was shielded by the sleeve of her dress. What would it be like to have more skin exhibited? How would she endure the agitation?

He snatched a pillow and slipped it onto her lap, resting her fist on it. Then he situated his supplies and, with a few broad strokes—they transpired so rapidly, she could barely follow the movements—he'd drawn her hand. He shifted it, and sketched it again. Then again. He kept on, until the empty pages were overflowing with variations on the same theme.

By the time he flipped to a sixth sheet, he was including her arm, then her shoulder and neck. With subtle pressure, he adjusted her position then continued on, incorporating a profile of her bosom and abdomen.

Mesmerized and impressed, she observed him, his slender, tapered fingers folded around the charcoal, his abundant, luscious hair flopping over his forehead. She'd never witnessed another so totally absorbed in his enterprise. No wonder he was so skilled!

He was immersed in his task, scarcely cognizant that she was in attendance, and there was something elegant and divine about beholding him.

Eventually, he was illustrating all of her, and she was forced to conclude that he was correct: Through his eyes, she was quite pretty, shapely, curvaceous and extremely feminine.

Was this how he really saw her? How glorious if it was!

From somewhere far off, a clock chimed, and she sighed. Their appointment was wrapping up when it seemed as though she'd hardly spent any time with him at all. How had four o'clock arrived so quickly? Prompt, dependable Mary would be waiting impatiently at the main house.

Would her hours with him always elapse in a blink? If this trend persisted, the entertaining engagements would pass so fleetly that, when their contract was terminated, she'd hardly have any memories to carry with her.

With the fourth bong of the clock, the reverberations penetrated his concentration. He peered toward the window.

Dazed and disoriented, he inquired, "Is it four already?"

"Yes." She was happy to discover that the minutes had progressed hastily for him, as well.

"Will your friend be punctual?"

"Aye."

"Then I suppose we must be done for today."

"I suppose," she concurred, sad all over again that it had ended so soon.

He scowled at the page upon which he was currently working, his engrossment gradually waning. The pictures he'd drawn were scattered about him on the floor, and he peered down at them as though he didn't recognize them. Then, he focused on one in particular—a silhouette of her upper body—and he picked it up, analyzing it, and her, as if comparing her to the finished product.

"How fetching you are!" he ultimately pronounced.

He submitted it to her, and she contemplated it as thoroughly as he'd just done. Amazingly, she looked pretty and young, innocent and pensive.

"I'm flattered."

"Don't be. This is truly you." He retrieved the sketch and tossed it on the pile with the others. "You're too hard on yourself."

"Perhaps," she allowed, and she pointed to the stack of amazing pictures he'd executed with so little effort. "May I keep them?"

"Not yet. I'll want to review them extensively before I begin with the actual painting."

She'd hoped to be given a token of the magical interlude, but she hid her disappointment, reminding herself that there would be other meetings, other lazy afternoons that would enchant and beguile as this one had.

"When would you like me to come again?"

As he considered his answer, he examined her so tenaciously that she was certain he would invite her back the next day, so she was greatly mystified when he said, "How about Friday? I'm free then."

Four days away! An eternity!

Yet she masked her displeasure, once more, despising how the intervening period loomed, a gray, barren void, where she would have nothing to do, and no responsibilities to oversee. Their imminent session beamed like a beacon on her individual horizon, the sole bright spot in her otherwise dreary universe. Her anticipation for the pending event only underscored the pitiful level to which her life had sunk.

"Friday will be fine," she graciously responded. "At two?"

"How about one?"

An extra hour! "Marvelous. What will we do?"

"I'll carry on with my sketching." The meeting adjourned, he stood, then assisted her to her feet. "Next time, I want you to dress differently."

"How so?"

"I need to see more of your arms. Your neck and back."

He cupped her shoulder, kneading the fleshy section just above the blade, startling her with the strength in his fingers. No one had ever stroked her similarly, not even when she was ill as a child, so the gesture was strange, but also pacifying, and she pondered what it would be like to have him caress her more exhaustively.

"I realize it's February," he mentioned, cutting into her reverie, "but might you have a summer dress available?"

"They're packed in my closet but easily located."

He perused her again, in that punctilious fashion at which he excelled. His right hand resumed its seductive massage, but his left trailed down her brow and chin, across her nape, coming close to, but stopping before, he caressed her breast.

She was paralyzed with expectation. Her heart skipped several beats, her breathing arrested, as she waited for him to slip lower, but he didn't. Instead, he simply gestured horizontally across her bosom, the motion nonchalant, as if he hadn't intended any naughty conduct.

"Wear a gown that's had the bodice cut back," he requested. "Choose one that you might don for a garden party. Something flowing and casual. Your most feminine side needs to shine through."

"As you wish."

She'd never paid much attention to color or chic attire, and fancy gala dresses had never been her style, but her mind was already awhirl with thoughts of what she might find in her dressing room that would be suitable.

Furtively, she peeked down at her conservative brown day dress. It sheathed her from neck to wrist to toes, and what she'd long classified as functional now seemed dowdy and old-maidish. Perhaps a new wardrobe was in order.

"Until Friday, then," he said as if they were polite strangers.

"Until Friday," she echoed.

"Let me escort you to the house."

"No. I'll see myself out. I know the way."

He was about to argue, so she walked to the door, opened it, and briskly stepped through, pulling it shut behind. She wanted her departing reminiscence to be that of him sheltered in the midst of his sensual retreat.

On the stoop, having abandoned the hot, muggy air, and the sultry, foreign surroundings, she shivered. A cold, fat raindrop plopped on her forehead.

"Ah, reality returns," she groused, realizing that she muttered the phrase constantly, *reality* having become so untenable. Abruptly freezing, she sped across the yard and into the town house.

Even now, she was counting the minutes, counting the hours, until Friday afternoon.

CHAPTER FIVE

JOHN Preston walked toward the receiving parlor where Mary Smith waited for Lady Elizabeth.

No doubt, Miss Smith was growing apprehensive about what precisely was transpiring between her friend and Gabriel. She'd been extremely reluctant to leave the lady to her own devices, and John had had to summon all his charm—a substantial amount—in order to ease her concerns as to her friend's decision to remain.

John was amazed, himself, by how freely the exalted noblewoman had agreed to privacy for her initial session. Despite his son's renowned way with women, Gabriel usually had to suffer through several appointments before his potential paramours were comfortable enough to meet *sans* a chaperone.

Surprisingly, Lady Elizabeth had seemed downright eager for solitude, but John wouldn't try to deduce what her early acquiescence might portend. He'd never comprehended women, their thinking or their motives, which meant that females had been the constant impetus for many of the snarls in which he'd become enmeshed.

A true gallant in the old-fashioned sense of the word, he was habitually plagued by their troubles, sucked into the middle of their trials and tribulations, and thus, he was perpetually besieged by the need to offer his services.

Women were the ultimate mystery which, of course, made them all the more fascinating. He'd rarely met one whom he didn't find to be incredibly appealing, except for that horse-faced shrew his father had demanded he marry when he'd been a mere boy of eighteen. Her nasty disposition, and her jarring nature, had grated ferociously.

Advanced age brought on reminiscence and, at the oddest times, he thought about that girl, and about the depressing episode that had followed his flippant renunciation of his planned betrothal.

His repudiation of his father's choice had been the supreme embarrassment to his family, the final straw, causing an irreparable rift that had left him penniless, adrift, and separated from all that was familiar and cherished.

After being threatened with poverty, then disinherited, he'd cut a swath through society that still had some elder members of the quality clucking their hypocritical, puritanical tongues over his antics: the liaisons he'd instigated, the duels he'd fought, the money he'd won and lost through gambling and vice.

Eventually, he'd fled to the Continent, chased out of England by creditors, the law, and a few irate husbands. As one of the scores of destitute, expatriated boys of the British aristocracy who traipsed around Europe with nothing to do and no visible means of support, he'd withstood hardship and disaster.

Yet, if he'd never traveled to Italy, he'd never have met Selena, Gabriel's mother. He'd never have fallen madly in love, would never have risked all to be with her, would never have sired his charismatic, gifted, dynamic son.

Life was a series of trade-offs. His misfortunes had led him to Selena, so he wasn't sorry for any of what had happened, though he did worry about the lingering effect events had had on Gabriel.

His son was the product of two noble houses—one in Italy, one in England—yet neither would claim him due to the fact that John could never have wed Selena. She'd already been married to another.

No relative from either family had ever met Gabriel, which was exactly how John wanted it, a petty revenge he wasn't beyond inflicting. As far as he was aware, none of the patriarchal men of his generation—on either side—had begotten an heir. His three older brothers were in their fifties and sixties, their wives childless. Selena's brothers' wives were proving equally infertile. Gabriel was the only boy birthed to any of them, yet he was a shameful love child, conceived in the worst possible scandal, the appalling circumstances of his procreation ensuring that any genealogical relationship had to be hastily and permanently denied.

Which meant that they could all go hang. They viewed Gabriel—his marvelous, talented, extraordinary boy—as merely a further example of how John's bad judgment and unrestrained comportment had ruined his life, when he didn't feel that his life had been *ruined* at all.

He'd known love and bliss to an extent few ever encountered, he'd endured turbulent, buffeting trauma, he'd survived Selena's heinous death—a depraved murder by her villainous male relatives—and had managed to carry on. Just himself and Gabriel against the world. He had no regrets, though he wouldn't have objected to having more money for the journey. A notable infusion of cash would have smoothed the ups and downs considerably. His affairs would have been easier to arrange, and Gabriel wouldn't be so set on increasing their finances through any disreputable method.

While Gabriel contended that he persisted in his devious schemes simply because he relished a good swindle, his conduct was more complicated than that. His cunning son practiced his treacherous techniques on lonely, gullible women, working to gain what he believed was fiscal reparation owed to John as compensation for what he'd been through.

Gabriel was well versed in every squalid detail of John's infamous slide to perdition, and he perceived every former slight as a wrong that needed to be righted.

As a young man, John's foes had painted him with a

sordid brush, and their memories were protracted and vicious. Some of the scorn that had been heaped upon him was deserved. Some not. He now lived peacefully, out of the public eye, and he did naught to alter those sporadic opinions that surfaced since his unobtrusive return to England two years earlier.

The convictions of others no longer mattered to him, but the snubs and censure continued to vex Gabriel. Gabriel couldn't let it go, but then he'd been refused much—wealth, status, material comforts—that might have legitimately been his but for his notorious parentage, so perhaps he had reason to be bitter.

Yet his rancor was misplaced. He was bound and determined to exact recompense for the affronts that had been visited upon John, even though John bluntly proclaimed that he'd provoked much of his own adversity. In defiance of how John insisted that he didn't require such dubious assistance, Gabriel persevered, and John ended up helping him in his various intrigues, the one currently in progress being an excellent example.

He stepped to the parlor door and unobtrusively peeked at his guest. She was nervous, furtively glancing at her timepiece, patently fretting over Lady Elizabeth's whereabouts.

His job, if one could call it that, was to entertain her, to take her mind off her companion. It wouldn't do to have her scurrying home, telling tales. Especially not when the current mark was Elizabeth Harcourt, daughter of his old nemesis, Findley Harcourt, Earl of Norwich.

Norwich was an ass, a selfish prig, an arrogant, pompous stuffed shirt, who had seriously mistreated his first wife—Lady Elizabeth's mother, Pamela. John had stood as her friend, and on one propitious occasion had even given Findley a sound thrashing for the egregious sins he'd committed against her.

Findley hadn't changed; evidence his failure to find Elizabeth a husband. For Findley's own purposes, she'd been exploited and used, so she could only benefit from an acquaintance with Gabriel, but they couldn't have Mary Smith spoiling the ruse before it had a chance to get off the ground.

He had honed his ability for flirtation and dalliance at the grandest courts of Europe, and he was a master at distraction. Gracefully, he waltzed into the room, tugging at his cuffs. He'd oft been told that he could charm the bark off a tree, which was near to the truth.

"Miss Smith," he gushed, "welcome back."

"Hello, Mr. Preston." She started to stand, but he waved her down.

"Don't you dare rise, my dear." He crossed to her, then he bowed attentively, kissing her hand, holding on to it much longer than was proper. "How enchanting to see you again so soon."

"And you, as well."

Momentarily, he paused to bestow a close-up, winning smile, designed to disarm and appease, but as his gaze locked with hers, he was the one caught off guard.

His breathing arrested, his heartbeat accelerated, and it dawned on him that he was feeling sexual desire. For pleasant, striking Mary Smith! A woman with whom he'd only been acquainted for three hours!

It had been so long since a woman had physically bewitched him that he barely remembered what attraction felt like. How incredible!

With that silvered blond hair, and that rounded, voluptuous figure, she really was stunning. Clearly, she'd once been a beauty, and she still was; an uncommon woman who had matured well and who wore her age with refinement and dignity.

She had the most exceptional blue eyes, a deep azure that was positively mesmerizing, and they evinced a perception that seemed ancient and wise. They were eyes that had seen the best and worst in life, and for the briefest instant, he imagined that he'd miraculously blundered onto a kindred spirit, someone who'd suffered and grieved, but who'd kept on, just as he had done.

Which was nonsense. After the tragedy his recklessness had launched with Selena, he never permitted himself to indulge in any fantasies involving romantic drivel. Such rubbish eventually led to heartache and disaster.

"Forgive me for staring." He gauchely stumbled over himself, still clutching her hand, and he forced himself to drop it, then eased himself into the chair that was positioned directly across from her.

"That's quite all right." She politely covered his lapse of manners, but she was assessing him much as he was scrutinizing her. Apparently, she'd felt some of the same odd sensation that had just swept over him.

Desire, too? Could it be? She appeared perplexed and confused by the prospect.

"I'm early," she mentioned.

"So we have the perfect opportunity to chat."

"Actually, Mr. Preston—"

"John, please." He interrupted her, absurdly overcome by the necessity of hearing his name on her lips.

She hesitated, not overly comfortable with the ramifications of familiarity, but then she courteously tipped her head. "As you wish . . . John."

When she didn't suggest reciprocal informality, he couldn't stop himself from requesting, "May I call you Mary?"

Once again, she studied him, but as there was nothing untoward in his entreaty, she acquiesced. "I guess that would be acceptable."

"Good, good," he inanely replied.

What was it about the woman? Her presence had him thoroughly tongue-tied!

An awkward silence ensued, as they gawked and evaluated each other. Finally, Mary broke the bumbling contact. "Do you think Lady Elizabeth will be long?"

"No, I'm sure they're almost done." Shifting on his

seat, he was dazed to recognize that his trousers were un- accountably tight. He was becoming aroused! Just by being near her! He exhaled very slowly. "For all of Mr. Cristo- fore's eccentric proclivities, he does keep to his schedule. I harp at him about it."

"So the session should conclude on time?"

"Right at four," he promised, which was likely a lie. "Would you care to see how they're coming along?" He extended the invitation even though he had no intention of letting her anywhere near the studio.

Although it was only Lady Elizabeth's initial consul- tation, there was no telling what one might stumble across in the sensually appointed cottage. After all, she was a beautiful, enchanting woman, and Gabriel a handsome, vir- ile man. They'd been sequestered for almost three hours; anything could have occurred.

He wouldn't allow Mary Smith within rock-throwing distance.

On cue, the maid entered, bearing a tea tray. She set it down on a table, then departed, shutting the door.

"It's such a dreary afternoon," he noted. "Let's warm up first, shall we?" Prudently evading his prior allusion that he would squire her outside, he proceeded to prepare a cup of tea to Mary's specifications.

As he extended it, their fingers touched, their gazes linked, once more, and he was visually trapped, held fast by her astute appraisal. The fire crackled in the grate, an icy rain pinged at the window, and he could have lingered forever in the cozy salon, watching her, and having her keen regard flit over him.

She broke off the connection, settling herself further onto the sofa, and sipping the hot beverage. Confounding him, she quietly said, "Is there some reason you don't want me to visit Mr. Cristofore's studio?"

He jerked upright. "Why wouldn't I?"

"You tell me."

"If you're worried about Mr. Cristofore's intentions toward Lady Elizabeth, I can assure you that—"

"He's your son, isn't he?" she interposed. "Why do the two of you pretend no relation?"

How did she fathom so blasted much?

He stammered and stuttered but couldn't respond coherently. There was no simplistic explanation for his and Gabriel's sustaining affection for Selena, or for Gabriel's need to honor her memory. They both held themselves responsible for her untimely demise. John, because he'd whisked her away from a desperate predicament, thus enraging her volatile male family members. Gabriel, because he'd been born, his very existence the precipitating cause of her slaying.

Mary scowled, the elemental gesture spurring him to silence.

"Your paternity is so blatant," she said. "Don't insult my intelligence by disputing it."

As she stared him down, he felt stupid. There was no point in defending the undefendable. The woman was no fool.

Lamely, he supplied, "It's just easier to avoid clarifications."

"Easier for whom?"

He wasn't about to get into the odious details, so instead, he confessed, "Gabriel would never hurt Lady Elizabeth."

"There are different kinds of *hurt*, John," she gently urged. "You understand that."

"Yes, I do."

"Lady Elizabeth has been very sheltered in her upbringing. A dishonest gentleman could effortlessly take advantage of her."

"I realize that."

"Your son seems very . . . worldly."

"He is."

"I care for Elizabeth. I've known her since she was a babe, and she's had a difficult life, particularly in recent months. I wouldn't want her maltreated. By anyone." She hesitated a beat, then inquired, "Will your son make her happy?"

"Yes, he will."

"Swear it to me."

"I swear it."

She nodded, accepting his vow, but her threat was clear: If Gabriel did anything to aggrieve Lady Elizabeth, Mary would intervene. What a catastrophe that would be!

He was inordinately curious as to what she'd just described as their lifelong relationship. "Are you a friend of Lady Elizabeth's?"

"Me? Goodness no. I'm her employee. Her head housekeeper, but I wouldn't like to—"

"*You* are the head housekeeper for the Earl of Norwich?" He was dismayed, and rude because of it.

"Yes."

"Then you're Findley's—" He didn't dare finish.

After a protracted delay, she sternly probed, "I am the earl's . . . what?"

He hadn't meant to refer to the earl, or to the secret confidence that Findley's first wife, Pamela, had shared decades earlier, but he was shocked at discovering Mary's identity.

She was a homewrecker! A jezebel! A strumpet!

How ironic! He'd finally met a woman with whom he possessed a liberal corporeal affinity only to learn that she was little more than a paid courtesan.

"Nothing," he insisted, coming to his senses. To where had his manners disappeared? For all his profligate habits, he was still a gentleman. "Forgive me. I was out of line."

"Yes, you were," she retorted sharply.

Flagrantly furious, she stood, as did he, and she marched to the hallway, plainly ready to stomp out to the cottage and retrieve her employer, but they were saved from an embarrassing scene by Lady Elizabeth's appearance in the corridor. She was energized and ecstatic in a fashion she hadn't been upon arrival, so something had obviously transpired. An embrace, perhaps? An ardent kiss?

She would definitely wish to return for a subsequent appointment, but would Mary Smith let her? How much control did the housekeeper have over the noblewoman? And in light of the earl's remarriage, what was the status of Mary Smith's ongoing, intimate relationship with him? Was she still in a position to voice her suspicions?

"Lady Elizabeth"—he smoothed over the perilous moment—"I trust your session went well?"

"It was marvelous," she replied animatedly. "Mr. Cristofore is a fabulous artist."

"His *son,* Lady Elizabeth," Mary caustically charged.

"What?"

"His real name is Gabriel Cristofore Preston. Mr. Cristofore is Mr. Preston's son." Mary Smith glared in his direction. Where before she'd looked at him with perplexity and an amount of affection, now he saw only scorn and contempt. "It's just a little game they play at the expense of unsuspecting women."

"Mary—" he tried, feeling horrid.

"Miss Smith to you!"

Lady Elizabeth's mood was too exuberant, her sentiments too distracted, so she didn't catch the import of Mary's disclaimer or the undercurrents of their discord. Pleasantly, she said, "Well, then, your *son* is a fabulous artist. I can't wait for our next interview."

"I'm needed at home, milady," Mary remarked. "The driver is out front. Shall we go?" She efficiently maneuvered Elizabeth toward the door where the butler proffered their cloaks. When John moved to escort them to their carriage, she cast a contemptuous glance over her shoulder. "We don't require your presence, Mr. Preston. We can find our own way."

He tarried at the parlor's threshold, watching them depart, while rueing his mishandling of the situation. What effect would his bungling have on Gabriel's venture? Had he imprudently wrecked the entire endeavor? More importantly, how would he ever make amends to Mary for his terrible gaffe?

Charlotte Harcourt, Countess of Norwich, dawdled at her mirror and made a final assessment of her coif and gown.

Her blue evening dress was modishly styled, emphasizing her inadequate breasts and unsuitable cleavage. She adjusted the bodice, yanking at her corset, striving to supplement fullness where there was none. The diamond necklace the earl had conferred as an engagement gift dangled over the swell of her bosom, catching the light and underscoring the dramatic turn her life had precipitously taken. She twirled back and forth, examining herself from every angle.

"Quite fetching." She blew a kiss at her reflection.

With her shimmering blond hair piled high, and her face delicately colored with paints, she was majestic, precisely how one of the most prominent women in the land should appear before going down to sup with her illustrious husband.

"Look at me now, you silly twits!" she muttered, thinking of the dozens of other girls who'd vied for the earl. But she'd wanted to be a countess more than any of them, and now she was.

Many of her former rivals were still green with envy, especially those who hadn't wed and who were now considered to be on the shelf. They were bitter, spreading rumors that—with her father only a baron—she'd married above herself, that the earl had been so smitten by her comeliness that he hadn't bothered to delve into the state of her dowry, or the condition of the properties she'd brought to the union.

They'd even maliciously gossiped that the earl hadn't really cared whom he married, that he'd merely been in a hurry. In their spiteful version, they claimed any girl would have sufficed, and as she'd been more eager than the others, his decision had been easy.

Well, she'd shown them all. Besides, as her mother frequently pointed out, the level of their grumbling was in direct proportion to their paltry jealousies, so she mustn't torment herself over any of the stories they disseminated.

Still, it was painful to realize how many covetous, resentful people there were in the world. With so many begrudging her her good fortune, she tried not to flaunt her ascendance, but honestly, how could a girl be expected to hide the boons she'd acquired through excessive planning and hard work?

She'd married one of the wealthiest, most respected men in the kingdom. He parleyed with the revered leaders of government and industry. Why, the Prince Regent himself sought out the earl's advice and counsel! He was lauded and extolled, fawned over, his favor curried. Underlings begged for his notice or assistance, and she was his wife. His countess. The most beautiful, ravishing female in all of London, which made it acutely difficult to comprehend why she hadn't been welcomed into high society.

From the instant her engagement had been announced, she should have been bumped to the top of the social ladder, a preferred guest for soirees, musicales, and teas, the best balls and parties. Instead, she was constantly overlooked or downright omitted.

Initially, she'd been bewildered. Then hurt. Finally, embarrassment had set in. A distinct pattern was clear, and the only conclusion she could reach was that she was being intentionally discounted.

Her mother insisted that, by now, she should have established herself as London's premier hostess. Her suppers should be the talk of the town, with people anxious for invitations, but the reality was that she could scarcely conjure up enough bodies to fill the chairs at the table.

A malevolent gleam came into her eye. It was Mary Smith's fault. The incompetent housekeeper's inefficiency had spoiled three banquets. Elizabeth was culpable, too, for rejecting Charlotte's attempts to fire the inept woman. Who did Elizabeth think she was, issuing orders and counter-manding Charlotte's edicts? The town house was no longer Elizabeth's domain, but she refused to recognize that fact.

If Charlotte could just get the earl to listen to her com-plaint about Mary Smith! Once briefly, she'd tried to raise the feasibility of termination, but the earl had cut off her complaint and brutally reprimanded her. Every time she recalled how he'd humiliated her, she bristled. The matter was so vital to her contentment, yet he wouldn't support her.

She'd have liked to give him a piece of her mind on the topic, but as always happened when she was around her husband, she'd held her tongue because, much as she hated to admit it, she was afraid of him.

He was so old, so large, so intimidating! He exuded power and authority, and he wielded both in a manner that was terrifying. His temper was legendary, and he used con-tempt like a weapon, repeatedly making her feel ten years old, completely helpless, and irrelevant. She despised him for his disrespectful treatment, but more often, she loathed him for what he did to her in the night when he visited her room.

Her mother had sufficiently apprised her of what would occur in the marriage bed, but still, she'd been so shocked, so repulsed, by his nocturnal thoroughness. She shuddered from contemplating the degradations to which she was steadily subjected. He brought a lamp, which he kept lit; he made her disrobe, made her touch him, turn over, and do disgusting things with her hands and mouth.

As a veritable innocent, how could she have predicted the secret horrors of the wedded condition?

Yet, she knew her duty, and she did it without com-plaint. As her mother had explained, it was the price she had to pay for the rest, but his preoccupation with the marital act certainly made it arduous to speak civilly with him during the day.

If she would just begin increasing! For the past six months, she'd submitted to him—oftimes twice and thrice a night!—and there was no babe to show for her submissive efforts!

With each successive month, the earl grew more displeased, subtly reminding her that she was failing to fulfill the sole obligation of marriage. To her chagrin, others were beginning to think the same. She could see the pitying looks from the staff, the whispers of so-called friends. Whenever she went visiting, people cast furtive glances at her stomach until she yearned to shout at them to leave her be! She was trying her best! At every task presented!

If only she could wrest control of her house from Mary Smith and Elizabeth! She would bring her mother to town from the country, so that she could receive valid counsel on social transactions, and sound guidance as to supervising the servants. With her mother in residence, everyone would shortly grasp that she was a force with which to be reckoned!

The clock chimed the hour and, as she was now forty-five minutes late, she decided to go down. The earl and Elizabeth would be impatient over the delay she'd caused.

The earl rarely addressed her, so tardiness was a sure technique for garnering his notice. As to Elizabeth, Charlotte loved to irritate and annoy the older woman. Punctuality was one of Elizabeth's premium virtues, and Charlotte strove to ensure that supper was unceasingly postponed just so that Elizabeth would be exasperated.

She left her bedchamber and strolled to the landing, carefully timing her steps so that—in case anyone was watching—she seemed to float down the curving staircase. Serenely, she approached the parlor. The door was ajar, and she was thoroughly piqued that no footman was attendant to announce her, thereby foiling her grand entrance.

Under Mary Smith's lackadaisical administration, the

staff was impossible! The servants were little more than hooligans who should be thrown out to fend for themselves in the vile neighborhoods where they'd been bred.

Well, she'd deal with the situation later! For now, she smoothed her frown and forced calm into her demeanor, as she fluttered into the salon. "Sorry I'm late, milord, I was just . . ."

The room was empty! They hadn't been waiting for her!

They wouldn't dare go in to supper without her! Would they?

Fuming, she tiptoed to the door that adjoined the dining room and peeked inside. It, too, was vacant, a lone retainer loitering next to the sideboard.

"Where could they be?" she seethed.

Sneaking to the hallway, she peered out, relieved that none of her slothful employees were lurking. She crept to the rear of the manor, and up the back stairs that covertly took her to the third floor and a guest bedroom, which boasted a conveniently located flue. All sorts of interesting discourse drifted up the expedient chimney. As a new bride, she'd stumbled upon it during one of her explorations, and the discovery had come in handy on numerous occasions.

Elizabeth and the earl would be in the library, his precious haven that was off limits to Charlotte. When she'd first arrived in the dreary mansion, he'd instructed her that she wasn't allowed inside, and she'd invariably complied, but he went there with Elizabeth, and the slight burned Charlotte with humiliation. The two of them disappeared into the private chamber whenever they wanted a discreet conversation—one to which Charlotte couldn't be privy, because she was the main topic.

Stealthily, she shut the door, and leaned against the wall, finding the vantage point that rendered maximum eavesdropping. Voices rose from below.

". . . I don't know how much more I can take, Father." Elizabeth was jabbering, and Charlotte squeezed her hands into tight fists. "Her behavior is becoming more outrageous with each passing day."

"She's just a child," the earl rebutted, his tone irritated and put-upon, and Charlotte cringed. She detested how he derided her! "It's a mystery to me why you can't be more tolerant of her fickleness and volatility. Learn to get along with her."

"It's not just me. It's everyone in the house."

There was a prolonged silence, then the earl scolded, "I've told you before that I won't listen to these recurrent lamentations. Domestic concerns are none of my affair. You women must come to terms with one another, and I—"

"She tried to fire Mary again today."

"She what?" The air fairly crackled with his ire, and the terse mode of his question had Charlotte straightening.

"I intervened and wouldn't let her."

"What was the reason?"

"She didn't like how her breakfast eggs had been cooked."

"Is Mary . . . is she all right?"

"Yes, but she can't take much more, either. She advises that she's going to start searching for another post."

Charlotte couldn't stifle her glee. The earl was adamant that Mary stay on, in spite of her slovenly conduct and defective management. If she'd just withdraw on her own! Her departure would solve so many of Charlotte's problems!

"You dissuaded her, of course."

"For now"—*Witch,* Charlotte mouthed—"but I don't know that I would a second time. She's been with us her whole life. She shouldn't have to abide such disrespect. Not from anyone."

Charlotte's rage spiraled to a new height. How could Elizabeth be permitted to make such impertinent comments! The earl should have her whipped for disparaging his countess! How could he not! Yet he totally disregarded

Elizabeth's audacity, focusing instead on placating Charlotte's adversary, Mary Smith.

"I've warned Charlotte to desist," he said, "and I've made it clear to Mary that I won't accept a resignation from her."

"If this nonsense persists," Elizabeth interjected, "I doubt your opinion will matter to Mary in the least."

"We'll see about that!" the earl blustered.

"Let her go, Father," Elizabeth chided. "Let me go, too. Buy me a small house—I don't need anything fancy—and I'll take Mary with me. Charlotte can arrange the house as she sees fit, and we'll be out of your hair."

"You've never been a bother, and I couldn't get along without Mary. You know that."

"Please, Father. Something's got to give."

"It's not as bad as you make it out to be."

"How can you say that? You're never here to witness how she acts!"

"I weary of this discussion," the earl barked. "I'll not have you living by yourself, like some notorious member of the demimonde. We'd be the talk of London. The scandal would never die down."

"But I don't belong here!" his darling Elizabeth sniveled.

"If you're so intent on a home of your own, perhaps I should select a husband for you."

"Why? So I can live in misery as you are?"

Well! The presumption of the harridan! Charlotte simmered with resentment. Her marriage to the earl was her foremost accomplishment! How dare Elizabeth deprecate it!

"That was uncalled for," the earl angrily rejoined.

There was a lengthy interlude where it was evident he was braced for an apology, but it wasn't extended. Charlotte could just picture them, toe to toe, furious, headstrong.

"This debate is over," the earl inevitably pronounced, "and I won't listen to your complaint again. Don't raise it with me. Now"—there was rustling as chairs were pushed back—"you've wasted enough of my time. It's been a trying day, and I would have my evening meal. Which I plan to enjoy in blessed silence. I'll not tolerate any feminine sniping."

For many minutes after the noises of their egress had faded, Charlotte huddled, brooding upon what had been revealed.

So . . . Elizabeth and the housekeeper were disgruntled, were they? They were bent on undermining Charlotte's dominion, on weakening her sovereignty by tattling their accusations to the earl. Well, Charlotte would not yield to their bewailing or criticism. She was the countess, and they both needed a reminder of her supremacy over them.

She wanted them gone. Immediately. Mary Smith, first. Elizabeth, second. She wouldn't have either on the premises, and she would take whatever steps were necessary to ensure their hasty egress. Apparently, they were both eager to leave, so with some provident plotting, she could shove them out the door with scant trouble. But what was the best way to commence?

CHAPTER SIX

"TAKE down your hair."

Lady Elizabeth stared at him as if he'd just grown a second head. "What?"

"You heard me."

How comely she was! The pink gown, with matching parasol, slippers, and gloves, that she'd selected for their afternoon session was the exact shade and style he'd have picked himself, if he'd been offered the chance. The bright color highlighted her dark hair, her ruby lips. The fashionable tailoring bared her shoulders and arms, stretching tight across the bodice to emphasize her full bosom, then billowing out in the skirt to stress her rounded hips, her long legs. She looked as though she'd just returned from a fancy garden party at which the members of the *ton* whiled away their summer days.

Her straw hat sported a wide brim and a green band that tied under her chin. A corresponding band circled her slender waist, and it was knotted into a large bow that swept down her back, further accentuating her lush curves. The emerald yards of ribbon intensified the green in her eyes, making them appear as verdant as mowed grass in a country meadow.

When he'd advised her to don something *summery* for their subsequent appointment, he hadn't really believed she would. She seemed so steeped in convention and ritual that he'd imagined it might take weeks to overcome her inhibitions so that she'd begin to accouter herself with more flair.

The brown, drab, functional attire in which she'd formerly garbed herself was gone. Young, fair, and alluring, she'd become a different woman entirely. Amazing what a new outfit could do.

"Take down your hair," he reiterated.

"I'm not sure if it would be appropriate to—"

"Do it for me."

With an impulse that bordered on desperation, he was avid to behold her hair flowing free and unencumbered. During the past few nights, he'd dreamt about her hair, had visualized how velvety it would be, how far it would hang. He'd pictured himself running his fingers through it, sinking his nose in it, burrowing his cheeks in the soft strands.

"All right," she ultimately acceded, "I will."

He breathed a sigh of relief as her graceful, manicured fingers rose and languidly unraveled the bow under her chin. She grabbed for the hat's brim and yanked it off, tossing it away so that it fluttered to the floor, then she plucked out the combs. As she worked, her corset pushed at and reshaped her breasts so that he was tantalized by the creamy swell of her bosom.

Vividly, he could conceive of her nipples. They would be elongated and erect, the areola rosy and contrasted with the white of the shapely mounds. The image was so stirring that his manly blood surged to his groin, filling his cock, and he inflated to an obscene length. Uncomfortable, aroused, distressed by how promptly her presence excited him, he moved out of her line of sight, over to one of the shelves that housed his sketching papers and chalks.

At the counter, he pretended to rifle through his supplies, and he used the interlude to calm his cravings. He was so hard for her!

She had an unusual power to inflame, and he wasn't accustomed to it. If mere thoughts of her could cause such anatomical upheaval, what would happen when their relationship progressed to the physical? How would he withstand the bodily stimulation she so readily induced?

Disturbed by his ruminations—disturbed by her!—he whirled around, forcing down the wave of longing that washed over him on seeing how winsome she looked. How trusting! She regarded him so innocently that it seemed she'd do whatever he asked.

If he was astute in his responses, he could eventually persuade her to commit many lewd acts. Clearly, she was ready. The restraint she'd possessed before they'd met had vanished. He could convince her to do anything and . . . for once, he didn't want to. He was a heel and a cad to be deceiving her for his nefarious purposes.

The notion of taking advantage of her was distasteful and wrong; he could feel it deep in his bones. His habitual urges—to dalliance, then larceny—had been quashed.

There was something about her, a patience or composure mayhap, that intrigued and called to him. On an intuitive level, he recognized that she was unique from any woman he'd previously encountered. Being involved with her was a circumstance to be treasured, coming to know her a boon, and she deserved better than to be duped by a bounder such as himself.

Yet as he watched her, as her incredible breasts molded against the front of her gown, as the hint of her nipples poked at the fabric, he conceded that he was smitten. That he lusted after her merely because she would render all of herself to a relationship, and the giving and sharing would be divine. He was attracted to her as he'd been to no other, and whatever obscure fiscal benefit he might receive from her in the future had ceased to matter.

She was proceeding too slowly, and he couldn't tolerate the suspense, so he hastened over and stepped behind her, shoving her hands away.

"Let me assist you."

She glared at him over her shoulder. "You're too impatient."

"Where you're concerned, I can't help myself."

For this rendezvous, he'd situated a stool in the middle of the floor, and she balanced upon it, the slight turn shifting her weight precariously. He leaned in, steadying her, and the more intimate position pressed her to him, and he could barely keep from pulling her closer, from flexing against her in an effort to allay the tension in his loins.

To his delight, she didn't flinch away, though worry furrowed her brow. She studied him, cognizant of the sizzling sensation betwixt their joined torsos. He hardly understood the novel stimulation himself, so she had to be utterly perplexed.

"How is it that you so freely undermine my sense of propriety?" She relaxed so that their bodies settled together more completely. "Why does it feel so right when you touch me?"

"We enjoy a peculiar affinity, you and I."

"Aye, we do. But why?" She spun on the stool, a leg now propped against his own, a hand at his waist. "You could suggest any deed to me, and I'd agree without hesitation. If you knew the kind of person I am . . . if you understood my background and upbringing—"

"Oh, but I do."

"Then you must realize how abnormal it is for me to be here. I'm behaving so strangely, so out of character."

She was begging him for an explanation, when he comprehended little himself about the secret chemistries that drew one particular individual to another.

"There's nothing *strange* about what's transpiring." He traced across her cheekbone, the fleshy section of her cheek. Her skin was smooth as silk, and she purred and stretched, much like a lazy cat seeking a caress. "Magnetism simply develops, sometimes, between a man and a woman. The first time I saw you—that night at the theater—I felt that there was a special connection between us."

"So did I."

"It seemed as if you were luring me to your side. I

shocked you when I spoke with you, but I could no more have avoided approaching you than I could have stopped breathing."

"After you departed, I felt so alone, as if the world was less bright."

"Precisely."

"And since then, I haven't been able to concentrate on any topic but you."

He smiled ruefully; he should have been celebrating the facility with which their association was progressing, but in all actuality, he was baffled. He'd never had a conquest commence so fleetly, or the woman primed to advance to the next stage with scant endeavor on his part. She was poised, enthusiastic.

"Will we always feel this way?"

"I suspect we will."

His irksome admission gave him pause. Never before had he come across desire and affection that refused to diminish, and the awareness that he might be at the beginning of more than a meaningless fling made him cautious.

How would he—the consummate scoundrel—deal with such an impossible consequence?

He wasn't interested in a lasting relationship. Intense devotion and commitment were absurd.

If he had any qualms about the folly of unchecked emotional involvement, he need only consider his own parents. Everlasting love was a fantasy, an excuse one used to justify passion run amok, and in his experience, passion waned. Promptly and unequivocally.

His father dubbed him a ruthless, unromantic pessimist. Gabriel labeled himself a realist who assessed the facts, who never lost sight of his objectives by allowing himself to be overwhelmed by ardor or fondness.

Elizabeth Harcourt was compelling him to reevaluate his established beliefs. Would they engage in a liaison that evolved far beyond his ability to control it? Was such an affair even feasible for a jaded man such as himself? Would he finally undergo the sort of soul-shattering attachment that had driven his parents to madness in their frantic compulsion to be together?

The concept was frightening, and he shook it away, declining to give it credence. Lady Elizabeth was a mark, a conquest, no different from the scores of other women who had passed through his studio over the years. She had a remarkable effect on his corporeal cravings, but it was no more than that and, as he'd learned through extensive practice, sexual appetites could be managed.

Still, he hated how she had him ruminating over irrational ideas and questioning the very tenets by which he lived. Weary of his tedious speculation, he decided to return to the realm where he excelled—seduction.

Stepping behind her, once more, he jerked at another comb, and her heavy mass of hair swished down. It shimmered and swirled, in varying shades of chestnut, auburn, and gold; the lengthy ends framed her figure, plunging past her buttocks.

"Your hair is magnificent."

"No man has ever seen it down but you."

"I'm glad."

There was a second stool a few feet away, and he grabbed for it and centered it behind her, then he sat, too, scooting it and spreading his legs, so that his body partially surrounded her own. His thighs cradled hers, and their positioning placed her shapely ass just inches from his incited loins, their indecent proximity stimulating and thrilling.

He bent nearer, his chest in contact with her posterior. At the unfamiliar melding of their torsos, her spine stiffened, and he circled his arms around her waist, resting his palms on her thighs, massaging, encouraging her to recline.

"I'm going to touch your hair," he clarified. "I want to discover its texture. Don't be afraid."

"I'm not."

"Good."

"I just wasn't ready for . . . so much, so soon."

"I know. This is very new to you."

She turned slightly. "Don't hold back on my account."

"I won't."

There it was again, that distinct perception that she grasped what he was up to, that she'd deduced that their meetings were about much more than painting and always would be.

He focused on her mouth, on those moist lips that beckoned and beguiled. Her breath was warm and soft against his cheek, her green eyes penetrating and full of wonder. A world of expectation hovered in the moment.

Were he brave enough, he could kiss her. She was blatantly anxious, yet he did nothing to initiate an embrace, for it unexpectedly occurred to him that he wasn't inclined to ascertain what *kissing* her would truly be like.

Without a doubt, it would be marvelous. He'd yearn to do it over and over, to persist until there was no stopping, and the prospect was terrifying. Such monumental insatiability led a man to ruin, made him vacillate and careen from one passion-induced, reckless decision to the next.

With a finger to her chin, he rotated her forward so that she couldn't entice him with that luscious mouth, those clever eyes, and he set himself to the more mundane task of exploring her hair. Sifting through it, he separated the strands, lifted it and let it drop like a mahogany waterfall. He nestled it in his hands, gauging its weight, its pliancy. Nuzzling in it, he inhaled the soap with which she washed, the smell of her skin.

She stoically submitted to his investigation, tipping her head or neck to give him a plentiful view and easier access.

"I'm going to sketch you from the back." A shiver jarred her, whisking down her spine, into her hips. She prickled with goose bumps. Disconcerted, he inanely mentioned, "I love this dress. It's exactly the type I was hoping you'd wear."

"It was difficult to conclude what you'd like best."

"You seemed to know." The insight was disquieting.

How could she so readily discern his tastes and preferences? He didn't want her to understand him so well! "The color and style are impeccable. They ideally emphasize your attributes."

As he talked, he laid his palms on her shoulders, rubbing the soft tissue, spurring her to release her pent-up tensions and accept his caress.

Once he could sense her muscles loosening, he massaged her until he grazed the rim of her bodice, then he urged the fabric down the slightest bit, exposing more of her stunning bosom. With his unconstrained handling, her breathing had elevated, each inhalation raising those two flawless mounds so that they prodded precariously against the edge of her corset.

Gad, but her breasts were so splendid! He couldn't wait to behold them in all their spectacular, naked glory. To have those hard, erect nipples in his hands, at the mercy of his tongue.

He continued on, his fingers blazing a trail, tracing the bumps, dips, and ridges of her spine, then he traveled on to her hips and bottom. Though her feminine figure was protected by skirt and petticoat, he could determine shape and substance. She was lush, curvaceous, a temptress who fueled his flights of masculine fancy.

"I adore your body," he whispered. "You're voluptuous, superb in all the ways a woman should be."

Intending to shock and provoke, he tossed her hair over her shoulder, revealing a broad expanse of her upper back, then he deftly unfastened the two top buttons of her dress. The maneuver instantly slackened the front so that it fell away from her bosom.

At his audacity, she gasped in dismay, clutching at her cleavage while whipping around to glare at him, shooting him with her teeming disapproval. She was breathtaking; she appeared to be disrobing for a lover, or perhaps, surprised in her boudoir as she rushed to don her apparel after hours of illicit sexual coquetry.

"Don't move," he commanded. "Stay just as you are while I draw."

Rapidly, he commenced recording her, but he couldn't sketch swiftly enough. How he wished there was a device that could immediately capture her likeness! That he could snap his fingers, and have her naturalness accurately illustrated!

Frustrated by his slow methodology, his hand nevertheless glided over the pages. She was an incredible model, centered, motionless, serene at her task, and with simple, stark lines, he scrupulously depicted what his eye so distinctly noted: her beauty, her sensuality, her suppressed, erotic disposition.

He drew more than she'd really revealed, using artistic license to widen the split in her dress, then to do away with it altogether, so that he was sketching bare back and buttocks, the naughty spots provocatively shielded by her hair.

Moving the stool, so that he was observing her profile, he took further aesthetic liberties, dropping her gown more than it actually was so that a breast was exhibited to the nipple. By examining her so thoroughly, by delving across skin and bone, he knew much and could infer the rest. While sharpening his talent, he'd meticulously analyzed the human form, had drawn thousands—if not tens of thousands—of people in his life. His imagination was vivid, and he could surmise how she would look unclothed.

He drew until his hand grew tired, until he glanced up and noted that she was exhausted from holding the pose he'd demanded. In mid-stroke, he halted.

"That's enough for now," he said, and she slumped down.

As always happened when he'd been in a frenzy of composition, his flourish of inspiration ebbed, leaving fatigue in its wake. His arms were tired, and his pencil slipped to the floor, his fingers no longer capable of sustaining its weight.

Diverse illustrations were scattered about them, like

leaves fallen from a tree, evidence of his stimulating burst of creativity.

He leaned down and scooped up several of them, scanning them for skill and precision. She appeared just as he'd wanted her to, just as he saw her.

Satisfied, he held them out.

"Look," he ordered.

Nervously, she peeked down, but she was apprehensive, even though she was exceptionally tantalizing in each one. He had the talent to correctly reproduce her handsome features, and his ability hadn't failed him.

"Look!" he repeated more gently.

Tentatively, she peered at the top one, a silhouette that showed her to be pretty, and so very, very sexy.

She scrutinized it for a protracted period, awed and astounded that he perceived her in a light so divergent from her own. "Is this really me?"

"*Sì.*"

Her eyes searched his, probing for equivocation or fabrication, but he was telling her the truth. She had a significant elegance, but she took great pains to hide it.

Upon accepting the depth of his sincerity, a blush reddened her cheeks, and her attention skittered away, resting, once again, on the drawing.

"It doesn't seem possible."

She was so unsure of herself! So unaware of her innate appeal and charm! Evidently, her comeliness had been disparaged and belittled for so long that she couldn't picture herself as remotely attractive, and his heart went out to her. What must her life have been like, growing up under Findley Harcourt's direction and authority?

As she inspected the sketch in detail, she was a lonely, tragic figure, and he suffered outlandish pangs of peculiar sentiment: to protect and shelter, to cherish and admire, to nurture and comfort.

With his previous lovers, he'd ceaselessly been conscious of their lack of self-esteem. He had a knack for detecting a woman's insecurities and utilizing them to bolster their pride and independence, but he'd invariably done so in order to achieve the end result, which was his financial enrichment.

Yet, as he assessed Lady Elizabeth, he was compelled to acknowledge that his misplaced affection for her had changed his original incentives. He had no ulterior motive. He truly cared about her and wanted her to be happy.

What a bizarre transformation! Just how was he supposed to deal with such a curious turn of events? If he wasn't pursuing her for economic enhancement, what was his goal? Certainly not a permanent relationship. Because of her status, they had no future. She'd never stoop so low; he'd never reach so high.

So what was his intent?

He couldn't define his objective; he only knew that he had to convince her that his appreciation was genuine.

Eager to wipe away her frown, to assuage her reservations, he slid his stool nearer, so that they were side by side, but facing each other, and he took the stack of renderings from her.

"I'm not lying, Elizabeth," he said, boldly pronouncing her given name, and relishing how it rolled off his tongue.

"Mr. Cristofore—"

"Gabriel," he declared. "You're the most extraordinary woman I've met in a long while."

He rifled through the stack, hunting for one of his favorites, where he felt he'd adequately portrayed her basic character: a profile of her naked shoulder, of the swell of her breast. It was a stirring, captivating drawing that animated and vitalized his male sensibilities.

"When I see you like this"—he gestured over the parchment—"I'm aroused and titillated. As a man. As a potential lover. You excite me with your sensual nature. I'm utterly bewitched."

"I want your words to be true," she murmured.

"They are."

Finally, she found the courage to wrench her appraisal from the sketch. She gazed at him, so ingenuous, and so damned fetching. Previously, he'd warned himself away from the foolishness of kissing her, yet abruptly, he couldn't recall why he'd chosen caution and restraint over intemperance and excess.

Circumspection wasn't part of his constitution and never had been. Without hesitating to debate the lunacy of what he was about to do, or to dissuade himself from his impetuous, dangerous course, he narrowed the distance between them.

His mouth brushed her own, and sweetly, deliberately, she permitted the tender overture. Her lips perfectly melded to his as if they had been sculpted for kissing him and no other purpose.

Ah, he thought, *this is what heaven must be like.*

His senses reeling, his blood pounding through his veins, his cock hard and braced for action, he closed his eyes and indulged.

CHAPTER SEVEN

As Gabriel's lips settled upon her own, Elizabeth wasn't shocked in the least. For the prior four days and nights, for longer than that—perhaps her entire life—she'd dreamed about this moment, and she was delighted to find that she had vastly underestimated the actualities of the event. In fact, her fantasies were nothing compared to the reality.

He gently cuddled against her, and she readily allowed the intimacy. Automatically, her eyes fluttered shut, and her senses engaged, heightening her enjoyment. She could smell the soap with which he bathed, the starch his laundress used in his shirt. There were other aromas, as well, of linseed oil and turpentine, of the fresh outdoor air, and another, more distinct scent that was uniquely his.

His chin brushed hers, and she felt the hint of whiskers on his shaved skin. The sensation was exhilarating, the experience absolutely too luscious for words, and she wanted it to never end.

With practiced ease, he nimbly and cleverly taught her how to react, how to respond, and she was amazed to note that she had an extraordinary aptitude for kissing, that she adapted to it as though she'd kissed him a thousand times.

Her world seemed to have tipped off balance with the onslaught of stimulation. She was alive in every pore, invigorated down to the smallest bodily particle. Her breasts swelled, her nipples throbbed. She was aching and restless, the mysterious womanly core between her legs contracting, her body crying out for a relief that was just beyond her ken.

She reached for him, steadying her hands on his forearms. The gesture was an approval of sorts, a surrender, a request for more, and he didn't disappoint.

Enhancing the pressure, thrilling her further, he deepened the kiss, a greater urgency in his motions and maneuvers. The move pushed her backward, but as there was no support on the rear of the stool, he stabilized her, holding her firmly in place so he could continue his masterful provocation.

Her front was snuggled against him, her breasts in direct contact with his chest. The collision set off a maelstrom of agitation. Her clothing was too tight, her corset a useless requirement.

She yearned to have his agile fingers coursing across every inch of her exposed flesh. Her torso screamed out for manipulation and handling. If he didn't touch her—immediately—she just might expire!

As if intuiting her increased perturbation, he intensified the embrace. His tongue flicked at her mouth, parting her lips. Asking. Asking. Instinctively, she perceived what he wanted; she opened and welcomed him inside.

He tasted like wine and tobacco, and she reveled in the novel flavors. Reeling, she tightened her grip, and he responded by pulling her off her stool and onto his lap. Her hip was wedged into his groin, and his tongue in her mouth. He explored, and as she acclimated, she grew more bold. With her own tongue, she eagerly stroked his in the rhythm he'd instituted, and the intrepid gesture caused him to growl low in his throat. The sound reverberated through her, encouraging her to augment her participation, rather than sit and passively receive his attentions.

She investigated the flex of shoulder, the width of chest, the strength of muscle. He was flat where she was rounded, hard where she was soft, rough where she was smooth, and she couldn't get enough. With mind and body, she endeavored to imprint every impression for later dissection and analysis.

She couldn't have guessed how long they tarried, hugging and caressing. The procedure was fiery and ardent, then tender and loving, and she was astonished by the myriad of methods and techniques to be learned in what she'd ceaselessly thought to be a simple phenomenon.

Gradually, the kiss wound to a subdued conclusion, but he didn't desist. He burrowed across her cheek, under her chin, down her neck, to bite at her nape. Goose bumps flared and tickled down her spine, all the way to her toes.

Snuggling against him, she was assailed by his heat, his masculinity. She rested, wishing she could stay forever, that she would never have to go, but then the dastardly distant clock began to strike four, once more signaling the conclusion of her idyllic escapade.

In an instant, her adventure in paradise was terminated.

"I'm starting to hate that clock," she murmured into the fabric of his shirt.

"As am I."

He chuckled, the undiluted pleasure of it making her feel connected to him as she'd never imagined it possible to be.

She had to withdraw, to separate herself, but she couldn't move. Once she detached herself, she'd have no reason to linger. Depressingly, she'd have to depart for her lonely, dreary home that was filled with such rancor and strife, yet now that she'd been kissed by Gabriel, she couldn't conceive of returning there.

By permitting him to slacken her dress, by sanctioning his free running of his hands over her person, she'd gone much farther than she'd ever supposed she might. She had to rein in her wanton behavior! Yet even as she scolded herself, and warned herself against greater involvement, she knew that she'd visit him again, and very likely would cooperate in whatever reckless acts he precipitated.

Where he was concerned, she had no willpower.

"I should go."

"Yes, you should," he concurred, but he didn't set her away, and she was somewhat mollified that he was in no rush.

There was no other option, though; she couldn't delay. Mary would be waiting in the main house and, considering Elizabeth's dishabille, she would require several minutes to repair the damage their outburst of passion had performed on her hair and clothes. Giving herself a mental shake, she forced herself away, sliding from his lap to the stool on which she'd originally been sitting.

As this was the first occasion she'd ever engaged in a tryst, she wasn't sure how to conduct herself now that the ardor had waned. She couldn't look at him, so she stared at the floor.

"Would you help me with my dress?"

"With pleasure." But he didn't stand.

Instead, he leaned in to her line of sight, so that she couldn't avoid him. "There's nothing improper with what we've been doing."

"I know," she said, for even though her comportment went against everything she'd ever been told, she wasn't sorry. Every second of the episode had been exceptional, and she'd take up with him again in a heartbeat if he but asked.

"Don't be embarrassed."

"I'm not. I just . . ."

Just what? How could she convey how special the afternoon had been?

Being in his presence made her feel as though she'd walked out of a dark room and into the bright sunlight. The interval stretching ahead, when she would have to survive without him, was gray and indistinct. Separation was overtly dismal, and apparently, she didn't hide her despondency very well.

"Why are you so sad?" he inquired.

"Am I such an open book? You read me too easily."

"I can't explain it. It seems we've always been acquainted. That we've always been close. I can determine your thoughts, almost before they enter your head."

Since she was suffering from the same heightened discernment, she was relieved by his confession. Perhaps her bizarre perceptions of cognition and affinity weren't so absurd after all.

"I'm not really sad," she said. "It's so marvelous when I'm with you. I feel as if I belong here, that it would be wrong for me to leave." And the concept of *home* had grown so distasteful that she couldn't bear the idea of going, but she was too proud to admit the sorry state of her personal affairs.

If only she could do more to change her life besides grasping at illicit, stolen moments with a handsome libertine!

"I wish you could stay longer," he surprised her by declaring.

"So do I."

"What a tangle . . ." he murmured, mirroring her musings exactly.

"Aye."

"There's so much I'd like to show you; so much I'd like to tell you."

What a positively romantic remark! What a silly ninny she was to be so affected by it! "And what would you tell me," she dared to query, "if you had all the time in the world to say it?"

"That I didn't understand how it could be between a man and a woman." He gestured between them, indicating what had just transpired, and he took her hand, linking their fingers. "Nothing similar has ever happened to me before."

The statement sank in, and she hesitated. She'd been anticipating something individual and fanciful, but unfortunately, the comment sounded like rehearsed seduction drivel. She tried to wrench her hand away, but he gripped it too tightly. "Don't utter such gibberish to me."

"What?"

"We both know it's not true, and—"

After a lengthy pause, he demanded, "And what?"

"And . . . you make me wish it was," she blurted out angrily.

She gave a fierce tug, yanking herself free, and she shifted on her stool, displaying her back to him. Blessedly, he remained where he was, watching her. His sizzling regard roved up and down her spine, but he didn't interrupt her attempts to compose herself.

Oh, but this was hopeless! What was she doing here? What was she seeking to accomplish? They could never have an enduring relationship. He wasn't the type to court a woman, and she wasn't the sort he'd choose even if he did desire a woman for more than a harmless flirtation. Dallying with him was torture, a slow, systematic torment that served no valid purpose.

She swallowed, forcing down the swell of emotion that was abruptly choking her. "Please button my dress."

He stood and laid his palms on her shoulders. "Why can't you trust me?"

"Because I'm quite sure," she dolefully replied, "that you've whispered those same words to any number of women, here in this very room."

"*Bella—*"

"It's difficult for me to be with you"—she glared around at him as he fixed her gown—"and to comprehend that this is the sole extent of what will ever occur between us. Don't falsely elevate my expectations. It wounds me when you do."

His responding gaze was so sincere that she could have been easily beguiled by his earnestness. "I meant what I said," he proclaimed. "Believe it or no."

As if he couldn't bear to delve into such contentious topics, he brusquely dropped the subject. "Let's get your hair up."

He rummaged around on the sofa and floor, searching

for her combs, and she straightened on the stool as he snuggled himself behind her. With an adept twisting, he had her hair anchored as carefully as any coiffeur might have done it.

Then, there was nothing else to do but go, and she rose, but she couldn't make her feet take those wavering steps toward the door. She assessed her surroundings as if she might never return. What a gloomy supposition!

"You'll visit again, won't you?" he asked.

Was there anticipation in his voice? Was he nervous? Unsure? "Yes, I will." She couldn't fathom any other alternative. "When?"

"How about Monday?"

Three days away! Infinity! Calmly, she answered, "Monday will be fine. What hour would be good for you?"

"Much earlier," he urged. "How about in the morning? You could share the noon meal with me. Spend the day."

"Oh, Gabriel—"

He wrapped his arms around her waist, and roughly jerked her to him, the unforeseen move cutting off the remainder of her reply. His fingers were spread wide and almost touching her breasts, spurring her to undergo an agonizing instant where she couldn't decide if she was hoping he would—or wouldn't—move higher.

"Say my name again."

He kissed the sensitive spot on her neck, just below her ear, and she shivered. "Gabriel."

Speaking his name aloud was a capitulation, a relinquishment of fortitude, a recognition of how much he'd begun to mean to her, of how much more important he'd be in the future.

She covered his hands with her own. "I don't want to leave."

"Then don't. Stay with me. We'll have supper together. We'll talk, and eat, and love—"

"I can't," she groaned in frustration. Pressing her back

into his chest, she squeezed her eyes shut against the picture his disreputable invitation painted.

Would she could do as he suggested! How sublime it would be to revel in his private company for a few more hours! To watch him as he went about such mundane tasks as dining and drinking! To avoid home and the tribulations that awaited her! But she couldn't acquiesce.

She couldn't justify a belated absence. While she could sneak away for a short portraiture session—the pretext was innocuous enough—she'd have to devise some clever fabrications if she was to be gone for a prolonged duration.

"Why is *home* so disturbing to you?" he gently probed.

How accurately he deduced her woes! She had no one in whom she could confide, had told no other save Mary how vile her home life had become, yet Gabriel Cristofore had effortlessly surmised her best-kept secret.

"There have been some drastic changes recently," she divulged. "My father remarried about six months ago. To a girl really; she's ten years younger than I. It's been hard . . . on all of us."

"Why don't you move out? You're an adult woman; you could establish your own residence."

Hadn't she proposed just such a drastic solution to the earl? Though many would deem such an arrangement to be scandalous, it wasn't unheard of for an unmarried female to live by herself. And it wasn't as if she'd be alone; she'd be surrounded by dozens of servants, with Mary to act as chaperone.

But in his customary, tyrannical manner, the earl had summarily dismissed her overture with a wave of his hand.

"If I had a pound to my name," she said, "I would do just that."

Gabriel froze. "You don't have any funds of your own?"

"Oh, I've a bit of pin money for incidentals, but nothing substantial. Not even my jewelry is mine; it's part of the family collection. I'm completely at my father's mercy."

He grumbled something she couldn't decipher. Was it sympathy? Commiseration? Incredulity?

"Is there any way I could help you?"

"Not unless you have a fortune you'd like to share with me." She shrugged away her disappointment.

"That, my dear, is the one thing I'm afraid I don't have." He sighed, the dire shape of her financial affairs seeming to have a greater impact on him than it was having on her. "Find an excuse for Monday," he finally entreated. "Pass the day with me."

"I don't know how I could."

"Say yes, Elizabeth."

On hearing her name roll off his tongue, she was putty in his hands, eager to throw caution to the wind.

"I'll try." Even now, she was recklessly running through a list of the feasible alibis she might employ to warrant an extended visit.

"Next time"—he leaned in, whispering naughtily—"the pictures I draw will be even more familiar."

A secret, feminine excitement vibrated through her, registering in the vicinity of her nipples, and she knew—without a doubt—that she would willingly participate in whatever indecency he requested.

"You are such a rake."

"I thrive on wicked behavior."

"I agree."

"Wear this dress again . . . just for me."

Playfully, he grabbed her hands and twirled her around, and he was smiling, his jovial, gay demeanor wiping away the dejection and doom that had momentarily engulfed her. They were grinning like a pair of enamored half-wits, and if the quarter hour hadn't chimed on the clock, she might have dawdled there forever.

"I'm glad you came." Scooping up her hat, he centered

it on her head, then tied the bow with a flourish. "I'm glad we did this."

"So am I."

"Now, go." He was ablaze with a fire and intensity that had to do with desire, carnal cravings, and appetites she was just beginning to heed. He was burning for her, and she was giddy at the realization.

Intrepidly, she tossed out, "I'll miss you every second until Monday."

"Go," he repeated, laughing, "before I lock the door and keep you here."

Elated, delighted, she turned and briskly strolled out without glancing back lest she shamelessly take him up on his offer to remain.

Mary Smith stood in the foyer of John Preston's home, impatiently tapping her toe against the tiled flooring. The butler had volunteered to show her into the parlor so she could wait in more comfortable environs, but she'd refused. After her initial visit, she wasn't about to relax as though she was happy to be a guest. She wasn't.

She wanted to retrieve Elizabeth and be on her way—without crossing paths with either of the Preston men.

Bored, irritated, and for lack of anything better to do, she studied her surroundings. Houses and their furnishings were her specialty. She knew more about décor and residential chattels than any person properly ought. It was her domain, her forte, so she couldn't help but scrutinize the table in the corner, the rug on the floor, the painting on the wall.

The fixtures and adornments were pleasing to view, well arranged and inviting, but the pieces were older and, if one looked closely—as she had a habit of doing—a tad threadbare. There was a dust ball under a chair, making her speculate as to just who, in this male den of iniquity, supervised and allowed such sloppy work by the maids.

How do those two knaves earn their money? she pondered.

They put on a grand display, pretending wealth and breeding, dressing and acting the part of cultured gentlemen. Their domicile was in a fashionable neighborhood, they had an acceptable number of staff, they kept a carriage, but she presumed it was all for show.

After furiously cogitating on the subject, she realized that she recollected John Preston from many years earlier. The dashing, dapper scoundrel had visited Norwich occasionally when they were both in their twenties. He'd regularly overstayed his welcome, ingratiating himself with Elizabeth's mother, exploiting her loneliness and country isolation.

He'd been an imprudent, obsequious lady's man, the talk of London, who had brought trouble and calamity wherever he went, and Mary suspected that he'd gotten his just deserts when his peccadilloes had eventually caught up with him. She'd never been apprised of the details—just a handful of bandied rumors—but whatever his sins, they'd been grave enough to see him disinherited by his family. Then he'd disappeared.

She was frankly curious as to what he'd been doing all that time. How was it that he'd returned to England, with a grown, incredibly gifted, half-Italian son in tow, who didn't even take his last name?

The image he and his son presented to the world was an expensive one to maintain, and obviously—from the condition of their belongings—it was costing more than they could afford to pay. She was quite confident that John Preston hadn't received a penny from his eldest brother in years, so how did they carry on?

While she was interested in the answers to her questions, she'd never pose them, for she truly didn't care enough about the contemptible gentleman to learn more. In her opinion, the too-handsome, overly sophisticated John Preston could go hang. If his treacherous son hadn't been working his wiles on Lady Elizabeth, Mary would never again have to tolerate the offensive cad.

The clock down the hall chimed the hour, and she stiffened with indignation.

Where was Elizabeth?

She had half a notion to march out to the backyard, to recover the girl, and save her from her folly, but it had been a long while since Mary had been responsible for watching over Elizabeth. Elizabeth was a capable adult who was assuredly able to make her own decisions, yet in this instance, Mary was torn.

For all Elizabeth's intelligence and maturity, she'd been sheltered and had had very little contact with men. Especially someone as elegant and dynamic as Mr. Cristofore. She was easy prey, and Mary couldn't discern what her role should be in the escalating situation.

Should she burst into the cottage, like some moral arbiter, intent on freeing Elizabeth from the man's lascivious machinations? If she stormed in and they were merely painting, as Elizabeth insisted, Mary would make a fool of herself. Yet if she caught them kissing, or worse, what would she do? Wrap Elizabeth in a blanket, fling her into the coach, and whisk her home? Then what?

At a previous juncture in her life, she'd have gone to Elizabeth's father, and would have taken action according to his instructions. Not now, however. For too long, she and Findley had been closer than two people ought to be.

In his domineering fashion, he'd set his sights on her when she was too young to make wiser choices. As a result, he'd been the obstinate force that had shaped her world, and she hadn't been strong enough to escape his subtle control. She'd spent the last twenty years in Findley's shadow, powerless to pull away. But no more.

Perhaps it was her advanced age of forty-five, or maybe it was the bodily changes she was undergoing, that had ultimately given her imperative strength. What had seemed a grand idea at twenty had evolved into a disaster two decades later, and she had finally faced the discouraging fact that she would be alone in her elder years.

With Findley's engagement to Charlotte, she'd severed their abiding relationship, kicking him out of her life and her bed, and doing what she could to restore their detached positions of employer and employee, but the rearrangement of status had proved impossible to attain.

His blasted pride and pomposity had perpetuated so much misery for her that she would never go to him with her concerns about his daughter. Elizabeth could be in grave danger, could be dying on the street, and Mary wouldn't utter a word. If the girl was bent on catastrophe, Findley would never hear of it from Mary. She'd choke first.

She had no idea how Elizabeth had fallen into Mr. Cristofore's clutches, but she conjectured that their meeting hadn't been an accident. Not on Mr. Cristofore's part, anyway. He was an unrepentant roué who, most likely, repeatedly charmed women out of their clothes and who could guess what else. Mary had never stumbled across a man who was quite so attractive, so smooth and polished, so suave in his demeanor and approach.

Except for his loathsome father, she thought crossly. She was still seething over his snide reference to her liaison with Findley. Though it had ensued clandestinely for many a year, it was hardly common knowledge, and regardless, she was acutely embarrassed that it had transpired.

How dare he have the gall to mention it! She was enraged enough to spit nails, profusely weary of all men and the havoc they wreaked in women's lives. She wished them all to perdition! Each and every one!

Footsteps sounded in the hall, and she turned, thinking it would be the butler with another lame evasion as to why Elizabeth hadn't appeared. She whipped around, only to find herself face-to-face with John Preston.

Oh, and isn't he just too handsome for his own good! she fumed.

With that thick, dark hair—a hint of enticing silver winding through the strands—those remarkable brown eyes, that toned body, and aristocratic face, he was one of those men who looked more distinguished with age. Dressed as he was in his flawlessly tailored suit, he was a cultivated, debonair gentleman who exuded charm and flair.

When they'd previously, disastrously, chanced upon one another, she'd been shocked to perceive a physical attraction. Though she was a spinster, she was no blushing miss. Her relationship with Findley had ensured that she was well versed in the sexual propensities of men and women. She enjoyed and craved what happened in the night, and it had been over a year—the evening he'd announced his betrothal, informing her after it was an accomplished fact—since she'd permitted Findley to slip into her bedchamber.

The blistering desire she'd felt for John Preston had disturbed and flabbergasted her. He'd felt it, too, and she'd been thrilled, ecstatic to comprehend that she still had the power to entice such a gallant, vital man.

But then, he'd recognized her through her position in the Harcourt household, and his rude comments had revealed his genuine character. His refinement and *savoir faire* only underscored the dissimilarity between them. He might have traveled far, and experienced much, from the era when he'd been the lauded fourth son of an earl, but he was no different from Findley or any of the rest of their kind.

He seriously believed he could say or do anything, that her modest station meant he could insult, affront, or otherwise offend without repercussion.

The stunning magnetism that had briefly flared between them made her view herself as wanton and dissolute, rekindling her worries about her depraved nature, and further quashing the image she had of herself as a gentile, upstanding lady.

"Mary . . ." He seemed honestly delighted to see her,

and he hurried toward her, extending both hands in welcome.

"Miss Smith to you," she barked nastily, and his smile faltered.

"I wasn't expecting you today"—he looked chagrined. Good!—"and I'm delighted you're here so that I might apologize for—"

She cut him off. "Is Lady Elizabeth ready?"

At the vehemence in her tone, he halted in mid-step. "I was just out in the cottage. Gabriel spent the afternoon sketching her."

Mary gave an impolite snort and rolled her eyes. "So they call it *sketching* these days, do they?"

He had the grace to blush. "They're finishing up."

"You should be ashamed, raising such a bounder, then allowing him to prey on innocent women. Under your very own roof!"

"He really is drawing her. And making her happy." Virtuous as a choirboy, he shrugged. "What's wrong with that?"

Slowly, he sidled nearer as though fearing she might bite like a rabid dog. Very brave, considering her careening emotions! "You're telling me that your son is thoroughly harmless? That his motives are completely legitimate?" Her glare could have melted lead; she let it connect with his own, then she dropped her eyes and tugged at her gloves. "I'll give her five more minutes, then I'm going out to fetch her."

"Don't be angry with me, Mary."

Her name was murmured intimately and low, an entreaty that rang through her, striking at her isolation and despair, pricking at the center of her broken heart. He inappropriately rested a hand against her waist, the heat of his palm singeing her through the fabric of her dress. She tried to step away, to remove her person from his allure, but her body wouldn't heed her mental command. Rooted to the floor, she was spellbound by the notion that his hand felt exactly right just where it was, and there was a small, insane part of her that yearned to relax, to confess her woes and unburden her regrets.

What ailed her these days? The most insignificant event pitched her into a sea of unconstrained turmoil!

"Please . . ." she implored, not sure what she was asking from him.

"I hurt you. I'm sorry."

She couldn't remember when a man had ever apologized to her about anything. There was such remorse in his voice that she was totally undone. A few embarrassing tears surged to the fore, and she blinked them away.

Both his hands were now on her waist, and he easily shifted her toward him, and she spun willingly. If she'd had the courage, she could have buried herself against that broad chest. Her current troubles would have balanced perfectly on those sturdy shoulders.

Without warning, she was swept away by the whimsy that she craved a solid familiarity with him, which was craziness. After all she'd suffered in her dealings with Findley, perhaps she'd finally been driven mad!

"The other day," he said, chastened, "I had no right to make insinuations about you."

"No, you didn't. You don't know me."

"But I'd like to."

He gripped her more firmly, easing her forward so that the toes of his shoes slipped under the hem of her dress. She could feel his warmth and substance and physical form. His legs tangled with her own, and her body leapt in response as though she'd been poked with a sharp stick.

"You're spewing nonsense."

"I behaved like an ass. Let me make it up to you."

"You couldn't possibly."

"May I call on you?"

"No, you may not."

It wasn't fair that a mortal man be so ideally put together, and she twisted away, refusing to hungrily gaze at him. He was already too full of himself by half!

"There's an affinity between us, Mary Smith."

"No there isn't."

"You sense it, too. Don't deny it."

She was delivered from participating in the unpalatable argument by Elizabeth's footsteps hastening down the hall. Relieved, Mary strode away, hoping her cheeks weren't as red as they felt, praying that there was no visible evidence of the tumult he'd generated.

"Mary"—Elizabeth hurried toward them—"I'm late again."

"I've only just arrived myself," she lied politely.

Mary made a rapid appraisal of her employer and friend. With hair coifed and clothing on, she seemed to be fine, yet something dramatic had occurred. Elizabeth's joy was tangible, rolling off her in waves. She looked vibrant, contented, and alive, as she never had before; she was bursting with bliss, and Mary shook her head in dismay.

Nothing good would come of this, but it wasn't Mary's place to speak out, or to stop what was happening.

"I had such a fascinating appointment," Elizabeth was merrily saying, "that I completely lost track of the time." She smiled at John Preston. "Mr. Cristofore—"

"My son," Preston corrected her.

"Yes, that's what Mary informed me! How fantastic! Well, your *son* is a genius." Elizabeth was so ecstatic from her afternoon of passion—or whatever it had been—that the undercurrents escaped her.

John Preston stared fervidly at Mary, apparently trusting that his admission of a paternal link with Mr. Cristofore would buy him absolution. His eyes were hot and pleading, begging for a forgiveness she wouldn't bestow.

"I love watching him work," Elizabeth said.

"I understand why you would. It's quite a sight to behold." Preston didn't bother to glance in Elizabeth's direction.

"He's miraculous, really."

The butler surfaced, holding out Elizabeth's cloak, and she donned it, but she was geared to launch into a lengthy diatribe about Gabriel Cristofore and his astounding attributes, and Mary couldn't stand to listen.

"Shall we go, milady?" she asked, preempting potential conversation. "I'm afraid I'm needed at the house."

"Oh, certainly, Mary," Elizabeth agreed obligingly. "I've been having so much fun that I'd forgotten about all else."

The butler opened the door, and Elizabeth waltzed out, so distracted that she forgot to make her good-byes to Mr. Preston. Dangerously entranced, she seemed to float on the air, and Mary followed after her, but not before meeting Mr. Preston's gaze once more. He stoically matched her accusing expression, and what she saw reflected back was potent desire, and a sexual hunger for her that was so tenacious it was frightening.

"Good day, Mr. Preston."

"John," he entreated, but she departed, and the door closed behind her.

CHAPTER EIGHT

GABRIEL stood in front of the mirror, checking the intricate knotting of his cravat. He was embarking on an evening of entertainment, and what he hoped would become a successful enticement of a new client. It had become patently obvious that he couldn't continue with Elizabeth Harcourt. In light of what they'd instigated, and considering what he'd learned in the process, prolongation of their relationship was not an option.

So he would make the social rounds again, would set his sights on someone else, although he wouldn't view the evening a failure if all he accomplished was to cross paths with a previous paramour who might be interested in a sexual dalliance.

If he didn't chance upon a prior lover, he would have to visit one of the brothels he sporadically frequented. While he generally hated the type of meaningless sex to be found in a whore's arms, his corporeal state had been reduced to a desperate point, and his masculine drives had to be assuaged. At the moment, numerous episodes of impersonal, detached sexual intercourse sounded like a remarkable idea.

After the hours he'd spent with Elizabeth, he was in dire straits. His body was on fire, his balls ached, and his cock was hard as a poker, painfully erect, and irritatingly protesting his failure to advance to the logical conclusion.

Needing alleviation, he pushed at his trousers where the rude bulge was embarrassingly apparent. Disgusted, he stared at his groin, studying the prominent ridge, and wondering how he'd go about town in such a condition.

How had she incited him to such heights of libidinous lusting? He'd done nothing but kiss her, yet he was completely distracted, walking around with an erection in his pants as though he was a randy boy of thirteen.

Kissing Elizabeth had been arousing, stimulating, and the most pleasant interlude in which he'd engaged in a very, very long time. The funny part was that he hadn't really wanted to do more. He could have pressed, could have spurred her to a deeper lesson in the carnal arts, but he hadn't fancied traveling any farther down that road.

In the past, he'd rushed toward the main event, where fornication was not only the goal, but the sole objective for participation. With Elizabeth, it was remarkably sweet merely to hold her, to tarry, to treasure every nuance that made her so unique.

When she'd been in the room, their limited interaction had seemed sufficient, but once she'd walked out the door, his body had revolted, loudly and clearly reminding him that he was burning for her and what should have transpired.

He'd tried to distract himself, but nothing had worked. As a rule, he could lose himself in his art so that he'd forget what was plaguing him, yet he couldn't draw, couldn't paint. The only topic upon which he could concentrate was her, so he'd changed tactics, forcing himself to review the sketches he'd executed. But observing her, with her hair down and her dress unbuttoned, had fueled the fire raging in his loins.

How he wanted her! He craved the opportunity to make her his own, to cherish and take, to debauch and deflower. Fast, then slow. Raucous, crude, tender, gentle, he'd guide her into the physical realm where he thrived.

Before venturing out into the night, he should tarry, unfasten his trousers and relieve his carnal predicament with a few deft strokes of his hand, but he wasn't about to slake his appetites so simply. It was important that he remain on edge, that he remember why he'd altered his plans, why he couldn't meet with her again.

Elizabeth Harcourt was dangerous. To his fiscal security. To his peace of mind. To his way of life. She made him foolishly covet things he'd never known he fancied, things he couldn't have. Like a wife, a family, a stable home life.

She made him want—dare he admit it?—to love and be loved.

Long after her departure, he'd sat in his prized studio, ruminating and stewing. Frustrated, uneasy, sexually testy, he'd dawdled in the quiet, peering at the spot where she'd been. The sun had set and the fire had died down, the room had grown dark and cold, but he hadn't moved.

In that defining instant, it had occurred to him that he was lonely. That he was weary of the dissolute existence he pretended to adore, tired of scrounging and scams, of seduction and immorality. He pined for balance and constancy. Most terrifying was his discovery that he liked Elizabeth very much. As a woman. As a person, and he didn't want to see her hurt, didn't want to maltreat her.

He loved his father, and though he'd never known his mother, he desperately loved her, too, and honored her memory. He'd been raised on tales of their doomed *amore,* of their cursed destiny. In his own fashion, he emulated them: a man who existed for the moment, who would commit any outrageous act, who would bask in any sort of appealing, corrupt indulgence.

His conduct was also fueled by revenge, at both the noble houses from which he'd been barred due to his illegitimacy. He wasn't fooling himself; many of his antics amounted to no more than his trivial attempts to retaliate against the kinds of horrid people who had shunned his father and killed his mother.

Since meeting Elizabeth, it all seemed petty. She didn't fit with his perception of the detestable aristocrats who inhabited that despicable group. The rancor, the retribution, was a waste. She had him doubting his motives, disputing his ideas, and questioning his convictions. Most of all, she had him wishing he could change his life.

Apparently, there was a secret, unacknowledged element of his character that sought normalcy and tranquillity, which was frightening. His world of superficiality and capriciousness had been just fine until she'd entered the picture. Why was he suddenly dwelling on principles and integrity? Why was he letting the infuriating woman intrude where she didn't belong?

Though she hadn't done anything to directly cause his upset, he wasn't about to persist with his confidence game. He needed to put an end to the painting contract, and Lady Elizabeth, herself, had given him the perfect excuse for termination: She possessed no money or other valuables.

On the table next to his bed was a page listing the other women John had recently heard about who might ultimately be induced into an affair.

Venality was what Gabriel understood. Vice and profiteering were the only processes by which he cared to support himself. Taking a final glance at the names, ones that he'd reviewed many times before selecting Lady Elizabeth, he strode into the hall and down the stairs just as John exited the parlor.

"Going out?" John asked, surprised that Gabriel was dressed at such a late hour. When Gabriel was involved in a swindle, there wasn't any reason for him to plod through the available amusements that constituted London's pretentious, expensive nightlife.

"Lady Carrington is hosting a soiree."

John raised a brow. "My, my!"

The lady was notorious for her decadent, ribald parties where licentious behavior was not only allowed but downright encouraged.

"I haven't been in a while," he said, feigning indifference. "I thought I'd attend."

"I told you she'd be a good contact."

"She has been." He assessed his father, who'd once been a diligent womanizer, but who now rarely met a female who could turn his head. "You haven't had a woman in ages. Would you like to join me?"

"At Lady Carrington's?" Melodramatically, he gripped the center of his chest. "I don't think my heart could stand the stimulation."

Gabriel chuckled. "You're only fifty. I doubt that a bout of excessive fucking would toss you over the precipice."

"All that nude flesh, all those unrestrained, wanton females!" John shuddered dramatically. "I believe I'll stay at home, finish the book I'm reading, then retire."

"You're becoming a virtual stick-in-the-mud."

"An absolute puritan," he agreed.

"Right!" Gabriel scoffed. His father was many things, but a moral, virtuous prude he was not. "Don't forget that I'm the man who shared a flat with you in Paris."

"How could I? You never let me."

They smiled at recalling their wilder days, and their exotic experiences on the Continent, before the familiarity of England had lured John back to where it had all started.

Gabriel turned toward the foyer, his father dogging his heels, and they chatted until Gabriel was ready to depart.

"By the way," he said, affecting nonchalance, "I've decided that Lady Elizabeth won't work out."

"What?"

"I'd invited her to sit again on Monday, but I'm going to cancel. Send her a note on the morrow, would you? Advise her not to return." He donned his hat. "Gently, of course."

"But why? I . . . I . . . thought it was proceeding so well."

"I'm sure she'd be amenable to temptation, but I find that I'm not inclined."

"But what pretext should I use?"

"Tell her whatever you suppose might suffice. How about that you just realized I'm overbooked? Scheduling conflicts and all that." He stepped to the threshold, hoping to leave quickly in order to evade John's in-depth quizzing. "And refund any retainer we've received."

"I just sent the bill to her father yesterday."

"Then it should be easily voided." John glared at him with the aggravated glower that had regularly had him squirming when he'd been just a lad, and he could barely resist fidgeting.

"Are you feeling all right?"

"Yes, why?"

"You've never backed out before. Not with any of them."

"Well, there's a first time for everything."

"This doesn't make any sense."

"It does to me."

John was upset, much more than he should have been. His father worried too much about their finances. He felt guilty, and blamed himself, for the earlier choices that had created the economic predicament in which they'd been perpetually mired, but Gabriel ceaselessly told him not to fret. It wasn't as though they were starving and about to be thrown into the streets.

"Look, *papà*"—he reverted to the affectionate term he'd used as a child—"Lady Elizabeth hardly has any funds of her own. I found out this afternoon. There's no incentive to carry on." At learning this disturbing shred of information, John was totally unmoved. "You knew!" Gabriel accused.

"I considered it a distinct possibility. Findley Harcourt was the worst penny-pincher I ever encountered."

John didn't exhibit an ounce of remorse and, exasperated, Gabriel inquired, "Then why did you encourage me to pursue his daughter?"

"Old habits." He shrugged, unrepentant. "I wanted to rub his nose in it once more."

"What happened between you two anyway?"

John, ever the gentleman, was impassively, noncommittally silent.

"Let me guess: It had to do with a woman."

He shrugged again.

"Well, I'm not playing a role in some twenty-year-old feud. Contact the lady in the morning. We're through with her."

"But don't you—"

Gabriel held up a hand, halting his objection. "The matter isn't open to discussion."

John scowled at him then, looking much older than his years, he sank into a nearby chair. "But if you recant with Lady Elizabeth, Mary won't ever . . ." He trailed off.

"Mary who?"

Fleetingly, John appeared as though he had a confession to make, then he shook his head. "It's not important."

"You'll send the cancellation, then?"

"Aye," he conceded dejectedly, "I will."

"*Grazie.*"

Gabriel strolled out, jumped into the coach, and signaled the driver. The carriage rumbled away, and he shifted against the squab, striving to alleviate the fullness in his trousers. Hopefully soon, his sexual hunger would be eased. If he was lucky, perhaps through multiple episodes of copulation, he'd achieve a dual benefit: satiation *and* relief from his asinine, sentimental yearnings. His musings were intolerable, and he couldn't permit himself to be encumbered by such ridiculous introspection.

Yet even as he approached Lady Carrington's residence, even as his cock stirred and his body sizzled at pondering who and what he might confront inside, the only subject upon which he could focus was Elizabeth.

How will she take the news?

Findley Harcourt, Earl of Norwich, crept up the staircase at the rear of his mansion. Without warning, he tripped, stubbing his toe and causing his candle to flicker and almost extinguish. He shielded it with his palm until it flamed strong once again.

"Like a burglar," he groused, "sneaking through my own damned house."

For many years of his life, brimming over with anticipation and expectation, he'd made the furtive trip up the back stairs.

As a much younger man, he'd enjoyed the stealth and naughtiness. His raging masculine drives had constantly pushed him to make the climb, even though he knew what he was doing was wrong for all concerned, but despite his misgivings, he'd never quit making the trek. Too much pleasure had awaited at the end of the journey. He'd kept on—with joy in his heart, as well as a bounteous, sweltering phallus in his trousers—and oh, what heaven he'd discovered, right under his very own roof!

The thrill of the chase, the wearing down, the final capitulation, followed by the covert appointments, the forbidden trysting! Each assignation had been more erotic and fulfilling than the last! Then, after the inaugural desire had waned—it had taken years—he'd settled into the routine, delighting in the gratification to be gained from long-term commitment. Familiarity and acquaintance, he'd ascertained, brought their own rewards.

A mistress, without the bother of one! Every man's dream! A ravishing, uninhibited paramour, who willingly engaged in any dissipation, who saw to his needs and whims, but who was in no position to mewl or complain about having too little or wanting more than she'd been offered.

For two decades, he'd been fortunate to have stumbled into such a facile arrangement, often preening over having gotten so lucky, and never taking for granted his fortuitous circumstances.

Nowadays, though, he just felt drained. And grouchy. And put-upon.

He was an earl, for pity's sake. A peer of the realm. A leader in Parliament. A luminary whose every word was law. His favor was curried by friend and foe alike. Yet, in his own abode, he groveled and beseeched like a pauper outside a wedding feast. Like a starving dog, he whined and begged, supplicating for a few scraps of feminine attention.

And would she provide him with any? No, she would not! The blasted woman had been an absolute boor since the day he'd announced his plans to marry Charlotte. In no uncertain terms, she'd let him know what he could do with his youthful bride, and just where he could put his rowdy, undisciplined fifty-year-old cock.

Why, she'd gone so far as to say that his decision was an insult! To her personally! After all she'd *endured*! Just what specifically was it that she'd deemed so insufferable? A roof over her head! All the food she could ever eat! An elegant room and an admirable salary. A job managing one of the grandest houses in all of England. The continuing respect of a wealthy, revered nobleman.

He'd always presumed that he'd never understood women, and her ungrateful attitude had slapped him in the face with the evidence that he didn't.

She had banned him from her bed, then she'd moved on, excluding him as thoroughly as if they were two strangers. If he heard her coldly address him as *Lord Norwich* one more time, he couldn't predict what violence he might commit.

So, he'd married Charlotte. What had that to do with anything?

He *had* to have an heir. Siring a son was a responsibility he'd evaded for far too long. Mary grasped his obligations to the earldom. She'd habitually advised and counseled, consoled and comforted, when the intermittent stresses of his exalted position had become difficult to tolerate. Her ability to extend succor was what he liked most about her.

The abominable woman knew him better than anyone ever had. How could she discount their past?

The temperature in the stairwell was brisk, and he tugged at the belt of his robe, covering too much of his pants. Out of deference to Mary, he went to her sufficiently clothed, just in case he encountered a sleepy servant out wandering the halls, but amazingly, he'd never stumbled upon one of his retainers. Either they were excessively heavy sleepers, or they didn't want to be up and about where they might accidentally unearth the actual goings-on of the large household.

No one had ever detected him on his nocturnal forays, or guessed where his true passions lay.

Except Pamela.

His first wife had never challenged him as to his sly philandering or his abundant infidelities, but he was positive that she'd uncovered his eternal, unrelenting ardor for Mary Smith.

Early on in their marriage, she'd somehow learned of his penchant for his housekeeper. She would never have demeaned herself by interrogating him, or verbally accosting him as to his proclivities and peccadilloes, but she'd known, and in a myriad of petty, shallow ways, she'd made his life intolerable because of it.

Born and bred to be a gentlewoman, Pamela had loathed her marital duties but had complied nightly. Bedding her had been a chore he'd stoically tolerated, but he'd needed more than she could ever have rendered. He'd supplemented her meager attempts by treating himself to a hot-blooded, eager partner, a commoner who wasn't afraid to bare herself, to let her prurient nature show through.

Who could have blamed him for choosing pretty, amenable Mary?

As with his prior marriage, he was compelled to bed Charlotte nightly. While assuredly, her nubile, juvenile body was arousing, and he effortlessly generated a cock-stand at the thought of visiting her bed, he'd promptly wearied of her passive, meek behavior when it came to their marital relations. No matter what he told her to do, how he threatened or cajoled, she declined to participate as he commanded.

If only she'd conceive! If she'd just begin increasing, he could desist with the unpalatable ritual, but the wretched girl was proving to be as infertile as Pamela had been.

What he needed—besides to dip his wick in a welcoming haven without having to degrade himself by coaxing and wheedling to get it there—was a bit of sympathy, of commiseration and condolence.

He needed Mary, but she was proving obstinate as hell. Who did she think she was? Daring to defy him! Denying him his lordly rights!

He was enraged by her rejection, and now, with the most recent information from Elizabeth that she was considering leaving his employ, that she would rather be out on the streets than in his home where he'd always watched over her, he was in a state. He wouldn't allow her to embarrass him with departure.

It was time she be reminded of her place. He was her friend, but more importantly, he was her master—by God!—and she wouldn't rebuff him again. He wouldn't permit it.

Still, as he raised his hand to knock, it trembled, indication of how vastly troubled he was about his reception. She was headstrong, no longer the biddable innocent she'd been when he'd initially seduced her. He had to handle her carefully, prudently, but after their last, bitter disagreement, he wasn't confident of how to gain lost ground. Her oft-voiced ultimatums seemed as foreign to him as those of an African savage might have been.

Well, temper or no, tears or no, she was about to learn how relentless he could be. Because of his fondness for her, he rarely showed her this side of his personality, but she was about to witness it, in all its insolent, shameless glory.

There was no answer to his knock, so he tried again

and was rewarded by her footsteps crossing the floor. The door opened, and there she was, her magnificent silver hair hanging down, her curvaceous body flawlessly outlined by the torso-hugging robe she'd cinched about her tiny waist.

"What do you want, Findley?" she asked, annoyed. There was no sparkle in her eye, not the slightest sign of hospitality, or any hint that she was glad he'd arrived.

He floundered, his bluster and bravado dwindling. "May I come in?"

"No."

"Mary—"

"We've been through this a hundred times."

"Well, we'll go through it a hundred and one, then." He straight-armed the door and sauntered inside. After all, it wasn't as if he hadn't ever been in her boudoir. He was hardly an intruder. "I won't dawdle in the hall like some underpaid footman."

Rankled, she acquiesced to his entrance with a resigned shrug and a sigh, and she shut the door behind him.

"There's nothing to discuss," she maintained.

"Yes, there is."

"What's left?"

"How long will you keep this up?"

"Keep what 'up'?"

"This insistence that we've separated! It won't do, I tell you. I've had enough."

"You have, have you?" She chuckled strangely, and foreboding tingled down his spine. "Well, perhaps I've had enough, too."

"Enough of what?" He jammed his hands on his hips, all six feet of him towering over her, but she wasn't cowed. Not even his superior size had an undue impact on her. "What is so terrible about your life? Everything was going so well! Then, poof! You stubbornly call off our affair, then you act as if none of it ever transpired." His voice was rising, and he reined himself in, appreciating from boundless experience that he never prevailed with her by yelling.

"Let's forget our differences," he said evenly. "Don't you remember how things were before all this . . . this . . ." What word should he use to finish the sentence? *Chaos? Discord? Pandemonium? Matrimony?*

She and Elizabeth firmly contended that the disruption was his fault, when his marriage was naught more than one—in a lengthy line—of the proscribed duties that came with his rank.

What would Mary and Elizabeth have suggested? That he not wed? Not endeavor to father an heir? Not secure the title?

Women! he grumbled peevishly. Nary a one of them fathomed the pressures and obligations a man faced. Better than anyone, he realized how horrid marriage was, so he hadn't made his determination lightly, and he was bloody sick and tired of shouldering the burden of their joint disapproval.

"Mary"—he switched tactics, focusing on her, rather than Charlotte and the friction the girl's presence had wrought—"I've missed you."

"I haven't missed you, Fin," she said hostilely. "Not for a second."

He took some comfort from the fact that she'd used his pet name. "You don't mean that."

"I really do."

He struggled not to sound as if he was sniveling and, striding nearer, he enfolded her in his arms, but she was so unaffected that it was like hugging a stick of wood. "I can't live without you, Mary."

"Yes you can," she said harshly. "You're like a child, Fin. You're angry that I keep saying no and, for once, you can't get your way."

"I have needs, Mary"—he leaned in, inhaling her familiar scent and kissing her cheek, but she flinched at the contact—"manly needs."

"Go to your wife, Fin. Let her slake them."

"But she can't furnish what I require. Having sex with her is like fucking a stone; you know that."

"I *know* nothing of the sort"—she jerked away, stomped to the door, and grabbed the knob—"and I refuse to lend a compassionate ear to any drivel about the sexual problems the two of you are having. How dare you expect me to listen!"

She was irate enough to cast him out yet again, and he rushed to her, resting his hand atop hers, quelling her effort at eviction. When he was by himself, it was simple to enumerate what he wanted to tell her, but when they were together, their association was on such a slippery slope that he couldn't explicate his intent; he came away from every meeting having bumbled like an idiot.

"Doesn't our history mean anything to you?"

"To which period would you be referring?" She impaled him with her steady blue gaze. "When we committed adultery against Pamela? When we broke her heart? When we clandestinely sneaked about, year after year after accursed year? Never affirming our acquaintance in public? Never acknowledging one another in the light of day?" Her vehemence made him lurch away. "Which part was so bloody excellent for me that I'd do it all over?"

"You can't be sure that Pamela was aware of our liaison," he lied, the only lame retort he could utter. "Even if she did suspect, what does it signify? It has nothing to do with Charlotte. Nothing to do with us."

"What an ass you are! To imagine that I'd suffer through such an unsavory episode ever again!"

"And just what was—"

She cut him off. "I was a girl when we started in. I didn't have any better sense. I was so flattered by you; the grand *earl*!" She spat his title as if it was an epithet. "By the fact that you'd deigned to shift your exalted attention in my direction. I had stars in my eyes, so I didn't comprehend how inappropriate my conduct was. But I'm a grown-up now."

She was advancing on him, her wrath driving her on, and with each forward step, he took one back.

"My *attention*, as you so baldly put it, has been real. My affection for you is sincere. You were always there for me; you stood as my lover and my friend. You've been my true wife, in every way that counts."

The sentiment rolled smoothly off his tongue, and he believed that he'd adequately conveyed his feelings, but from the fervent rage that overtook her, it was clear that he'd misread the entire situation, once more.

"I've been your *true* wife, Fin? Oh, Lord, how clueless you are!" She stalked to the door, yanking it wide so that any fool walking by might hear the hideous conclusion of their quarrel. "Is that why you wouldn't let me bear any of your children? Why I'm now forty-five, and so alone? I could have waited a hundred years, and you'd never have stooped so low as to ask me to marry you."

"Of course not," he scoffed. "How could you conceive that I would?"

"Precisely." Disgusted by his obtuseness, she motioned toward the hall. "Go away, before I call on one of the male servants to assist me in throwing you out."

"See here"—he was confounded as to how he'd lost control of the argument, and he blustered to re-establish dominion—"this is my home, and I won't be ordered about. I'll withdraw when I'm damned good and ready."

"Go!" she shouted, making him jump, and she pushed him over the threshold. "You're not wanted here!"

In a blink, he'd been tossed out! Just like that! Behind him, a lock—that he wasn't notified had been added—clicked portentously.

A new lock! To which he didn't have the key! In his own house! What next! How had their dealings fallen to this insupportable level!

Totally confused by her rejection, by her impassioned reaction, he stewed, about to bang on the door, to create a commotion and demand reentrance, but he declined to engage in the sort of emotional spectacle that he abhorred. Besides, he was done imploring. When she came to her senses, *she* would have to come supplicating to him.

He stormed off. What did she want from him? Had she gone mad? Well, he'd show her! He'd get a bloody mistress; that's what he'd do. A respectful, gracious gentlewoman who could utilize her mouth for some purpose other than spewing sass and impertinence.

In a snit, he trudged down the stairs to his room. Furious, he paced, calming himself to where he wouldn't effect violence on any of his belongings.

The clock downstairs struck two, and he still hadn't had his customary tussle between the sheets. From the day he'd turned fourteen, and his father had surprised him with a proficient whore as a birthday gift, Findley had not retired without emptying his cock beforehand, and he wasn't about to set a trend on this horrid evening.

Mary wouldn't oblige him? Fine. He had a wife in the adjoining chamber who would.

Though he could scarcely tolerate the youngster, he liked fucking her. Just pondering the eventuality predictably made him hard as a rock. This night was no exception. If anything, he was more provoked than usual, his ire at Mary adding an extra edge to his carnal discomfort.

He stripped off his trousers and slippers, then, clad only in his robe, he headed to her room. Charlotte appeared to be asleep, though he couldn't be sure. Occasionally, she feigned slumber, believing it would dissuade him from exercising his privilege, but her pathetic ruse never succeeded. She had to provide routine, intimate favors until she produced the heir she was duty-bound to render.

Nearing the bed, he saw that she really was in a torpor, which irked him. He was being unreasonable, bearing in mind how late it was, but she had strict instructions to wait up for him.

He set his candle on the table, then bent over and shook her. Groggily, she rotated onto her back, her eyes fluttering.

As she struggled to awaken, he watched impassively, removing his robe and climbing in next to her, so that when she was cognizant of what was happening, his naked body was pressed along her side.

"Lord Norwich?" she asked.

"Bloody right! Who were you expecting?" He fumbled around under the covers. "You have your nightgown on."

"I was cold."

She was to attend him in the nude! "Remove it! Now!"

He'd trained her well, and she snatched the hem up past her hips and breasts. He assisted by tugging it over her shoulders and hurling it on the floor, then he stared down at her.

What man would fail to be aroused by beautiful, adolescent Charlotte?

Yet her breasts were too small for his taste; he liked buxom women, and her underdeveloped, slender physique made it seem as though he was cohabiting with a child—a perversion that had never titillated him as it did some other men.

Her distaste for the act accentuated their marital discord, for in spite of how he scolded, urged, or explained, she wouldn't participate. However, her aversion to coitus had an upside: She was so tense and inflexible that she never relaxed, so fucking her was like having a virgin over and over.

Surely, there was some excitement to be had from such a contingency!

He covered her resistant, immature body with his large, much older one, his fingers immediately on her breasts, ferociously kneading the two inadequate mounds. Her nipples were contracted into tiny buds from their sudden exposure to the frigid air, and he suckled and bit, moving back and forth, rooting and nuzzling.

Ordinarily, he tried to be more accommodating, considering her youth and naiveté, but not tonight. He'd had enough abuse from women recently.

He shifted to the side, clutching her hand, and wrapping her fingers around his shaft. "Stroke me," he decreed. "You know what to do; I've given you sufficient instruction." She vacillated and, out of patience, he tweaked her nipple. "Do it."

Hesitantly, she complied with a loose-fisted grip he could barely feel. He gave her a minute or two to redeem herself, and when she didn't, he rose up on his knees, straddling her chest, and he directed his cock to her mouth.

"Lick across it."

"Please don't make me," she pleaded, eyes wide. "I don't like to."

"I don't care. With the mood I'm in . . ." He flicked the tip across her pursed lips, cognizant of what a perfect haven he'd come upon once he pried them open. "Kiss it."

She did, just a slight peck, and he was too irritable to press for more.

"Now open up," he commanded, but she refused, staring up at him, fearful and defiant, which only enraged him further. "Suck me inside—this instant!—or I will beat you; then you'll have to do it anyway."

He'd actually had to take a strap to her on a handful of occasions, so she grasped that he was serious. Her lips parted, and he took advantage, propelling himself inside an inch, then another. With a smile of pure triumph, he went to work, having her in the fashion he relished most.

Bracing himself, he carried on with no regard to her plight. Charlotte deemed everything to be unpalatable, so he was beyond worrying about what she thought of the repellent ordeal. Besides, it wasn't as if he finished in her mouth. Though he often required her to go down on him, he'd never ravished her to the end, so he wasn't about to listen to any complaints over her having to submit to a bit of thrusting.

Her imperviousness was a potent aphrodisiac. The more she resisted, the more stimulated he became. At the brink, he scooted down and centered himself between her legs, yanking her thighs apart, and probing with his cock. She was dry, unwelcoming, and he shoved inside, ignoring her intake of breath, her moan of pain.

He'd never been much of a one for aggression in his lewd endeavors, but currently, the indelicate handling suited him. He'd bestowed more than enough chances for her to acclimate, and he couldn't discern any reason to be obliging when she was so intractable.

Commencing again, he scurried to the brink of fulfillment and jumped off. In a fiery rush, he came, his seed surging out in a powerful wave, and he strove to picture it flooding her, inundating her with little pieces of himself.

Eventually, his pulse slowed, his body relented. Then, his duty done, he crawled off her, got out of the bed, and stuffed his arms into the sleeves of his robe. She was facing the other wall, curled into a ball, and he strutted out, not bothering with a good-bye.

He proceeded to his room, shut the door, and scrambled into his bed, wrenching the covers high against the chill. Peering at the ceiling, he observed the shadows, and attempted to catalog just how he'd arrived at such a sorry, miserable state.

No Mary. At odds, and constantly arguing, with Elizabeth. And incompetent, immature Charlotte to allay his masculine appetites.

"Cold comfort," he muttered. "Cold comfort, indeed."

CHAPTER NINE

THE carriage jingled to a stop, and Elizabeth peered out the window, glad to see that they'd arrived at Gabriel's residence so fleetly. If she'd encountered the slightest delay en route, she might not have survived.

The ghastly note she'd received earlier was tucked into the bodice of her dress, and it crinkled when she moved, vividly reminding her of his ruthless insensitivity. It hadn't even been signed by Gabriel! Apparently, he couldn't be bothered with such a minor detail as breaking her heart. His father had penned it for him.

The cruel, impersonal words of regret rang in her head. *So sorry to inform you . . . No longer able to . . .*

Surprisingly, she'd committed them to memory, despite the downward spiral into which they'd flung her. Or perhaps, reading them over a hundred times had done the trick. She'd been so stunned by Gabriel's decision that she'd had to copiously review the content in order for it to make sense.

How could he do this to her? Didn't he grasp how much she anticipated their visits?

She'd never felt so joyous, so excited about the future. Being in his presence gave her confidence; she was maturing, changing, and she wasn't about to revert to the person she'd been before they'd met.

The transformations had occurred rapidly. If she and Gabriel continued on, what would she be like in a month? In six? A year from now, she'd be unrecognizable!

The prospects were frightening and tantalizing.

Fidgety, she shifted on the seat, which made her recall how he'd wreaked physical upheaval on her body. It was killing her.

During the prior, unending night, she'd interminably examined each delicious second of their protracted kissing, and the in-depth analysis had only increased her perturbation. The vivid reminiscence had exacerbated her longing so that, at one particularly desperate point, she'd even massaged her breasts in an effort to calm their strident disquiet, but the naughty palpation had only elevated her turmoil.

In the wee hours of the morning, as she'd paced across the icy floor of her bedchamber, it had dawned on her that Gabriel would comprehend how to remedy her unnatural bodily cravings, so she'd decided to allow him further liberties. She was more than amenable to any depraved conduct so long as he promised mitigation at the conclusion.

Wan, exhausted, grumpy, she'd gone down to breakfast, only to be handed his offensive letter, canceling any subsequent appointments.

How could he recant? She'd thought matters were proceeding nicely, so he was in for a rude awakening. She might seem complacent and accommodating, but she was her father's daughter in many ways, too.

She intended to pursue their affair, so Gabriel was about to witness a side of her that few ever saw, but then, she rarely showed it. In her staid, tedious world, there were infrequent reasons to exhibit her stubbornness; it was easier to acquiesce to the wishes of others.

Gabriel was a different circumstance entirely.

The coachman was lowering the step and preparing the door, and she peeked again. No one inside the house appeared to have noted her arrival. She turned to Mary, who occupied the space beside her.

"This may take a while. Won't you come in?"

"No," she said. "You go on."

"You'll catch a chill."

"I'll be fine. I've got the blankets and the warming pads."

"If you're sure."

"I am," she insisted with waning vigor.

Elizabeth hesitated. Mary hadn't seemed to be herself lately, but then, in light of Elizabeth's *own* distraught state, she probably wasn't in any shape to form an opinion. She studied her companion, wondering if she should pry. Mary was a private person, who rarely discussed those incidents by which she was intensely troubled. Still, in the gray of the winter afternoon, she looked ill.

"Are you feeling all right?"

"Yes. Just tired."

"Well, then"—Elizabeth wavered, desperate to depart, but speculating as to whether she should take Mary home and have her put to bed—"I'll try to be quick."

Mary stared at her, then glanced away. "Are you positive you should do this?"

"Why wouldn't I be?"

"It might be better if Mr. Cristofore *didn't* paint you."

So . . . there it was. Mary had never been enthusiastic about Elizabeth's determination to fraternize with the man. "You don't like him, do you?"

"It's not for me to judge."

"Mary," she chided, "tell me what has you so concerned."

"He doesn't have your best interests at heart."

Elizabeth smiled and patted her friend's hand. "I don't have any illusions on that score; he's a bounder, all right."

"Even though you appreciate his failings," she wisely cautioned, "doesn't mean you can't be grievously hurt."

"I won't be."

Mary flashed her a shrewd look that made her feel naive and out of her league, and she wanted to elucidate the forces that were driving her, but she hardly understood her motivations, herself, so she couldn't explain them to someone else.

Lamely, she offered, "I'll hurry."

"Take all the time you need." Mary leaned against the squab and closed her eyes. "I'm in no rush to return home."

Hmmm . . . What an odd statement!

Elizabeth wanted to probe further, but they'd never had a relationship that lent itself to intimate revelations. To delve into Mary's confidential affairs would be the height of discourtesy.

The coachman saved her from a decision by opening the door, and she slipped out as he steadied her on the ground. Vacillating, she stared up at the house and debated whether to bang the knocker, but she had no desire to encounter Mr. Preston, no patience to endure his charming prattle, or to brook his running interference.

She absolutely had to speak with Gabriel, and she couldn't let Mr. Preston prevent her.

Nervous, she walked through the front gate. Off to the left was a stone path that disappeared around the corner and into the backyard where Gabriel's cottage was discreetly hidden. If he was working, he'd be sequestered there.

After mentally deliberating for the barest instant, she pursued the path to the rear of the house. Though it was all manner of folly, she couldn't stop herself. Even her awareness that he might have another woman with him couldn't deter her.

She neared the cottage. Smoke curled from the chimney, and she was heartened, deciding that he had to be inside. Heating materials were extraordinarily expensive, and no one would be so frivolous as to waste them.

Holding her breath, she peeked in the window, sagging with relief that there was no female lounging on the fainting couch. Emboldened, she went to the door and rapped loudly. There was a mumbled male reply, and she entered without waiting for invitation or rebuff.

To her delight, she discovered that he was present and by himself. And hardly dressed!

The room was warm, as he enjoyed it, and he was facing the opposite wall, focused on dozens of sketches he'd tacked up in haphazard rows. She narrowed her eyes, elated to detect that he was perusing the drawings he'd made of her during their two previous sessions.

He wore a pair of tan-colored knee breeches; no shirt, no shoes or stockings, and she curiously scrutinized his mostly naked form. His shoulders were broad, his waist slender, his buttocks and thighs rounded and outlined by the tight pants. His calves were muscled and dusted with dark hair, as were his feet, and she blushed, inanely cognizant that she'd never beheld a man without his footwear.

"Set the tray on the floor, then leave me be," he imperiously pronounced, obviously assuming she was a servant bringing him a belated noon meal.

"Sorry, but I don't come bearing food."

He froze, then he whipped around. His brow furled, and he glared at her as though he didn't recognize her.

"Lady Elizabeth?"

"Hello, Gabriel." As he articulated her title, she kept her smile firmly in place, refusing to let him perceive how the slight hurt, concentrating instead on the marvelous fact that they were alone, and he was magnificent.

From the front, he was even more intriguing, with an ample chest that was covered with a thick mat of black hair. It tapered to a thin line that vanished into his trousers. The top two buttons were unfastened, providing her with a glimpse of much more *man* than she'd counted on viewing.

Her naughty, inquiring gaze followed that descending trail of hair, wishing a few more buttons were unhooked so that she could better peruse his masculine secrets. They were carefully shrouded—a lump here, a bulge there—and she'd have given anything to see him completely unclothed.

He looked like an angel, albeit a slightly messy one. With a smudge of blue paint on his cheek, chalk on his fingers, he was rumpled and mussed, cute, adorable, but also hardy and vibrant. She tingled with an urge to run her hands across all that visible flesh.

He scowled. "What are you doing here?"

"I had to talk to you." Boldly, she strolled away from the door, as though distance from it would hamper him from tossing her out.

"I'm terribly busy. Didn't you get my note?"

"Yes, your letter was very explicit, but"—she approached until she was next to him, until she could smell the sweat on his skin—"I didn't believe it."

"Why would I lie about something so mundane?"

He was staring at a spot over her shoulder, her proximity inducing him to squirm, which she took as a very good sign. "For some reason, you're trying to get rid of me, when I'm not even certain what I've done or what I—"

"You're no longer welcome here." He curtly cut her off, then whirled away and went to the shelf where his supplies were stacked. "Please go."

"You don't mean that."

"Oh, but I do." He made a great show of rearranging his brushes that were stacked in a jar. "I don't care for drafts; shut the door on your way out."

He'd dismissed her as if she was naught more than a serving maid. He was cold, indifferent, a stranger, and to her horror, tears welled into her eyes.

How could he disregard what had happened between them?

She'd thought that he'd come to like her—at least a little—but perhaps she'd been mistaken. Perhaps after he'd sampled a minuscule amount of the delights she had to render, he had concluded that the meager sum wasn't worth his investment of energy.

The demeaning notion was as alarming as it was depressing. The puddle of tears escalated to a flood, surging so fast that she couldn't contain them, and the wayward drops slid down her cheeks. Mortified, she swiped them away, but there were too many.

Without planning to, she sniffled.

"You're crying!"

On stating the obvious, he leapt around and glowered at her with a mixture of dread and aggravation.

"I'm sorry."

"Why are you so upset?"

"Because . . ."—she swallowed past the lump clogging her throat—"because I miss you already. I can't abide the thought of never seeing you again. And I . . . I thought you felt the same."

If she'd expected a tender rejoinder, he solidly dashed her hopes. "I simply made a business decision, based on my excessive number of clients. I intended no personal affront."

"I see." Dejectedly, she studied the floor. "So we're through, then? Just like that?"

A grown woman, she didn't require a response.

Feeling imbecilic and ridiculous, she started toward the door, chastising herself for her impetuosity that had sent her charging ahead before she'd weighed the consequences. When she'd received his message, it had never occurred to her *not* to come, not to talk with him, not to try to dissuade him, so she hadn't foreseen or evaluated the probable scenarios that might unfold.

She'd presumed he was experiencing the same riotous swings of emotion. How stupid she was!

"You're correct," she mumbled. "I shouldn't have visited. My sincere apologies."

Just as she reached for the knob, he stopped her. "Lady Elizabeth." His footsteps moved in her direction. "*Bella,* wait."

Then, he was behind her, his hands encircling her, and he turned her so that she was wrapped in his arms and hugged close.

"Don't make me leave," she begged, burrowing her nose into his warm, furred chest.

"No, I won't." He rained kisses along her hair, her

cheeks, murmuring over and over, "I didn't mean what I said . . . I'm sorry . . ."

He nuzzled and caressed, his deft fingers removing her cloak so that it fell to the floor. Their lips met, tenderly and cautiously at first, then the urgency flourishing until they were locked in a torrid embrace.

His tongue invaded her mouth, plundering and demanding all that she was, all that she could ever be. She eagerly responded, her own tongue joining with his in a steady rhythm that had her pulse racing, her nipples aching.

They engaged in a spirited dance; his hands were everywhere, seeking and exploring, delving and beguiling. He fondled and stroked, driving her to insane heights while he whispered indecent, delicious Italian love phrases into her ear.

She pressed herself to him, the merger of their bodies flattening her breasts so that the merest shifting rubbed him against her, easing some of the building, unalleviated tension.

"Touch me," he ordered harshly. "With your hands, your mouth. Touch me all over."

With his strained command, she perceived that she'd been standing like a statue, accepting his sumptuous attentions but extending none of her own. As if his dictate had given her permission, she jumped to the task of investigating his heavenly anatomy.

Her zealous fingers roamed, avidly inspecting every inch of exposed torso. Not a speck of skin eluded her thorough investigation. She traced across ridge and bone, muscle and sinew, his brawn and superior size enchanting her.

More brave with each passing minute, she sifted through the pile of springy hair on his chest. She'd never seen a man's chest before, had never supposed that it might be so tempting. The furred pile tickled her hands, and she reveled in the novel sensation by resting them over his breasts, the tiny pebble of his brown nipples poking at her palms.

The gesture had an immediate effect on him. Tensed, he gritted his teeth, and forced her back against the door.

"Stroke me. Like this." He set her fingers to his nipples, teaching her how to pinch with just the right measure of pressure, and a moan of pleasure rumbled through him.

How exotic! How satisfying! She had the knave completely at her mercy, and she couldn't help but ponder how proficient she'd become after she'd had a few lessons. With some extensive tutoring, she'd be a veritable master at the sexual arts. How thrilling!

"Lick me," he decreed. "There. Where you're touching me." He bent nearer, his nipple at her lips. "Put your tongue on me."

Jolted, she recalled the woman he'd suckled in that shadowed theater box. Did a man delight in the same wicked maneuver?

Apparently, yes.

Her tongue flicked out, wetting the nub, and his sharp intake of breath told her she was doing it correctly. She repeated the procedure over and over, growing more audacious, more indelicate.

"Now, suck me into your mouth," he urged, "as a babe would at its mother's breast."

Fervently, she acceded, her lips closing around the delectable morsel.

"Harder," he counseled.

She enhanced the pressure as he clasped her neck, spurring her on. His fingers spread through her hair, the combs flying, and the heavy mass swished down.

With another lusty groan, he wrenched his breast away, his respiration labored, his heart thundering behind his ribs. He gripped her bottom and picked her up, shoving her against the wall. Ablaze, he clutched her thighs and rucked up her skirts, opening her so that she could circle his waist with her legs, a scheme with which she ardently complied. Then he flexed into her, his groin pushing into hers, and the move ignited an indescribable frenzy in her 'loins.

"I'm so hard for you." He stole a fervid kiss. "Do you have any idea what that means?"

"No. No."

"I want to fuck you so bad."

She'd never heard the term before, didn't know its definition, but it lewdly reverberated through her feminine passages. "Do what you will."

"Don't say such a thing to me," he growled, "or I just might. It would serve you right for coming here."

"I couldn't stay away."

"No," he said, resigned, "I don't suppose you could."

Spinning about, holding her to him, he carried her across the room as if she weighed nothing at all. He glided down onto the decadent sofa, slouching so that she was sprawled across him.

She was positioned over his lap, kneeling, her skirts bunched up, and he spread her, widening her further, so that her private parts were in direct contact with his lower torso. They were connected in a fashion she'd never conceived, yet her body welcomed the conjunction, what it heralded, what the subsequent act was to be. He thrust his hips, and she adopted his tempo.

After a protracted indulgence, he murmured an unintelligible phrase then, sounding and looking pained, he halted his efforts.

"Am I hurting you?" she inquired, worried.

"Only in a good way."

Not comprehending his answer, she endeavored to move off, to give him more space, but he held her in place, impeding retreat by sliding his hands under her skirts and resting them on her thighs.

"Is your bottom bare under your dress?" he queried irreverently. "You're not wearing any of those newfangled drawers?"

"No, I never do."

"*Buono*. I hate them."

She confidently met his stare, and she was pleased that

she seemed so self-possessed, precisely the type of urbane woman who could discuss her lack of undergarments with a lover.

He smoothed his hands higher, until he clasped her rear, then he used the leverage to tip her toward him. She tottered forward, balancing her weight on an arm.

"You have such a great ass," he mentioned. "I'm going to draw you without your clothes someday. You'll allow me to, won't you?"

The notion was scandalous, but she didn't automatically discount it. The abstraction of being naked for him was no longer shocking. In all actuality, she couldn't wait for the chance and, if she'd had the slightest inkling of how to brazen it out, she'd advance to nudity forthwith. Her constricting garments—especially her corset—were a confinement from which she was more than willing to escape.

"I suppose I will."

"I won't let you refuse me anything."

"I'm beginning to realize that fact."

At her tractable capitulation, he smiled arrogantly, silently telling her that he'd never had any doubts. He would get his way, and she would gladly revel in her fall from grace.

Deftly, he unhooked the back of her dress, yanking at her bodice, then loosening the strings on her corset. With several clever moves, which gave her no opportunity to prepare or panic, she was exposed to the waist, her breasts dangling before him.

"Gabriel!"

She snatched at her attire, her initial instinct to hide what he shouldn't see, what no one had ever seen. Even at her bath, she wasn't naked! She washed in her chemise! He prohibited concealment by bracketing her hands behind her, so that he had an unimpeded view of the two breasts that she had always thought too large and unwieldy.

With an artist's attention to detail, he analyzed her, his

regard potent as his hands might have been. Then, he caressed her, with finger and thumb squeezing, shifting, testing weight and mass.

"Ravishing. As magnificent as I'd suspected they'd be." The compliment prickled down to her toes. "You were made for a man like me to appreciate."

With a gentle nudge, she was tipping, once again, her breasts over his mouth, and he sucked her inside, his teeth and tongue voraciously sampling her nipple. He nipped and played, teased and bit, until she was squirming in unrelieved agony, yet he didn't ease up.

He went to the other, bestowing the same fierce application. An extra torture, while his mouth suckled on one, his fingers toyed and manipulated the other, so that both nipples were overwhelmed.

This was simply too much sensation for a mortal woman to bear!

"I can't stand any more," she protested. "Desist!"

"No," the rogue insolently declared.

He rotated them, until she was on the bottom, and he was stretched out on top of her, then he continued to nurse, her nipples raw and inflamed, and still he didn't cease. He insinuated and centered himself between her thighs, the fabric of her skirts a cushioning pillow for his loins and, slowly, languidly, he thrust against her. Of their own accord, her hips matched his pace.

An alarm blared in her head, and she intuitively recognized that she'd traveled past an acceptable limit, that he was about to go precisely where she shouldn't permit him.

"Gabriel . . ."

Before they'd commenced, she'd presumed that she was capable of carrying on to whatever conclusion he desired, but the reality was much more complicated than she'd surmised, and he was progressing so quickly, his hunger for her inciting them both to recklessness.

"Gabriel," she tried again, more forcefully. "Please."

Being so involved in his task, he made no response;

he just persisted with his meticulous flexing, a ridge of flesh pressuring into her through his trousers, pushing into her just where she needed it most. Only when she began to struggle in earnest did he quit.

Grappling for control, he lowered his weight so that his groin was in unlimited union with hers. His burning expression seared her, so powerful and magical that she was glad she was lying down when it fell upon her.

"This is happening too fast," she said apprehensively. "You're scaring me."

"*Buono*," he remarked again. "You should be very afraid."

He rolled to the side, but he kept a thigh thrown over hers. With a last look of acute longing, he tugged at her corset and bodice, so that her breasts were shielded, then outrageously, he fumbled beyond her petticoats, lowered his hand and cupped her betwixt her legs. His hand was . . . there! She writhed uncomfortably.

"You're so wet."

"Aye."

She flushed as she admitted the humiliating detail. Ever since she'd met him, her private parts had been moist and stimulated. Just now, she was slippery, her bodily juices thick and coating the entire area.

He left the couch to traipse across the room. When he returned, with a towel, he reached under her skirt and wiped between her legs, blotting up the peculiar moisture. Her damp core was swollen and tender, and the nap from the towel's fabric had an arousing effect.

"You're so ready for me." He chuckled crudely as he pitched the towel on the floor. "I'm going to love fucking you."

"You keep saying that word, but I don't know what it means."

"It *means* that I'm going to fondle you here; kiss you here, and much more."

He rubbed his thumb across the saturated area, both fascinating and disturbing her. "No!"

"Sì," he insisted.

"Why would you?"

"Because it will please me. And you. That's why you shouldn't have come here today." He kissed her forehead, lingering as if it was an atonement. "I'm sure you don't believe me, but by sending you that note, I was trying to protect you."

"From what?"

"From me."

He hauled her to a sitting position, and knelt behind her, relacing her corset and securing her dress. His actions told her they were done—for now—and she waited as he finished with her clothes and pinned up her hair, his competence reminding her yet again of his extensive amorous experience.

Once he had her presentable, he rose, then assisted her to her feet and, his eyes inscrutable, his thoughts unreadable, he asked, "Will you be my lover, *bella?*"

"Yes, I will."

He nodded somberly. "We have an appointment on Monday. Think carefully about attending, because if you show up, there'll be no retreat. You'll be ruined, totally compromised."

"I'm twenty-seven. I'd say it's about time."

"After I'm through with you, you'll never be able to marry."

"I don't care."

"You may. Someday."

"I sincerely doubt it."

He scoffed. "You can't know what you're assenting to until it's too late to repair any damage."

"I'll take my chances."

"I let you call a halt today, but I won't again. If you walk in my door on Monday, I won't allow any restraint." He stroked over her breast, vividly prompting her to recollect what they'd just achieved, what they would accomplish if she dared another visit. "I won't be denied merely because I might offend your virginal sensibilities."

"I understand."

"No, you don't. But you will." He retrieved her cloak, settled it over her shoulders, and fastened the clasp. "I'm an adult man, with a healthy sexual drive. If you're rash enough to offer yourself, I'll take and take until there's nothing left, and I'll suffer no stabs of conscience over my behavior."

"I don't believe you'd ever do anything nefarious to me."

"Then you're a fool." He shrugged and rested his hands on her waist. "Our affair will conclude one day, in the not too distant future. You realize that, don't you?"

"Of course I do." Her heart sank at his blunt assertion, but she declined to dwell on the negative. He was bent on disparaging himself and discouraging her, while she proposed to concentrate on the possibilities.

"When I grow bored with you, I'll move on, and I won't look back."

"Perhaps I won't, either," she lied, hoping to appear worldly and sophisticated.

"Not bloody likely," he mocked, and he shook his head, rankled by her obstinance. "Just remember this: I'll never apologize for what transpires from here on out, and I won't be sorry when it's over. Despite how badly you're hurt. That's the kind of man I am."

"You'll never convince me that you have such a base character."

"Well, you can't say I didn't warn you."

"No, I can't." She smiled tremulously, relishing his adjacency, his body's heat and smell. "I'm nervous."

"You should be." He stepped away, intentionally creating distance. "On Monday, I plan to strip you to the waist. To draw your naked breasts."

"I don't know if I'm ready to—"

"It's what I want; what I'll expect. You have to decide if you're mentally prepared."

"As you wish." Her rational self derided the impudent suggestion, but her more wanton self—the woman into whom she seemed to be turning—was secretly titillated. "I don't want to go."

"You have to. Right now, or there's a fair chance I'll keep you here all night."

"Ask me to stay."

For many long seconds, he assessed her, and she could almost see the thoughts spinning through his head. Emotions warred; he was conflicted, vexed, aroused, and she braced herself, certain that he'd invite her to tarry.

Then, the moment passed.

He pulled the door wide. Cold air surged in.

"Go," he said quietly.

"I'll be here Monday."

He raised a brow, questioning her resolve. Obviously, he didn't anticipate that he'd entertain her again. Well, he didn't know her very well, but he was about to become much better acquainted.

Exhilarated, on fire, she strode past him, but not without pausing to plant a hasty farewell kiss on his mouth. Then, she strolled out, eager and ecstatic, but also despondent over how tediously the hours would pass.

Monday seemed an eternity away.

Chapter Ten

As John passed an upstairs window, he happened to notice a carriage parked on the street. He halted, peered closer, and could make out the Norwich crest. It wasn't the earl's grand coach-and-four, but a smaller vehicle, used by his daughter.

John hadn't heard the butler announce callers, and no servant had advised him that Lady Elizabeth was in the parlor, having arrived unexpectedly and unannounced.

"What is she doing here?" he grouched.

He'd sent the note Gabriel had impelled him to write, politely but succinctly informing her as to the cessation of the painting contract, but when he'd dispatched a footman to deliver it, he'd never thought to be on guard against a potential visit. Such a gently bred woman wouldn't dare drop by without an invitation.

The realization of how attached she'd grown to his wayward son was disturbing and irksome. Gabriel had a knack for selecting the appropriate type of paramour—one who wouldn't ask for more than he could ever give. His amorous affairs didn't spill over into his life outside his studio, so John never had to be drawn in to any emotional conflict, and he assuredly hoped that this would not be the first time.

Lady Elizabeth was amiable and beautiful, but the concept of having to soothe and cosset Findley's daughter was distasteful. Not because he didn't like Elizabeth, but because he couldn't abide her father.

Her indecorous level of fondness may have been the reason Gabriel was so adamant about terminating their relationship. Perhaps Gabriel had noted a partiality in her that was bothersome and that he couldn't foster.

Well, there was trouble to be dealt with now.

He sighed, starting down the stairs, praying that he wouldn't stumble upon a weeping, morose Lady Elizabeth, who would be begging for news of Gabriel, pleading for help or an intervention that John would never supply. Gabriel was eminently capable of beginning and ending his own liaisons without assistance. John was proficient at many things, but having to explain his son's incomprehensible conduct, calm ruffled feathers, or ease a broken heart, seemed far beyond the pale.

On the landing, he paused, listening for voices, or servants scurrying about, but there was nothing out of the ordinary. He leaned against the rail, an ear straining toward the parlor, when it dawned on him that he was trying to decipher if Mary was also present.

Had Mary accompanied the lady? The likelihood had his male senses soaring with anticipation.

His musings often strayed in her direction, and he rushed down, anxious to learn if he would have an opportunity to converse with her.

He hadn't yet figured out exactly what it was about the bristly, cantankerous housekeeper that had him so intrigued, but he couldn't quit thinking about her.

She was pretty, smart, mature. Rounded where a woman should be, and thin where she should be, too, and he couldn't get her out of his head, which was absurd. Despite the reduced financial circumstances with which he'd persistently struggled, he was still an earl's son, and his standards were particularly high. She was a commoner with an abrupt, no-nonsense personality, and she was diametrically opposite the sort of soft, gracious, accommodating noblewomen he was wont to choose.

Raw lust was driving him—a mystifying attraction—

and he knew from experience how rapidly and readily car-
nality could overwhelm a man's saner impulses, so there
was scant reason to fight it. Lust always won out, and he'd
lain awake the past several nights, contemplating the ramifications of progressing, and pondering as to where he
might end up if he did.

The pathetic fact of the matter was that he was lonely.

After his doomed *amour* with Gabriel's mother, he'd
assuaged his guilt and despair by engaging in numerous
wild flings—some more protracted than others—but he'd
never generated much enthusiasm for any of the women
with whom he'd dallied. He'd never been much of a one
for permanency, but he'd just turned fifty, and besides his
magnificent son, sired so long ago, what did he have to
show for all that wasted time?

He'd fucked a libidinous trail through the majestic
courts of Europe, so he could properly boast that he'd had
his share of ravishing, refined woman, but after Selena's
murder, he'd sworn off monogamy, never hoping for more
than the fleeting connection obtained through passionate
sex. With his advancing age, he'd started to pine for more
than pointless, sporadic couplings with aloof, reserved
women.

That's why he'd stopped accompanying Gabriel on his
nocturnal rounds of philandering. John wanted companionship, trust, joy, the emotions to be encountered in a true
romance, but he was never lucky enough to cross paths with
a female who raised his pulse rate, let alone his cock.

Yet, Mary Smith did.

He couldn't recall when a woman had tickled his fancy
so thoroughly, and the enchantment ran deeper than his
usual quest for sexual alleviation. She perplexed and delighted him, made him fuss and stew over who and what
she was, over who *he* was and what he was searching for
in his life.

Her, perhaps?

Yes, he desired her as a lover—if he could ever lure

her anywhere close to a bed, they'd have fabulous, outrageous sex—but surprisingly, he also wanted merely to talk with her. He yearned to hold her hand during a walk in the park, to spend a quiet evening reading to one another in front of the fire, to probe and investigate until he'd unearthed every minor detail: her favorite color, her favorite food, what leisure pursuits she enjoyed, what she wore to bed for her nightclothes.

Her lack of regard for him, and her feigned disinterest in him as a man, played a key role in his fascination. Her vocal disdain jabbed at his vanity, making him impatient to chase after her just to see if she could be caught. With her prickly, cool nature, that hint of temper buried underneath, her surrender would be sweet, indeed.

Outside the parlor door, he slowed, intent on being calm and collected when he entered. Once he'd gained sufficient control, he stepped inside, only to find that no one awaited him, and his disappointment was enormous.

A maid was down the hall, and he quizzed her. "Has Lady Elizabeth arrived?"

"No, sir," she said. "The knocker hasn't sounded all afternoon. I'm quite sure of it."

He went to the window and peeked out. The Norwich driver and a coachman were down the street, balanced against a stoop where they had a clear view of the house and the carriage, and where they could be shielded from the frigid drizzle by the branches of a large tree.

Was Elizabeth sitting in the chilly, dank carriage, mustering the courage to come inside? Or had she gone to the cottage by herself? She must have.

Fortunately, there wasn't another *client* scheduled—what an unqualified disaster that would have been!—so there was naught to worry about on that score, though if she'd interrupted Gabriel when he was immersed in his work, she'd probably wish she hadn't. His son focused more intensely than anyone John had ever met and heaven help the person who disturbed him.

Feeling put-upon, John decided to check her whereabouts. After all, he couldn't have the foolish noblewoman loitering in front of the house, moping and languishing for hours on end. Imagine the neighbors' gossip!

He grabbed for a coat and exited into the brisk weather. Though it was just before two, the dreary sky cast winter shadows that made it look as though dusk would fall shortly. Icy drops of rain spattered his head as he proceeded to the vehicle. The step was down, indication that Lady E. had alighted, but he opened the door just to be certain.

To his astonishment, Mary Smith was huddled under a pile of blankets, and resting so peacefully that he suspected she might be sleeping.

"Elizabeth . . . finally!" she said, blinking and snapping upright. "I'd about given up on you."

Plainly, she'd mistaken the identity of her visitor, deeming him to be her employer. She straightened away from the squab, and she appeared to be discreetly drying her eyes. Had she been crying?

His heart lurched at the notion. Had someone hurt her? Who? And why?

"Mary," he murmured, loving the chance to speak her name, "it's me, John Preston."

"Mr. Preston?" She jumped, whirling so that her back was to him. "What are you doing out here?"

"I could ask you the same," he replied more testily than he'd intended.

"I'm waiting for Lady Elizabeth," she responded stiffly. "We'll be out of your hair straightaway."

Was that a hitch in her voice? A sniffle?

He peered into the confines of the conveyance, only to observe her stuffing a white kerchief—one she clearly hoped he wouldn't notice—up the cuff of her sleeve.

"You've been awaiting Lady Elizabeth for some time."

"What if I have been?" she queried irascibly. "I have duties where she's concerned, and I don't see how they could possibly be any business of yours."

Composed enough to face him, she turned around, pretending that all was well when it was so bloody apparent that she was excessively distraught. Gad, but he could read her so easily, and the idea that he was attuned to her mental state was exciting.

Their gazes locked, and the air seemed to sizzle. Sparks were crackling between them, and the erotic sensation jolted him to the tips of his toes.

"I want you to come inside," he said gently.

He extended his hand, but she glared at it as though it was a venomous snake. "Thank you kindly, but no."

Her rebuff rankled and annoyed him. "You're still angry with me."

"Don't flatter yourself. I haven't spared you a thought."

"I apologized for my gaffe." The accursed woman! Didn't she grasp the rules of civilized behavior? "Aren't you ever going to forgive me?"

"I can't fathom why garnering my pardon would be important to you—or to me."

Well, she'd told him, hadn't she? "Mary," he admonished, "you're being ridiculous. I demand that you come into the house. Right now."

"Don't order me about, Mr. Preston. I've been ill-treated by loftier men than you, and I won't have it."

She grabbed for the door to yank it shut but, riling her immensely, he kept it just out of reach. Oh, but he loved to see her in a temper! She was teeming with suppressed bad humor. What would happen if all that pent-up emotion was rattled loose and permitted to tumble out?

"Fine then," he agreeably rejoined, "I'll stay out here with you."

She gulped with alarm. "Mr. Preston, you absolutely will not!"

Ignoring her wishes, he climbed in, tugging at the door and setting the lock, sheltering them in a dark, muffled cocoon. With great relish, he slid onto the seat and scooted across until he had her wedged into the corner, then he lifted the blankets in which she was swaddled, and snuggled under.

Warily, she scowled at him. "What are you doing?"

"Keeping you company."

"I don't require your *company*."

"I don't care." Proximity revealed her eyes to be reddened and puffy, evidence of a prolonged bout of weeping, and ere he could restrain himself, he inquired, "Have you been crying?"

"Honestly! You are the most rude, insensitive beast! Is there no comment too discourteous for you to utter?"

"When the reply pertains to you, no there's not." He reached out and stroked her rosy cheek. It was very cold. "You madwoman! You're freezing! You'll catch your death."

"I'm perfectly all right," she contended, but a shiver moved across her shoulders, so he slipped an arm under her knees, the other behind her back, and allowing no protest, hoisted her onto his lap, then hastily adjusted the blankets to preserve their combined bodily heat. Underneath the covers, it was warm and snug, her pleasant ass directly over his loins, and his cock hardened.

Scandalized, she shifted around, her hip digging into his groin, and her eyes widened in surprise. Praise God, the rumors he'd heard about her were true: She was no virginal miss! She knew exactly what was pressed so intimately against her thigh.

He urged her forward so that she was off balance, having to prop herself against him. One of her breasts was flattened to his chest, the nipple erect and poking at him through her corset and dress.

Unashamed of his animated predicament, he flexed against her, letting her feel the full extent of his situation. She inhaled sharply, her lush, succulent mouth only an inch away, and he ventured all and closed the distance between them.

His lips touched hers, and she gasped in dismay and

jerked away, exposing her cheek, and he nuzzled and kissed it.

"Please, John, don't," but she'd completely relaxed against him, her face buried at his nape.

"Shush, Mary." He kissed her hair, her ear, her neck. "It's meant to be."

"We can't do this."

"We *can*." He dipped lower until he located her mouth, once more.

Totally compliant, she attempted no evasion. With a sound that was near to a sob of joy—or was it a wail of resignation!—she opened herself to him, and they joined together in a bliss-filled, staggering embrace, the likes of which he hadn't luxuriated in since his first tryst with Selena.

Would he be twice blessed in his sorry life? Would he be lucky enough to find the same sort of encompassing, exhaustive passion a second time?

He deepened the kiss, his tongue seeking and mingling with hers, and he suffered the strangest impression that he'd come home, that after all his wandering, he'd ended up where he was truly supposed to be.

"God, it's been so long," she mumbled, almost to herself, as he cradled her breast in his hand.

"For me, too." He was glad that there'd been no one else before her for such a lengthy period.

The rain outside started to pour down in earnest, pinging on the roof, and he cuddled her nearer, reveling in sensation. She was a hot-blooded woman, proficient and torrid in her actions and movements. Her fingers explored as avidly as his own, across his chest, his stomach, and lower, to where she unabashedly manipulated his cock through the fabric of his pants.

Craving bare skin, he unfastened the top of her gown so that he could slip inside to pinch and squeeze her nipple. Initially, she succumbed to the manual stimulation, welcoming the interplay of tension and stress, and she continued to acquiesce as he migrated to the other breast, as he gave the nipple the same explicit attention.

But as he began to remove her dress, as he pushed it off her shoulders so that he could suckle against her, he met with resistance.

With a moan of desperation, she wrenched away. "I can't," she asserted. "I can't go any further."

"Mary . . . I need you."

"I know you do, but I just can't."

"At least let me see you; don't deny me such a stunning gift."

Before she could stop him, he shoved her bodice that final inch, displaying a pert nipple, and he bent down and took it into his mouth. Her hiss of pleasure was his reward, and he went to work with teeth and tongue, as she strained against him and goaded him on.

With such precious coaxing, he couldn't prevent himself from investigating under her skirt, roaming up to the moist, mysterious haven between her legs. He hastened through the springy cushion of hair and, with no finesse or hesitation, delved inside her lush pussy.

Her level of titillation was patently evident; she was wet, her bodily juices flowing, and she flexed for him as he flicked across her clit, discovering it to be enlarged and ready. Greedily, he latched on to her nipple, and with his naughty thumb, he effortlessly tossed her over the edge into a shattering orgasm.

She bucked and thrashed, and he clutched her to him, treasuring how she battered his abused phallus. He rode the tempest with her, until the savage episode gradually abated, then she slumped against him and burst into tears.

He melted. It had been a long while since he'd consoled an anguished woman, and he didn't really care why she was so upset, for he'd crashed through her wall of reserve, her defenses were destroyed, and he was holding her while she wept.

With love words and soothing hands, he comforted her.

Eventually, she quieted, and with tranquillity came the embarrassment he'd anticipated. She was a proud woman, and not one who freely yielded to visible scenes, and he was ecstatic that she trusted him enough to lower her guard.

"Feeling better?" he asked, somewhat arrogantly. How he adored that he'd reduced her to quivering jelly! He'd been out of practice, and it was gratifying to ascertain that he hadn't lost his touch!

"Yes, but don't act so damned pleased! I can't believe I let you do this to me."

"Hush, now. It was wonderful, and I won't hear any complaint."

"But you must think I'm a ninny. Or a whore." More tears gushed out. "Or both!"

"Mary"—he kissed the tip of her nose as if she was a young child—"I think no such thing!"

"You overwhelm my better sense!"

As she scolded him, she tugged her bodice into place, concealing her splendid breasts, and he sighed with disappointment as she fumbled over the fastenings on her dress. Her fingers were unsteady, and she couldn't match button to hole.

He shoved her hands away and assumed the task, but he couldn't resist a final nuzzle into her cleavage. The move reignited the fire in his loins, and he flexed, reminding them both that only one of them had been fulfilled.

"You're still aroused."

Staring down at the atrocious ridge in his pants, she gaped as if she couldn't fathom how he'd attained such an untenable condition, then she drove the heel of her palm across the engorged apex, and he gritted his teeth in unrelieved agony.

He couldn't help wishing she'd undo his trousers, that she'd take him in hand or mouth, but he perceived that she'd gone as far as she could for one day. Besides, if he had his way—and he definitely intended to—there'd be plenty of occasions in the future to extensively spill himself in her charming presence.

"I'm so attracted to you," he said, smiling sinfully. "You make me so hard."

"But I can't satisfy you," she lamented. "I can't make you come! Oh, I can't do anything right anymore."

The odd confession induced a new wave of weeping, and he nestled her against his chest, permitting her to fret for a bit, then he cajoled, "Tell me all about it."

"There's nothing to tell."

"Isn't there?" He lifted her so that she had to look at him. "Is it Findley?"

The simple question spoke volumes as to the hidden secrets to which he'd been privy. Years earlier, Pamela Harcourt had professed her discovery of the liaison, and John suspected the relationship might be enduring, that Mary was miserable because of it.

His interrogatory brought a fresh surge of tears and, ashamed, she bowed her head and swiped at them. "I don't know what I'm going to do. I can't keep on as I have been."

"Are you in love with him?" John braced, not sure what he'd do if she said yes.

"I thought I was once"—she chuckled bitterly—"but it's recently occurred to me that I might have been mistaken."

He chuckled, too. "By any chance did your revelation materialize about the time he remarried—to a sixteen-year-old girl who is young enough to be his granddaughter?"

"The bastard!" Shocking herself with her vehemence, she blushed. "Sorry."

"Don't apologize for loathing Findley Harcourt. I've perpetually considered him a bastard, myself."

The disclosure mellowed her, and with the topic out in the open, it wasn't so painful. "I've always understood his duties and responsibilities," she said, "and I've clearly comprehended my place in his life, too—or at least I thought I did—but the night he crawled into my bed and bragged about how he was marrying again, he's extremely lucky I wasn't holding a pistol."

"He announced his engagement while you were in bed together?"

"Yes! Can you imagine?"

"The man's an ass!" He laughed, elated when she laughed, as well.

"I tossed him out, and I never let him back."

"That's my girl." He patted her on the rump, even as he was calculating how long it had been since they'd been lovers. Six months? A year? "So your affair with him is over?"

"Aye, but he wishes it wasn't."

"Why?"

"I made things so convenient for him."

"Then I take it all is not well with his wife?"

"They have their problems." Acridly, she grumbled, "I don't know how he could have expected any result but adversity. The girl's a pain in the rear."

"How is she to you?"

"She's horrid. She almost slapped me once."

"You're joking!"

"Unfortunately, I'm not."

"What did Findley do?"

"Elizabeth and I agreed not to inform him."

He groaned in disgust. "Mary—"

"I'm more cautious now. I stay out of her way, and Elizabeth helps."

"You're not safe there. You must leave."

"But I don't have anywhere to go. I've worked for the Harcourts since I was a girl, and I'm not even sure how to find another job. Especially one that would correspond with my abilities. I can't picture myself starting out elsewhere as a scullery maid."

"No, no. That would be terrible for you. And beneath your qualifications." His mind was whirling, searching for viable alternatives. "Would Findley pension you off?"

She snorted disdainfully. "He's too proud. I could re-
sign, but he'd refuse to allow it. If I insisted, he might
throw me out in the street with just the clothes on my
back!"

"Would he really?"

"He's capable of all sorts of unscrupulous conduct."

"Yes, I know." He recalled how Findley had treated
Pamela. In his more turbulent days, John had pummeled
Findley as punishment.

Not wanting to dwell on Findley, or their old feud, he
hugged Mary instead, and ruminated on her plight, when
he recognized that he had the ideal solution.

"Why don't you come and work for us? We need an
experienced housekeeper, and we could use a woman's
touch around the house."

She stiffened, then pulled away. "John, shame on you."

"What?" he queried, puzzled. "What did I say?"

In a huff, she moved to the opposite seat. "I've been
the housekeeper for one nobleman, and look where it
landed me."

"I'd never mistreat you!"

"Mistreatment can take many forms." When he would
have argued, she held up a hand. "You're already planning
where to situate my bedchamber so that you can sneak up
the back stairs at night."

He shifted uneasily, for that's exactly what he'd been
thinking! Drat her for being so astute! Defensively, he
asked, "Do you have such scant respect for me?"

"Your kind has a separate standard for behavior."

"My *kind*! What's that mean?"

"It *means* that I know much more about you than you
realize; much more than I wish I did." She frowned at him,
making him marvel as to how they could have made such
sweet love only minutes earlier. "I remember when you
used to visit Pamela at Norwich. Flirting with her, playing
on her insecurities and woes. When you were rampaging
in London, gambling and womanizing, I heard the stories."

"And you believed them, of course." Though most of them were true, he'd wearied of defending himself some thirty years later!

"It's not so much that I believed them. It's that I know of your rank, of your family."

"So? I have no contact with any of them. I haven't had for decades."

"Yes, but even though you're estranged, it doesn't change who you are. Deep down, you remain the fourth son of an earl."

Since her observation was accurate, he could hardly argue, so he countered with, "But what does my status have to do with us?"

"Everything." She stared at him as if he was a dolt. "I deserved better than Findley Harcourt. And I deserve better than you. If I ally myself with any man ever again, it will be in order to obtain a husband, a home of my own, and the respect that goes with them." She paused, shrewdly dissecting him. "You'd never stoop so low as to offer me that type of security, would you?"

Under her obtrusive scrutiny, he twitched and chafed. Her words were a blatant challenge, a dare he couldn't meet. He would have loved to wed her, to grow old with her by his side, and a proposal was poised on the tip of his tongue, but he couldn't force it out.

She certainly has my number, doesn't she?

What a despicable coward he was! What a snob! A stuffed shirt! He couldn't budge beyond the societal restrictions that had formed the bedrock of his beliefs, that had shaped his vision of the world.

A man in his position never wed a woman in hers. She was available as a mistress, but never as a wife. She could never be more to him than she'd been to Findley. How humiliating to be lumped together with such a detestable fellow!

"When will I see you again?" He already felt her loss and was astonished by how arduous it seemed.

"You won't. Our paths need not cross."

He clasped her hands in his. "I'm not willing to have it conclude like this. Before it's had a chance to commence. Are you?"

"What conceivable purpose could there be to our meeting? So that we can roll around in a parked carriage like a pair of lusty adolescents?" Contemptuously, she shook her head. "No, I want more. I've earned a different future."

"But . . . but . . . don't you want us to be lovers?" Disconcertingly, he was begging, but he couldn't desist.

"No, I don't."

"But it was so extraordinary!"

"Temporary madness on my part, I assure you. It will pass." Brazenly, she reached between his legs to condescendingly pat the enlarged phallus that bulged his trousers. Disgracefully, it leapt in response. "You're aroused, so you're confusing your excited physical state with elevated affection. After I depart, you'll forget about me. As it is, I'm sure there are any number of serving girls in your household who would be willing to intimately oblige you."

He fumed at the insult but didn't respond to it. What had he done to give her such a low opinion of his character? Why would she discount their connection? How could she spurn him so casually?

"You're mistaken about us, about how it could be," he entreated inanely.

"Just go away, John. Elizabeth will return shortly, and I don't want to have to explain what you're doing here."

His initial reaction was to protest, to argue, to convince her as to her folly, but from the firm set of her shoulders, he knew extensive discussion was fruitless. Furthermore, she was correct: What lies would they provide to Lady E. if she suddenly appeared? In his haste to alleviate their sexual tensions, he'd forgotten about the incorrigible noblewoman.

Mary's domestic circumstances were dire enough without his exacerbating them by involving her employer's daughter. Sighing with frustration, he moved to the door and opened it.

"This isn't over," he contended as he stepped out without waiting for her reply.

He hurried up the walk and went inside where he peeked out the window, spying on the carriage until Lady Elizabeth arrived from her jaunt to the backyard. The driver and coachman sprang to attention, helped her in, then mounted to their posts.

The conveyance rumbled off, and he stared after it, hoping for a final glimpse of Mary—perhaps a peek of her own out the carriage window, or a wave of good-bye—but regrettably, she made no gesture of farewell, and he keenly felt the slight.

Behind him, Gabriel insolently sauntered down the hall as if he had the world by the tail, and John speculated as to whether the lady was still a virgin. As his son neared, he glanced around but didn't abandon his post. He couldn't propel himself away from where he'd last seen Mary.

"What are you looking at?" Gabriel inquired as he beheld his father who was oddly—and longingly—gazing out the window.

"Lady Elizabeth's departure," John said. "What did she want?"

"What do you suppose?"

"The *painting* contract will continue?"

"She was quite persuasive."

John chortled with repugnance. "After your mood yesterday, this can't be a good idea. What are your plans for her?"

"You shouldn't have to ask."

"But she has no money. Why persist?"

"Why not?"

"So, it will be just for the sex, then?"

"Aye." He shrugged impertinently. "Just for the sex."

"If you persevere, you'll be sorry."

"Perhaps," Gabriel allowed.

"I guarantee it."

John spun away, not wanting to protract the debate. Gabriel would do as he pleased, and damn the consequences. He was strong-willed, and once he'd selected his course, John had little sway.

In any event, John didn't care to fret over Gabriel and Elizabeth. He ignored Gabriel, wanting only to be left in peace, but his son's astute regard cut into his back.

No doubt, he was behaving peculiarly, but he couldn't defend or explain his eccentric manner; he could only focus on Mary and how their destiny would evolve. Blessedly, Gabriel walked on, not eager for an extended quarrel, either.

John could smell Mary on his fingers and tongue, could vividly recall the shape of her breasts, the taste of her mouth, the tightness of her pussy.

Long after the coach disappeared, he dawdled, reflecting upon her and what they'd done, and one fact was indisputable: He would see her again!

CHAPTER ELEVEN

GABRIEL stood at attention, legs braced, arms behind his back, much like a ship's captain. Elizabeth vexed him from across the room, and how he wished she hadn't come!

After their last meeting, he hadn't believed she would return. Barring that eventuality, he'd decided that if she was reckless enough to show up, he would have the fortitude to save her from herself. He would sketch her, as he'd agreed, then send her on her way.

But with those marvelous breasts thrusting out at him, he was forced to recognize the mistake in his calculations: When he was in her presence, he simply couldn't resist.

Well, he'd warned her, hadn't he? He'd explicitly spelled out his intent. He was only human, after all, and he wasn't about to refuse what she was so willing to give.

For this rendezvous, the pink party dress was absent. She was attired in a severe, drab gray dress—and she resembled a no-nonsense missionary, or perhaps a washerwoman about to see to her chores.

"I hate seeing you in gray and white. It washes out your facial color."

"I know, but the outfit matched the excuse I devised to escape the house all day."

"Which was?"

"Charity work. It was the only lie I could concoct on such short notice."

He nodded, impatient to have the offending clothes off. "Let's begin with your hair." It was wound tightly around her head. "That austere braiding has to go."

At his stern command, she briskly complied, her hands pulling at the combs until the brunette mass swished down in a shimmering wave.

"Shake it out; run your fingers through it."

"Like this?"

"Exactly." Not taking his eyes off her, he reached for a glass of wine, sipping the red liquid as he contemplated her. "Your gown. Unfasten the top button. But slowly. I like to watch. It arouses me."

Not accustomed to his sexual banter, she blushed becomingly, then submitted, fussing with the first closure, ultimately freeing it, then she froze, unsure of how to proceed.

"The next, if you please."

The second one fell away.

"You're not wearing a corsct, are you?"

She shook her head, but he hadn't needed to ask. The flow and sway of her breasts jolted him, made his cock awaken and harden.

"I've never gone without one before; it feels strange."

In light of her background and upbringing, it was an extreme feat of courage and audacity to forsake the contrivance. That she would have relinquished it at his instigation, and for his gratification, was thrilling. By the simple act of eschewing the undergarment, she'd demonstrated her unconditional trust in him—misplaced though it might be.

He approached and tipped his glass in her direction. "Another."

A third button was liberated, and he shoved the lapels aside, exposing a good share of her bosom. Her two gorgeous breasts were covered by a cream-colored chemise, and he slipped his hand under it, caressing and fondling her.

"When you were here on Saturday, I loved kissing your breasts." He massaged her more thoroughly. "You reveled in it."

"You know I did."

"I want to kiss you here again. You'll let me, won't you?"

"That's why I'm here."

"What was your bodily condition the past few days? Were you aching for me?"

"Of course I was."

He'd pined away for her, too, though he'd never admit it. "I'm going to show you how a man makes love to a woman. Would you like that?" He applied extra pressure, causing her to fidget and hiss out her breath.

"What will it entail?"

"Does it matter?"

"I guess not."

She stared up at him with those verdant eyes, beseeching him to be kind, to progress gradually, but he couldn't slacken his pace. If he relented, he'd be holding her in his arms, cherishing and comforting her in a fashion that was perilous to his freedom and autonomy.

He couldn't allow her to burrow any further under his skin! Being in her company put him in danger of relinquishing control, of ceding power, of permitting her to discover how much he cared about her. Lest she ingratiate herself more fully, he had to remain aloof, or there'd be no telling in what sort of quagmire they'd end up.

"Finish with the buttons." He dislodged his hand from her person, distracting himself by sipping at his wine.

She swallowed, vacillated, then carried on with her task as he avidly observed. When she reached her waist, she tugged at the bodice of her dress so that it hung loosely, furnishing glimpses of cleavage, but she couldn't locate the necessary strength to shed it altogether, so he assisted her by yanking at the tight sleeves, stripping her to her chemise.

The undergarment was dreary and functional but exquisitely tailored, and it flawlessly hugged every delectable inch of her breasts, leaving nothing to the imagination as to their shape or size.

"Very nice," he murmured.

Languidly, he circled around her, studying her form. At the rear, he moved close, assessing her. His proximity made her apprehensive, and she tried to gaze at him over her shoulder.

"Don't turn around." He leaned in, his front flattened to her back, his phallus against her ass.

From his angle, her breasts were stupendous. They protruded from her chest, the nipples jutting out. He nipped at her nape, and she tipped her head, providing unlimited access, and he gripped her hips and clasped her shapely bottom into his raging cockstand, taking a deliberate flex.

"Have you been thinking about me?"

"Yes, but I'm not about to say how much. You're well aware of your devastating effect on women. You hardly need your vanity stroked by me."

He grinned. "Did you contemplate what we did? How we kissed? How I suckled at your breast?"

"Every minute. I was in agony, you cad!"

"In your suffering, were you dreaming that I was with you so that I might do it over and over again?"

"I confess," she said crossly. "Since meeting you, I've become an absolute wanton."

Chuckling, he ventured on, completing his journey so that he was facing her once more.

"Sit for me." He urged her backward toward the sofa, and initially, she acquiesced, but once her thighs encountered the cushions, she resisted.

"Are we going to—"

"Not yet. I simply want to draw you."

This piece of information mollified her, and she relaxed onto the pillows.

They had all day, and he planned to prolong the pleasure, to attenuate the anticipation, so that when he actually progressed, they would both be burning with unfulfilled passion. Drawing her would moderate the momentum, would ease her into total nudity, and give him something to do besides fall on her like a wild beast. An additional benefit, he'd have a stack of erotic pictures after she'd departed.

He arranged her, gathering her hair to the side so that it flowed down her arm, and tilting her chin up so that she appeared haughty and unobtainable, then he snatched up his sketching materials and a stool.

"Lower the strap on your chemise."

She acceded, but moved it only the slightest inch.

"More."

She tried again, still not far enough, so he intervened, jerking it nearly to her elbow, revealing most of her breast. The rim of the areola was visible, the edge of the bodice balanced precariously and held in place solely by being caught on her elongated nipple.

"Much better. Wet your lips."

She stroked her tongue across her lush bottom lip, and the gesture was so ingenuous, so carnal, that he felt it clear to the tip of his cock.

"What a vixen you are."

"How? I'm not trying to be."

"You don't have to do anything special. You're tempting just as you are. When I look at you, I want to make you mine. In every way that counts with a man."

"Will I—" She stopped, perplexed by her budding sexuality.

When she couldn't finish her question, he posed it for her. "Will you please me?"

"Aye."

"Without a doubt. Now, don't move. I need to capture your essence."

Desperate to record the provocative pose, he frantically set to drawing, each sketch growing more suggestive. She was sexy, rumpled, a seductive enchantress about to disrobe for an unseen lover.

Eager to behold more of her, he yanked at the chemise so that it dipped below her nipple, unveiling a perfect breast.

His regard was tangible as any touch, and her nipple hardened even more. "Would you like me to kiss your breast?"

"Please, Gabriel—" she begged.

"Not yet." He decreed, "Take your breast in your hand. Squeeze your nipple."

"I couldn't!"

"I insist."

Tentatively, she submitted, caressing herself for what he was positive was the first time, but she scarcely pinched the elongated nub. "With more pressure," he dictated, "and rotate your finger and thumb to increase sensation."

"I don't like how it makes me feel."

"How is that?"

"Unsettled. Out of control."

"Look down. Watch what you're doing to yourself."

She nearly refused, but then her eyes sank to her chest and the forbidden sight she witnessed made her hand still. Her brow creased with awe. "It's quite enticing, isn't it? A woman's breast. I hadn't ever realized it."

"Yours are particularly exquisite."

He shifted her so that she was cupping the precious mound, the nipple impudently poking from the center then, with a few swift strokes, he'd drawn her, thoroughly depicting her sensual temperament.

How quickly she'd evolved!

"Here." He proffered the sketch. "Who told you that you aren't beautiful?"

"My father."

"He's an idiot," he spat out, glad he'd never met the man. "Let *my* opinion be the only one of import from now on."

He pitched his supplies on the floor, then he hauled

her off the pillows and steadied her on her feet, so that she was standing.

Gripping her chemise, he maneuvered it off, then he clutched her buttocks and bent down, inhaling and nuzzling her cleavage, but he wouldn't allow himself the luxury of nursing at her breast. He wanted the tension to mount until neither of them could tolerate any delay.

"Remove your dress."

"What? I thought you only wanted to see my breasts."

"I have, and now I'm inclined to see the rest of you."

"That seems too much."

"You promised to do whatever I asked."

"Yes, but I didn't grasp that you proposed to . . . to . . ."

"To what? Corrupt you? Debauch you?"

He was behaving badly, giving her no opportunity to adapt or acclimate, but he was beyond placation. He was anxious to forge on, to use her in every despicable manner.

"If I agree," she dubiously inquired, "what do you intend?"

"What do you imagine? I'll draw you naked." Kneeling down, he rooted against her abdomen, and he ground the heel of his palm into her mons. "When I'm finished, I'll be extremely aroused in a masculine way, so I'll fondle you here, and kiss you here."

Her head fell back, and she groaned. "Why are you handling me like that? Why is it so incredible—and so awful—at the same time?"

"It's your pleasure center. I'm going to relieve some of the bodily anguish you've been enduring." He replaced his hand with his mouth, breathing through the fabric of her skirt, and she flailed restively. "That's what you expect from me, isn't it?"

His fingers rose, alighting on her nipples, and she complained, "You don't play fair."

"Never." He laughed, then sobered. "Let me do this for you. I guarantee it will be phenomenal." His hands dropped to her waist, and lingered there, waiting for her submission, which came rapidly.

"Bounder," she chided, but she was smiling.

A row of tiny buttons descended down her hip. Because of their size, it took her forever to detach them, and he watched, greedily following every flick of her wrist. Finally, the last button was unhooked, and her dress billowed around her hips. She clutched at it as though it was a lifeline.

"Let it fall to the floor."

Irked, she hissed, "I'm not wearing anything underneath."

"I'm so glad."

Exasperated by his licentious constitution, she wavered, but he wouldn't be deterred. As if she was about to jump into a cold pond, she took a deep gulp of air, opened her fingers, and her gown slithered away.

He visually tracked its descent, then determinedly meandered back up, assessing her soft leather shoes, her off-white stockings, the frilly garters tied at her knees. Her thighs were sleek, smooth, and he traveled on, treating himself to her rounded hips, her sloping abdomen, her adorable virgin's pussy, covered with a cushy pile of dark hair.

He couldn't resist parting her and sliding a thumb into her secret, slick crevice, and she was literally dripping with want. Oh, but he couldn't wait to fuck her! She would be so tight, so fine!

"You are so wet for me."

"Gabriel!"

He withdrew, and cupped her instead, letting her adjust to the unaccustomed stimulation.

"What are you doing?"

"I'm caressing you as a man caresses a woman. I'm making love to you with my hand."

"It feels . . . terrible."

"Liar." He was gratified as her hips began to respond. "I'm helping to spur you toward the end."

"What end?" she wailed. "Cease this torment!"

"Soon." His suspicions—that she'd never previously brought herself to orgasm—were correct, and he preened at the knowledge. "It will abate."

"But how?"

"I'll show you." He propelled her onto the sofa so that she was sufficiently reposed.

Modesty inciting her, her primary instinct was to shield herself, a forearm over her breasts, the other across her lap, but he pried them both away, situating them at her sides.

"I want to look at you."

"This is so embarrassing."

"No, it's not, *bella*." Titillated beyond measure, his phallus was raging with its need for immediate satiation, so he mitigated some of the building urgency by pressing into the frame of the sofa. "Anything . . . everything . . . is allowed when we're here alone. Remember that."

While he slipped off her shoes, he left on her stockings and garters, and he grasped her ankles and raised her knees so that she was curled into an alluring ball. Up until this point, he'd really and truly meant to draw her in the nude, so that he'd have some body sketches, but on having her so flagrantly displayed, his artistic intentions flew out the window.

Dramatically altering his course, he spread her, opening her so that he had an unimpeded view of her core. Her nether lips parted, her pink pussy winked at him from behind the wall of her womanly hair. She was slick and glistening, ready for his male attention, and the copulation that would ultimately ensue.

The spectacle inflamed him, and he couldn't resist kissing up her calf, past her knee. He nibbled at her inner thigh, and she went rigid, striving to secure her legs, but he was sufficiently positioned that she couldn't.

"You can't proceed much higher." She scowled. "Can you?"

"Of course I can."

"You're not going to . . . to . . ."

"*Assolutamente.*" He was ablaze with lust, every pore crying out for surcease from misery. "Lie back. Shut your eyes."

He neared his target, and her whole body tensed. "Gabriel! Let me up!"

"No." He scorched an impassioned, insolent trail up her torso until his gaze linked with hers. "You trust me, don't you?"

"I most affirmatively do not!"

He laughed, long and loud. "Good, then. Your anxiety will make your leap from the pinnacle more profound."

"I don't understand you. Stop talking in riddles."

"I'm overcome by desire, and I'm beyond caring about what you want. That's a man's tendency. That's why you shouldn't offer yourself unless you're prepared to follow through."

"I'm scared."

"Of what?"

"Of what I don't know."

If he'd been any kind of gentleman, he'd have slowed, he'd have taken her trepidation into account. Unfortunately for her, he'd never been a gentleman, and his masculine drives were demanding satiation.

"I informed you of the consequences if you visited today. I wasn't joking." More gently, he appended, "Try to relax."

He widened her, then he eased down and burrowed into her pussy, flicking at her with his tongue. Piercing her succulent abyss, he delved far inside, thrusting and prodding at her until her hips began to skirmish and flex against his seeking mouth.

"Yes, *bella*," he encouraged, "that's it."

"What's happening?" she lamented. "I don't like this. It makes me—oh, I can't describe it."

"It's your passion rising. You're struggling toward a peak of gratification. I'll lead you to it."

He wound his hands under her legs, flinging them over his shoulders, while he reached up and found her breasts. Fiercely, he kneaded her nipples while he bothered her from below. She strained and grappled toward release, and he toiled to give her what she inherently craved.

He laved her clit, the nub swelling and throbbing. With each stroke, she stiffened and gasped.

"You're there, *bella*. Let go."

"I can't."

"Yes you can. Do it for me."

He latched on to her clit, sucking hard while he harassed her nipples, and her body hurled her to where she needed to be. With a cry of alarm, she vaulted into a powerful orgasm.

Lurching and bucking, she battled to escape his clutches and the overload of agitation, but he wasn't about to let her avoid the onslaught. He held her down, riding out the tumultuous undulations with her.

She soared to an amazing zenith, then gradually floated back to earth, and he was there beside her. He'd abandoned his perch between her legs, and had kissed a path up her enchanting, sweat-soaked body. As her perception was restored, he peered down at her, holding her and kissing her, letting her taste the salty tang of her sex on his mouth and tongue.

Upon seeing her so discomposed, something in the middle of his chest reeled and spasmed, and it dawned on him that it must be his heart. The ice in which it had perpetually been encased was melting, sensation returning, and it was painful.

What he'd fought against for so long, what he'd shunned and deftly eluded, what he'd sworn would never transpire, was starting to occur: He was becoming absurdly, senselessly attached to her. In precarious and risky ways, the tentacles of connection were extending, taking root, binding them so tightly that there could never be a separation.

While a part of him rebelled by signaling an alarm, another part impelled him to welcome the circumstance, to delight in it, to cherish her forever.

Near to love, he thought.

She stirred him in an unfathomable manner, making him crave and yearn and want. Every remarkable thing he'd ever longed to obtain suddenly seemed within his grasp.

Which was ludicrous. They'd done nothing more than engage in a rousing episode of sex. That's all there was to it. He was confusing lasciviousness with more gallant sentiments.

There'd never be anything more between them than a brief, heated dalliance. They'd never marry, or have a family. Even if Gabriel went temporarily mad and decided that Elizabeth was the love of his life, that their combined lack of money didn't matter, her father—and very likely his own—would never consent to it.

A bastard, a confidence artist, a user and abuser of women, was hardly the sort of man who would be selected to wed the daughter of an earl. Besides, they didn't suit. Their antecedents were too diverse.

They currently enjoyed an invigorating physical attraction, which he intended to exploit, but if by some quirk of fate they ended up together, tragedy would result when they were confronted with their incompatibility.

Sex was their sole common thread, but from lengthy experience, he appreciated how rapidly sex became stale and boring, and he had no doubt that the same would eventually happen with her. They'd be naught but two wretched people for whom fornication had been the only uniting factor and, into perpetuity, they'd both be unhappy.

Even if she'd have him—with his eccentric routines and queer habits, with his night hours and hectic schedule, with his demanding, domineering disposition—he'd likely drive her crazy within a fortnight.

Still, it was fun to dream, fun to conceive of what might have been. Yet, that's all it was: a dream. Though he'd sporadically fantasized about a wife and family, it was not a lifestyle he could ever embrace.

Shaking himself, he stumbled back to reality, sustaining only a twinge of regret as he cast aside his whimsical notions.

Why be saddened, he asked himself, *over something that was never meant to be?* He'd never wanted children anyway. Had he?

He was behaving like a fool. The woman had had an orgasm. Nothing more, nothing less, and he needed to maintain his perspective.

With his resolve for distance firmly in place once again, he shifted away from her and sat up. Straightening his clothes and hair, he fussed with his trousers, endeavoring to find some ease for his unassuaged cock as the ill-mannered rod pulsated against the placard of his pants.

While he'd originally resolved to fuck her relentlessly throughout the day, he now recognized his folly: He'd momentarily forgotten the inherent pitfalls in growing close to her, so there'd be no sexual alleviation. Not this day, and perhaps not ever. He needed to keep his wits about him.

His craving for Lady Elizabeth had spiraled him to new heights of covetousness, and he wouldn't careen down such an insane road.

Determined, in control, he stood, searching the room for chalk and parchment. Sketching her was the best method for reducing his ardor, for keeping his libidinous impulses at bay. He scooped up his materials, centered the stool, and sat on it once more.

Concentrated on his enterprise, he glanced up, cleared his throat, and said, "Could you scoot up on the pillows? With you slouched like that, I don't have enough light."

CHAPTER TWELVE

"WHAT'S wrong?"

"Nothing. Why?"

Disconcerted, her head whirling, her body drumming with stimulation that was just beginning to wane, Elizabeth sat up and glared at Gabriel. He was staring at her as if she'd committed a huge sexual gaffe, and she desperately sought to hide the proof of how thoroughly she'd unraveled, for he plainly didn't care to witness it.

Where a moment earlier, he'd been holding her close and whispering soothing love words, now he was distant, aloof, acting as if he scarcely knew her and couldn't fathom how she'd come to be nude and lounging on a sofa in the middle of his studio.

Disturbingly, she couldn't help but wonder if perhaps the sumptuous peak to which she'd ascended had terminated her chastity, and thus, he was finished with her. For her entire life, she'd been warned that men despised defiled women. Had he gotten what he wanted, and now, in the fickle way of males everywhere, he had ceased to be interested?

"Am I still a virgin?"

"Yes, of course you are."

"So when I . . . I didn't . . . you weren't . . ."

She had no capacity for making such a confidential inquiry. She wasn't sure what virginity entailed, or how it was surrendered.

"Don't worry. Your virtue remains unsullied."

When they'd been in the throes of passion, she'd felt pretty and adored, but with him detached and being so haughty, the splendid bond they'd generated had vanished. She simply felt naked and foolish. And cold!

Her skin was speedily cooling, and she glanced around, searching for a throw or shawl with which she might cover herself, but there was none to be had. She was exposed, on display, and didn't wish to be.

She stood, meaning to stomp over and fetch her cloak.

"What are you doing?" Gabriel asked, surprised.

"I want my clothes."

"Well, I'm ready to draw you again. Sit down."

"I'm sorry, but I'm not in the mood for posing. And I'm freezing."

He was perched so closely that she couldn't move around him. There was no avenue of escape. Arrogantly, he settled a hand on her waist and eased her down, and she had to admit that she was glad he had, for after what she'd just endured, her legs were shaky and unsteady.

"Stay there," he commanded in his imperious, tyrannical fashion.

Marching to the back room, he returned with a gauzy length of red cloth. In a futile effort to furnish warmth, he draped it across her lap, but the material was so flimsy that it offered scant protection.

Dawdling behind the sofa, he fluffed and fussed with it, adjusting it so that it shielded her privates but nothing more. Irritated, she yanked it away from him, and fully covered herself, erasing his exact positioning with a flick of her wrist.

"Elizabeth! I had you arranged!"

"I don't plan to lie about while you're looking at me like that."

"Like what?"

"Like you've never seen me before. Like you're angry with me." She gulped down a surge of tears. How could he jump from ardent lover to reserved artist in the blink of an eye? "What have I done to upset you?"

"Nothing."

"Then why are you acting like this?"

"Like what?" he echoed.

"Don't be obtuse; it doesn't become you."

At her admonishment, he spun away and went to his shelf of painting supplies, effectively ignoring her as he pretended to scour through bowls and jars, hunting for an unrevealed object she was quite sure he didn't need.

"I've never been with a man before." She spoke to his unyielding back. "If I did something inappropriate, then tell me. I'm eager to learn. Just show me what's required, and I'll try my best."

He uttered an odd choking sound.

"You did fine," he insisted, though from how he was avoiding a rational discussion, she was positive she'd made an unforgivable mistake, but she was so unschooled in libidinous matters that she couldn't begin to speculate what it might have been.

The erotic conduct he'd disclosed was breathtaking, stupendous. He had pushed her to a shocking summit, and the rise and fall had transpired so swiftly that she hadn't had opportunity to reflect on whether or not she had performed adequately.

Her eyes a virtual pair of daggers digging into his shoulder blades, she challenged him to face her, but he didn't. He was stiff as a statue, except for a hand that pressed against the front of his pants as if he was suffering some major discomfort.

"Well, then"—she rose and wrapped herself in the scarlet fabric, determined to reach her clothes with her head held high—"I'll be going. I'm sorry I didn't perform as your other lovers obviously have."

"My *other* lovers!" He whipped around, blazing with temper, when she had no idea why. Would she ever understand him?

"I'm not an idiot, Gabriel. I imagine dozens of women have dallied with you on this accursed sofa. Apparently, they know something about this sort of activity that I don't. I apologize that I failed to meet your amorous expectations."

Overtly furious, he stomped across the floor, until they were toe to toe. "You believe I'm disappointed in you?"

"What else should I think?"

"You're mad!" He clasped her hand and laid it on the placard of his trousers. A prominent ridge was manifest. "Do I feel like I'm *disappointed*?"

He stroked her palm against it, and the strange crest seemed to come alive. "What is that thing?"

Almost violently, he shoved her hand away, the red wrap slipping so that she was nude, once more, and he gripped her hips and ground his loins into hers. Automatically, her legs spread, allowing him access to her intimate parts, and he took advantage, flexing slowly and meticulously. The precise thrusting instigated a myriad of explosions deep inside her.

"It's my cock. My phallus."

"What is it for?"

"For mating. For coupling with you in sexual intercourse."

"How does it—"

Ere she could complete her sentence, he clutched her buttocks, lifted her, and twirled her around so that she abruptly found herself lying on the sofa with Gabriel insolently kneeling between her legs. He lowered himself, crushing into her core with more force than ever before, the action patently agonizing for him.

Through gritted teeth, he muttered, "*Dio!* I want you so badly."

"Then show me what you mean," she brazenly declared.

"Don't tempt me."

He braced himself, arms locked, as he worked his hips

in a brutal rhythm. Her body recognized the maneuver, and her thighs widened, so that she presented him with a welcoming cushion against which he could lean and push.

With each impact, his pants roughly inflamed the area betwixt her legs that was still sensitive from his prior ministrations. A sizzle ignited, one that she now identified as the initial spark of passion, and she was delighted to realize that the marvelous diversion he'd initiated minutes prior could be repeated. Her anatomy was responding with avid enthusiasm, ready for a second round.

"Why are you making this motion? What are you attempting?"

"It's a prelude to fucking," he crudely explained, then with his fingers, he fumbled through her womanly hair and fondled her extensively. "Men and women are formed differently."

"How?"

"A man has a kind of staff between his legs. When he's preparing to fornicate, it enlarges." He placed her hand on his trousers once again, so that she could handle the curious appendage. "He rubs it back and forth, and the increased friction causes a white cream—his seed—to gush from the tip. The eruption is accompanied by a great wave of pleasure, much as you enjoyed when I licked you with my tongue."

"But your bodily cream didn't emerge. You derived no satisfaction from the event. Is that why you're so annoyed?"

"Woman!" he scolded. "I'm so bloody hard for you that I'm about to burst the seams in my pants."

He thrust, letting her perceive his size and shape, and the agitation was indescribable, instigating tingles of corporeal excitement and a renewed throbbing in her breasts.

"I desire you," he said. "You're the only topic I ever contemplate. All that I crave. Do you hear me?"

"Yes"—she nodded hesitantly—"I hear you."

"Then I shouldn't be forced to listen to any nonsense to the contrary."

What was his point? The blasted fellow was a walking, talking enigma. Riddles! That's what he was spewing! Was he irate or not? Dissatisfied or not? Unhappy or not?

"If you lust after me so intensely," she cautiously ventured, "why did you reject me just now?"

"Because I . . . I . . ." His cheeks flushed, and he couldn't expound upon what was inciting him to such asinine comportment.

She watched in stunned silence. The bounder was embarrassed! My goodness! What a peculiar turn of events!

"Tell me," she prodded.

Every possible emotion—regret, ire, yearning, concern, tenderness—played across his beautiful face. He appeared lost, perplexed, unable to rationalize his rampant bewilderment, and her animosity faded.

Dared she hope that he was experiencing some of the same maudlin upheaval that routinely plagued her?

Despite how deliberately he endeavored to feign apathy, he was fond of her; she was convinced of it. But he was a man. And a proud, vain, imposing one, at that. Presumably, any number of elegant, charming women had drifted through his life, but very likely, he'd never developed an attachment to any of them. Maybe the affection he was encountering was as novel and confounding to him as it was to her.

She took pity on him, resolved to ease him through his arduous predicament. "Had you determined that you've been moving too quickly for me?"

"Precisely," he admitted, then he heaved a sigh of relief that she'd granted him a means of wiggling out of his dilemma.

"You know"—she strove for nonchalance—"when I ponder my relationship with you, it frightens me."

"Why?"

"What I feel for you is so overwhelming. Nothing like this has ever happened to me before. And I'm not referring just to the physical. I mean the emotional, too. I care about you; much more than I ought."

"Aye," he said neutrally.

"But I'd never deny myself the joy of spending time with you, or of becoming better acquainted." She caressed his chest, and his heart beat fiercely behind his ribs. "Do you worry that I might develop into a complication?"

"Occasionally."

"Well, don't. Worry, that is. On the day you decide you're tired of me, just say so, and I promise I'll go peacefully. I'll never contact you again."

"Bella—"

"Hush, now." She pressed a finger to his lips, cutting him off. It had been difficult enough to offer him such an easy conclusion to their affair. She couldn't abide having to listen to whatever justifications he might have provided as to why her sentiments weren't reciprocated.

"You make me sound so cold-blooded."

It wasn't that she found him to be callous. She just had no illusions about their liaison. They had no destiny—that fact was a given—so there was no reason to pine over some frivolous by-and-by that would never arrive. If he could affect equanimity, so could she, and if she could bestow peace of mind by conferring a facile summation to their amour, then she would. She wanted him concentrating on her, and not on some nebulous apprehension about the morrow.

Determined to keep him from focusing on issues that just didn't signify, she trailed her hand down till it was on the protuberance in his pants.

"What did you call this thing a bit ago? A cock?"

"Sí. Or a phallus."

She massaged it, liking how she had him squirming. "Is it painful when it's so enlarged?"

"It can be."

"How do you alleviate the situation?"

"I told you: with friction, so that the seed erupts."

"Could I make that occur?"

"With scarcely any effort at all."

"What would I have to do?"

"Stroke me with your hand, or your mouth. Or, I could put it here"—he grazed across the opening in her body that she hadn't ever really considered before—"but that would result in my taking your virginity."

"So that's how it transpires," she mused. "You propel this . . . this cock inside of me?"

"Quite vigorously."

"Does it hurt?"

"Just the first time. And you'd bleed."

"It doesn't seem very pleasant."

"The initial episode usually isn't—for the woman."

"But for the man?"

"A man can spill his seed at the drop of a hat. It's an indulgence he hungers for above all else."

"Why isn't it as fulfilling for the woman?"

"It can be—if her partner is an adept lover. The female needs to relax before she can comfortably accommodate a phallus." He shrugged. "Many men don't grasp how to accomplish the feat. Or if they're too provoked, they can't bear a delay."

"Is that why you kiss and touch me?"

"I'm helping you acclimate to what's coming."

"Why would I bleed?"

"There is a thin piece of skin protecting the entrance to your womb, ensuring you're a virgin. Your husband breaks through it on your wedding night."

She laughed. "We don't have to fret over that contingency."

"You might regret your decision later."

"I doubt it."

She chortled with disgust. As if some swain would ask her to marry! Apart from her lack of suitors, since meeting Gabriel and ascertaining what a wife's duties truly entailed, she couldn't picture herself submitting to another. The idea of any man having her—besides Gabriel—was thoroughly repugnant. She'd begun to fancy herself as belonging to him and him alone, and she could never ally herself with another. It would seem like a sin.

"If I begged it of you," she shamelessly inquired, "would you take my virginity right now?"

"I don't think so."

He frowned down at her, mulling over his refusal. Obviously, this was not how his trysts typically progressed. He looked baffled, as if the words were the last he'd ever expected to spout from his own lips.

"Why won't you?"

"I'm confused about us. I'm not persuaded that I should relieve you of your maidenhood."

If he wasn't interested in compromising her, what were they doing? "Why not?"

"Because we can't predict the future. Once you lose your virginity, you can't get it back, and I would never want you to lament that I'd been the one to steal it from you."

"That's very sweet, Gabriel."

He blushed at the compliment, as if gallantry was out of character for him. Perhaps it was.

"And . . . I like you," he said, smiling, melting her determination and softening her opposition to a more serious involvement. "I could never harm you."

After such a profession, what woman could resist falling in love?

She'd spent long hours counseling herself, preaching restraint, establishing priorities, and forcing herself to remember that he was not the man for her. That she couldn't count on him, or anticipate an enduring association. That she couldn't permit her heart to become affected, but unfortunately, her heart seemed to have developed a will of its own. She was falling in love with Gabriel and falling fast, but she could never so much as hint to him that she was forming a stronger bond.

If he suspected that her emotions were engaged, he might not agree to see her again. Though the moment of separation would arrive someday, life without Gabriel would be unbearable, and she couldn't tolerate that her own precipitous demeanor might hasten the inevitable.

She changed the subject to carnal relations.

"May I look at you?"

"I shouldn't disrobe."

"Whyever not?"

"I'm horridly aroused. I'm not confident I can control myself."

What fabulous news! If he was already at the point of no return, just imagine what might ensue once he was naked.

"At least remove your shirt." She was careful not to let an inkling of her conniving creep into her voice, but she wanted him unclad and if she had to scheme in order to accomplish her goal, then that's what she would do! "Surely you wouldn't find it too dangerous?"

He brooded over her request, then acquiesced. "I suppose I could."

Tugging the hem out of his waistband, he wrenched it up and over his head, while she greedily assessed how his muscles shifted, his arms extended.

His shirt hit the floor, and she grazed his chest, combing her fingers through the springy hair, and she toyed with his nipples, squeezing and pinching until he hissed out an afflicted breath, then she lowered a hand to his crotch, bedeviling his cock.

"Show yourself to me. Let me see how you're put together."

Their gazes locked, and he vacillated, but he couldn't prevent himself from complying any more than she could check her incorrigible impulses when he suggested she participate in a naughty exploit.

Daring her to proceed, he unfastened the top button, but did no more, leaving the rest up to her, as though he wished no part—or blame—for what was about to tran-spire.

As if she'd shy away! She readily seized the chance she'd been offered, fumbling and rushing to free the re-mainder, which was difficult considering how his erect member stretched the enclosure. His body was tensed, on edge, and very much like a wild animal in a cage that was chafing to burst out from its confines.

The last button came undone, and she stared at his crotch, wondering what to do next, but he was beyond wait-ing.

"Don't be timid."

"I'm not," but she didn't move.

"Touch me," he ordered irritably.

At her indecision, he guided her inside his pants, wrap-ping her fingers around his staff. Mesmerized, she halted, deciphering the exact proportions. It seemed huge, and she could barely circle the breadth of it.

His hand enveloped her own, and he directed her, in-dicating how to add pressure, then he flexed, the adamant rod propelling into her closed fist. With his trousers in place, their disposition was awkward, and she couldn't pro-vide him with as much manipulation as he required.

Frustrated, he jerked away. Freeing himself from con-straint, he pushed his pants down to his haunches.

"Look at me," he decreed.

"Oh my . . . It's so large!"

"I'm a big man; bigger than most."

Amazed and astonished, she couldn't wrest herself away from the sight. The appendage—reddened and swol-len—jutted out from a nest of hair that shrouded his groin. The extremity was an acrimonious, pulsating organ, and he settled himself on the other end of the sofa, and he brought her with him, so that she was on her knees and hovering over it.

This time, she didn't falter. Using both her hands, she eagerly applied herself to the prurient task. A zealous pupil, she rapidly deduced what he liked, what titillated him the most. She alternated tension and tempo, every machination causing his cock to swell, and it appeared to grow—and become more demanding—with each handling.

She goaded him until the crimson tip was oozing with a slippery juice, and he was like an overstretched bow string, ready to snap from the strain.

He took her hand and situated it so that she cradled one of the sacs dangling between his legs. With a much lighter stress, he showed her how to pet him.

"What are these?" she queried.

"My balls," he bit out. "They shelter my seed."

"They're so soft."

"They're very sensitive."

She'd already gathered as much and, as she nestled the prized pair, he nearly exploded from pent-up perturbation.

"Take me in your mouth."

"What?"

Initially, she didn't grasp his objective, but he eased her down so that he could rub the crown across her lips, and his aim was abundantly clear.

She froze, once again unsure. These physical acts definitely escalated in a hurry!

"I can't take much more," he disclosed, "and I want to be inside you at least once before I reach the end."

"Will it hurt?"

"Only me." He chuckled, alluding to matters she didn't comprehend.

"Will you . . ." She couldn't pose the questions to which she suddenly needed explicit answers: Would he spill his seed in her mouth? How would it taste? How would it feel?

"I won't come in your mouth," he assured her, reading her frantic introspection.

She wasn't certain if she was relieved or not. "Why?"

"You're a novice. The first few instances can be . . . unpleasant. I'm aroused, so I won't be gentle. This sort of sexual play can take some getting used to. For the woman."

Not for the man, evidently. "Then why would you so-licit it from me?"

"Because it will please me more than just about any-thing you could possibly do." She hated it when he plugged at her willpower, when he made it so difficult to decline. Even as he requested the libidinous indulgence, she was tempted beyond her limits.

Very much like the snake in Eden, she thought, *luring Eve to her doom.*

"Will you stop if I ask it of you?"

He snorted derisively, and she couldn't figure out if his reply was yes or no.

"Go down on me, *bella.*"

She stared up into his blazing blue eyes. He was scru-tinizing her almost violently, as if he hadn't decided what he might do if she refused. She wasn't fearful of trying it; it was merely the newness of the deed that instilled her trepidation. However, everything he'd shown her up to this point had been remarkable.

Tentatively, she licked him with her tongue, moisten-ing the apex, and the moment she touched him, she was so glad she had. In a flash, she'd pushed him much farther than she'd ever conceived she could.

"Like that?" she questioned.

"Exactly like that," he groaned.

She went to work, savoring his taste, his smell. With great relish, she laved at the juice that continued to flow, but she couldn't get it all. The more she brushed across the crown, the more saturated it became.

"Open for me now."

No longer fearful or concerned, she did as he bade, easing her lips over the crest. She stretched to accommodate him, and as soon as he'd breached the portal, he flexed, just a small bit at first, then conferring a tad more with each thrust.

As he increased the depth to which he entered her, he

was constantly whispering exotically in foreign languages that she didn't recognize, and it seemed that he was murmuring love words, of flattery and adulation, and she pretended that she knew their definition.

She snuggled into the pillows, spinning onto her side and bracing against the sofa so that he could penetrate more fully. Expeditiously, she adapted to the abnormal exploit, and her world shrank to the barest elements: Gabriel, his cock, her mouth. The maneuver was so rudimentary, so essential, that she could have lain there forever.

Then, without warning, he pulled away, and she reached out to him, hating the loss, but he dragged her beneath him, then he scooted down until his cock was between her legs.

"I've got to come. Now."

"What are you—" she started, but he blocked any interrogation with a fiery kiss.

"I love the taste of my sex in your mouth." He adjusted himself on her stomach. "You were made for fucking. Made for me."

He commenced flexing, approaching an elevated precipice much as she'd struggled to attain, and she smiled, thrilled that she'd inspired him to such a drastic edge.

"Tell me what to do."

"Put your arms around me," he instructed. "Hold me tight."

"I will."

"Don't let go."

She hugged him with all her might, as he buried his face into the pillow next to her, then he lunged and lunged again. His body stiffened. A haunting moan reverberated through her skin and bones. Down below, on her abdomen, the heated spew of his seed erupted, a pungent odor filled the air, then he collapsed onto her, his heavy weight pushing her into the cushions, and she crushed him to her breast, cherishing every aspect of the torrid exhibition.

How could she ever have guessed that lovemaking

would include such a personal unveiling of self and soul? When she'd unraveled earlier, had he encountered the same staggering sense of connection? Was that why he'd seemed so disturbed, so unsettled, at the conclusion?

After such a fervent interlude, she wasn't sure what to expect, so as his heartbeat slowed, as he mellowed, she struggled for composure, prepared for any eventuality.

When he finally rolled off so that he was lying beside her, she took it as a very good sign that he kept her close. His thigh was thrown across hers, his arm massaged her back and dipped down to lazily caress her bare bottom.

He rained kisses on her hair, her brow, her cheek, his lips seeking and ultimately finding her own. His tongue tenderly mated with hers in a delicate dance of affection and what had to be close to love, but with him, she wouldn't try to put a name to his emotions. It was enough that he was so moved by what had just happened, and she was overjoyed that he would share such a unique, private experience with her.

Their lips parted, and he was smiling bashfully. He looked young, dear, puzzled, his confident arrogance temporarily tucked away.

He traced across the corner of her mouth. "I didn't hurt you, did I?"

"No."

"When I'm excited, I don't always mind my manners."

"I noticed, but it's quite all right with me."

"My little strumpet!" He swatted her rear.

She chuckled, but her heart ached. How she longed to comment on what she was feeling! Yet she couldn't describe her escalating affinity. He'd never want to be apprised of how much she'd come to value their relationship.

Besides, if she made some moronic affirmation of devotion, where would it leave them? The alliance they'd just established had left them both overly sentimental. If she mentioned the slightest indication of elevated regard, he likely would do the same, and there they'd be, in a coil of love and ardor from which there was no logical retreat.

Better to remain silent.

"It was different than I imagined it would be."

"How so?"

"More physical, I suppose. More special."

"Wait until I'm inside you—between your legs. It's a thousand times more intimate."

Just considering it made her tingle with anticipation. "Will you today?"

"I don't know," he said vaguely.

He sat up, and for a panicked second, she thought he was leaving, but he simply grabbed for his shirt, wiped his drying seed off her stomach, then stretched out once again.

"I hadn't intended to do anything today. Except, perhaps, to send you home immediately after you arrived. I can assure you that I wasn't going to do anything approaching this." As if he couldn't fathom his conduct, he gestured at their naked torsos. "When I'm around you, despite my best laid plans, I can't seem to behave."

"I'm delighted."

"So am I."

"On Saturday, you seemed so sure that we would . . . would . . ." How she wished she possessed the appropriate vocabulary! "Why have you changed your mind?"

"Over the weekend, I cogitated our situation at length, and I'd determined we shouldn't be lovers, but then"—he scrutinized her breasts, her stomach, her thighs—"I set eyes upon you, and I simply had to have you. You're driving me mad."

He shifted so that he was underneath her, and she was stretched out on top of him, her nipples dangling over his mouth. With a shock, she realized that his cock was promptly elongating.

"Blissful insanity," she said.

"I want you incessantly." He clasped her bottom and held her against his erection, perplexed by his swiftly accelerating passion. "Yet I'm so afraid that—if I persist—I'll end up abusing you terribly."

"You never could," she gently pronounced.

"How can you make such a claim? You don't know what—"

Alarmed by what he might disclose, she silenced him with a kiss, declining to listen to a confession of sins. She didn't need to be apprised of all the ways he would inevitably break her heart for she'd learn them all much sooner than she wished.

"Let's focus on what *is*," she said, "and let it be enough for now."

He searched her eyes, then blurted out, "I care about you."

His declaration was wrenched from some inner spot where it had been solidly buried, and she nodded prudently, accepting it as a priceless gift. "Then I'm sure everything will work out."

"I'm hard for you. Again! Already!"

He was severely disturbed by the discovery, but she could only laugh at his discomfort. How phenomenal to observe him so bothered! It could only mean that his feelings ran much deeper than she'd suspected.

"Then take me, you silly man"—she leaned down, so that her nipple brushed his lips—"and quit fretting about the morrow. It will arrive before we expect it to."

Evidently, he concurred, for he sucked her breast far into his mouth and, easy as that, his consternation was forgotten.

CHAPTER THIRTEEN

MARY paced back and forth across John Preston's slightly worn parlor.

She hadn't meant to visit him, yet here she was, stewing, nettled, and impatient for his arrival. The pending encounter couldn't be avoided any more than she could stop breathing. A destiny had presented itself, and much to her dismay, it appeared to involve John.

Since their tryst days earlier, her world had been turned upside down. She couldn't eat, couldn't sleep, could barely attend to her duties in the Norwich household. The sole topic upon which she could dwell was John. While formerly, she'd vehemently denied any affinity, she had been lying—to him and to herself.

He was the only person she'd ever met who truly understood her, he read her mind, he comprehended her worries and woes. She was desperately lonely, and it was a relief to stumble upon someone who cared about her wellbeing, and even though he'd made her an indecent offer, she was convinced that his underlying feelings were genuine.

Though he would never propose anything more than an occasional tumble, she was thoroughly disposed to acquiesce. In her current state, she craved the attention and friendship he would provide, not to mention the salacious joys he would lavish upon her in an illicit liaison.

Over the years, she'd heard many stories about him and his lascivious habits. Where previously, she'd snob-

bishly condemned him for his behavior, now she was glad
he'd had such extensive experience as a roué. After enduring a small sampling of the prurient delights in which he'd
been schooled, she couldn't wait to willingly submit to further indoctrination.

She was neither a starry-eyed girl nor a chaste virgin,
and definitely not the proper, upstanding lady her mother
had raised her to be. To her undying shame, she'd played
the part of whore to Findley Harcourt. The reasons were
convoluted, complicated, and difficult to rationalize, so
she'd quit trying.

Even though she was an intelligent, assertive woman,
she'd let him take advantage of her in humiliating ways,
notably the libidinous. He was her sole sexual partner, and
what she knew of mating games, she'd learned from him.

But from her condensed interlude with John, it was
eminently apparent that much had been brushed over—and
downright omitted!—in her erotic education. Findley was
a selfish man, so she'd adapted to his wants and needs,
perceiving her role as that of intimate confidante who was
there to soothe and comfort.

She'd never been bold enough to seek her own gratification, for it had never occurred to her that her bodily
requirements might equal his own. Whenever she'd achieve
satiation, she was invariably surprised that it happened, and
she even hid her violent reactions from him, not wishing
to have her response interfere with his.

Yet, with John, from the very first, he'd been intent on
her satisfaction, and his enjoyment escalated simply by
pushing her to heights of ecstasy. After having discovered
this novel approach to lovemaking, she was absolutely enticed and could not stay away.

Footsteps sounded down the hall. She recognized his
determined step, and her anxiety spiraled.

Would he be glad to see her?

A proud man, he'd been sorely vexed by her snub of
his proposition, and she hadn't heard from him since—

though why she would have expected to after scolding him so hideously, she couldn't explain.

Was he angry with her? Or was he—hopefully—in her same predicament? Irritated. Out of sorts. Ready to carry on, despite her absurd insistence that they shouldn't.

He halted in the threshold, cryptically assessing her as if he hadn't quite believed the footman who'd announced her.

"Lady Elizabeth isn't here," he said as his welcome.

"I know. I came alone."

He entered the room and walked to her until he was so close that the hem of her dress swirled around his trousers. "Why are you here?"

There wasn't a trace of emotion in his voice, and she panicked, but she'd never been squeamish or shy, and vacillation could prove fatal. For once in her sorry, disorganized life, she was prepared to reach out and grab for what she desired.

"I missed you, and I had to see you again." He didn't reply, but merely studied her enigmatically. Her heart sank. Nervous, worried that he might toss her out on her ear, she hurriedly added, "I had thought we might—"

Before she could finish, he held a finger to her lips, silencing her, then he clasped her hand and yanked her out to the hall. Loudly—for the benefit of any servants who might be lingering in the vicinity—he pronounced: "Gabriel has numerous paintings scattered around the house. I would be thrilled to show some of them to you."

Then, he was rushing her up the stairs. He whisked her along so that her feet scarcely touched the floor, rapidly climbing two flights to a quiet corridor, and he dragged her to the room at the end. She had only a brief second to observe that he'd led her to his bedchamber before he sheltered them inside.

Without hesitating, he folded her in his arms, grabbing her bottom and twirling her around, pinning her back against the door. Fighting for balance, she gripped his shoulders as he lifted her, jerking at her skirts and petticoats, until he had her thighs wrapped around his waist. He steadied her, pinioned, her privates splayed wide and pressed against his loins.

"You madwoman!" He was wild for her, taking her mouth in fervent, savage kisses. "Do you have any idea how furious I've been with you?"

"Yes, yes. I didn't mean—"

"Sending me away! Insulting me! Questioning my intentions!"

"I'm sorry. So sorry."

"I've cursed you a thousand times over."

His fingers were between her legs, stroking her, pushing inside in hard moves that made her whimper and beg. The pleasure was so intense that she had to bite at her hand to keep from wailing and having a passing servant guess what they were up to.

His thumb circled her clit and—just that fast, just that easy—she was on the edge and ready to spill over into orgasm. She tensed, struggling to escape the primitive torrent, but he wouldn't let her go.

"Tell me you love me," he decreed.

"No, I can't . . . I won't . . ."

"Say it!"

"John—" He flicked at her clit. Again. Again. Her orgasm started, a blistering, fiery explosion.

She cried out, and he covered her lips with his, catching her rapture and sharing in the lengthy ascension to paradise. As her senses returned, he was fumbling with his pants, opening the front. He positioned himself, his hips flexing, and easing him in the slightest amount.

"Tell me," he repeated, but gently. "I want to hear you admit it."

"I love you."

With a smooth thrust, he drove into her, and she lurched at the sudden invasion. He was much larger than she'd anticipated, and he felt so bloody wonderful. He retreated, then deliciously slid in to the hilt.

"Oh, God . . . John—"

"I love you, too."

They both froze, the significance of their pronouncements so extraordinary that time seemed to stand still. She stared into his luscious brown eyes, and it dawned on her that she'd known this man forever. The magnificent perception caused a flutter of euphoria to ripple through her, and he nodded arrogantly, as if to affirm that he grasped her insight and heartily concurred.

"Show me how much," she said.

He laughed in response, a full, robust sound, and their gazes remained locked. Leaning in, he clutched her hips, his cock an inflexible wedge that impaled her. With great relish, he worked at her, taking her boisterously and emphatically, prolonging the episode so that when he finally came, she joined him.

As he let himself go in a turbulent flood, her body contracted and spasmed around him, and she could feel the heat of his seed against her womb. She crushed her lips to his, snaring the groan of fulfillment that erupted as he emptied himself.

"Sweet Jesu, woman, I'm fifty years old." His pulse was racing, his breathing labored. "You'll be the death of me."

"Not too soon, I trust. I plan to have you a few more times before you expire."

"I must lie down. I'm so undone, my legs can scarcely support me."

He whirled them around and staggered toward the bed, dropping her, then tottering after her. As they bounced on the mattress, the ropes swinging from their combined weight, they were giggling like frivolous schoolchildren.

Rising up, he knelt between her legs, his trousers loose around his thighs, his cock prominent and imposing, ready to be serviced, once more. Delighted with his ample size, she shoved him back, scampering up and over so she could suck him into her mouth, and he expelled a hiss at her startling action.

She hadn't meant to behave so rashly—at least, not in the beginning!—but she couldn't resist tasting him.

Within seconds, he wrenched away, threw her on the pillows, and wrestled her down.

"You strumpet," he teased.

"I wasn't finished."

"Neither was I, but I want you naked."

He was tearing at her clothes so frantically that she was afraid he'd rip the fabric, and she'd never be able to account for her condition when she arrived at home.

"Slow down." Batting at his questing fingers, she couldn't recall when she'd last joked and frolicked. It had been so long. Too long.

"I can't wait."

"Well, we have all day. I don't have to be back until four."

He wiggled his brows in naughty invitation, then rolled her over to unlace her corset. Now that he had ascertained that they had plentiful, decadent hours stretching ahead, he languidly disrobed her. As each piece of clothing disappeared, he oohed and aahed, kissed and fondled, tormenting and entrancing in equal measure. He continued undressing her until she was wearing nothing but stockings and garters.

"I love your tits," he said irreverently as he cupped one of them.

"They're not as firm as they used to be." She flushed at the disparaging comment and couldn't conceive of why she'd expressed it. What did it matter if John found her breasts attractive or not? She was forty-five years old; she didn't need reassurances as to her appearance. Did she?

Perhaps her spirit had taken more of a beating than she'd suspected when Findley had married his young, pretty wife!

"Do I look like I care?" He pointed at his crotch, where his erect cock rudely protruded.

She chuckled and shook her head. "No, you don't."

"Then don't insult me with stupid statements. I think you're beautiful." He bent down and started to suckle, but she prodded him away.

"Not yet." She came up so that they were both kneeling, their bodies melded, thighs tangled. "I want your clothes off, too."

"Well, never let it be said that John Preston refused a lady's request."

He extended his arms, primping and posing, so that she could proceed as she liked. She dawdled, leisurely removing coat, cuff links, cravat, shirt, shoes, trousers, tarrying in between each piece of attire to kiss and caress. Finally, blessedly, he was naked, and she shifted nearer, their nude torsos connecting.

"Oh, Mary," he sweetly declared, "how lucky I've suddenly become."

He kissed her, a dear, almost chaste peck and, as he laid her down, tears prickled her eyes. She wasn't sure if it was the simple kiss or the precious remark that had moved her so, but she was abruptly filled with such joy that she felt she might burst.

Before a single tear could fall, he kissed them away, then idly entered her, inch by glorious inch. He tarried, cherishing and treasuring her, and when they came together, the teardrops swarmed and overflowed onto her cheeks.

With his cock still semihard and planted inside her, he tipped them to the side so they were facing one another. He hugged and petted her, calming her with his hands, his lips, his body. But nothing could stem her swell of emotion.

"What is it, *chère*?"

"I'm just so happy." Flustered, she swiped at her cheeks, but he reached for the corner of the blanket and promptly assumed the task.

"So am I."

"I feel so . . . so . . ." She couldn't describe the sentiments that were coursing through her. Any attempt would have brought on a wave of weeping.

"Like you're walking on clouds?"

"Every minute."

"I have a confession, darling."

"What?"

"Mere moments before I was informed you were downstairs in my parlor, I'd decided I was heading over to Findley's house to speak with you."

"You weren't!"

"I was!"

She climbed on top of him and conferred her most stern glare, but the practiced scowl had no effect on the overbearing man. "To what end?"

"I had to talk some sense into you." He flashed a cheeky grin. "If you'd forbidden me entrance, I was prepared to beat down the door."

"Now that's a sight the neighbors would have paid to witness! John Preston demanding an appointment with the earl's housekeeper!"

The smile left his face, and he grew serious. "I absolutely hate that you believe me to be such a snob, and I'm sorry for my conduct the other day when we were in the coach."

"Sorry for what? Making love to me?"

"No. For not telling you what was on my mind, though in my own defense, I must acknowledge that I wasn't sure myself. It took me a while to realize exactly what I wanted."

"And that was . . . ?"

"Will you marry me?"

Out of the blue! Just like that! With no warning!

"What did you say?" She began to shake, terrified that he meant it, terrified that he didn't.

"You heard me, Mary Smith." He eased her onto her back so that he was directly over her as he professed his intent. "I'm crazy about you, and I want to spend the rest of my life with you. I don't presume I'm the best match you might have made, but I'll always provide for you, I'll always be faithful, and I'll never stop loving you."

He paused and cleared his throat, braced for her reply, but she couldn't produce one, couldn't force out a single rejoinder. She tried, tried again, but nothing coherent emerged.

"This is where you reward me with an answer"—he swatted her on the rear—"and it had better be yes!"

Just then, the bedroom door swung open. They'd been so wrapped up in each other that neither had discerned any footsteps and, as she was aware, when they'd initially dashed in, John had been too preoccupied to turn the key in the lock.

Their heads swung around in tandem to discover the identity of their uninvited guest, and Gabriel strode in, not cognizant that his father was entertaining a naked woman.

"Father, I need to . . . *Dio santo!*" he exclaimed on witnessing their antics.

The three of them were paralyzed. Gabriel especially was stunned and shocked, and she took some small comfort in the fact that he obviously didn't often encounter his father in the throes of a sexual romp in their home in the middle of the morning.

Totally amazed, he peered from her to John, her and John, over and over, and she supposed they were a humorous tableau. She might have laughed if she hadn't been utterly mortified.

"*Merde!*" John cursed in French, bringing them all back to their senses.

"Pardon me, Father, Miss Smith. I had no idea . . . I was simply . . . I was . . ." Gabriel couldn't complete a sentence. His poise and aplomb had vanished. Blushing, he hastily exited the chamber, slamming the door behind him.

They hesitated, listening to his speedy retreat. Then,

John spun toward her, and when he did, he was smiling like the cat that had just eaten the canary.

"What?" she asked on observing the disturbing gleam in his eye.

"My son has impeccable timing."

"No he doesn't!" She was so embarrassed, and blushing so badly—much worse than poor Gabriel!—that she felt as if she might ignite from the shame. "What must he be thinking! Let me up! I've got to get out of here!"

But the odious cad simply chuckled and wouldn't budge. He was too heavy to dislodge, so she was trapped.

"You'll have to have me now, Mary girl. You can't say no."

"Just watch me!"

"If you decline my offer, my only child will conclude that I've been consorting with a lightskirt!"

"A lightskirt?" she sputtered.

"A virtual jezebel." He was gloating! "I'll have to unburden myself as to how you seduced me, how you wore me down with your feminine wiles."

"*I* seduced *you*? You insolent cad!"

"Yes," he mused irritatingly. "You'll have to make an honest man of me. To save my reputation."

"You bounder! You don't have a reputation worth saving!"

"Precisely, Mary." He stole a kiss, then another. "Now accept my proposal, and I'll be the happiest man in the world."

Charlotte sat in her chair at the foot of the table in the family dining room, purportedly a spot of prestige and distinction befitting her elevated status of countess. As usual, her husband of seven months sat at the other end, reading his paper and completely ignoring her.

Silently, she toyed with her breakfast as she raged over recent circumstances that had swirled out of her control, but she was powerless to rectify the situation.

The previous night's supper party—with the prime minister in attendance, no less!—had been an unqualified disaster. The food had been inedible and poorly served, the servants sloppy and inattentive. Even the seating chart had been incorrectly drafted, with a baron's son ahead of an earl's. She'd never been so humiliated; she'd never live it down!

Of course, the fiasco was that wretched housekeeper's fault. Mary Smith had had weeks to make ready for the grand event, and she'd failed unconditionally, leaving Charlotte dangling like a fool in front of her peers, and as she stared across at her contemptible spouse, she was seething.

On one prior occasion, she'd broached the subject of Mary Smith, awkwardly justifying why she wanted the housekeeper gone. The earl had declined to heed her complaint, but then, Charlotte had to admit that she'd done a shoddy job of clarifying the older woman's lack of initiative and supervisory skills.

She'd barely commenced with her list of grievances, when the earl had cut her off, informing her that Mary Smith would never be fired. He'd then had the gall to pronounce that Charlotte didn't know anything about running a large household, and that she needed all the expert guidance Mary Smith could bestow. Charlotte was prohibited from raising the topic of Miss Smith's aptitude—or dearth of it—again.

Well, Miss Smith had certainly fixed it for Charlotte! It seemed as if the servant had intentionally plotted to make Charlotte look bad. If that was her ploy, it had definitely succeeded!

The earl blamed the entire debacle on Charlotte, when she didn't comprehend how any of the disaster could be her fault. What was the housekeeper paid to do, if not to correctly manage their important entertaining? Why, from some clever eavesdropping, she'd learned that Smith wasn't even in the house most afternoons, evidently stealing the family carriage and gallivanting off to destinations unknown, returning at all hours with no explanation for her lengthy absences.

No wonder the house was in such disarray, the banquet such a calamity! But could Charlotte say anything in her own defense? Could she disabuse the earl as to the actual basis for the catastrophes? No, she could not! Heaven forbid that the lady of the manor make any disparaging comments about one of the employees!

After the guests had departed, the earl had come to her bed and had roughly slaked his manly needs, but not before giving her a potent tongue-lashing for the ruined supper. She'd stoically suffered through it all, and she was still extremely angry, yet she struggled to maintain a serene smile, a cultivated restraint. She'd never permit the pompous ass to deduce how much he'd upset her.

How she despised him! Her ire was so profound that, if she'd been a man, she might have lunged across the table and stabbed him with the butter knife! If he had a blade sticking out of his cold, black heart, he wouldn't be able to ignore her!

How dare he reproach her for Mary Smith's shortcomings! Would she be forever imputed for the chaos the inept retainer instigated?

In the months before her marriage, Charlotte had fantasized about how marvelous it would be to be a countess. How she'd be respected, esteemed. Never in her wildest dreams had she imagined that the reality would be so impossibly horrid!

If only her mother could come from Yorkshire! She'd put domestic matters in order straightaway! But the earl had rebuffed Charlotte's request for so much as a visit, let alone a lengthy stay.

Oh, what was she to do? How was she to gain control of her own home?

Gripping her teacup so tightly that she worried she might break the fragile handle, she determinedly set it on the saucer just as Elizabeth floated in. She was oddly attired for the chilly, dreary day, having donned a bright pink dress, with an off-the-shoulder neckline, frilly lace around the bodice, and a flowing, billowy skirt.

Her hair was unbound, hanging in lavishly curled ringlets. A straw hat, the wide brim trimmed with a green ribbon that matched the piping on her dress, drooped haphazardly from her fingers. A cheerful, delicate shawl was draped over her arm.

Charlotte examined Elizabeth carefully. Something strange was happening with her. She appeared younger, prettier, merrier, her hairstyles looser and less severe. She was spending a fortune on new clothes, the styles more colorful and fashionable, the tailoring and hues plainly picked to flatter her abundant figure. Decked out as she was, she was downright winsome, an occurrence that had Charlotte grievously irritated.

Each day brought about subtle transformations. Whereas Elizabeth used to be a housebound drudge, she now had places to go, people to see, things to do. Instead of moping about, lamenting her dire plight, she was bustling, constantly active, leaving early and arriving late, with nary a word of explication or apology to Charlotte for her truancy.

When Charlotte had first moved into the town house, she'd gloated over the fact that she so easily outshone stodgy, boring Elizabeth, that she'd usurped her role and responsibilities. Without question, Charlotte was more beautiful, more refined, and she had more aptitude in household transactions, more influence and visibility in society. She'd privately exulted over Elizabeth's loss of stature and influence.

Yet now, their fates had altered dramatically, and Charlotte wasn't sure why or how it had transpired. She and Elizabeth were in opposite trajectories. As Charlotte grew more gloomy, her disposition more doleful, Elizabeth was radiant, glowing, vivacious. She categorically bubbled with enthusiasm and excitement.

How Charlotte loathed her for the changes! Elizabeth

hardly seemed to remember that Charlotte existed!

"Good morning, Charlotte," Elizabeth gushed.

Charlotte bristled, convinced there was an underlying sarcasm in Elizabeth's voice. She nodded regally. "Elizabeth."

"Isn't it a spectacular morning? Father, you're looking particularly dapper. Is that a new suit?"

The earl grumbled unintelligibly, and Charlotte was appeased when he didn't bother to glance up.

She couldn't help but chide, "You're costumed rather peculiarly, aren't you, Elizabeth?"

"I should say."

Elizabeth glided to the sideboard and filled a plate, and the footman assisted her without instruction or prodding. Charlotte bristled again. She had to beat the miscreants before they'd lift a finger on her behalf!

Sipping her morning chocolate, she pretended scant interest in Elizabeth's affairs, when in reality, they consumed her. "Are you invited to a garden fete in this weather?"

"Me? My heavens, no." Elizabeth pulled up a chair and dug into her meal as a starving sailor might, eating as though there was no tomorrow, totally shunning any feminine inclination toward daintiness. "I'm having my portrait done. I thought you knew."

A portrait? How exotic! How romantic! Just one more petty modification to abhor!

"No, I didn't." Her response was too petulant, but she detested it when incidents occurred in the house and she wasn't informed. How was she to remain in charge if no one apprised her of pertinent details?

Another sin to lay at Mary Smith's feet!

"I've been attending sessions for weeks. The artist has been sketching me, and he's finally ready to paint."

"In a party dress?" Charlotte scoffed.

"He's depicting me in a pastoral setting. On the steps of the gazebo at Norwich." The illustrious family estate Charlotte had yet to be granted permission to visit! "I merely described the place, and he re-created it exactly. He's amazingly talented."

"What's his name?"

"Gabriel Cristofore."

"I've never heard of him."

"Really?" Elizabeth's condescension was palpable. "He's one of the premier artists in the city."

As if he could be that renowned when Charlotte didn't know of him! "It sounds quite fun. Perhaps when you're through, I'll have him paint me."

A queer noise gurgled from Elizabeth, and Charlotte was certain Elizabeth was laughing at her! The shrew!

"You do that, Charlotte. I'm sure he'd be more than eager to discuss a contract with you." Her repast gulped in haste, she shoved her plate aside, and stood. "I'm off to my appointment. Have a pleasant day."

For some reason, her *adieu* garnered the earl's attention. He lowered his newspaper and scrutinized her as though he didn't recognize her.

"Elizabeth, my . . . but aren't you fetching!"

"Do you think so?" Gaily, she shifted back and forth so that he could have a better glimpse of her ensemble.

"I've never seen you so pretty. I'm enchanted."

Charlotte nearly choked with outrage. In the entire year she and the earl had been acquainted, he'd never once uttered a flattery! Suddenly, he deigned to lavish a fawning attestation, but he directed it at another! The blackguard!

"Why, thank you, Father."

"You look just like your mother in that dress."

Elizabeth blushed becomingly, and with a start of astonishment, Charlotte realized that Elizabeth was positively striking, comely and graceful in a fashion Charlotte had never noted before.

"Are you going out?" the earl inquired, as if he was genuinely curious.

"I'm having my portrait done," she said again.

"How nice for you."

"It's been an amusing diversion."

"And when am I to view this superb masterpiece?"

"I don't know the artist's schedule. He's extremely busy, so I'd guess in a few more weeks."

"I'm looking forward to it."

"As am I," she said. "Good-bye," and she waltzed off.

A telling hush descended. The earl reverted to his reading. The servant left for the kitchens.

Charlotte glared at her plate, an unanticipated surge of tears flooding her eyes.

She hated her husband! Hated her stepdaughter!

Hated her life!

At the notion of Elizabeth's prancing off to enjoy a carefree adventure, jealousy poured through her. How she wished she could get even for the contentment Elizabeth had found! If only Charlotte could detect some method of reducing Elizabeth's elevated circumstances! It wasn't fair that Elizabeth was so gay, while she, Charlotte, was so miserable!

How gratifying it would be to bring her down a notch or two, and how splendid if, in the process, she could demonstrate to the earl a few of Elizabeth's defects. He acted as if his daughter could do no wrong. Well, Charlotte would eventually force him to confront the truth.

Elizabeth wasn't anything special! Charlotte would show him!

She rose, placidly and sedately withdrawing from the salon and proceeding to the stairs, but no one noticed her departure.

CHAPTER FOURTEEN

GABRIEL stood at the window, dressed solely in his trousers, ready to paint, but he couldn't. An arm braced against the sill, he gazed out at the rainy day, but saw nothing. Nothing, that is, but the sight of his father and Mary Smith. He couldn't put the scene behind him. Whenever he closed his eyes, he pictured them together: John blithe and joyous; Miss Smith rumpled and well loved.

He couldn't figure out why he was so upset by his discovery. Over the years, his father had had many lovers. His amorous exploits had never been a secret, even when Gabriel was a young boy, but it had been a long while since John had displayed more than a passing fancy for any female.

The man was fifty years old, and he'd encountered limited contentment, as well as inconceivable heartache, so Gabriel should have been glad that John had found someone with whom to share his future. Yet, John's marrying was painful to contemplate.

For some reason, Gabriel equated his disturbing reaction with the loss of his mother. He'd been a babe when she was murdered, so he had no recollections of her but, in many unexplainable ways, she had had more influence on his upbringing than John.

The woman's life had been a tragedy, one that John had recounted in numerous melancholic moments, so Gabriel felt that he'd known her, had suffered for her, and had loved her.

Wed at fourteen to an elderly, bitter Italian count, she'd been a gifted artist, supposedly more talented than Gabriel, yet her husband wouldn't permit her to practice her craft. Driven to create, she would slip away to hidden studios, using pilfered supplies, only to be caught and beaten, then locked in her room to prevent her from continuing.

At age nineteen, she'd met and fallen in love with John. His father had always imagined himself as a modern-day knight in shining armor, bent on rescuing damsels in distress, and he had fled with her to commence their doomed, bittersweet affair.

Eventually, her brothers had located them, had killed Selena for the disgrace she'd wreaked on their family. They would have killed Gabriel, too—the ultimate evidence of her grave sin—if they'd had the opportunity, but luckily, he and John had been out of the house when his uncles had arrived, and John had immediately whisked him away upon learning the dreadful news.

This event, and the torment that followed, had bound him more closely to John than any son could ever be, and though Gabriel's sentiments made no sense, it seemed as though John was tarnishing Selena's memory by succumbing to ardor again. The notion was asinine, but he couldn't set it aside.

He couldn't discuss his feelings with John. His father was buoyant in a manner Gabriel could never recall witnessing before, and Gabriel would never hurt him by implying that he wasn't ecstatic, too. He loved his father, and if Mary Smith could make him so exhilarated, then Gabriel yearned to be happy for him.

Unfortunately, the two women, Selena Cristofore and Mary Smith, were jumbled together in his head, having both vied for and received John's undying devotion, which Gabriel knew from individual experience to be a vast amount. He couldn't get past the annoying, infantile conviction that Mary Smith would be stealing John away, that John's regard would be forfeit and showered on another, that the fealty they'd unceasingly had to Selena's memory would fade with John's remarriage.

John had been the shining center of Gabriel's existence, the guiding force, the calming influence. For so long, it had been just the two of them against the world, running, traveling, living life to the fullest, while thriving on their bonding reminiscence of Selena. He couldn't predict how things would change with Mary Smith plopped into the middle of their relationship.

He was acting like a child. A spoiled, coddled, selfish child, yet he couldn't desist. He didn't want the woman insinuating herself into his family. As he'd never had a mother, he wasn't sure how to adapt to having a female constantly on the premises.

If that attitude wasn't immature enough, he didn't want her interfering with his time with John, meddling and intruding into their male business. Without a doubt, she'd insist that he modify his methods and habits—both public and private—and he was petulantly, pettily opposed to obliging her.

The door opened, and he glanced over his shoulder, inordinately pleased to see Elizabeth. He was terribly glad she'd come early, that she'd spend most of the day. Perhaps after copious hours in her sweet company, some of his agitation and apprehension would wane.

She's my best friend.

The thought popped out of nowhere, and the realization was refreshing and pacifying. She was someone in whom he could confide. She wouldn't judge or ridicule; she would empathize and offer advice upon which he could depend.

How extraordinary that he hadn't appreciated it before! He'd been so focused on the sexual, on her blossoming carnal proficiency, that he hadn't peered beyond the surface. From the beginning, he'd cherished her, which was why he battled to keep her at arm's length, but on this hideous occasion, distance wouldn't do.

He needed compassion and commiseration, so he intended to lean on Elizabeth for the duration of her visit, letting her shower him with her precious attention, and sate him with her lush, magnificent body.

Meticulously, he assessed her as she removed her cloak and hung it on a hook. She was so charming in her pink dress, in her hat with its green bow tied appealingly under her chin, with her luxurious hair cascading down. It was difficult to recognize her as the same demure, retiring noblewoman he'd stumbled upon such a short time ago.

"Hello, *bella*." He struggled for composure, for equanimity, and prayed his greeting had been sufficiently pleasant to have masked his level of anguish.

"Are you all right?"

Instantly, she perceived that he was unsettled, and he should have guessed that she would. Where he was concerned, she had an uncanny knack for discerning his emotional condition.

She untied her hat and tossed it on the floor, then stalked across the room and slipped her arms around his waist, scrutinizing him exhaustively. Considering his vexation, he couldn't abide such an exacting appraisal, so he pulled her tightly against him, burying himself at her nape, breathing in her scent so he could be soothed by her familiar essence.

"I'm fine," he contended once he felt more poised.

"Liar."

She tilted back to look at him, and he shrugged. "Well, perhaps I'm not feeling all that great."

"I should say not." Standing on tiptoe, she brushed a kiss against his mouth. "Want to tell me about it?"

The entire sordid story of his chancing upon John and Mary was perched on the tip of his tongue, but he simply couldn't speak of the incident aloud. Turning away from her shrewd evaluation, he proceeded to the small room at the rear of the cottage. She followed, tarrying in the doorway and watching his every move as he crossed to the nightstand next to the bed.

He slept in the bed when he was working late, and he'd had a lover or two upon its comfortable mattress. As he rooted around in a drawer, he wondered if she suspected. In situations involving his comportment, she was incredibly astute, so he wouldn't be surprised if she'd surmised his rampant, dubious proclivities.

"What are you doing?" she asked as he concluded his search.

"I have a piece of jewelry I'd like you to wear with your dress." He held out a silver necklace, with a heart-shaped locket.

"Oh, Gabriel, it's lovely."

"I want to draw you with it on."

She spun around and lifted her hair, and he stepped behind her and hooked the clasp. The locket nestled just above her cleavage, a stunning focal point to her gorgeous breasts.

"Is there something special inside?" She fussed with it, then flipped the pendant open to reveal two miniatures of a woman's face—one a front view, one a profile. "Who's this?"

"My mother," but as soon as he'd divulged Selena's identity, he felt horrid, and his anxiety spiraled.

He shouldn't have asked Elizabeth to model the price-less keepsake! The heirloom was too exceptional! Should he take it back? Put it away?

Was she cognizant of any of his parents' history? What if she made a disparaging remark?

No, no, she never would!

His fractious, careening introspection was making him crazed! He was a mess!

"She was very pretty."

"Aye, she was. My father always said she was the most beautiful woman he'd ever met."

"Did you do the paintings?"

"From his descriptions. I never knew her; she was ah . . . killed when I was a wee child."

"Killed?"

"By her brothers." Oddly, he blushed with shame, as if the disclosure made him partly responsible.

"Oh, Gabriel. I'm so sorry." She laid her palm against his cheek, a tender gesture that—disgustingly—brought a sheen of tears to his eyes, and he whipped away, lest she notice.

"She was compelled to marry very young, and she was desperately forlorn. She ran off with my father and . . . well . . ."

He couldn't finish, and he wasn't certain why he'd started. In his twenty-nine years, he'd never imparted a single detail to another soul. Yet, to Elizabeth, he'd hinted at the squalid particulars. It was almost as if he *wanted* her to comprehend some of the grief he carried, which was nonsense. He wasn't the sort to go around pounding his chest and supplicating for sympathy!

Behind him, he heard her shut the locket.

"Thank you," she said. "I'm honored that you'd have me wear it."

"I want you to have it," he suddenly proposed. "It's yours."

"Gabriel . . . it seems too dear. Are you sure?"

"It would please me tremendously."

She clasped her arms around his waist, burrowing herself against his naked back, her breasts flattened on either side of his spine. "What's wrong? Can you talk about it?"

He gulped in a huge breath of air. If he didn't exercise some discipline soon, she'd deem him to be insane! Yet, the next words out of his mouth proved that a trip to Bedlam was nigh. "What do you know about Mary Smith?"

"Mary . . . Smith?" Curious, she circled around him, and braced her hands on his waist. "Our housekeeper?"

"Yes, her."

"She's a valued employee and a respected friend. Although I'd say she's an extremely private person; she has her own life."

"Yes, yes"—he waved impatiently—"but what's she *like*?"

"Kind, smart, generous, patient. Why?"

"Has she ever been married?"

"No. She's a spinster."

"Has she ever been in love?"

"Well, there were rumors that she was once infatuated with a gentleman when she was a girl, but he couldn't marry her because of their disparate stations."

"So . . . she wouldn't be the type who would toy with a man's affections, or try to—"

"Honestly, Gabriel, what it is?"

"My father is going to marry her."

"What!"

"She keeps refusing him, but John insists he's about to change her mind. I'm sure he'll succeed."

"Mary and . . . Mr. Preston?" In shock, she sank onto the mattress, her hips balanced on the edge. "I can't believe it."

"Trust me, it's true." She was extremely dubious, so he confessed, "I walked in on them when they were naked. In my father's bed."

"No!"

"Yes!"

"How embarrassing! For all of you!" Baffled and dumbfounded, she shook her head. "I didn't realize they had more than a passing acquaintance. How—when—did this happen?"

"Well, I'd suppose we weren't the only ones dallying when you came to visit."

"Obviously not."

She chuckled, then flopped onto the mattress, staring up at the ceiling and worrying her fingers in the blankets. He climbed onto the bed so he could lie with her. "Will she be a worthy wife to him, do you think?"

"Absolutely, Gabriel." She shifted, so they were facing one another. "Is that what has you in such a state?"

"I've been in a complete muddle."

"Their affair has been stirring up memories of your mother, hasn't it?"

"Yes," he acknowledged. He crawled up to repose against the pillows, and he hauled her along so that she rested with him, her torso positioned between his legs. "I wish there'd been some means of contacting you. I was dying to tell you the news."

He paused, reflecting on what he'd just admitted. As his misery and confusion had intensified, the only person with whom he'd wanted to discuss the situation had been Elizabeth. It was frivolous daydreaming to presume that he could turn to her in times of trouble, yet there it was: He was smitten, captivated, bewitched.

Dared he give it a name? Was he in love?

"I wish I could have been here for you." She rubbed her hand over his heart, as if she knew how badly it was aching.

"As do I."

Their comments hovered in the air. Dangerous, risky, and foolish they were, so he tried to formulate another remark to fill the gap, but the only topic on which he could dwell was how splendid it would be if she was really his.

What was he contemplating? Had his recent mental ramblings left him so irrational that he imprudently hoped they might wed?

Elizabeth saved him from his folly, raising up to kiss him. "I hate that you're so distressed. Let me comfort you."

"There's no need."

"That's what I'm here for, aren't I? To make you happy?"

Yes, but it had become so much more! So much more than sex and naughty conversation and lewd interaction, and he longed to confess the sentiment, but she was nuzzling across his chest, licking at his nipple.

She kissed a trail down his abdomen, rooting across his trousers, biting and nipping at the hard ridge of his erection. Eagerly, she unbuttoned him, and he nearly cried out with relief as she reached in and freed him from the confines of his pants.

Without dawdling, she grazed the crown, teasing and tormenting until he was writhing against the bed. Her lips parted, and he thrust into her, holding her close as he languidly conferred all she could handle and a little bit more besides.

She'd come to relish the indecent maneuver, had fully adjusted to nuance and subtlety, using teeth and tongue in a practiced fashion that never failed to drive him wild. Thoroughly afflicted, he rapidly surpassed his limit, and he removed himself—as he habitually did—disappointing her with his reticence, but even though she performed like a skilled courtesan, he wouldn't culminate in her mouth.

He'd taken advantage of her in dreadful ways, so at least he could restrain his worst impulses by spilling his seed in a less disturbing, more innocuous manner.

"You never let me finish," she pouted.

Taking her into his arms, he kissed her, a lengthy, total ravishment that kept her quiet and kept him busy. His cock was temporarily distracted from its unrelenting demand for satiation. When she aroused him so terribly, he never could control himself, and the act was regularly terminated much before he was ready.

As he made love to her mouth, he gradually stripped her until she wore naught but his mother's necklace, and he blazed a path down her neck and bosom, pressing and squeezing her breasts, torturing the nipples. When her hips responded, he moved on, to her navel, then her mound.

He sniffed at her womanly hair, then opened her with his tongue. She was well schooled now, aware of what was approaching, and her thighs parted, allowing him easy access. He laved and tasted, prodding her higher and higher. When she could abide no more, he latched on to her clit, while roughly fondling her nipples, and she came in a brutal rush, crying out as she soared to what seemed the maximum pinnacle she'd yet achieved.

As she wound down, the tang of her sex was a powerful aphrodisiac that made him frantic to seize the moment, and damn the consequences. During their prior trysts, he'd reined in his baser instincts, but abruptly, he was prepared to risk all. If he violated her, if he crudely stole her maidenhead, if he pilfered more than she'd ever intended to bestow, he no longer cared. His level of passion had ascended to an apex from which there was no feasible retreat.

Previously, his ironclad discipline had prevented him from stepping beyond that decisive line to deflowerment. However, the recent familial upheaval, coupled with his elevated dolor, had him eager to wrongly purloin the remaining bits of her chastity in spite of the damage that might result to both of them.

As if a raging, savage beast had overtaken him, his only concern was alleviation. Without warning, he was so sexually provoked that he *had* to be the one.

He rubbed his cock over her wet center. She was slippery, inviting, and he shoved in just the tiniest inch, and her eyes widened with virginal alarm. They'd never journeyed this far down the road before. Although she'd sporadically asked, and had even begged for the normal conclusion, he'd persistently rejected her entreaties.

Continued restraint was stupid. What purpose was to be gained by spurning such gratification? This was what she'd repeatedly implored him to show her. He'd cautioned her as to the perils, but he'd had the fortitude to shield her from the genuine hazards. Until now. He couldn't locate the necessary mettle to deny himself.

He eased his hips forward so that he began to stretch her, and she stiffened, promptly afraid of what he planned.

"Are you going to—"

"Yes. Lie back."

He increased the pressure, and instinctively, she rebelled. "Can we discuss—"

"No. I should have done this long ago."

"Gabriel—"

She was sincerely frightened, and he should have slowed to cajole away her maidenly fears, but he was beyond reasoning, beyond the ability to placate or wheedle her into compliance.

"Try to relax," was the best he could do. He thrust again, and he butted up against her maidenhead, but he couldn't disengage.

He lifted her thighs and draped them over his own. Peeking downward, he was tantalized by the carnal spectacle: his cock slightly immersed, her pussy hairs tickling him, urging him on and in.

"You're mine," he declared. "No matter what happens in the future, I had you first."

She nodded hesitantly. "Will it hurt?"

"Yes. I'm a big man, and you're a virgin. It can't be helped."

More agitated, she grappled against the novel predicament in which she'd landed, but he wouldn't release her.

"It doesn't seem like you'll fit."

"Your body's resisting," he explained. "It's natural. You'll eventually adjust."

"Will I—"

"Hush!" He couldn't delay, and his hands went to her hips, steadying her. "Never forget: You're mine!"

With a groan of pleasure, he penetrated to the hilt. She lunged up, and called out, but he hugged her and held her still, capturing her wail of dismay with an ardent kiss. For as long as he could bear it, he was motionless, her ravished body acclimating to his incursion, but the second he felt the slightest slackening of tension, he had to carry on.

Her pussy was a saturated cauldron, slippery with her virgin's blood, and his passion escalated to a critical zenith. Proceeding deliberately, then with more force, he strained, catapulting himself until his loins spasmed, and his seed charged to the tip. He plunged once. Again. His orgasm began, and with his final grain of strength, he withdrew, saving her from calamity and ultimate disgrace by spewing against her stomach.

He was nestled into the crook of her neck, drenched with sweat, his muscles wearied with exhaustion, and he strove for calm. Driven by lust, he'd acted outrageously, like the bastard he actually was, but he'd never desired a woman as ferociously as he'd desired her. His climax had been stupendous, astounding, yet with his ardor waning, guilt flooded in. Shifting away, he compelled himself to look at her.

She was crying!

He wrenched with alarm. How was it that he systematically moved her to such displays of woe?

He . . . he *loved* her! And he hated that he could behave so contemptibly, that he could maltreat her.

"I'm sorry." He kissed her mouth, her cheeks. "I'm sorry. I didn't know I'd hurt you so much."

"You didn't," she bravely contended, but he knew it was a lie.

He was an ill-bred dog! An uncivilized beast! He never trifled with innocents! His lovers were sophisticated women who were versed in sexual procedures, their chastity long absent, and he'd obviously forgotten how affecting the incident was on the female's end of things.

Appalled with himself, he lurched away, his skin assaulted by the cold air, and he stomped across the floor to a pitcher of water on the stand by the door. He poured the cool liquid into a bowl, then swished a cloth and returned to her, blotting at his seed that was smeared across her abdomen.

Avidly and quietly, she watched as he refolded the cloth, then gently pressed it to her mistreated, swollen loins, swabbing at the swatches of blood smudged on her thighs. He finished with his cock, dabbing away the traces of his carnal sin, then he snuggled next to her, grabbing a throw and shielding them under the blanket.

"I should have gone slower; I should have—"

Amazingly, she kissed him, silencing his apologies and justifications. "I'm not injured," she declared. "Well . . . not badly."

"Then why are you crying?"

"It was just so different from how I'd assumed it would be. So much more . . . more personal. More intimate." Shyly, she professed, "I liked it very much."

He wiped her tears, relieved that they were quickly disappearing. "It's difficult to describe."

"I understand that now."

"That's why I've been so cautious."

"You're forgiven for your circumspection."

She extended her legs and winced with discomfort, causing his heart to twist and flutter.

"The pain will fade," he was constrained to clarify, "and after you heal from this initial attempt, it won't ever bother you again."

"Good. Because I find myself in a hurry to augment my licentious education."

"Minx!"

Unexpectedly, she looked embarrassed, blushing and peering off to the side. "I didn't mean to act like a ninny. There at the end . . . I panicked."

"I should have taken more time."

"There was no need. You gave me exactly what I'd sought, and very much more besides." She wiggled her brows mischievously. "I was just getting the hang of it. When may I have a repeat performance?"

"You shameless hussy! Give me a minute to catch my breath."

"If you promise you won't loaf too long."

She suggestively rubbed her crotch against his own, inciting an instantaneous stir in his satisfied phallus.

"Roll over," he grumbled.

Without waiting for her to agree, he rotated her and curled her so that her backside was spooned to his front, her shapely ass burrowed tight. His cock energetically reacted, and she laughed and pressed herself nearer.

"It doesn't feel like you need a break."

"Well, I'm taking one." In light of his enamoration with her, he probably could have copulated all day, but she had to be sore and tender, and she was so accommodating that she would never complain. "Let's rest."

"I'm not tired."

"Neither am I."

"Then why—" She tried to peek at him over her shoulder, and he settled her down.

"Because I want to hold you in my arms."

"Really?"

"Yes. I can't predict how many more chances I'll have."

In accord, she smiled, and soon, her respirations moderated and stabilized, and he could tell that she slept. He waited a few minutes then, confident that she couldn't hear the pointless confession, he whispered, "I love you."

Overflowing with gladness and contentment, he shut his eyes and joined her in slumber.

CHAPTER FIFTEEN

ELIZABETH awoke in a strange bed, but she suffered no confusion over where she was or what she was doing.

Gabriel was nestled behind her, his cock limp and flaccid against her bottom, his breathing regular and steady behind her ear. She tarried, reveling in the marvelous moment, wishing it could go on forever.

How many more times could she sneak away? How many more excuses could she concoct to explain her absences? How often could she evade Charlotte's questions? And most disturbingly, how long would Gabriel welcome her as a guest in his wicked cottage?

The pretext she'd used to start their affair and to continue it—his painting her portrait—wouldn't provide cover much longer. The artistic endeavor couldn't proceed indefinitely; there had to be an end.

Even if she could devise a means to account for the slowness of the project, her dilemma wouldn't be rectified, because Gabriel would never agree to an interminable dalliance.

After extensive reflection, she had developed a niggling suspicion that he sought out lovers from whom he could gain financially. Initially, he'd been after her money, but she didn't have any. When he'd learned of her dire financial straits, he'd tried to cancel their contract, but she'd refused to surrender peacefully. She wasn't certain what she'd said or done to persuade him to keep on. Perhaps he simply liked her more than he had some of the others.

He'd made numerous affectionate comments, and while she wouldn't try to read too much into his statements, she was satisfied that he harbored a genuine fondness for her.

She shifted so that she could clandestinely analyze his beautiful face, his splendid physique. Her leg muscles rebelled, her delicate, overused privates twingeing and reminding her of just how recklessly she'd behaved earlier.

In sleep, he looked young, adorable, and it was difficult to believe he was so full of passion and intensity, that he could employ his body in such raucous, fascinating, and brazen ways. In his own chivalrous fashion, he'd attempted to protect her from his nefarious propensities, but she had declined to heed his admonitions. As a result, she'd garnered an intense dose of sexual instruction.

She smiled a wise, sly feminine smile, as she recalled how aroused he'd been, how incapable of restraint. She'd had no idea a man could become so focused, so adamant, so dangerously driven to unstoppable conduct. But she couldn't say she hadn't been warned. Throughout her life, she'd been counseled about men and their sinister motives, and Gabriel, himself, had cautioned her against incitement, but she hadn't listened, and she was glad she hadn't.

She was a woman now, one who knew the mysteries of male-female relations, and she wouldn't trade the knowledge for anything in the world. That Gabriel had been the one to show her how it could be, made the event even more wonderful.

Her stomach tickled as she recollected how aggressively he'd taken her. She'd loved every electrifying, stimulating second of the magnificent episode, and she couldn't wait to do it all over again.

The interlude had been lewd and risqué, yet they'd barely scratched the surface. As she'd determined from handling his cock with her mouth and her hands, there were tricks and adaptations, unusual methods to try, unique approaches with which to experiment.

Desire was an interesting commodity. With Gabriel, she never grew bored, never wearied of the procedures he suggested, and the excitement of joining with him never decreased. Each new maneuver was more delightful and satisfying than the last. The more she practiced on his fabulous anatomy, the more she wantonly craved repetition.

Their intimacies had formed a deep, unbreakable bond that would never have evolved had they been mere casual acquaintances. A talented, flamboyant man, he habitually interacted with scores of women, yet he was an extremely private person, too. He showed others only those traits he wanted them to see, and he hid the rest. Yet, with her, he'd dropped his guard, had let the defenses fall away, trusting her so much that he'd confided details of his mother's untimely death, and his worries about Mary and his father.

Why, he'd given her his mother's locket! She'd demurred due to the preciousness of the gift, but he'd insisted she keep it. Surely, there was no better evidence of their emotional attachment. From how he'd held her when they'd drifted off, she yearned for his level of involvement to match her own.

Oh, what was she to do when their time together was terminated?

He'd come to mean everything to her. When she was with him, she brimmed over with joy and serenity. When they were apart, she spent every hour thinking about him, speculating as to where he was, what he was doing, and if—by chance—he might be missing her just the slightest bit.

Her prior melancholia, her ennui, her irritation over her lack of responsibilities, none of it mattered anymore. Even her exasperation with Charlotte had faded into the background. Her stepmother had become, much like a bothersome insect, little more than an annoyance.

Gabriel had so thoroughly pervaded her life that the rest was simply clutter.

When they separated for good, which would be soon,

she didn't know how she would bear it. Just the thought of farewell made her palms sweat, her heart pound.

Disturbed by her introspection, she needed distraction, but Gabriel was sleeping heavily, and she didn't want to wake him. She glanced around, searching for diversion, and through the door that led to the studio, she saw his easel with a canvas balanced on it. Dozens of sketches were tacked up on the wall behind. Intrigued, she decided to explore, something she'd never previously had occasion to do since she was always preoccupied when in his presence.

She carefully scooted around him and climbed off the bed. He didn't stir, although he did reach out toward her empty space on the mattress, and a frown curled his brow as if—even in slumber—he realized she was missing.

On tiptoe, she went into the studio. The fire had died down, so the temperature was cooler, and she cast about for a wrap. His shirt was discarded on the floor, and she picked it up, stuffing her arms into the sleeves. It fit her like a dress, the hem hanging past her knees, and she swathed the lapels around her body as she walked to see what was on the easel.

Just as she stepped to it, her attention was diverted by the sketches. There were pictures of herself everywhere. The entire wall was covered, a comprehensive and total study, spread out and arranged as though he'd spent multitudinous hours inspecting the variations.

Happy, sad, pouting, angry; diverse idiosyncrasies were articulated. In some, she was partially clothed, in others naked. Surprisingly, the grouping included the pieces he'd drawn while she was posing, but also many others, as if he'd been fantasizing about her and had been desperate to record his imaginings.

What a reassuring discovery! She'd ceaselessly contemplated whether he ever thought of her when they were apart, and she had her answer! The man seemed positively obsessed!

As she moved down the line, assessing and scrutinizing

each one, she stumbled upon a collection in which Gabriel had added himself into the pictures with her. They were erotic illustrations of the two of them making love—in some of the ways they'd already explored, but also in other ways he'd never initiated. The renderings were so lifelike and so graphic that they made her blush.

There she was, crouched before him and sucking at his cock, a maneuver she enjoyed and had perfected. But there she was, as well, lying beneath him, legs spread, in the manner they'd just accomplished in the adjoining room. In still another, she was on her hands and knees, her breasts swinging down, her hair off to the side, and he was rutting on her like an animal.

The depictions were disturbing, titillating, provoking. They were authentic and precise, a haunting beauty to the facial expressions and bodily positionings. She hadn't known that a person might create such disquieting art, yet as she examined the pictures, she was tempted, lured, held spellbound by the indecency, captivated by the depravity.

Uncomfortable with how the illustrations mesmerized— and wary of the immodest ruminations they generated!— she forced herself away, turning instead to the easel so that she could review his latest work-in-progress.

Unexpectedly, she encountered the portrait for which she'd contracted. The background was filled in, the south garden at Norwich verdant and lush under a startlingly blue summer sky. The white gazebo was done, too, contrasting with the grass, shrubs, and blooming pink roses that wove up the trellis.

Only the center of the painting remained to be executed. It was a blank space, as though she was about to magically step into the middle of the pastoral scene.

She hadn't realized he'd started the portrait, let alone nearly completed it, and dismay inundated her. He was ready to paint the final section. When that portion was incorporated, there would be no reason for her to persist with her visits.

How could that be?

She stared over her shoulder, at the dozens—perhaps hundreds—of drawings, then at the canvas once more. Her exotic idyll had been reduced to these few compositions of charcoal, chalk, and oil, and she trembled with the awareness that this was all she'd ever have when it was concluded. Just a handful of any sketches he might deign to give her, and the enchanting canvas he would painstakingly finish and her father would buy.

How wrong it suddenly seemed that her great love for Gabriel would be reduced to just this—and no more.

Unbidden, Mary Smith and John Preston came to mind. Would they marry as Gabriel had claimed?

A huge wave of jealousy swept through her. How unfair that Mary should wed and live happily ever after, that she be afforded the opportunity to move on, while Elizabeth was doomed to wallow in her untenable domestic situation. The idea of never seeing Gabriel again was beyond contemplation.

Despondency swamped her, just as his voice sounded from across the room.

"What do you think?" he asked.

"You have such a remarkable gift."

She peeked at him from around the easel. He was rumpled from his nap, his hair on end, and he lazily leaned against the doorjamb, sinfully, blissfully naked, and totally unconcerned that he was.

"I didn't like it when I awakened and you weren't in the bed. I was afraid you'd gone without a word of farewell."

"I would never do that."

He neared and hugged her. "I like having you in my shirt."

With a roguish hand, he rummaged under the dangling hem and rubbed her bare bottom, and she chuckled half-heartedly. He really was the sweetest man, despite how vigorously he tried to hide it. "I like wearing it," she admitted. "It makes me feel closer to you."

"Now, tell me how much you love what I've done—so far—with your portrait."

The consummate artist! she mùsed ruefully. *Needing constant adoration and acclaim!*

"It's very nice."

"Nice! Is that the best you can do?" he scoffed, pretending affront. "I'm sure you mean, Magnificent! Stupendous! Brilliant! The finest art you've ever laid eyes upon. Correct?"

"Absolutely." She nodded and struggled not to laugh.

At her tempered adulation, he sobered, rocking her gently. "What's amiss, *bella*?"

"I hadn't understood that you'd actually commenced with the painting. I thought you were still sketching me."

"I started with the oils yesterday afternoon, and I couldn't stop."

"You worked all night?"

"Aye."

"It's so near to completion." She didn't need to clarify what she really meant: that their affair was so close to being over.

"Very soon it will be." He was responding to her unspoken comment. Softly, he added, "We can't keep on forever. You know that, don't you?"

"Yes, of course I do." Her spirit lurched at the reality abruptly confronting her. "But I don't wish it to be true."

"Each time you drop by, we risk detection."

"Perhaps"—she boldly revealed her fantasy—"I wouldn't care if we were *detected*."

"But then your father would be calling for my head on a pike; perchance demanding we wed. Is that how you'd like our relationship to resolve?"

Marriage! To Gabriel! The tantalizing concept hovered between them. Such a startling, phenomenal possibility!

She never once considered it. What a fantastic denouement it would be!

She was as intrepid as Mary. She could dare all in the name of everlasting love. Couldn't she?

"What if I did want things to end that way between us?" She defiantly lifted her chin, replying to his question with one of her own, while fervently hoping that she really was as brave as she supposed herself to be.

"Do you seriously expect me to believe that you're prepared to debase yourself? I'm an unrepentant bastard, so you'd suffer untold shame and disgrace if you stooped so low."

He raised a brow, obstinately contesting her audacious suggestion. "Don't forget, you'd be allying yourself not just with me, but with my scandal-ridden father. You'd have to move into our home, where you'd be an equal with your former housekeeper. You'd be a laughingstock among the members of your precious high society. They would ridicule and mock you—if they deigned to acknowledge you at all. Why, your very own father would probably never speak to you. You'd be barred from Norwich, prohibited from calling on your relatives, refused admittance at the town house. Disowned, disinherited." He paused for effect. "Is that what you really want?"

Bending nearer, he appended a decisive wallop. "And I'm poor as the dickens—by your standards. Except for those rare days when I'm lucky enough to sell a painting, I seldom have two pennies to rub together. I could never support you in the lofty manner to which you've been accustomed."

Straightening, he regarded her strangely, and she wasn't sure if he was being facetious or not. His impudent stare seemed to inquire: *Well? What say you to all that?*

He was challenging her to offer a rejoinder, to state her opinion as to his antecedents, or to deny that her elevated status made them such a mismatch, but she couldn't utter a single retort that wouldn't come across as horrid or vain, as though she considered herself far above him.

Her confidence wavered as she frantically replayed all he'd just said. Every word was correct—when she didn't want any of them to be—and her optimism sparked and fizzled out, as she recognized how ludicrous and foolish she was acting.

If she'd told herself once, she'd told herself a thousand times: They had no future! He was larger than life, a bright star in her dull universe. His days—and nights—overflowed with illicit romance, amorous artifice, and torrid trysting.

What man would be insane enough to abandon such carnal latitude and liberty for the prospect of staid, monotonous, stable domesticity?

While he might currently be enamored of her, she could never keep his interest. She'd witnessed the sort of female with whom he typically consorted, and she didn't compare. He'd tire of her, and she could think of no other, more painful eventuality than having to suffer through the awareness that Gabriel was no longer enticed, that he was weary of her and chafing to break it off.

She couldn't survive such a wrenching circumstance, and she declined to put herself into a position where it would inevitably happen.

Any extended affiliation was unattainable, and daydreaming for a different finale was a waste of effort and energy. She needed to focus on the present, on what lasting memories she could build with him.

"You're right; we would never suit"—she regained her equilibrium, and smiled flirtatiously as if she'd simply been joking—"but I don't have to like the fact."

For the briefest second, his eyes narrowed and he tensed, as if he'd taken a hard blow, and she was overcome by the absurd notion that he'd been testing her, that he'd been fishing to ascertain her precise inclinations. His disparaging observations about himself and his father, and about what she'd have to forgo in order to be with him, had been but an experiment or a trial that she'd failed. Miserably.

Which was preposterous. He didn't want to settle down, to forsake his freedom and bachelor's lifestyle. Did he?

She blinked, and just that quickly, whatever she'd momentarily beheld had vanished, leaving her to surmise that her mind had been playing tricks. Regrettably, she was so desperate to win Gabriel's love that, apparently, she was beginning to presume and infer deep emotion where none existed.

He liked her very much, but he'd done naught to indicate a stronger partiality, had never intimated that he desired her for more than occasional companionship that ultimately led to improper intercourse. He'd certainly never hinted that he was predisposed to change his habits, to rearrange his life, or relinquish his independence, just for her.

Like a fatuous girl, she was waxing on over impossibilities, chasing after windmills in the sky, and it was high time she came back down to earth.

Resolute, she spun away, not wanting him to perceive her visible distress, and she went to the lewd pictures he'd produced of the two of them.

"These are quite something. What motivated you to draw them?"

For a hesitant moment, he didn't respond, then he let out a ponderous sigh, one that was heavy with disappointment, as though he couldn't credit her nonchalant attitude, and she was left with the distinct impression that she'd hurt him grievously, when she couldn't fathom how or why.

Yet just as she noted his dolor, he shook it off and cuddled himself behind her, his hands on her waist. "I think about you every second."

"Really?" She smiled at the unanticipated confession and peeked at him over her shoulder.

"Yes, and my reflections are not always chaste."

"So I gather."

He nestled his loins against her, and immediately his cock stirred and hardened. "When I'm here alone, I get these images in my head of how you look, of how I see you, or how I *hope* to see you, and next thing I know—"

"You're creating indecent pictures?"

"Yes."

"You have a very vivid imagination."

"So I've been told." Aroused, he flexed against her.

"If you could pick any of these renderings, and bring it to fruition right away, which would you select?" She pointed to an illustration where she knelt and sucked at him. His hand was fisted in her hair, an expression of exquisite pleasure on his face. "This one?"

"That's definitely a favorite." His inhalations increased, his grip tightened.

"How about this?"

She gestured toward the drawing where he was taking her from behind. Her thighs were braced, and she was splayed wide, his patent enjoyment evident by his posture and demeanor.

"It's so difficult to choose."

"This one tickles my fancy." In it, he was lying on the fainting couch, and she was on top of him. His tongue teased her nipple, his palm stroked her flank. "I'd like to—"

"Elizabeth?"

"Hmm?" She turned as much as she could with him clutching her so tenaciously, and hot desire flared in his eyes. His lust for her was at a severe level. At least for now.

"Come back to bed."

"I thought you'd never ask."

He twirled and lifted her, moving so fast that he made her dizzy, and she squealed with delight. Holding her to his chest, he carried her to the small bed, cradling her as if she weighed no more than a feather, as if she was delicate, or terribly fragile.

Gently, he deposited her on the mattress then followed

her down, and as his lips joined with hers in a tender, loving kiss that swiftly animated, she closed her eyes and irrationally prayed that—just this once—all her dreams could come true.

CHAPTER SIXTEEN

MARY accepted a final hug—for courage and support—then she scooted off John's lap and leaned toward the carriage door.

"Are you sure you don't want me to come in with you?" he asked for the tenth time, but she was determined to do this on her own. Besides, in light of John's history with Findley, his presence would likely make matters worse.

"I'm positive."

"I'm afraid he might hurt you."

"I'm not," Mary insisted. John scoffed, and the sound brought a smile to her lips.

"The man's an ass."

"That he is," she agreed, "but he'd never stoop so low as to physically abuse me. Despite what I said or did."

"There's a first time for everything. Losing you"—he took both her hands in his and stole a kiss—"would provoke any man to new heights of outrage."

"You are too sweet, my darling husband," and her heart did a flip-flop as she referred to him as her spouse.

She couldn't figure out how he'd worn her down so rapidly, or why she'd acquiesced. He'd been so persistent, and before she'd had much of a chance to consider what she was about, she'd been standing at the altar in the small chapel near his home and repeating her vows with only Gabriel and the minister's shy, young wife as their witnesses.

The past two weeks had been a whirlwind of panic and indecision, as she'd vacillated and fussed, wondering how to terminate his tenacious pursuit without damaging his manly pride, of which she'd discovered he had a huge amount.

But late one night, in her lonely bed, as she'd desperately wished he was there with her, or that she'd had the courage to sneak out and be with him, it had dawned on her that she was being foolish.

Why deny herself? Why forsake the opportunity John had offered?

Her entire, wretched life, she'd craved a home of her own, a family. While the worldly, sophisticated John Preston and the flamboyant Gabriel Cristofore weren't exactly what she'd ever envisioned for herself—a woman she perceived as quite plain and conventional—she had tossed aside her misgivings.

Lack of confidence had been making her feel unworthy and unsuited, so she'd decided to forge ahead, to form a kindred unit with the two dynamic men.

During the prior, bliss-filled fourteen days, they'd loved and talked and listened, and she'd learned that he had suffered great trauma and survived. A devoted father, he'd raised a magnificent son, but he saw his job of parenting as finished. He wanted more for his elder years than to grow old alone.

Funny, kind, smart, interesting, he was possessed of all the traits she admired, and he had a flair and a zest for living that she'd never seen matched in another—except, perhaps, in his son. He'd gone places and done things about which she could only fantasize. His view of the world was much larger than her own, and she'd worried that he might become bored with someone as reserved and unassuming as she pictured herself to be.

Yet at the same juncture, she liked to think that she had valuable qualities to render to him in return. Her steady influence and her balanced existence, her seeking of routine and simple pleasures, would introduce a dimension and a stable harmony that he clearly needed.

John Preston had withstood a series of excessive swings—joys and sorrows, fortune and hardship—and he would profit immensely from her constancy.

That's not to say there wouldn't be gales of tumult and melodrama. The two rogues who now comprised her family had a definite knack for creating chaos and instigating turmoil, but after her years of repressive obligation at the Norwich household, she didn't regard a little sporadic upheaval as a bad thing.

No, life with the Preston men would never be dull. She was excited, ready for her future, but before commencing it, she had to tell Findley what she'd brought about. How that horrid conversation would proceed was anybody's guess.

She was geared to go in and terminate the whole, sordid business, but she couldn't help but pause first, to admire her handsome husband. A rush of tears clouded her eyes, and even in the dark confines of the carriage he could observe them. He soothed her by rubbing her shoulders and arms.

"What is it, my dear?"

Gulping down a swell of emotion, she murmured, "Thank you."

He was exceedingly surprised. "For what?"

"For having me."

"Oh, Mary—"

"You've made me so happy."

"And I plan to make you happier still. Each and every day."

She hugged him as tightly as she could, then she moved away, and he could readily infer that she was distraught and unenthused about their parting, so he delayed it further. As if she was a child, he bothered with her suit, her hair, straightening and adjusting, until his fussy ministrations had restored her composure.

"I shouldn't be too long," she promised.

"I'll wait a half hour," he said, "but if you're not back, I'm coming inside, and I won't hear any objection. I'm totally against your handling this by yourself."

"All right," she agreed. How marvelous to have a champion!

"And if he says or does anything inappropriate, leave immediately and fetch me." Gleeful at the prospect, he said, "I'll thrash the living daylights out of him for you."

"That won't be necessary." At least, she hoped it wouldn't be. Findley was a vain, narcissistic individual, so she couldn't see him stooping to insults or threats. His excessive pride would prevent him from debasing himself. "Anyway," she teased, "you look as if you'd enjoy pummeling him far too much."

"I'm sure he's overdue for another trouncing."

"Well, I'm not about to give you a second opportunity. Especially not on my wedding day. I want you in good condition for tonight."

He chuckled. "Hurry back, love."

"I will."

Their footman assisted her in maneuvering the steps, and as the door was closed, John peeked out from behind the curtain. He flashed a thumbs-up, extending his silent encouragement and support. She returned the gesture, then faced the imposing residence.

Squaring her shoulders, she walked to the front door and entered. And why shouldn't she come in the front? She was no longer *just* a housekeeper, but a respectable gentlewoman. Who had wed the fourth son of an earl! The gilt had definitely faded from the golden ring John had once gripped as a younger man, but the fact remained that his birth status was extremely high, and she stood imperiously, braced to eagerly pronounce her good fortune to whoever crossed her path.

Taking in her surroundings, she assessed the immaculate foyer. From birth, she'd been groomed to manage and care for the extensive properties of the Earl of Norwich. The job was an enormous burden and an incredible honor that she'd cherished and treasured.

Diligently, she'd seen to her duties to the best of her ability, and she was pleased with how she'd carried on, with what she'd achieved for the renowned family.

Yet, her success hadn't been enough. Cold marble and polished wood had been her sole companions, and they glimmered back at her. The tiled floor, the sweeping staircase, sparkled in the brilliant lamplight, and she realized that the satisfaction once gleaned from scrutinizing their upkeep had vanished.

Throughout her arduous toil, she'd been lonesome, pining away for love and affection, contentment and fulfillment. John had given them all to her on a silver platter.

Initially, she'd wondered if she would miss her position in the palatial manor, but she hadn't needed to fret. Nothing she was forsaking in the luxurious pile of bricks could begin to compare with what she'd gained in exchange.

With a perceptive smile, she climbed the stairs to her unpretentious room, not encountering a soul on the way. She retrieved her portmanteau from under the bed and, in minutes, she was packed. Her tiny pile of belongings was pitiful.

What a meager amount she had to show for her investment!

After a conclusive, nostalgic inspection, she descended to the ground floor, intending to head toward the rear of the house where Findley would be sequestered in his library and awaiting the butler's call to supper. Unfortunately, just as she reached the bottom, Lady Norwich was advancing down the hall.

"Where have you been?" the juvenile woman angrily barked.

"Milady." She replied politely while secretly celebrating that she'd never have to see the horrid termagant again.

"I've been searching for you all afternoon."

"My apologies." Of an equal height, she stared the girl down, not contributing a word in her own defense, or an explanation as to her absence, which caused the lady to bristle with outrage.

"Well, what do you have to say for yourself?"

"Nothing, actually. Now, if you'll excuse me—"

"I do not excuse you!"

The countess's cheeks were mottled purple, her inhalations fast and irregular, an inevitable sign of a pending temper tantrum. Any abominable disturbance might shortly occur. Valuable objects could be smashed, food thrown, people slapped. Mary had witnessed many untenable incidents, and she was heartily glad that this would be the concluding episode. She'd never be required to protect herself or others from undue injury, or have to spend innumerable hours after a fracas, calming the waters and cleaning up whatever mess Charlotte Harcourt deigned to incite.

"I have an appointment with the earl"—Mary stepped around the countess—"and for once, I'm relieved to point out that I don't have time for your nonsense."

"Why . . . you disrespectful, insolent harridan!" She was sputtering, incapable of forming words that sufficiently clarified her affront.

"Good-bye, Lady Norwich."

"Of all the nerve! How dare you speak to me so contemptuously! I'll have you whipped, then thrown out on the street with only the clothes on your back!"

"I'm trembling with fear."

She was baiting the girl, and she should have kept her mouth shut, but she'd stomached so much that she couldn't seem to remember her place. Besides, hadn't her *place* been drastically altered since eleven o'clock that morning? She wasn't about to be servile before the despicable brat.

Still, she had every intention of avoiding a confrontation, so she took another step just as Lady Norwich grabbed her by the wrist and whipped her around. Holding her in a crushing grip, she swung her other arm to deliver a slap to Mary's cheek, but Mary swiftly reacted, blocking the assault and preventing contact.

"Don't even think about it!" Mary quietly warned.

Footsteps sounded above them on the landing, and Mary glanced up, embarrassed to discover Elizabeth who was absorbing every detail of the deplorable scene.

"Charlotte!" she ordered, aghast. "Unhand her this instant!"

Astoundingly, the countess complied. For some reason, she usually bowed to Elizabeth's influence, and she jerked away as Elizabeth rushed down.

"What are you doing?" Elizabeth chided. "One of the other servants might walk by! Imagine the gossip should they witness you in such a state!"

"Ask her where she's been!" Charlotte seethed.

"I will." Impeding further strife, Elizabeth situated herself between Mary and the lady. "Go upstairs. I'll send for you when supper is served."

Charlotte hesitated, as if contemplating refusal, but she was intimidated by their advanced ages and loyal association. Mary and Elizabeth both scowled at her, an impenetrable bastion of combined offense and condemnation.

She stomped off, stopping to hiss over her shoulder, "I'll have you jailed, you witch! Just see if I don't."

They watched the countess's retreating backside as she stomped up the stairs and disappeared. Momentarily, a loud crash ensued, as if she'd snatched one of the priceless vases in the corridor and had shattered it on the floor.

They tarried in the silence, then Elizabeth turned to her. "Are you all right?"

"Yes," Mary answered, although she was trembling. "I'm sorry, but I couldn't keep a civil tongue in my head."

"I don't blame you."

A maid scurried toward them, investigating the commotion, and Elizabeth directed her to return to her evening meal, then she practically dragged Mary into a nearby parlor and shut the door.

"Where *have* you been?" Her concern was elevated and authentic. "I've been hunting for you for days myself."

"Come. Sit." Mary led her to a sofa by the fire, then tugged off her glove and held out her left hand. The wedding band John had recently placed there glowed thrillingly. "I've gone and married John Preston."

"So . . . he was correct," she murmured.

"Who?" Mary kindly inquired.

"Mr. Cristofore had mentioned you might wed."

"Really?"

Amazed, Mary raised a brow, tickled that Gabriel had been talking about her. She'd been debating how to become friends with him and sought any approach that might bring them closer.

"I've been dying to ask you if it was true," Elizabeth said, "but you haven't been home."

"I've been busy with decisions and arrangements."

"When was the ceremony?"

"This morning."

"Why didn't you invite me?" Elizabeth's distress over the slight was genuine. "I would have come."

How to explain?

Elizabeth had been a friend, like a daughter in some ways, but their employer-employee relationship had invariably prevailed, and Mary's absurd, lengthy affair with Findley had forced her to erect barriers to ensure a distance that couldn't be breached by either of them.

"It happened so fast, Elizabeth," she submitted as a rationalization. "There wasn't so much as a second to deliver invitations," which was a lie. She could have invited anyone she'd wished, but the ceremony had been so special to her that she hadn't been inclined to share it with anyone. Not even Elizabeth.

"What are your plans?" Elizabeth appeared lost and

confused over this latest transformation, making Mary rue that she hadn't been more forthcoming.

"I'm quitting my job and moving out."

"Now?"

"Well, it is my wedding night." Her mouth quirked up in a smile.

"Where will you live?"

"With John and Mr. Cristofore. Where do you suppose?"

"How lucky for you," she mumbled, without regard to the implications of what she'd uttered. "But . . . but how will you support yourself?"

"I've spent little of my salary over the years. I had no need of anything, so we'll have a moderate income from that, and Gabriel has his art, although"—on alluding to the touchy subject, she shifted uncomfortably—"he'll be painting more families and children, and not so many women. Plus, John and I have decided that we must find him a patron, a nobleman who will appreciate and nurture his talent."

"That's a superb idea."

"Isn't it? And I've persuaded John to negotiate a financial settlement with his family. He's never received a dime in almost three decades."

"My goodness," Elizabeth said, "the Preston men will never be the same."

"No, they won't, but as you can deduce"—she patted Elizabeth's hand—"I shall get along just fine."

"Yes, you shall, but how will *we* get by without you?"

"I'm sure you'll manage." She peered around the salon that she'd been charged with overseeing for so many years, but she suffered no regrets. "I haven't had much of an effect on these rooms—or your lives—in quite a while."

"That's not true. You're the best part of us."

"Oh, Elizabeth . . ." Overwhelmed by the expression of sentiment, she noted that the emotional swings of the extraordinary day were taking their toll, and she stood, desperate to be off as she was running out of energy for the tribulation she had yet to endure. "I must be off. I still haven't conferred with your father."

"He's in the library. Would you like me to accompany you?"

"No. This should be a private chat."

They strode into the hall, suddenly awkward together, and Elizabeth queried, "Will you visit again?"

"No. But you know where I'll be. You're always welcome."

"Thank you."

Elizabeth moved first, enfolding Mary in a fierce hug, and Mary hugged her back for all she was worth, and when they separated, Elizabeth had tears streaming down her cheeks.

"I can't believe you're really going," she said.

"It's for the best."

"I'm sure it is," Elizabeth conceded, but she was obviously forlorn over being left to face Charlotte's chaos without Mary's support.

Mary sincerely felt sorry for her, but there wasn't any solution she could provide. Findley should have rectified the escalating domestic situation months earlier—perhaps by selecting a husband for his daughter—but in view of Elizabeth's current experiences with a particular extravagant Italian artist, a spouse was likely now an impossibility.

After Elizabeth had been assailed by Gabriel Cristofore's propensities and charm, how could Findley locate a man of whom she would approve?

"Good-bye, dear." Mary embraced her once more. "Try to be happy."

"I will."

Mary left her weeping in the foyer, and she didn't look back, unsure of how to respond or how to remedy Elizabeth's problems. They were beyond Mary's ken, and moreover, she had bigger matters to attend. Findley would be livid, she was convinced of it, and in case another fervent scene developed, she had to preserve her remaining stamina.

She knocked on his door, utilizing the specific rapping pattern that let him know it was she, and he hastily bade her enter. They'd regularly convened in his restricted sanctum, but she had ceased visiting after he'd announced his engagement, and his delight over her appearance was palpable.

"Mary"—he was drinking a libation, and he tipped the glass in welcome—"how pleasant to have you here."

"Hello, Findley."

He was in the high-backed chair behind his glossy, impressive desk, and she confidently walked to him, the clicking of her heels muted by the expensive Persian rug. She halted directly across and set her bag on the floor, and he assessed it carefully, nervously.

"Are you going somewhere?"

"Actually, I am." She had drafted a letter of resignation, and she laid it on the desktop and slid it over. "I'm resigning from your employ. Effective immediately."

He picked up the letter she'd composed, scanned the contents, then, as she'd surmised he might, he tore it to pieces. With a dramatic flourish, he threw them over his shoulder, and they fluttered down. "Well, I don't accept it. Return to your duties."

"It's not that simple, Findley."

"It most certainly is *that* simple. As if I'd permit you to leave me! What are you thinking? Have you gone stark raving mad?" Never one for in-depth conversation, and never supposing that she'd decline to obey, he dipped his pen in the inkwell, and continued writing on the document that had had him engaged before her arrival.

She observed him, pondering how speedily love could blossom, how it could abide through so much, how it could wane. Had she ever felt anything for him? Other than misplaced passion? Now that she'd met John, now that she'd ascertained what love and desire were really about, she couldn't recall what it was that had originally attracted her to him. Their affair had begun so long ago that it was difficult to recollect how and why she'd allowed herself to be so intricately bound to him.

Early on, she'd been flattered by his attentions, and too young to know any better, but after the incipient lust had worn off, how did she justify her persevering? Maybe it had been too easy for both of them; maybe there was no viable answer.

"Findley, listen to me." The stern tone in her voice had his head swinging up, and he glared at her as though he assumed she'd already departed. "There's no simple way to tell you this."

"Tell me what?"

"I got married today."

"You what?" He rose up as though he would stalk around to her, but his legs gave out, and he sank into his chair. "You can't mean it. Say it isn't true."

"It is." As evidence, she held out her ring so he could inspect it.

"How could you?" He did advance on her then, hastily moving to her side and taking both her hands in his. "You've been angry with me since I married Charlotte, but I thought it would pass. I thought you'd eventually forgive me."

"There's nothing to forgive. You did your duty."

"Then why?"

He was earnestly perplexed, as he had been during every heated discussion they'd had, and she was sorry for him, but she couldn't save him. He'd engineered his fate.

"I merely need more out of my life."

"But I love you, Mary! I've always loved you!" He squeezed her fingers so forcefully that she worried her bones might crack, and he waxed on as though he hadn't heard a word she'd articulated. "You know how much I love you still! From the very beginning! You remember the day I came to Norwich, don't you? Your mother had died, and you'd been given her position. I hadn't seen you in years, since you were a girl, but there you were, all grown. I barely recognized you. You were wearing that blue dress I liked, and your hair was up. I decided, then and there, that you were the loveliest creature I'd ever laid eyes upon."

"Findley," she scolded, "let it go."

"How can I? I've been waiting for you to change your mind. All these months, I've been hoping you'd welcome me back to your bed, to your life! I've been so patient! You can't say that I have no chance left. I've apologized a thousand times, and I'll apologize a thousand more if that's what it takes!" He was nearly begging. "I *had* to marry Charlotte."

"I grasp that fact, Findley. Charlotte never signified to me."

"Then why do you persist? You know what Charlotte is like: she's a child, a spoiled, pampered child who could never give me what I need as a man. You keep stating that you understand why I wed her, so why can't you grant me your pardon?"

They were mired in the circle in which they unceasingly landed, with Findley declining to acknowledge—or even try to comprehend—her insupportable plight. Previously, she'd wasted many words, attempting to clarify or account for her actions and opinions, but she'd been through this repeatedly! It was her ancient history. Her destiny awaited in the carriage that was parked out front. There was no reason to hash it out, once again. Findley never listened anyway.

"Good-bye, Fin." She picked up her bag and forced out the next. Her gratitude was mostly bona fide—if she disregarded the rest of what he'd accomplished at her expense. "I appreciate the opportunities you gave me, and the faith you had in my abilities."

"I won't let you go." Vehement, undeterred, he pulled

himself up to his full height. "I'll have you locked in your room till you come to your senses."

"You're being absurd." She rolled her eyes at his predictability. No one ever told him no or contradicted his wishes. "My husband is waiting for me outside."

"Your *husband*!" he derided snidely, spitefully, and he seemed assured of the base sort of scoundrel who'd have her. "Who's the lucky fellow? Anyone I know?"

"You two are well acquainted." Casually, she drew on her glove, covering her ring, and eager to gauge his reaction to the next. "I'm Mrs. John Preston. You recall John, don't you? Years ago, you two quarreled. If I remember correctly, it was over your abominable treatment of Pamela."

"John . . . John Preston?" The tidings were so outrageous that he collapsed slightly, leaning for support against the edge of the desk. "You married . . . Preston?"

"Yes. Isn't it splendid?"

"What's that knave doing back in England? No man's wife is safe! I should have him deported!" Baffled, bewildered, he asked, "Did you do it intentionally to hurt me?"

"When I made my decision, I didn't think about you at all." She strolled to the door, then turned. He looked older, crushed, defeated. "All those times, Findley, when you sneaked up the back stairs to crawl into my bed, you constantly insisted that the secrecy was imperative to protect my reputation. But guess what I finally figured out."

"What?"

"You were protecting your own. You never wanted anybody to know that I was your lover." She strode across the threshold. "Shame on you. I was always worth it."

As a parting shot, it wasn't bad, and she was grinning as she paraded down the hall. Loudly, he bellowed her name, but blessedly, he didn't follow.

As she entered the foyer, she was glad that none of her staff was lingering so she wouldn't have to explain or say farewell. She was seeing herself out, just reaching for the knob, when the door burst open, and John marched in, impatient and mad as a hornet.

"Your thirty minutes are up!" he curtly declared.

Laughing, she stretched on her tiptoes, and kissed him on the mouth, not caring if Findley or anybody else witnessed her behavior.

"Let's go home," she said, and she slipped her hand into his and led him out.

But I love you, Mary! I've always loved you!

Charlotte sucked in a piercing breath, feeling as though she'd just been punched in the stomach. Her ears were playing tricks! She'd misheard! This couldn't be true!

After Elizabeth's brusque dismissal, she'd been too furious to loiter in her room like a naughty child being punished. What she'd really wanted to do was to lash out, to vent her unruly temper that had spiked to a new high.

She'd never been more livid, and a colossal dose of revenge was called for. Aware that Elizabeth and the housekeeper would be gaggling like a pair of hens in the Receiving Parlor, she'd gone to eavesdrop next to the flue that conveyed so many secrets to the upper floors. But who could have expected this horror?

They were lovers! Her husband and her housekeeper! Why . . . they'd been carrying on right under Charlotte's very nose! In her own house! The audacity! The gall!

The earl habitually chided her that she was a failure at her marital obligations, but to learn that the hideous oaf had deigned to review her dreadful bedroom deficiencies with his paramour!

How could he condescend to such a flagrant, monstrous breach of fealty and privacy? His criticisms had caused her sufficient chagrin and embarrassment. How could he compound matters by announcing her personal ignominy in such a repulsive manner?

Reeling, unable to listen to more of the abhorrent dialogue, she crawled to a nearby chair, gripping the arm and using it to brace herself as she clambered to her feet. Raging and shamed, she lurched into the hall and down the stairs, blindly stumbling into her room, not caring if a passing servant viewed her in such a deranged condition.

Shuffling to the window seat, she stared out at the rainy night and the dreary garden below, as she fought to regain her equilibrium. Composure gradually returned, and with it, she was overcome by a glaring clarity.

Her husband was the sort of despicable swine who would consort with a woman of dubious character in an upstairs bedroom while his wife slept, blissfully ignorant of his sins. Then he would require that selfsame abused wife to tolerate the degradation of being waited on by the harlot in the light of day.

While in the throes of their illicit passion, had he and Mary Smith laughed and joked about her? Had they poked fun and ridiculed her for her copious carnal ineptitudes? How many of Charlotte's painful secrets had the earl wrongly shared?

Charlotte couldn't believe her naiveté. Her folly. Her foolishness.

She would never forgive Findley Harcourt for this mortification as long as she lived. But she would get even for it. Just see if she didn't.

CHAPTER SEVENTEEN

GABRIEL stood before the wall of pictures he'd drawn of Elizabeth during their numerous sessions. He tried to study nuance and form, but as happened so often of late, his excessive ability to concentrate had vanished, and he couldn't focus on his work with his usual level of passionate commitment.

Behind him was the portrait he'd begun of her. The background had been filled in with his customary meticulous attention to detail. The pastoral setting tickled the senses, so lifelike that he could detect the aroma emitted by the roses climbing up the trellis. But the center was blank, as though the person who had been posed there had simply strolled away.

He couldn't finish it. Although it was absurd to think so, he was convinced that as soon as he painted Elizabeth into the scene, their interval together would abruptly terminate, so he couldn't constrain himself to put brush to canvas.

At some point, however, a portrait had to be presented to the Earl of Norwich for payment. Once delivery was made, what fabrication could they possibly use to persist with their trysts?

Elizabeth was clever and could certainly devise other pretexts for getting out of the house, but those excuses were few in number, and they would quickly dwindle until there wouldn't be any valid alibi she could offer as to where she was going or where she'd been.

She'd already pushed herself to the allowable amount of absences. Her adolescent stepmother was interrogating her with a curiosity that went beyond general interest and into the realm of preoccupation, so it was only a matter of time before circumstances compelled them to cease.

Morosely, he stared at the copious renderings he'd sketched, while wondering how he would get along without her when their affair wound to its logical conclusion. God willing, that day would arrive many weeks in the future, despite how his father and Mary were insisting on an earlier date.

A smile quirked his lips as he thought of them. They carried on like a pair of lovebirds, so attuned to one another that it was embarrassing to be in their presence. The morning after their wedding, they had departed for a brief honeymoon in the country, and Gabriel was heartily glad.

He hoped that by their return, they'd have slaked some of the overt passion that was almost shameful in its intensity. With their cooing and kissing, fawning and cuddling, he was constantly blushing. He had endured many carnal episodes with his father, had seen him woo any number of potential lovers, but watching John with Mary was disconcerting. Gabriel invariably felt as though he was spying on them during intimacy.

His father had actively and regularly enjoyed associations with bored, jaded aristocratic women. Never commoners. He'd sought them out for physical alleviation, for diversion from tedium, but never for emotional connection.

Gabriel had never seen his father in such a state. He neither understood, nor was comfortable with, the burgeoning affection John displayed, although after spending many hours in Mary's company, Gabriel was relieved to discover that she was much different than he'd assumed her to be.

Even before she'd moved in, her devious, crafty mind had been busy, concocting the methods by which they could improve their fates. A no-nonsense, straightforward female, she exhibited none of the coquetry or simplemindedness to which they were accustomed. A virtual genius at organization and planning, she objected to Gabriel's tendencies to earn money by less than reputable means, and she wanted changes. Immediately.

She had many ideas as to how he and his father should support themselves, and Gabriel wasn't persuaded that he could accept any of her suggestions. Out of deference to John, he hadn't refused her outright, but battles were looming, which he hated to consider.

With ease, she'd convinced John that much of their financial situation could be rectified if Gabriel obtained a patron. She was also imploring John to approach his eldest brother for either an allowance or a cash settlement. Her brashness knew no bounds. She'd even propounded that they hire a solicitor to contact Selena's family in Italy, that Gabriel's wealthy uncles be coerced into coughing up a stipend to reimburse Gabriel for the loss of his mother.

How did the sly woman form such diabolical suppositions?

He liked her style, but unfortunately, he was vehemently opposed to all three proposals. John would have to go, hat in hand, to those who had shunned him when he was young and foolish. Gabriel would be impelled to acquire cash by performing, like a circus animal, for the very bastards who had scorned and disdained his father. And to have any contact—though it would transpire through a third party—with his Italian relatives was extremely abhorrent.

Still, there was another side of him—his mercenary, corrupt, greedy side—that promptly grasped her schemes as justified and logical. If their appeals for sustained funding were successfully wrangled, he would gain immense, protracted satisfaction, because the payments they received would be from villains he'd perpetually loathed.

No doubt about it, Mary Smith Preston had the heart of a genuine confidence artist. She was a virtual master at shrewd posturing, and Gabriel could feel himself being drawn in by her persistent, tenacious determination to transform his behavior. Though perhaps it was more elemental than that: perhaps he was merely ready to oblige her. He was so elated by her obvious, undeniable fondness for John that he might have acquiesced to any supplication she voiced.

His frantic worries about her motives had vanished. She was as devoted to John as John was to her, a fact repeatedly demonstrated in countless small ways. They were an excellent combination, a balanced couple, with strengths and weaknesses that complemented and offset each other's attributes and faults.

How John had stumbled upon her remained a mystery. He'd been unusually reticent about what had led to their falling in love, just when Gabriel wished he'd spill all. He was dying to ascertain how John had been so effortlessly won over, how he'd tossed aside his reservations and qualms.

Gabriel wished he'd been brave enough to inquire, for he might have learned how to utilize the same bluster and bravado to snag Elizabeth. He might have determined how to wear her down, to alter her opinions so that she'd be amenable to the potentialities that existed between them.

During their prior appointment, it had seemed that there'd been a major shift in their relationship, that Elizabeth's emotions were becoming engaged. Preposterously, he'd imagined that she was prepared to grasp at the chance to build a life together, but he'd been wrong and had been stung by her rejection.

If she'd given the slightest indication that she was interested, he'd have jumped any hurdle to be with her, but when he'd brutally specified the reasons they didn't suit— their disparate statuses, his poverty, her father's disapproval—she'd flung aside his overture. He'd hoped that she cared about him enough to defy the odds, to gamble on the unknown, to recklessly seize the turbulent perils of love, but she'd been totally indifferent, readily dissuaded, so he wouldn't raise the possibility again.

He couldn't deny it: He was a proud man, and he wouldn't place himself in a position where she could rebuff him a second time.

While he wanted to be angry with her, to be bitter or disillusioned by her repudiation, he grasped the strictures that governed her. She'd been born and bred to embrace certain truths and realities, and it was utterly impossible for her to set aside such an extreme indoctrination.

She could no more cast off society's rules to marry him than she could leap in front of a runaway carriage. His insane, misguided assumption that she might lower her standards was ludicrous and laughable.

He had to stop ruminating about her! He'd made a fool of himself, but he wouldn't repeat his mistake. As with his previous paramours, he would use her for the duration, then he'd move on. Their parting would be more difficult than any of the others, but he wouldn't dwell on it.

The door opened, and in she came, a burst of cool wind whooshing in behind her, inducing the fire to spark and flare. Spring was rapidly approaching, and he could smell fertile earth, ripe air, and growing flowers. Green shoots were poking up all over in the garden, and regrettably, with the appearance of the first blossoms, his affair with Elizabeth Harcourt would likely be but a memory.

"Hello, Gabriel." She smiled, pushing the door against the stiff breeze.

"*Entri pure!* Let me have a look at you."

She was wearing her pink dress as she always did for her visits. When she departed for his house, she made the excuse that he was painting her, which wasn't exactly a lie.

Frequently, he sketched her—he loved having her pose, relished the opportunity to languidly study and assess her—but now when he drew her, she was naked. In dozens of illustrations, he'd captured her in nude repose, and he never tired of engaging in the naughty artform. She was a willing model, and he had produced many superb renditions that emphasized her beauty and enchanting femininity.

Eager, happy, he swept her into a torrid kiss, reveling in how her torso fit to his own, the brush of her soft hands over his bare back, the push of her tongue as it mated with his, the slow flex of her hips as she thrust into him.

What an adept, proficient lover she'd become! She'd mastered the techniques and procedures of sexual intercourse, and he could hardly wait for their carnal play to commence, for he was well aware of just how raucous, glorious, and satisfying the event would be.

"My goodness," she said, laughing as he broke the kiss to nibble down her neck, "I'd say you've missed me."

"Every minute we were apart."

He was yanking at the back of her gown, freeing the buttons, and he forced himself to slow lest he rip the fabric in his desperation to feast his eyes on her luscious breasts. They were the most delectable pair he'd ever seen, her nipples sinfully sensitive to his manipulations, and at each rendezvous, he gave them extra attention, suckling and fondling until she was wet and crying his name.

Impatient, out of sorts, he ceased with the fastenings. Grabbing her by her bottom, he lifted her up in order to press against her so that she could discern how hard he'd grown while he'd been awaiting her arrival. He prodded at her through her skirts, earning a giggle at her realization of how aroused he was.

Abruptly, he set her down and stepped away, reaching for a glass of wine as he went to the sofa and reclined. "I want you to disrobe for me. Very slowly. While I watch. Then, I want to draw you in the nude."

"A marvelous notion."

"I thought so."

"By the way"—she winked wickedly—"I missed you, too."

He had loosed enough of her attire so that she could proceed without assistance, and he avidly observed as she merrily complied with his indecent request. Accentuating each flick of her wrist, every snap of her fingers, she loosed the bodice of her dress and let it shimmy down her hips and over her thighs.

Next were the ties on her petticoat, the laces of her corset. She tarried and dawdled, turning and shifting so he was gifted with the most stimulating view. So expertly did she taunt and tease, that she might have been a high-priced courtesan, and he stroked the stem of his wineglass across his loins, pushing at the painful erection she'd inspired.

Her undergarments fell away, her chemise was tugged over her head, and momentarily, she wore only her slippers and stockings. With deliberate provocation, she situated the stool directly in front of him and steadied her foot on it. Her nimble, slender fingers toyed with her garter, untying it, then rolling the stocking down her leg, unveiling a lengthy expanse of smooth skin.

She bent over, her abundant, rounded breasts swaying delectably, her nipples rigid and inducing him to greater heights of titillation. Her pussy tantalized, her mound located so that her cleft flirted with him from between her womanly hairs. As she finessed the other stocking, he could scarcely remain seated. His entire body screamed for abatement, begging to progress, but he did nothing, letting the tension escalate, the tumult increase.

"Are you hard?" she asked as her stocking drifted to the floor, but she needn't have inquired. He was aching, hungry for her, the crest in his trousers providing ample evidence of his condition.

"You know I am."

"If you could have me do anything for you, what would please you the most?"

"Having your mouth on me."

"A delightful sentiment."

With a mischievous grin, she scooted onto the sofa, her hip next to his, and she unbuttoned his pants, proceeding so resolutely that by the time she slipped her fingers inside and wrapped her hand around his hot, burning shaft, he was fit to explode.

She tongued him, licking him with tiny strokes that drove him wild, then she eased over the crown, taking the tip, then more and more until he was mostly impaled. As unceasingly happened when she slaked him in this fashion, he spun out of control, and he was in instant need of satiation, but he declined to allow the ending to occur so swiftly.

Retreating, he hauled her up and over his body. Spreading her thighs, and centering himself, he penetrated her so rapidly that she hitched out a breath at his invasion. She squirmed and adjusted to his immense size, and he focused on her breasts, caressing and massaging them, urging her forward so that her nipples dangled over his mouth. He sucked and trifled with one, then the other, spurring her to the edge of assuagement, but never quite all the way.

He fondled her at the spot where his phallus had her stretched wide. She was slick, her sexual juice oozing from her core.

"You're so ready." He thumbed her clit, making her tense and strain. "Should I let you come?"

"Yes . . . please." She tried to flex, to enforce the motion that would cede ecstasy, but he wouldn't assent, pressuring her thighs and holding her in place.

"Not just yet."

"Gabriel!" It was a plea, as well as a command. He scooted away, his cock sliding out of her saturated pussy, making her pout and scowl. Chafing, she pronounced, "I hate it when you play these games!"

"And I love it when you're so unsettled." He rolled her onto her side, then stood, and she was sprawled on the sofa by herself. "You're so cute when you're angry."

"You can't mean to leave me like this!"

"Just for a few minutes, my little wanton."

"Beast!"

He fluffed the pillows behind her, chuckling as she grumbled and complained about his baser tendencies, but there was a fire in her eye, and a constriction in her anatomy, that he'd never recorded before. He'd never depicted her when she was this close to the precipice of desire; he'd never drawn her when *he* was so discomfited by passion. His elevated disposition would bring an intensity and depth to his creativity that he'd previously attained only on the rarest occasions.

As he arranged her, she looked so appetizing, so enticing, and he stroked his exposed cock, then stuffed it into his pants as she greedily watched.

"Would you like me to tend that for you?" She licked her lips, vividly reminding him of what she'd just affected, of how he'd landed in such a throbbing predicament.

"Eventually." He answered casually, though he was nearly ready to toss the vixen onto her back and finish what he'd started. "Stick your finger in your mouth."

"Like this?"

"Yes. Now rub it across your nipples."

They were thoroughly stimulated, but the excess dampness contracted them further, and his lust peaked as he beheld her fondling herself. He didn't often solicit it for the concept made her uncomfortable, but he was sensing such urgency as to the finite duration of their relationship, and he wanted to push her as far as he could.

"Squeeze your nipple."

Glowering, she contemplated refusal, but then she did as he'd demanded. She was so aroused that the procedure had an instant effect; she groaned and hunched against the pillows, arching her pelvis.

"Do you touch yourself like this in the night, when you're alone?"

"No."

"I want you to. Tonight. When you're in your bed, snuggled in the dark under the covers, stroke your breasts and think of me."

"And how about you?" she caustically queried. "Will *you* touch yourself in the dark and think of me?"

"As I do every night."

Skeptical, she stared at him. "Why would you?"

"So that I can achieve carnal pleasure, even when you're not with me. My desire for you never wanes, so in your absence, I close my eyes and imagine you sucking me off, and I come in my hand."

"And it gives you relief from these . . . terrible bodily urges?"

"Temporarily. I'm assuaged until I can be with you once more." He nodded to her chest. "Touch yourself again." She submitted more willingly, and he dictated, "Don't move."

He sat on his stool, snatched up his sketching pad, and began. Her head was tipped back, her hair flowing across her shoulders, her legs widened so that he could make out the dusting of curly hair shielding her mound. Cupping her breast, she cradled it in her palm, the nipple directed toward him as though she was offering herself. She was a fey nymph, an erotic sprite, a beautiful mermaid, her siren song luring him to his doom.

Craving a naughtier vantage point, he abandoned the stool and stationed himself between her legs, so that his vista was of her pussy, her inner thighs, her stomach and cleavage. He portrayed her from the lewd angle, the decadent arrangement thrilling as he strove to chronicle a glimpse of her that no one had ever witnessed but himself.

Desperate to document this dramatic alteration he'd wrought in her character, his hand flew over the page.

"Done," he finally murmured, more to himself than to her.

He scrutinized his work, his critical appraisal roving over it, and a smile crept across his face. It was extraordinary; he'd exactly caught her sense of expectation and excitement. She was ravishing, primed and prepared for loving.

The representation was sensational, enormously sensual, and he wished he had the low scruples that would allow him to sell it into the prurient art market. He could transform it into a full-sized painting, and make a bloody fortune, but he never would. He had many faults, but such depravation was beyond him.

"Let me see." She held out her hand, but he pitched the illustration on the floor. She was so damned seductive, he could no longer resist.

"Give me that!" she complained, but he cut off her protest by leaning in, opening her. Breathing deep, inhaling her scent, he inspected her core, then he licked her cleft, piercing her with his tongue, implanting her taste. Moving to her clit, he laved across it, and within moments, her passion peaked and she was writhing beneath him. He gripped her nipples, rubbing furiously, and she started to come.

His original intent had been to ride out the storm with her, but she had driven him far past delay. He could only pursue his own end, seeking ultimate gratification.

While she was still in the throes of her orgasm, he whirled her to her stomach. Dragging her to him, he entered her pussy from behind and initiated a savage thrusting. He worked against her, her shapely ass slapping his crotch. Inspiring himself to the limit, then beyond, his body spasmed and his seed surged from his loins.

Frantically, he clasped at her, endeavoring to withdraw and spew himself over her back, but in the confined space, their positions were awkward, and he couldn't retreat. Plus, she bore down on him, pressing her hips into his groin, and he tried to halt his emission, but he was incapable of restraint.

With a ferocious gush, he came inside her, planting his very essence, and he couldn't remember when he'd ever spilled himself in a woman's body. While his lovers generally took him to the end with their mouths, he was never so reckless as to ejaculate between their legs, even when they begged him to. The danger of siring a child had always been too great.

The indiscretion of his act was profound, yet he was

delirious. Even the prospect that his carelessness might result in a babe had no effect on diminishing his exultation. He'd now made her *his* in every way that truly counted.

Later on, there would be plenty of opportunity for recrimination and regret, but with his cock still rock-hard, and her internal muscles clenched around him, he was too overcome to worry about some nebulous circumstance that might—or might not—come to pass.

The jarring effects subsided, and he held her close, sitting on his haunches, and bringing her with him, so that they were kneeling on the sofa. He was embedded inside her, her backside nestled to his front, and she stretched lazily.

"You never came inside me before," she tentatively said. "Might we have—"

"No"—he briskly cut her off—"not from a single time."

Though he knew his statement to be false, he declined to speculate on the forbidden potentiality when he was so pleased, and he forced down words of joy as to how amazing the experience had been. He could never say. What good would it do?

Shifting, she peered at him over her shoulder. "I liked it. Very much."

"So did I."

She was studying him strangely, as if she, too, had been acutely moved by what had just happened, but her silence was as incisive as his own. Moving off his lap, she turned so that they were facing one another, and she wrapped her arms around him and initiated a heavenly kiss that went on and on, and when they parted, he couldn't meet her gaze. He was seized by an upwelling of pure melancholy so potent that it yielded an incredulous sting of tears.

"Have you completed my portrait?" she queried.

"No. But soon."

Doggedly, she tried to impel him to look at her, but

he couldn't permit her to ascertain how acutely disturbed he was.

"Do you ever wish—"

She halted in mid-sentence, leaving him to stew over what she might have said, and he inquired, "Wish what?"

He located the courage to stare her down, but he carefully masked his careening emotions, and she shook her head as though she hadn't intended to pose the question.

"Nothing," she grumbled on a sigh. "Nothing at all. Do you have any idea when you'll be done?"

"No, although I must confess that my father asked me to terminate at once—as a favor to my new mother."

"Mary?"

"Yes. On their wedding day, she beseeched him to intervene and convince me to desist."

"They're both aware of what we've been doing?"

"Aye."

"How did your father—"

"He's always known, *bella*," he said kindly, hoping she wouldn't probe as to how, dreading that he might ever have to explain that she had started out as one in a long line.

She blushed prettily. "And he told Mary?"

"No. She guessed."

"Will you do as they've requested?"

"I told them I'd think about it"—he lifted her hand and kissed the middle of her palm—"but I'm in no hurry."

"What about your other painting *contracts*?" She flushed a deeper shade of red. "Will you discontinue them, as well? As a favor to Mary? Or is mine the only one to go?"

He couldn't fathom why she supposed there were other women with whom he was currently consorting, but then, she'd ceaselessly been too astute. For once, he was relieved to confess the truth. "I have no other contracts. I haven't worked on any other portraits since I met you."

"Swear it," she fervently entreated.

"I swear."

With his vow, she snuggled against him, burrowing her nose into the hair on his chest. "I'm glad."

"I promised her you'd be the last." He kissed the top of her head. "She's thoroughly determined to find me a lucrative method of earning my living. But for now"—he tipped her onto her back and followed her down, stretching out and covering her with his body—"there's no rush. We have all the time in the world."

CHAPTER EIGHTEEN

CHARLOTTE banged the knocker, her third attempt, and she was impatient for footsteps to sound. None came winging in her direction, which she couldn't understand. Elizabeth had insisted that Gabriel Cristofore was a man of some means, and from the house and neighborhood, he certainly seemed to be. While his residence wasn't situated on the grandest lane in London, it assuredly wasn't the stews, either. He had some sort of decent income.

Surely such a famous artist didn't live alone and would have his own set of retainers!

Sensing a need for stealth in her journey, she'd traveled without her maid, and she bristled irritably as a few drops of rain splatted on the brim of her hat and pelted her shoulders.

"Doesn't the blasted gentleman have any servants?" she griped to herself.

She studied the windows facing the street, hoping she might see activity, a curtain fall, but no one appeared to be at home. Yet, Elizabeth had to be inside. Her carriage was parked down the block, her slovenly driver hanging about on the corner and neglecting his duties by vigorously flirting with a pretty girl who'd walked past. He was so busy with his mischief that he hadn't noted the rented hansom that had pulled in behind him.

A fourth time, she tried the knocker then gave up and retreated from the stoop. Tapping her toe with displeasure, she assessed the dwelling, the yard that was shielded from prying pedestrians by its wrought-iron fence, and she wondered about the fellow who inhabited the property, as well as Elizabeth's odd and growing attachment to him.

Since Elizabeth had met Mr. Cristofore, she'd become a different person, and Charlotte couldn't stop speculating as to what part he'd played in effecting the alterations. While Elizabeth contended that her visits were solely for the purpose of her portrait being painted, Charlotte was dubious.

For an artist to render such modifications merely by touching brush to canvas, he'd have to be a sorcerer.

Without a doubt, she shouldn't have followed Elizabeth, chasing after her like a pet lapdog, but she'd been so annoyingly curious as to Elizabeth's comportment.

The other woman's clamoring—that she'd crossed paths with an artistic genius—rang false. Her disposition was too changed, her attitudes too varied, from how she'd been in the months Charlotte had known her, and Charlotte was convinced that Elizabeth was up to no good.

Even if, in the end, she learned that Elizabeth had been telling the truth as to her goings-on, Charlotte would be satisfied with her day's work. Pitifully, she couldn't put any of it to rest until she found out what was transpiring.

She abhorred that Elizabeth was keeping secrets, that she had events occupying her that didn't involve Charlotte. Anymore, Elizabeth acted so utterly happy, as though Charlotte had no business being apprised of her whereabouts. Charlotte was incredibly jealous about whatever transformations had occurred to have brought about Elizabeth's radical reformation, and she was fit to be tied that she had ceased to be a controlling factor in Elizabeth's life.

When Charlotte had married the earl, Elizabeth had been beside herself, regularly complaining to her father about how Charlotte's command of the house had left her with nothing to do. Now, Elizabeth was totally removed from the worries that had previously absorbed her.

Where formerly, she'd hated that Charlotte had

usurped her position, suddenly Elizabeth couldn't care less. She had no interest in their stifling domicile, or the horrid home life they endured, and she scarcely noticed Charlotte's handling of the servants. Her behavior was so out of character! Why?

Obviously, no one was available to answer the door, and she knew she should depart, but she couldn't withdraw until she discovered concrete information. There was something fishy about Elizabeth's coming here so often, especially now that Charlotte had tried to gain entry with no success.

She cast about, searching for an explanation, when she noted the garden path leading around the side of the house. Without pondering the proprieties of strolling about uninvited, or how it would look should the Countess of Norwich be caught snooping, she strolled down the path as it disappeared into the rear yard.

Surprisingly, a tiny cottage was located in the back, and from the smoke curling out of the chimney, it was apparent that someone was on the premises. She glanced over her shoulder toward the main dwelling, but nobody stared back at her, or rushed out to question her presence, so she walked over and peeked in the window.

On witnessing the sordid scene inside, she sucked in a stunned breath.

Elizabeth was kneeling on a sofa, naked as the day she was born! An incredibly handsome man—Gabriel Cristofore; it had to be!—was crouched behind her. He was naked, as well. One of his large hands cupped her breast, the other reached to the front of her torso and touched her . . . *there!* . . . between her legs.

From their bodily configuration, Charlotte was sure that the knave had impaled his masculine rod, Elizabeth spread wide that he might enjoy his disgusting pleasure at her expense.

Charlotte's initial reaction was one of horror. Had the artist forced himself on Elizabeth? Was she being ravished, even as Charlotte watched? Why didn't she cry out in alarm? Or scream for help?

Despite how little Charlotte liked Elizabeth personally, she lurched back, ready to pound on the door and rush in, where she would save the woman by rescuing her from the ultimate disgrace. But just as she would have initiated Elizabeth's emancipation, Elizabeth arched her back, a sly smile crossed her lips.

Why . . . Elizabeth was participating voluntarily!

Charlotte shuddered with derision and repugnance. Had the strumpet no morals? No principles to guide her conduct? What type of gentlewoman would willingly submit to such a foul, wicked procedure? How could she allow such odious liberties?

The scandal! The shame! Elizabeth was no better than a whore!

Narrowing her focus, she scrutinized the nuances of the spectacle. Cristofore leaned nearer, whispering into Elizabeth's ear while nipping and biting her neck. She murmured in response, then spun into his arms. As she did, Charlotte managed a swift, unimpeded glimpse of the man's phallus. It was cocked as a pole, wet and slick from being lanced in Elizabeth's body.

Brazenly, Elizabeth instituted a long, ardent kiss, and Cristofore lustily joined in, his tongue in her mouth, his erection pressed against her belly. His hands were everywhere, at her nipples, on her bottom.

Charlotte covertly spied on them, and as the lovers concluded their impassioned kiss, her heart was pounding. Seeing them together was obscene, yet at the same juncture, she was thoroughly mesmerized. Their physical exploits were revolting but fascinating, their gestures strangely elegant in a manner that was puzzling and enthralling.

The gentleman, in particular, vexed her. With his slender, graceful physique, and his undivided attention focused on Elizabeth, Charlotte was transfixed, amazed that the vile deed could evolve so tenderly. Perplexingly, her own body reacted to his maneuvers.

She hadn't known that the male anatomy could be so magnificent, that viewing it could incite a woman's baser instincts. Distasteful as it was to admit, her nipples responded to what he was doing, and she shifted, uncomfortable with her corporeal reaction, with her state of mind.

They were conversing, and Charlotte edged to the window, wishing she could decipher their comments, but she couldn't hear a word, so instead, she analyzed their demeanor, the tip of a head, the stroke of a hand, the penetration of a gaze.

Whatever the topic, they were immersed in an urgent, serious discussion. Their devotion and blatant affection was provoking and irksome, and Charlotte was astounded to have stumbled upon Elizabeth's delicious, decadent secret.

Cristofore laid Elizabeth down, distended her legs and, with no consideration for her feminine condition, brutally entered her with his loathsome staff. Elizabeth was such a harlot that she didn't even flinch. If anything, she opened further, allowing him greater access. Nauseatingly, the man began to thrust, as he sought his filthy conclusion, and Charlotte whirled away, incapable of additional observation.

Repulsed and unexplainably titillated, she ran to her rented carriage, not concerned if anyone had witnessed her indecorous, hasty flight. The driver helped her in, and she was so distressed that she couldn't speak, not even to deliver the simple command to depart.

Her thoughts were in chaos, and she blindly stared out at the passing streets. She'd prayed for a method by which she could revenge herself for the slights and insults Elizabeth had heaped upon her since her marriage. Likewise, she longed to prove to her pompous, cruel, elderly husband that she was a force with which to be reckoned. That she wasn't a child, as he'd callously described to his despicable paramour, but an adult whom he'd underestimated.

The ruthless remarks he'd uttered to Mary Smith continued to stab like a dagger, and the animosity he'd generated through his betrayal festered like an infected wound. She would never forgive him, and she wanted to hurt him as badly as he'd hurt her, but he seemed so powerful, so omnipotent, and she so insignificant to him, that she hadn't been able to conceive of a single retaliation she might perform that would affect him in any manner.

Clearly, Elizabeth's ruination provided Charlotte with the tools she needed to wreak havoc. The earl thought Elizabeth was perfect and held her up as the model to which Charlotte should aspire. Wouldn't he be crushed to be apprised of how wrong he'd been?

Many scenarios were feasible, numerous courses of action warranted. But which would be most beneficial? And in what fashion should she implement them?

The earl had to be enlightened as to what a jezebel he'd raised, but how best to utilize the knowledge she'd gleaned? What would be the most precipitous finale? How could Charlotte garner the maximum advantage?

The carriage rumbled to a stop just down from the Norwich town house, but she was only vaguely aware of her arrival. Once again, the driver assisted her with the steps, and she floundered, blindly heading into the house, then up the stairs to her room, where she locked the door so that she would have privacy while she contemplated her next move.

Findley Harcourt sat at the head of the family dining table, swirling the last of his wine in his goblet as he glared at his plate, not entirely positive what he'd just been served. He was frightfully glad it was just the three of them—himself, Elizabeth and Charlotte—and that there were no guests to whom they'd presented the terrifying repast.

After the second course, he'd deigned to question Charlotte, to which she'd replied that Cook—their eighth since his marriage—had walked out in a snit for no reason at all the day after Mary left. Charlotte claimed to be in the process of interviewing for another, her workload apparently compounded by the fact that, after Mary's abandonment, she was also currently endeavoring to locate the ideal housekeeper.

His temper boiled anew over Mary's rejection. She was the most disloyal, perfidious, treacherous of women! How dare she desert him! For that roué, John Preston! What was the world coming to?

After all he'd done for her, she repaid him by walking out with barely a good-bye. If she'd still been at her post—where she belonged—he wouldn't be starving at his own supper table! He was wretched without her! Absolutely wretched!

As if Charlotte could find someone to take her place! She wouldn't recognize a suitable housekeeper if the best candidate bit her on the ass!

He snorted into his cup, both women glancing at him, inducing him to realize that he'd probably had too much to drink. No surprise there! He certainly hadn't filled his belly with food! Red wine had had to suffice.

After his criticism of the poor quality of the cuisine, he hadn't probed further into the fiasco. Charlotte would have sworn that nothing was her fault, that the mistakes were beyond her control, that every member of the staff was an imbecile.

He couldn't abide her justifications. Besides breeding an heir, she had one job and one job only: to supervise the house. He'd scolded her on numerous occasions, but with this latest culinary disaster, he'd been too angry to civilly address the recurrent situation. Perhaps it was the wine making him more irascible than usual, but if a man couldn't return home after long hours of commerce and politics to enjoy a pleasant, appetizing meal, what was the purpose of coming home at all?

Before their betrothal, he'd extensively interrogated her mother as to the instruction and grooming that had been done to prepare Charlotte to assume the varied, exhaustive role of countess. Her mother had insisted that the girl had received the finest tutelage in the land, but as he perused her over the rim of his glass, he was compelled to concede that her mother's assurances as to her fitness might have been an out-and-out lie meant to marry her off in a hurry to the first man stupid enough to ask.

Well, he had no one to blame but himself. Once he'd decided to tie the knot, he'd forged ahead with his customary intensity, much like a bull in a china shop. After he'd set eyes on Charlotte, the choice had seemed easy. He'd been in such a dither to finalize the contracts, and Charlotte's parents had been so amenable, that he'd scarcely checked into her background or habits.

Clearly, he should have been more judicious and circumspect, but who could have imagined that such a slip of a girl could perpetrate such discord?

She had the appropriate lineage—although her rank hadn't been as high as he'd have liked—and she'd been the prettiest of the season's crop of eligibles, which had definitely made the idea of sex more palatable. The few times that they'd been in each other's company before the wedding, she'd been deferential and respectful, creating the false impression that she'd be a biddable, conscientious, and submissive wife.

In reality, she was never tractable, rarely agreeable, and she didn't comprehend anything about prudent regard for her duties.

He furtively examined her, trying to recollect why he'd ever found her attractive, and instead, he caught himself ruminating over how, of late, she'd been awfully peculiar. Furious, morose, captious, she pretended not to hear him when he spoke to her; she acted as though she didn't notice when he entered a room. While she'd constantly been fussy and acrimonious, she'd recently grown more obstinate.

Once, she'd even had the gall to refuse him sexual services when he'd visited her bed, but he'd set her to rights with the back of his hand and hadn't had to brook any subsequent nonsense.

About what did the bloody girl have to be despondent?

Just when he'd supposed she'd be more contented than ever, her attitude had soured. For months, she'd been harping about Mary, demanding that she be fired, that she be turned out, and now Mary had departed.

But was Charlotte happy? No, she was not!

There was no understanding women! What they wanted. What they needed. He'd never previously figured it out, and obviously, he hadn't gleaned a clue by the ripe old age of fifty.

Unable to fathom his wife, he shifted his attention to his daughter, when it dawned on him that he didn't grasp anything about her, either. She'd undergone significant changes, as well. There was a glow about her, a sparkle, a spring in her step, that he hadn't formerly perceived. She regularly dressed in brightly colored, gadabout clothes that were flawlessly tailored to enhance her demeanor and charm.

While she'd habitually been quiet and somber, she was now carefree, lighthearted, and gay. In fact, as he pondered the circumstances, it seemed that Elizabeth's conversion into a livelier, more vivacious person directly correlated with Charlotte's descent into the doldrums.

How odd.

He held out his glass, and a servant automatically replenished his wine. With liquid courage at the ready, he was braced to expound on the meal and Charlotte's role in the debacle, but just as he opened his mouth, Charlotte leapt into the void.

"Elizabeth, how was your afternoon?" Charlotte was inexplicably rancorous, her query conniving and malicious.

"My afternoon?" Preoccupied, Elizabeth was overtly startled that Charlotte had addressed her. "It was exceptional."

"Really. Where were you?"

"I was sitting for my portrait." Elizabeth was plainly exasperated by the inquisition. "Charlotte, I've explained my whereabouts time and again. Why do you persist in bothering about it?"

Findley stared from one to the other. There was a queer undercurrent to the conversation that he couldn't interpret. Both women were in an elevated state of volatility, with Charlotte quarrelsome and hostile, Elizabeth animated and exuberant.

"How is your *portrait* coming along?" Charlotte sipped her wine, using it to cover a snicker.

"Marvelously well."

"So it's almost finished?"

"Almost."

"Pity," Charlotte said snidely. "You'll soon run out of reasons to call upon your distinguished *friend*."

"Yes, it is too bad. He's been wonderful to me, and I've learned a great deal about the creative process. I wish I had the money to be a patron. I'd support as many artists as I could afford."

"A patron! For *dozens* of artists!" Charlotte smothered a strangled sound by pressing her lips to her glass. "What stamina you have!"

"What?" Elizabeth queried, confused.

Abruptly, Charlotte turned to him, and she was ablaze with a bizarre sort of venom. "Milord, I would speak with you privately after our supper has ended."

Taken aback by her malevolent expression, he cleared his throat and sat up straighter. "I would speak with *you* now."

His anger peaked in harmony with her own, the excessive wine causing his temper to flare over matters about which he ordinarily couldn't have cared less. "This food is atrocious."

"But I've accounted for why—"

"No more quibbling." He slammed his fist on the table, making the silver—and the two women—jump. "You have one week to correct your shortcomings in home management. If I dine at this table next Friday night and endure anything similar, I will strip you of your responsibilities"—he leaned toward her, his larger size reminding her of his dominion over her—"and I will confer them upon Elizabeth, once more."

There! Let her stew! Charlotte's pride was one of her few redeeming qualities, therefore, there was no worse insult he could level, no more demeaning renunciation he could pronounce. "I will no longer tolerate your deficiencies or lapses. Have I made myself clear? Unless you show serious improvement, I will have no choice: Elizabeth shall run this house."

"Actually, Father"—Elizabeth flashed the most annoying smile—"I don't fancy having the household chores bestowed upon me ever again. As you counseled, I've involved myself in various other activities, and they adequately engross me. I'm much too busy to superintend the house or the staff. I really have no interest in reestablishing our prior arrangement."

He analyzed her protractedly, thinking that she had metamorphosed into someone with whom he was not acquainted. She didn't want to oversee the house? She was too . . . too . . . *busy?*

His marriage, and how it had produced a vacuum in her life, had been an incessant protest for months! What was wrong with her? Had the damned woman gone batty?

"If I command it," he imperiously decreed, "you *shall* handle it for me. And I shan't listen to any objection. My residence will be put in order!" Rampageous, he rose, violently tossing his napkin. "Now, if you'll excuse me—"

"May I speak with you, milord?" Charlotte repeated her solicitation, springing up and blocking his exit, determined to hash out whatever petty dilemma weighed on her.

"No, you may not."

Gripping her forearms, he lifted her, and physically deposited her to the side, then he stomped out and stormed down the hall to his library, the sole sanctuary he possessed in this madhouse of crazed females.

As he passed the butler, he curtly decreed, "I am not to be disturbed! By anyone!"

He slammed the door and poured himself a stiff whiskey, gulping down the contents. On his empty stomach, with his supper uneaten and the wine sloshing about, the amber concoction gurgled and burned, and he plopped down in the chair behind his desk, rubbing his tender, unsettled abdomen while cursing Mary. Charlotte. Elizabeth.

Tired and aggravated, he closed his eyes, relishing the quiet, when to his shock and consternation, the door squeaked, the noisy hinges apprising him of an interloper.

His temper simmered. Had he no authority left in his own home? Was there not an individual remaining who paid heed to anything he said? Who dared contradict his mandate for privacy?

He whipped his eyes open, and to his amazement and fury, his visitor was Charlotte. She had deigned to confront him! Despite his current ill humor! He truly could not bear any trivial feminine complaints!

"Am I now to add *deafness* to your many faults, Charlotte?" He stood, his body a rock of tense muscles and ire. "I could have sworn I just told you that I am in no mood to deal with whatever it is you're intent on sharing. Begone! At once!"

"But milord—"

"Go!" he roared, cutting her off. "Leave me be!"

"This can't wait."

"I don't care!"

"It has to do with Elizabeth." Ignoring his directive, she waltzed in, sitting across from him in one of his favorite chairs.

"What about Elizabeth?" His jaw was clenched so tightly that he worried he might crack a tooth.

"I would discuss the artist she's been seeing."

As she was fairly glimmering with spite, he was

swamped by the impression that she was up to no good. She thrived on trouble, mischief was her forte, so he was instantly on guard.

"What about him?"

"His name is Gabriel Cristofore."

Elizabeth had sporadically mentioned the man. "And . . . ?"

"He's not painting her."

Suddenly, she was blushing, her cheeks so red that he prayed she might burst into flames and put them all out of their misery. "What's he about then, Charlotte? If you have something to say, say it and be done!"

"He's . . . he's . . ."—she choked it out—"having marital relations with her."

Findley assessed her composure, while he calculated the impact of what she'd just contended. "Are you maintaining that Elizabeth and this artist are—"

"Yes." She nodded eagerly, believing she wouldn't have to clarify.

"In the middle of the afternoon, in his studio, where anyone might walk in on them"—a tic started in his cheek, and he speculated as to whether her accusation was genuine, or if she was simply stirring a pot of adversity— "they're getting naked and . . . and . . . *fucking*? Is that what you're claiming?"

At his use of the indelicate term, her bravado faded. She studied the floor, her nervous fingers fiddling with her skirts. "Aye, Lord Norwich."

"And you know this because . . . ?"

"I saw them."

"Today?"

"Yes, that's what caused the problems with supper. I was so distraught! I couldn't supervise the kitchen."

"No, of course not." He toyed with the chain of his watch. "Just how did it happen that you stumbled upon them?"

"Well, Elizabeth had waxed on about Mr. Cristofore's

talent, so I proposed to visit him and request his doing a portrait of me, but when I arrived, I . . . I . . ."

She couldn't finish her sentence, and she continued to scrutinize the floor. Either she was too embarrassed to specify what she'd observed, or she couldn't concoct a satisfactory lie on the spur of the moment. He couldn't deduce which problem harried her. He prodded: "You walked in and . . . ?"

"Well, no one appeared to be at home, although Elizabeth's carriage was parked out front, so I looked in the window."

"My Countess of Norwich was spying from the lawn like a bloody Peeping Tom?"

"It wasn't like that," she warily attested.

"What was it *like,* then?" Out of patience, he crudely postulated, "Were they rutting like beasts in the forest? Going at it like a couple of dogs in a barnyard?"

"She was . . . she was on her knees, and he was roughly taking her from behind."

"Did he spill his seed inside her?"

"Yes! Then, they kissed for a long while and started in again. With Elizabeth on her back, and the artist on top."

Gad! Could it be true? He couldn't imagine Charlotte inventing such a horrid story, notwithstanding how the two women disliked one another. Not even Charlotte would stoop so low. Would she?

And what about Elizabeth? She'd always been so well behaved, so trustworthy. Would she comport herself so reprehensibly?

A remote hope flared, and he asked, "Might you have been mistaken, and he was forcing himself upon her?"

"No. She was willingly participating."

The pathetic wench had spied on them long enough to know! Though he needed solitude to assimilate the dreadful tidings, he pointlessly inquired, "Why have you come to me?"

"I felt you had to be informed."

"So that I could do what?" He wasn't interested in her advice; he was merely curious about what selfish methods she'd formulated as to how he should pursue a resolution.

"Well, my original opinion was that we must find her a husband, but then"—finally in her element, she tenaciously stared at him as if they were coconspirators—"I realized that she's ruined herself. Why . . . she might even now be with child. No gentleman would have her."

The irony was not lost on him: His unwed, spinsterish daughter might be sinfully, shamefully increasing, while his young, healthy wife consistently exhibited—month after disappointing month—her inability to conceive.

What next? he petulantly wailed. How else would the women in his life torment him?

"If not marriage, then what do you suggest?"

"She should be sent to Norwich, in perpetuity, so that she's secluded from decent people."

"Such as yourself, you mean?"

"Absolutely." Charlotte missed his sarcasm. "I shouldn't have to be sullied by her wicked presence."

"Barring that move?"

"She must be confined to the house. To her rooms. Not let out. Ever. Not to socialize or fraternize, not to shop or mingle about town, not to attend her charitable functions or those musicales she enjoys."

"Who would act as her jailer? You?"

"If you asked it of me"—striving to seem demure and sympathetic, she bowed her head—"I would gladly assist you."

She was elated over the notion that he might isolate or incarcerate Elizabeth, joyous over a detention and what it might engender. His wife was an enigma, a disconcerting mystery, an amalgamation of devious plots and machinations. If she put half as much energy into correcting her personal flaws as she did poking her nose into the business of others, she might eventually achieve some contentment.

As it was, he couldn't predict what would become of

her. Or himself. How was he to trudge through the remainder of his years with her? The concept was so depressing that he couldn't bear to contemplate it.

"You may go to your room."

"But what about—"

"I will investigate your allegations." He gestured toward the hall, indicating that their appointment was concluded and—praise be!—she stood to go. "I will uncover the facts, and you had better hope that what you've divulged is the entire truth."

"It is. You'll see."

Her vehemence persuaded him as to her veracity, and his heart sank. Still, he was compelled to add, "If you've been lying, my wrath shall descend upon you. There will be no way to redeem yourself."

"Aye, sir."

"A terrible whipping will be only the first of your punishments."

"I'm not afraid."

Indeed, the more adamant her declarations, the more he was satisfied as to her probity. "I will handle this, and in the meantime, you will not utter a word to anyone."

"But I ought to be able to—"

"Tell no one! Especially Elizabeth. You'll not so much as broach the subject with her. No snide comments. No insinuating remarks." His fury shut her up. "You and I will not speak of this again, either."

"That's not fair," she said, mutinous. "I'm the one who discovered her fall from grace. I should be permitted to—"

"We shall not discuss it again!" He stalked around the desk, yanking at the door and motioning toward the hall. "You're excused."

She hesitated as though she would argue or instigate further debate, but on witnessing his determination, she decided against such an unwise course. In a huff, she lifted her skirts and floated out.

With her egress, he went to the sideboard and poured another whisky, then he wearily slumped into a chair.

What to do? What to do?

CHAPTER NINETEEN

As the footman pronounced their caller, John wasn't certain he'd heard correctly.

"Findley Harcourt?" he inquired in astonishment. "The Earl of Norwich. You're positive you have the name right?"

The servant didn't appreciate having his abilities disputed, and he hid his indignation as he tendered the earl's card.

"Well . . . I'll be damned," John murmured as he passed it to Mary. "What the devil could he want?"

"Lord only knows," Mary grumbled. She stood, brushing at her skirt, patting her hair, then marching for the door.

"Where are you going?"

"I'll handle this."

"You will not."

"He's obviously come to speak with you. About me."

"You're sure of that, are you?" Her irritation was so great that he almost felt sorry for Findley.

"Don't trouble yourself, dear. I'll send him packing."

"Actually, Mrs. Preston"—the footman interrupted, before she could rush downstairs to box Findley's ears—"he's not here to see you or Mr. Preston. He asked for Mr. Cristofore."

"Gabriel?" Abruptly, Mary halted and spun around, glaring at John. "Did he say why?"

"No, ma'am," the retainer responded. "He requested a private meeting, though, claiming it was a matter of some gravity that couldn't be delayed."

"Gad, what next?" John sighed, abhorring that he'd been drawn into the brewing debacle. He rose and went to Mary's side as she cast him a scathing look that clearly said *I told you so.*

Just to discover how fiercely she'd bristle, he grinned and queried, "You don't suppose this has to do with Elizabeth, do you?"

"It has everything *to do* with Elizabeth, as you well know."

"I hate to go in blind. What will he demand?"

"Your son's misbehavior has finally caught up with him. I'd guess we're about to gain a daughter."

Her comment stopped him in his tracks. "You think Findley will insist that they wed?"

"Don't you?"

"I hadn't given the situation serious contemplation one way or the other."

"What other recourse does he have?"

"I can't conceive of Findley stooping so low. Gabriel is quite a bit beneath what he must have always pictured as a son-in-law."

"Trust me," she smirked. "Gabriel's about to become a husband. I understand Findley better than anyone. He won't let the outrage pass with no recompense. There's about to be a wedding."

"I wouldn't count on it."

"Why? Don't you like Elizabeth?" She scowled at him. "She's a fine woman."

"That may be, *chère,* but Gabriel will never marry her."

"How could he refuse? Her ruination is entirely his fault." She was furious enough to skewer any man lingering too closely.

"I'm not disagreeing," he hastily maintained. "I'm just clarifying. Despite what he's done, he'll never acquiesce to matrimony. Especially not when a horse's ass such as Findley is ordering it." He smiled, hoping to defuse some of her ire. "He's contrary."

"So is Findley."

"This won't be pretty."

"No, it won't."

"Do you expect there'll be a great deal of shouting?"

"Absolutely."

"And Findley will be totally unreasonable."

"As will Gabriel."

He sighed again, wondering how he and Gabriel had managed to persevere for so many years without these types of calamities occurring on a daily basis. But then, Gabriel never seduced chaste innocents. He sought out widows, or unhappy wives, so there'd never been an irate father waiting in the wings.

"I detest emotional scenes."

"So do I, but don't worry"—she slipped her hand into his—"we'll get through it together."

"*We* most definitely will not!"

"Don't be ridiculous. Of course I'll accompany you."

John assessed her fierce stance, the rigid set of her shoulders. Even though she despised Findley, and he'd abused her horridly, she was ready to leap into battle, never imagining for an instant that she'd abandon John when he might need her.

What a lucky fellow he was! Every morning when he awoke with her snuggled next to him in his bed, he patted himself on the back for being so smart.

He'd forgotten how satisfying it was to have a female about the house. While he'd enjoyed residing with Gabriel in their bachelor abode, it didn't render quite the same rewards. It was grand to be pampered, to be coddled and scolded, to have someone who noticed him, who fretted if he didn't get enough sleep, or if he stepped out in the cold without a hat.

Such unpretentious worries brought out the best in Mary. She was a natural fusspot, a meddler who encountered problems and fixed them. She advanced, full speed ahead, taking charge and mending what needed to be repaired—including himself and his headstrong son.

How he loved her! "For better or worse," the vows had been written, and he'd plainly wrangled some of the "better" for himself.

He wrapped his arms around her waist, gently kissing her, reveling in his good fortune.

When their lips parted, she stared him down. "You're not about to sweet-talk me out of it."

"I wouldn't dream of it."

"I know how Findley's mind works, John. Let me attend you."

"*Chère,*" he said, "stay here. For me."

"But—"

"They'll likely utter hideous remarks to each other, and I don't want you to hear."

"I'm not a child. I won't swoon over a few offensive words."

"I realize that," he said, chuckling. "It's more than the words. Elizabeth is your friend. She'll be the main topic of discussion, and if the conversation's heated, it won't be pleasant."

"That's precisely why I should be present."

"To defend her honor?"

"Someone must."

"I'll see to Elizabeth's *honor* for you." He nestled her tighter. "Mary, temperaments will be at a fever pitch, and I won't provide Findley with any excuse to hurt you."

"I'm not afraid of Findley Harcourt."

"I grasp that"—he kissed her again—"but if he was rude to you, I'd be forced to commit murder."

"You'd be tried and found guilty."

"Hanged for it."

"I'd be a widow."

"Exactly."

"Men!" she complained as he crossed to the threshold

without her. "Give your son a message for me, will you?"

"What is it?"

"If he doesn't do the right thing by her, he can't continue living with us."

"It's his house," John said.

"Then *we* shall move out."

"I'll tell him, but I can't guarantee it will have any effect."

John yearned to be mistaken. The older he grew, the more appeal a stable family held for him. The notion of the pattering feet of grandchildren running about was extremely enticing but, while he secretly wished Gabriel would marry the girl, he was convinced it would never happen.

If only he had the authority to command that Gabriel wed! But John was hardly the person to advise another on affairs of the heart. He'd never been what one could describe as an expert on romance, and he wouldn't begin to make recommendations on how others should proceed. His own choices—until lately—had been disasters.

He started down the hall, griping to himself: "Why couldn't Gabriel have been a store clerk? Or a farmer? A stodgy, tedious banker . . ."

Behind him, Mary laughed, and the sound brightened his mood as he descended the stairs and braced for the pending strife. He thought about parlaying with Gabriel first, to warn him and to probe his opinion, but he decided against it. There was very little he could impart to Gabriel as to how he should behave. The younger man wouldn't heed his counsel.

Gabriel was the most obstinate, stubborn individual he'd ever met. He'd do as he bloody well pleased, in spite of who was pressuring him, or the fact that someone as exalted as the Earl of Norwich was screaming for his head on a platter.

At this belated juncture, John could only support him by suffering through whatever bad solution was selected, and intervening should Findley be too obnoxious. Findley could be irrepressible and relentless, but then, so could Gabriel. Perhaps Findley had met his match!

The footman who'd announced Findley had followed him down, and as they reached the foyer, John whispered for him to retrieve Gabriel from the studio, to show him Findley's card and inform him that the earl awaited his attendance.

"Make sure," John added, "that he knows I'm here, too, and that if he doesn't arrive in fifteen minutes, I'll be out to drag him inside."

The usually stoic retainer smiled discreetly as he walked away. Their employees were conscious of Gabriel's nocturnal haunts and odd daylight habits. They were in awe of his talent and genius, and they did their part to sustain his creativity by strictly obeying his instructions regarding solitude when he was working—which was most of the time.

When in the midst of an artistic binge, he often didn't surface for days. The servants would inconspicuously deposit trays of food on the porch of the cottage. When he came up for air and emerged, a maid would hurry in to clean the premises so that it would be ready when he locked himself in once more.

If a new composition had captured Gabriel's interest, he wouldn't feel like chattering to Findley, and he'd ignore the summons, which John couldn't allow. This imbroglio had to be resolved.

He entered the parlor, and Findley had discerned his footsteps. Anticipating Gabriel, he whirled around, then he blinked, and blinked again, flustered and striving to make sense of whom he was observing.

John could grasp Findley's bafflement. It had been over twenty-five years since they'd laid eyes on one another, and John had been somewhat of a recluse since returning to England, so few of his former associates were aware that he was home.

John evaluated his venerable nemesis, finding him

gray-haired and overweight, but haughty and disdainful as though he was God's gift, and John conceded that he still couldn't abide the man. A single glimpse, and his temper was goaded.

"Preston . . . ?" As recognition dawned, Findley viewed John with such disgust that John could tell the antipathy was mutual.

"In the flesh."

"What the hell are you doing here?"

"I live here."

"But I'm here to see this . . . this painter"—he muttered *painter* as if it was an epithet—"Cristofore."

"He'll join us shortly."

"And your connection to him is . . . ?"

"None of your damned business."

John didn't care if Findley learned that he and Gabriel were father and son, but he childishly liked keeping the arrogant prig in the dark.

"So you help him carry out various scams." Findley scoffed. "I should have guessed! This sort of thing is right up your alley."

"What the hell do you mean?" John strolled to the sideboard and poured himself a whisky, but discourteously, he didn't offer one to Findley, intentionally slighting him. He wasn't about to drink with the boor as though they were friends. They weren't.

"You always were a miscreant." Findley frowned at John, then he indicated a satchel he'd placed on the table. "I've had Cristofore investigated. I've uncovered several of his dubious swindles. I'm quite sure you two reprobates must get along famously."

"And just what trespass has Mr. Cristofore committed that has you—bastion of virtue that you're renowned to be—so up in arms?"

"He preys on naive women." He puffed out his chest and stuck his nose in the air. Such a pompous knave! "He's a master at seducing them, then stealing their money."

"Really?" John smiled maliciously. "He's a thief of women's purses and hearts, is he?"

"An indisputable brigand."

"What has that alleged exploitation to do with you?"

"Well I . . . I . . ." Findley blushed furiously, unwilling to divulge the incentive for his visit, not wishing to impute Elizabeth, and John was humored at watching him squirm.

Findley stammered and strutted, unable to devise a valid motive for calling on Gabriel, so he changed the subject. "Where's Mary?"

The query blindsided John, when he should have been anticipating it. "Upstairs—where she won't have to see your despicable face."

"I can't believe she left my protection, only to wallow in this male lair of immorality." Caustically, he glanced about, as though he might step in something foul and have to wipe it off his shoes.

"She married me because I love her."

"Love, bah!" Findley derided. "As if you understand the definition of the term."

"Since she chose me, and not you," he chided, "I must have some clue."

"As if I'd have asked her!" Findley jeered. "You've certainly come down in the world, haven't you? You were one of the cheekiest lady's men ever—the irresistible John Preston—and you wind up shackled to my housekeeper! Hah! I can't wait to spread the news at my club!" He leaned toward John, leering. "I'm still a member. Are you? Your downfall ought to furnish weeks of laughs."

"As least I was gentleman enough to marry her," John said quietly.

The exchange had strayed into dangerous territory. It was one thing for Findley to denigrate Gabriel—he didn't know of John's and Gabriel's kinship—but it was quite another for him to slander Mary. Perhaps—despite his earlier joking with her—the contemptuous nobleman would be dead before the afternoon was over.

"I'm not like some bounders," he couldn't resist pointing out, though he'd never be so crude as to directly refer to Mary's affair with Findley. "You know the sort, don't you, Norwich? Those cads who would perpetrate any abominable act against a respectable lady, without apology or remuneration?"

Findley paused. If he'd been speculating as to whether Mary had confessed her indiscretions, he had his answer, and wisely, he didn't pursue the topic. Instead, he switched to firmer ground: denigrating John. "Has Mary been apprised of your squalid history?"

"Which part of it?" John asked impertinently.

"When we were younger, you were the biggest scoundrel in town. No man's wife was safe in your company."

"Especially not yours." John couldn't prevent the jibe from slithering out, even though his conduct with Pamela Harcourt had never involved more than letting her cry on his shoulder.

Findley grimaced, their antiquated feud alive and well. "Now that you've wed, will you rein in your licentious tendencies? Or do you intend to persist in your adulterous copulations with every lightskirt who tickles your fancy? Although, considering Mary's proclivities, perhaps she won't—"

John didn't wait for the rest. He tossed his libation onto the sideboard, stomped across the room, and clutched Findley by the lapels of his coat.

"Last time I beat you to a pulp, I was twenty-one years old." He lifted Findley up, the blackguard's toes off the floor, the seams on his jacket straining and popping. "I may be fifty, but I'd relish the opportunity to discover if I possess the vigor for a repeat performance."

"Lecherous bastard!" Findley spat out.

"You haven't changed a bit, you overbearing toad, presuming you can saunter into my home and insult my wife." He tightened his grip, giving the wretch a hearty shake. "If

Mary's name ever crosses your lips again—for any reason—I'll kill you."

Findley had just opened his mouth to retort, and John stiffened, excitedly enthusiastic for whatever moronic comment might dribble out. It had been many years since he'd wildly engaged in a nasty brawl, and he was eager to confer an unbridled thrashing, but Gabriel picked that precipitous moment to arrive.

"Well, well, what have we here?" he sarcastically remarked from behind them as he insolently ambled in. "Now, Father, is that any way to treat a guest? Unhand the man."

John glared over his shoulder at Gabriel, relieved that he'd bothered to don some clothes, but his outfit had to be a far cry from what Findley would have expected for the portentous meeting.

Gabriel had come from the studio, where he'd been painting through the previous day and night, and he looked like a damned gypsy, with those baggy breeches and a loose, flowing shirt that was half-buttoned, the tail hanging out. His hair was swept back and standing on end from his running his hands through it as he concentrated. His fingers and a cheek were smudged with various smears of paint, and he smelled like the turpentine he utilized to clean his brushes.

John was accustomed to Gabriel's disarray, his typical state after a lengthy bout of inspiration, but for this auspicious occasion, he'd outdone himself. He was definitely a sight.

What must Findley think of his dishevelment? Bearing in mind the purpose behind Findley's visit, he'd likely deem Gabriel a lunatic.

There was a fire in Gabriel's eye, a kind of maniacal gleam that John recognized as having developed after hours of lost sleep and intense labor. On edge, restless, jittery, he would be in no mood for nonsense. He'd never been one to dally with idiots—Findley being a prime example—and he had no patience for inanity or balderdash. In his current heightened condition, he'd be even less inclined to endure Findley's bombast.

The conflict hadn't even commenced, and it was shaping up to be a catastrophe. Any fantasies John had harbored about Gabriel marrying, settling down, supplying a houseful of grandchildren, faded into the woodwork. All John could do was to salvage the showdown by keeping it from spiraling into a hideous altercation.

He gave Findley a final shake for good measure, then released him, and the other man stumbled, regained his balance, then whipped around to grimly scrutinize Gabriel. Though they hadn't been introduced, there was no mistaking who he was.

"He called you . . . *Father!*" Findley accused, his fury settling on John once more. Aghast, horrified, he straightened his clothes, then brandished a castigating finger. "*You* are this man's father?"

"Yes. Sweet, isn't it?"

"You planned it!"

"What?"

"Why would you? For revenge? For vindication? Out of sheer malevolence? What could possibly matter after so much time has passed?" Findley's face was mottled red with rage, and he spun away from John to confront Gabriel, examining him as though he was a fascinating specimen of insect.

"Mr. Gabriel Cristofore?" he inquired formally.

"*Sì, signore,*" Gabriel answered, exaggerating his accent.

Findley snorted. "What type of progeny are you, anyway? Have you so little respect for your sire that you don't even take his name?"

John winced with exasperation. Gabriel was touchy about appellations, and he wouldn't kindly suffer the domineering aristocrat's questioning of such a personal decision. While Gabriel was legally a Preston, he honored his mother by using Cristofore, and John had never felt slighted by it. Besides, the Italian surname was much more flamboyant—just as Gabriel was—and they both believed that it brought in more clients. ·

"Have you some objection to my name?"

There was a menacing air about him as he converged on Findley. Gabriel was a few inches taller, and he advanced till they were toe to toe. Not cowed by the man's elevated status, he rudely inspected Findley, refusing to back down under the earl's visible antagonism.

Gabriel bounced on the balls of his feet, his years of fencing lessons having increased his agility, and he was disposed to pop off at the smallest provocation. He had a temper that could be easily incited—Findley being exactly the type of clod who could exacerbate it. In the past, John had intervened in numerous spats that might have resulted in injury to Gabriel's precious hands, so he watched nervously, ready to jump into the middle of the fray the instant it appeared that a fist might fly.

"Why are you here?" Gabriel asked sternly, after giving the earl a thorough once-over but, as he had to be amply cognizant of Findley's driving motivation, he seemed exceptionally cool.

Amazingly, Findley was the one who was unnerved by Gabriel's cocky approach. He stepped away, putting more space between them. "I would confer with you privately. On a subject of some urgency."

"Whatever you have to say, you can say in front of my father."

"I would rather not."

"Depart, then." Gabriel shrugged. "It matters not to me." He roved to the sideboard, poured himself a whisky, then lounged on the sofa, sprawling casually and showing no respect for their visitor. He blindly sipped his drink, then gazed at Findley as though puzzled to find him still on the premises. "Are we done? If so, I'd like to return to work."

For his part, Findley stared as if Gabriel was an uncouth savage. "Do you have any idea who I am?"

"Yes, *Lord* Norwich, and I'm busy. You're wasting my time."

"I could break you like that!" Findley loudly snapped his fingers.

"Better men than you have attempted it." Gabriel gestured to John. "Close the door, Father. The earl has something he needs to get off his chest."

"Listen to me, you little bast—"

"Tut, tut, Norwich," Gabriel reproached, cutting him off. "If you disparage me—or my beloved mother—I'll have my footmen throw you out. Bodily."

"You wouldn't dare," Findley huffed.

"Try me."

Findley was fit to explode. No one risked his displeasure by sassing him. The powerful nobleman had been pampered and humored from birth, and wherever he went, people begged for the chance to promptly do his bidding. Effrontery and discourtesy were unheard of.

Briefly, John fretted that Gabriel had pushed Findley too far, but then he remembered that Gabriel had been around men of Findley's ilk his entire life. He knew them well; that's why he loathed them.

"Findley," John said, diffusing the volatile banter, "you can speak candidly. I serve as Gabriel's secretary."

"Why am I not surprised? I'm sure you taught him everything he knows."

"Not *everything*," Gabriel impudently interjected. "Some things I learned with none of his assistance at all."

John endeavored to arbitrate. "Gabriel and I have no secrets." He skirted Findley and shut the door, then returned to his side and waved toward a chair. "Why don't we sit down, and you can tell us what's wrong."

"I will not *sit* with that scapegrace."

"Fine, then. We'll all stand." John cast Gabriel a quelling look that had no effect. He remained impolitely reposed on the sofa, so John forged on. "What has you in such a dither?"

Findley dawdled, sharing nothing, the sheer intensity of his glower hot enough to burn a hole through the drapes. Gabriel met the stare full-on, not recoiling, not retreating, but audaciously braced.

The silence became oppressive, then Findley cursed and muttered, "He knows why I'm here." He narrowed his focus. "There's no need to spell it out, is there, Cristofore?"

"No, none." Gabriel smiled maddeningly, and John longed to strangle him.

"She has no money," Findley abruptly mentioned. "She's poor as a church mouse."

"So I was informed. From the very beginning."

"Then why do you persist?"

"Why not?" Gabriel sampled his libation, completely indifferent to Findley's affront. "She's quite lovely."

Findley was so outraged he couldn't reply, but perhaps he was a tad disconcerted, as well. He was infuriated on behalf of his disgraced daughter, permeated by a heavy dose of a father's justified, righteous indignation, yet he couldn't get so much as a ripple of remorse from the villain who'd accomplished the ruining.

John pitied him. Even if Findley was a buffoon, Elizabeth was a charming girl and worthy of this exhibition of paternal offense.

"Findley, are we talking about your daughter, Elizabeth?" By feigning ignorance, John thought to imbue the discourse with a touch of rationality before it launched into the emotional. "She's been having her portrait done, and I—"

"Shut! Up!" Findley hissed venomously.

"Are you intimating that our children are physically involved?"

"I'm not *intimating* it," Findley declared. "I'm flat-out imputing your son in her utter defilement." Findley turned to John, astounding him with the depth of his wrath. "Your son is a profligate fornicator, a shameful violator of women, a libertine of the worst sort."

"Harsh charges."

"I would hear his defense—with my own ears—before we proceed."

John challenged Gabriel. "What say you to these accusations?"

"I have nothing to add."

"So the earl's allegations are true?" John implored in vain.

"Each and every one," Gabriel admitted, unrepentant.

"Have you any rejoinder?"

"Yes: I make no apologies, and I submit no explanations."

"Filthy scum," Findley seethed between clenched teeth. "I'll see you hanged for this!"

"Findley!" Frightened, John sharply admonished him. Findley was an omnipotent member of the nobility, a peer who could exploit his authority and rank to procure any conclusion he desired. "You'll do no such thing!" But Gabriel was already orating, making his case much more dire.

"But then you'd have to acknowledge what transpired," he said. "How your daughter willingly debased herself. Your prized jewel would be publicly humiliated, ridiculed, and scorned. Your family disgraced." Aggravatingly, he swirled the contents of his glass. "Is that what you want?"

"Findley, calm yourself," John interposed. "We accept the appropriate remedy for Gabriel's conduct. You arrange for the special license, and Mary and I will start planning the ceremony."

"This blackguard"—Findley's vehemence was ghastly—"will *never* marry Elizabeth. I'd murder him with my own two hands before I'd permit it."

"You don't wish them to wed?"

"Never," Findley reiterated.

John was confused. Findley wasn't the type to rail and

bemoan his fate. He'd crave action, results. "Then why have you come?"

Findley nodded at Gabriel. "Your son can tell you."

"I believe I can."

"What?" John was bewildered. The two combatants seemed to be conferring in a foreign code to which he wasn't privy.

"The earl is prepared to offer me money to break off with her." Gabriel condescendingly mirrored Findley's acrimonious expression. "Am I close?"

"Dead on target."

At Findley's response, John threw up his arms in defeat and fell into a chair. "How will such an agreement benefit Lady Elizabeth? She's the one who's been harmed, yet neither of you is contemplating her welfare."

"I'm thinking *only* of her," Findley contended. "I want her removed from his dastardly clutches. Today!"

He retrieved the satchel he'd brought, extracted some papers, and spread them on the table in front of Gabriel. It was a contract. Gabriel picked it up and carefully perused the terms, then he glanced up at Findley, flashing a wicked smile that made John panic.

"Is that all her reputation is worth to you?" Gabriel raised a brow. "Why . . . it's a mere pittance."

"I won't give you a single farthing more."

Gabriel tossed the papers down. "Then I'm about to become your son-in-law." Suddenly pensive, he tapped a finger against his lips. "You realize, of course, that with hardly any effort, I could persuade her to marry me. Since she and I have no funds, you'd have to support us. We'd likely have to move into the Norwich town house." He chuckled spitefully. "My painting supplies are hideously expensive. Just ask John; he keeps my books. My steady upkeep would be a huge *drain* on your resources."

"You wouldn't dare!" Findley choked out.

"Wouldn't I?"

"A hundred more."

"I'd best be going." Gabriel stood. "I've an appointment with my tailor so I can be measured for my wedding clothes."

"Five hundred."

Gabriel strolled toward the door.

"A thousand!"

Calculating, Gabriel assessed him. "Ten thousand more. I won't settle for a pound less."

"And you'll disappear?"

"Forever."

"No midnight trysts? No messages passed through her maid? No clandestine love letters to keep her pining away? No persisting contact of any sort?"

"None."

"Swear it."

"I swear." He held up his right hand, as though taking an oath.

"As if you'd honor your vow!" Findley sneered. "You must deem me a fool! You'll sign an amended agreement."

"Naturally." Gabriel pointed to the document that lay condemningly on the table. "Add on ten thousand, and no one in your family will ever hear from me again."

"Absolutely not!" John exclaimed, leaping to his feet. "That's an outrageous amount! I won't allow it!" But both men ignored him.

"As of this afternoon?" Findley asked of Gabriel.

"I'll pack my bags as soon as we're finished."

"Money well spent," Findley groused.

"Gabriel," John entreated, trying to inject sanity into the debate. "Don't do this. Not to yourself, and most assuredly not to Lady Elizabeth. You'll be eternally sorry."

"I doubt it."

"Listen to you!" John was shocked by his son's callousness. While Gabriel could act the charlatan, deep down he had a benevolent heart. He understood the difference between right and wrong. What had come over him?

He tried another tactic. "There are worse things than marrying someone who cares about you."

"I can't conceive of any."

"Don't accept his blood money."

"Why shouldn't I? It's a fortune. More than I could earn painting in several lifetimes. I'd be an idiot to pass it up."

"Good boy," Findley patronizingly intoned.

"Do be silent, Findley." John was frantic to dissuade Gabriel, and he struggled for a rationalization that would pierce through his hardened demeanor. "What if Lady Elizabeth finds out what you've done? She'll be terribly hurt."

"She won't ever learn of it, will she, Norwich?"

"Over my dead body."

"But what if she does?" John pressed. "Her last memories of you will be of this betrayal! I thought you liked her. At least a little."

"It was just the sex, Father. You're aware that I consort with them solely for the riches that can accrue, and she doesn't have any fiscal assets, so I took the only other item she had to contribute that was of value. But now that I'm to be remunerated for my troubles—"

"Your troubles . . . ?" John gasped, appalled.

"—there's no reason to persevere."

"I don't know who you are anymore." John was sick, depressed over the entire, repulsive episode. How would he ever explain this to Mary?

"There you have it, Preston." Findley preened, quashing John's efforts to alter their course. "The deal is executed to our mutual satisfaction."

Findley scanned the room, locating an inkwell and pen on a writing desk in the corner, and he sped over to them. Hastily, he modified the original draft, endorsed it at the bottom, then held out the pen to Gabriel so that he could validate it, too.

Gabriel inspected the accuracy of the revisions, then inscribed his signature with a flourish. Findley regained the

pen, affixed a blank line, then extended the pen to John.
"Sign as a witness."

"I won't," John reproved. "You two are mad."

"Even if you won't ratify our transaction, I retain my
right to call you as a witness. Your son swore to the terms.
I'll never let either of you deny it."

"As if I would take part in this . . . this infamy."

"We'll see." He pulled an empty sheet out of his
satchel, and commanded of Gabriel, "Compose a note to
her."

"Specifying what?"

"Good-bye. What do you suppose?"

John watched in astonishment as Gabriel did precisely
as he'd been bid. He went to the writing desk where, for
just a second, he tarried, organizing his justifications in his
head before committing them to parchment. With a few
scrawls, he'd sealed his fate. And Elizabeth's.

He sanded the message, then began to fold it, when
Findley stomped over.

"I don't trust you. Let me read it."

"Will this suffice?" Gabriel proffered it as Findley dissected his *adieu.*

"Succinct. Concise. This will do nicely." He slid it into
the satchel.

John's incredulity ratcheted up another notch. "You
won't show her that insensitive piece of rubbish?"

"Only if I'm forced to."

"Aren't you concerned about Elizabeth's feelings?"

"I *am* thinking of Elizabeth," Findley maintained. "Of
her and her alone."

"What if there's a babe?" he prodded.

"There isn't," Gabriel guaranteed, but with much less
confidence than John would have liked, and his heart con-
stricted. The possibility that Gabriel could sire a child, but
that they would never see it grow, was unimaginable.

He turned to Findley, beseeching. "If there is a child,
promise me that you'll bring it here, so Mary and I can

raise it. I realize that you don't care for me, but you once felt some affection for her. Please say you'll do it as a favor to Mary."

Findley flinched, as if the appeal had stabbed at his very core, but he swiftly recovered. "If the worst happens, and there is a babe, I would drop it on the church's doorstep before I'd deliver it to you."

John was stunned. A babe would be his and Findley's lone grandchild! Could he so easily discard it? "You can't mean that!"

"Oh, but I do," he said, sweeping away John's complaints with a flutter of his hand. "I'm rapidly losing my stomach for the details. Let's get this finished."

He then removed another item from his pouch. It was a bank draft—made out in advance to Gabriel. Findley had been so confident of Gabriel's base tendencies!

Findley filled in the appropriate amount, then displayed it to Gabriel who studied the numbers with much more enjoyment than the deplorable moment warranted.

Outcome achieved, Findley smugly stuffed his contemptible papers into his portfolio, then readied to leave. "This afternoon, Cristofore?"

"As soon as I have the cash."

"Go to my banker immediately. He has orders to accommodate you."

"Marvelous. I'm looking forward to it."

"I'll show myself out. Don't bother getting up," he said to John. With that, he departed.

John scowled at his intractable, incomprehensible son, and a deafening silence ensued as they listened to Findley securing his belongings. As he exited, he was whistling with delight over how successfully the event had transpired.

With the click of the door, John's temper boiled over. "Are you proud of yourself?"

"Not particularly."

"Well, I can go you one better: I'm thoroughly ashamed of you."

"I did what I thought was best."

"Really?" John snorted derisively. "I'll be sure to tell that to Lady Elizabeth next time I run into her."

Feeling much older than his years, he retired before Gabriel could respond with any lame excuses. Despondent and despairing, he climbed the stairs, intensely glad that Mary would be waiting for him.

CHAPTER TWENTY

ELIZABETH rushed down the stairs, the skirts of her pink dress rippling behind, her hat dangling by its ribbons from her fingers. Gabriel's locket swayed from a chain around her neck, a simple, pretty complement to her gay attire. Absently, she rubbed across it, liking how its presence made her feel closer to him.

Three days! Three long, miserable, unending days since she'd visited! Their prior tryst on Friday seemed to have ensued eons ago, and now, with their Monday appointment rapidly approaching, she could barely stand the suspense.

The waiting was over! Shortly, she'd be in Gabriel's studio, in his arms, in his bed, and she quivered with delight.

Why did the bounder mean so much to her? He'd become the sun and the moon, the stars in the heavens, air and water and life itself. What a foolish, foolish woman she was to have succumbed to his charm and manipulations. With every fiber in her being, she conceded her folly, yet she couldn't desist.

Having to endure a single hour—a single minute!—without him was torment. He had given her purpose and direction, had compelled her to evaluate her present and her future. She'd been so doleful and disconsolate, then he'd burst into her staid world, like a blazing comet shooting across the sky, and nothing had been the same since.

The trivial worries about Charlotte, the irrelevant

fretting over her loss of status, her boredom and listless-
ness, none of it mattered. There was only one certitude that
carried any weight: She loved Gabriel! With her whole
soul! Peripheral factors were naught but petty distraction.
What did they signify in the face of the grand passion she
harbored for the audacious scoundrel?

On light feet, she fairly skipped along, thinking about
how glorious their preceding rendezvous had been. They'd
made love over and over. Rough and crude, slow and gentle, and every fashion in between, he'd shown her how
much he desired her, but he had displayed an abundant
quantity of devotion for her, as well. With soft professions
and tender ministrations, he'd amply proved that his heart
was fully engaged—though he continued to pretend no permanent affection.

After their fond farewell, she would never again believe his assertions that they had no destiny. She'd stood
at his door, not wanting to ever leave. Both of them had
been rumpled and sated, and he'd kissed her lingeringly in
good-bye, incapable of stopping until the clock had chimed,
signaling the conclusion of their assignation. She'd fled,
like Cinderella at the ball, but not before he'd held her tight,
whispering in Italian, then he'd touched her hair, her face,
as though committing them to memory because it would be
his final opportunity.

"Not if I have anything to say about it!" she vowed to
herself.

He might claim that their liaison was about to end, but
she wouldn't give up on them so easily. There had to be a
way by which she could persuade him that they belonged
together.

She couldn't remember precisely when the obvious solution had emerged, but it had formulated, and she couldn't
set it aside because it seemed so absolutely right: she
wanted Gabriel as her husband, and she would settle for
nothing less.

On several occasions, they'd skirted the topic. Once,

Gabriel had even intentionally attempted to scare her off. Frostily, he'd asked her if she was prepared to weather the storm that would arise if they wed.

Ashamed as she was to admit it, his ploy had worked. He had temporarily frightened her into lamenting over all she'd be surrendering if they proceeded, so she'd slinked away, too timid to broach the prospect again.

But since then, she'd critically pondered the morrow, had ruminated over the pitfalls and perils if she persisted with him, and it had dawned on her that, through matrimony, she'd be relinquishing naught that was important to her.

What did she care if others scorned her for her selection of a spouse? Why concern herself with others' opinions? If she forged ahead, what would she truly be renouncing? A few friends who'd never been close. A father who'd never been interested in her happiness. A dreadful domestic situation that consistently deteriorated and wasn't about to improve.

When the alternative was a life and family with Gabriel, the choice was so elemental, so perfect.

Yes, he'd done things in the past of which she wasn't proud. He'd had a difficult childhood. As an adult, he'd earned his income through dubious enterprise. Some might refer to him as a swindler, a cheat or a charlatan, and she was definitely cognizant of his tendencies as a libertine, but she couldn't move beyond the impression that he'd be willing to change—just for her.

They'd had many intimate discussions, and she was convinced that he was lonely, weary of his precarious existence, and eager to start over. Notwithstanding his history or his former inclinations, he was sincere, kind, and reliable, and she was confident that she could make no better decision as to whom she would marry.

Now, if she could just get the obstinate oaf to agree! As she reached the foyer, she grinned, imagining the devious, naughty ways she could wear him down. She knew exactly how to achieve her goal, too. The man couldn't resist sexual play and, as she'd detected early on, when he was physically aroused, he was putty in her hands. This was love; this was war, and she intended to win every battle.

If it took every ounce of her carnal proficiency, utilization of every lewd technique he'd taught her, he would ultimately acquiesce. She was determined to succeed, and she laughed merrily, incapable of preventing a bit of her exultation from bubbling over.

Gabriel Cristofore had never witnessed this side of her! She'd have the knave standing at the altar before he grasped what she was about!

A maid appeared with her wrap, and as she threw it over her shoulders, she glanced outside, assuring herself that the carriage was ready. She turned to go when, to her consternation, Charlotte strutted down the hall, and she groaned inwardly. She didn't have the patience to suffer through another bizarre conversation with the wretched girl!

Elizabeth couldn't figure out what had befallen Charlotte. She'd always been difficult, but now, she was acting downright strange, constantly lurking and making odd innuendos.

She seemed to be jealous or resentful of Elizabeth's newfound distractions, suspicious and watchful as to Elizabeth's conduct, though Elizabeth couldn't fathom why. Charlotte was so self-centered that she scarcely heeded those events or people who didn't directly affect her. Previously, Elizabeth's exploits had hardly registered.

"Going out?" she snidely inquired.

"Yes," Elizabeth said, offering no details.

She assessed Elizabeth's dress. "Off to visit your . . . *artist*?"

"Do you have some problem with my having my portrait painted?"

"Me?" She looked so ingenuous, so deadly. "Whatever gave you that idea?"

"You're terribly bothered by my activities." Elizabeth drew on her gloves, conferring a fierce tug for emphasis. "If there's something on your mind, spill it and be done with it."

"I have nothing to say to you, although"—she had a peculiar gleam in her eye and a feral smile on her lips—"the earl has arrived, and he might have a *word* or two he'd like to impart."

Marvelous! Just what she needed! An interview with the earl! She hadn't seen her father in days. He'd been notably absent, not even making it home for supper as he regularly did, and now that he'd deigned to surface, she couldn't be pestered with whatever trivial quandary ailed him.

Let Charlotte handle it! That's why he'd married her!

"Well, he'll have to catch up with me. I'm off."

Unfortunately, her father took that moment to approach from the rear of the house, and she bristled with frustration; she'd never escape!

"Elizabeth, I must speak with you."

"I can't, Father. I have an engagement." Hoping to avoid a conflict, she walked to the door, boldly behaving as though he'd granted his permission for her to depart.

With a pained grimace, he studied her outfit. "Are you bound for a portraiture sitting?"

"Yes." He generally paid no heed to her plans, so she was amazed that he recollected.

"You won't be able to attend."

Charlotte chuckled meanly, and Elizabeth ignored her. "But I'm expected."

"You'll have to cancel. I'm afraid this can't wait."

"Told you," Charlotte childishly chimed in.

As if he'd just noticed his wife, the earl scowled, and Elizabeth billowed with annoyance. Why, oh why, had the foolhardy man married her when—seven months later—she was all but invisible to him?

"Go to your room, Charlotte," the earl ordered.

"But I—"

"Go!" he said so forcefully that she spun away without argument and began to climb the stairs.

Before she disappeared, she smugly peered at Elizabeth over the railing. "Enjoy your *chat*."

The earl dawdled until her footsteps faded then, without comment, he left, too, and Elizabeth trudged after him, when it occurred to her that he had aged recently. He looked haggard and less forceful, having lost some of his imposing disposition, and she was overcome by the sudden conviction that he might be ill. The concept distressed her, for he'd invariably been such a powerful, compelling figure that she pictured him as being invincible.

They plodded on to his library, and he entered and went to his desk. "Please close the door."

She complied, then walked across the room and pulled up a chair. He toyed with some papers, abstractedly shuffling through them, unable to commence. She decided to ease him into what was apparently a laborious revelation. "Are you unwell, Father?"

"I'm fine." He frowned, uncharacteristically unsure of himself. "Actually, I'm not fine. I need to discuss a particular issue with you that's extremely delicate, though vital, and I'm not certain how to begin."

"You can tell me anything; you know that."

He scrutinized her in a manner that was unsettling and puzzling. "We've always been honest with one another, haven't we?"

"Yes." Anxiety escalated her pulse. Was he dying? "What is it?"

"I received a note over the weekend. It was mistakenly directed to me, and I opened it without realizing it was for you."

"A note?" Frantically, her mind whirled. Who would

have written? And what subject could have reduced him to such a state?

"Yes. I'm sorry I read it. I didn't mean to."

He retrieved the mysterious letter from a drawer, and he passed it to her, but she simply stared at it. She was frightened to touch it, which was silly, but she was discomfited by the overwhelming impression that by perusing it, her life would be forever altered.

Shaking off the absurd perception, she lifted it, and instantly, her breath hitched in her chest. Gabriel's ornate handwriting leapt off the page, and with a speed that bordered on madness, she scanned the concise content.

"This can't be . . ." She trailed off, the room dwindled to black, and she was no longer conscious of her father or her surroundings.

Gabriel never wanted to see her again! He had another paramour! He claimed that he'd met a widow with extensive funds, so he couldn't pass up the chance to become better acquainted. Brutally, he explained that she daren't drop in on him, because there was no telling what she might stumble upon, and he didn't wish her to be hurt.

Could he be so cruel? So ruthless? Had she meant so little to him?

While she'd been viewing them as star-crossed lovers who needed time to reconcile their differences, he'd been out scouring the theater lobbies, questing after more booty to plunder from some other unsuspecting female!

How could she have been so wrong about him?

As the insulting question rang out, she wrenched herself back to reality. Gabriel loved her! He did! No ridiculous letter would ever cause her to mistrust him. The inexplicable correspondence made no sense. The entire incident—the letter, his hasty *adieu*—had developed suspiciously, had left her dazed, prompting her to impugn his veracity and integrity.

Well, she wouldn't credit his disavowal! Yet, at the same juncture, a disturbing voice kept goading her: What did she really know about Gabriel? Could he have forsaken her so clumsily? If his farewell was genuine, where did that leave her?

"I did some checking, Elizabeth"—her father poked through her despair, yanking her back to the discourse he was bent on pursuing—"and I learned all about Mr. Cristofore and his licentious propensities, so I must ask you—"

"What?" She blinked as though she'd just stepped from a pitch-dark room into the bright sunlight.

"Have you been having a sexual affair with him?" When she refused to grace him with a response, he gently prodded, "I would hear it from your own lips, daughter."

Insolently, she stared him down. She couldn't discuss her remarkable romance. Not because she was abashed or embarrassed, but because the meetings at Gabriel's cottage were among her few precious memories, and she wasn't about to share them with anyone.

Seizing the offensive, she shot back, "How did you find out?"

"So you admit it, then?"

"Tell me how you discovered it!"

"It doesn't matter."

"It does to me." They glared at one another, and it dawned on her that she already knew how it had come about. "Charlotte, was it? Did you urge her to sneak about after me, or did she take the initiative on her own?"

"Don't impute Charlotte because you were caught in a peccadillo of your own creation."

Too true, she thought bitterly. "No wonder she's been acting so curiously. She must be positively gleeful."

Without warning, tears flooded to the surface, not due to Charlotte's perfidy or her father's censure, but from the staggering sense of loss that was swamping her over the likelihood that she'd never see Gabriel again.

How could she bear to carry on?

"What now?" she queried.

"There's no easy way to raise this." Nervously, he

drummed on the desktop. "Might there be a babe?"

"I'm not sure . . . ah . . . how I would know."

"So, it's a possibility?"

At the query, she peered down at the rug, finally too chagrined to maintain eye contact. When she'd been locked in the throes of passion with Gabriel, any capricious outcome had seemed desirable—even a babe—but with her father diligently appraising her in the quiet of his study, his disappointment and displeasure patently clear, she merely felt imprudent and immature, a woman who had recklessly and heedlessly plunged ahead with no regard for the consequences.

Well, they would rain down on her now and, as her father had pointed out, she had no one to blame but herself for whatever shame she would reap, for whatever punishment the earl would deign to mete out.

"Well, darling," he soothed, "don't fret over it. We'll have our answer in a few weeks."

Elizabeth could only concentrate on the endearment. In twenty-seven years, he'd never referred to her as *darling*, and it ignited a spark of optimism that perhaps things wouldn't end too badly.

"I'm sending you to Norwich," he said. "If circumstances take a turn for the worse"—she assumed that he meant a pregnancy—"we'll reassess our position."

"Why?"

"We'll need another location for your confinement. Someplace secluded and private so that no one will ever know of your disgrace."

As he dismissed her *amour* with Gabriel as nothing more than a humiliation that had to be hidden from others, the tears that had been hovering flowed profusely, and she swiped at them.

How could her great ardor be terminated like this?

"Now, then"—he continued placating her, appearing incredibly sympathetic, more so than she'd ever supposed he could be—"you'll pack your bags and leave for Norwich today. You'll be gone for at least a month. Maybe two." He came around the desk and patted her shoulder. "We want to provide Mr. Cristofore with plenty of opportunity to vacate the premises, so he won't ever plague us again."

She was still staring at the floor, when the import of his statement sank in, and she lurched upright. "You saw him," she accused. "You spoke with him."

She jumped up and, taken aback by her vehemence, he scurried away, seeking the security of his desk once more. "Don't be absurd. As if I would personally confer with such an unrepentant villain!"

"You're lying." Abruptly furious, she braced her palms on the desktop, and leaned across. "Father, what have you done?"

"Nothing. You're spewing nonsense."

She whipped away, berating herself for being so quick to doubt Gabriel. "I don't believe anything you've said."

"You have to, Elizabeth."

"You coerced him into writing that letter, didn't you?" Panicked, alarmed, she could just imagine how dastardly her father might have behaved. "I must talk with him."

"I can't let you."

She cast about, so overwrought that she couldn't spot the doorway. Before she could gain her bearings to flee, the earl was by her side, a restraining hand on her arm.

"Elizabeth, listen to me: the man isn't who you think he is."

"Don't try to convince me of what he's like!" she contended in a near shout. "You don't know anything about him."

"I know more than I wish I did." He was holding tight on to her arm so she couldn't retreat, and he propelled her toward his desk, picking up the papers that had been so neatly piled and shoving them under her nose. "Look at what I have here! Just look! *This* is how little regard he has for you!"

At first, in her distraught condition, she couldn't focus,

but gradually, she began to decipher the words, and they were devastatingly harsh.

"*I, Gabriel Cristofore, do admit and affirm that I have had illicit sexual intercourse with Lady Elizabeth Harcourt, daughter of the Earl of Norwich . . .*"

Frenetically, she skimmed bits and pieces.

"*. . . the relationship was at my complete inducement and instigation . . . I am fully responsible for any and all damages, including loss of her chastity . . .*"

She wasn't proceeding rapidly enough to suit her father, and he yanked the pages from her and shifted to the last one. "Here. Read this!"

"*As compensation for my agreement never to contact Lady Elizabeth again, I consent to accept the proffered amount . . .*"

Her attention was riveted on the bottom line, where his signature condemned him.

Yet, even though the inscription was there, and plainly visible, she couldn't believe it. "This is a forgery. It has to be. And the letter, too. You faked them!"

"No, they're real as I am." .

"They're falsehoods you conjured. To confuse me. To dissuade me."

"He *volunteered* to write the damned letter, and he couldn't wait to sign the contract."

"You pressured him into it somehow."

"I confess it! I did! With money! *He* negotiated the price for which he'd settle!"

"No, no," she wailed. "Gabriel would never do that to me."

"You'd be surprised at the sins a man will commit if enough cash is waved in front of him."

"So, you're alleging it was all his idea? That he was eager?" She was enraged, incredulous.

"I offered, and he snatched it up like that." The earl snapped his fingers.

"Oh, Father, how could you?" She jerked free of his

grasp. "He was the only thing that mattered to me. The only thing I cared about." Tears gushed down her cheeks, and she swallowed past the lump in her throat. "The only thing that brought me any joy."

"He never deserved you!" the earl asserted hotly. "Neither your loyalty nor your love, and he assuredly doesn't now! Not after this . . . this treachery!" He grabbed her shoulders and shook her, hard. "Don't you understand? You were a mark, a prize to be auctioned off when the time was right. He made out like a bloody bandit."

"It wasn't like that! *He* isn't like that." She took a step away, then another. "I'll never forgive you for this as long as I live."

Then, she twirled around and ran as fast as she could.

"Elizabeth!" he bellowed.

Exasperated, he paused for a lengthy period, and his delay permitted her to gain momentum. Then, he was chasing after her, his heavy, authoritative footsteps lumbering down the hall, but rage and anguish were propelling her beyond his ability to catch her.

She had to meet with Gabriel, face-to-face. She had to look him in the eye and ask him if what her father maintained was accurate. If she was standing before him, he couldn't lie to her, he couldn't vacillate or prevaricate. Lest her heart be rent in two, she had to ascertain the facts: how the confrontation had been joined, how the encounter had evolved, how the bargain had been sealed.

Had Gabriel betrayed her? Had her father? Had they *both* schemed against her, neither of them having any authentic compassion or affection for her?

Grievously agitated, she dashed outside, and vaulted into the carriage, barking out Gabriel's direction to her driver who'd been patiently anticipating her arrival. Sensing her perturbation, he cracked the whip so that the horses raced down the drive and into the street, and they were well away before the earl followed her out, still shouting her name.

*   *   *

Charlotte slid away from her covert post next to the hearth, then tiptoed to the corridor and peeked out. No servants were passing by, so she nonchalantly strolled to her bedchamber. As she deliciously replayed the quarrel she'd just eavesdropped upon, a malicious smile crossed her face.

Revenge was so very sweet!

In her room, one of the maids was tidying up.

"You, there! Have my carriage brought around," she decreed. "It's such a splendid day. I believe I'll go shopping. I'm in the mood for a new gown. Perhaps a new hat."

As the inept servant scuttled away, Charlotte tarried at her mirror, primping her curls, and waiting for the announcement that her coach was ready.

CHAPTER TWENTY-ONE

GABRIEL tossed a last handful of clothes into his portmanteau, then walked to the stairs. It had been a long while since he'd packed his bags and fled on the spur of the moment. He and John had escaped numerous locales over the years of Gabriel's childhood, chased by crazed relatives, debt collectors, or angry husbands who'd had enough of John's lecherous habits.

As a youth, Gabriel had enjoyed their hasty exits, viewing them as a grand lark. Upon adult reflection, he was sure they'd been more frightening than he'd ever surmised, but John had always acted as though they were off on another fabulous adventure, carefully hiding the precise level of peril.

He was used to living out of a valise, making do, getting by, but as he reached the foyer, he conceded that he hadn't missed those daft times one bit. There was something to be said for stability, for constancy and balance, and though he hoped his departure would be transitory, he resentfully regretted that he was constrained to leave at all.

For the foreseeable future, he couldn't remain. Elizabeth would come; he was certain of it. Norwich would temporarily restrain her behavior to prevent her from visiting—either through cajoling or more drastic measures—but eventually, she'd sneak away. She'd be determined to learn why Gabriel had broken off with her again.

Hadn't she previously rushed to him, demanding answers, when he'd tried to separate himself? And that was before they'd become lovers!

She would badger him for an explanation and, coward that he was, he simply couldn't face her. He couldn't justify what he'd done. He could only run—and hide—a trick at which he'd excelled for most of his life.

John's current sentiments also had to be considered. In light of his father's pique, absence was preferable. He and John were two strong-willed individuals, so they'd had their share of differences, their squabbles and spats, but there'd never been any lingering hostility. They were too close, and had endured too much, to be at odds.

Yet on this occasion, John was fit to be tied, more angry than Gabriel had ever seen him, and not inclined to forgive as was his wont. For once, Gabriel had pushed him beyond his limits, but with the way Gabriel was feeling, he wasn't about to apologize.

He was the one who'd had to stomach the insult and abuse from Norwich. *He* was the one who'd had to bite his tongue as the pompous ass had spewed and strutted in their parlor. *He* was the one who'd perceived the perfect opportunity for enrichment and had grasped it, but was John satisfied?

No. And Gabriel was furious that he wasn't.

Norwich had swaggered off, arrogantly and foolishly assuming that he'd been the victor when, in all actuality, he was too stupid to realize that Gabriel had swindled him out of thousands of pounds—without expending any effort!

The earl had paid Gabriel extravagantly to do what he'd been preparing for all along, that being to end the *relazione* with Elizabeth, but John hadn't so much as patted Gabriel on the back for his quick thinking or his clever resolution of a desperate situation. There'd been no congratulations. No compliments. No celebratory toasting to their success.

Instead, John claimed that a grave injury had been done to Elizabeth, when nothing could be further from the truth.

John and Norwich were bitter enemies, and Gabriel had routed the toplofty boor in the easiest deception in which he'd ever engaged, but John couldn't be bothered to display a hint of gratitude. Gabriel was righteously fuming, and he couldn't guess when he might calm.

His affair with Elizabeth had been winding down, but he hadn't been strong enough to end it, nor had she possessed the fortitude to say good-bye and really mean it. They'd continued on, into the realm where discovery was likely at every turn.

Due to their folly, the worst had transpired. Her father had exposed their peccadillo, which had caused the farewell to ensue a tad sooner than expected, and it had been more abrupt than either of them might have anticipated, but the clean break was an apt result. He was convinced of it, so John could go hang.

Despite John's clamoring, Gabriel's ploy—to dupe the earl out of his money—was a fantastic solution that had never occurred to him prior to the earl's unwelcome appearance. He was ecstatic that he'd been shrewd enough to react beneficially, that an extreme profit had been attained from the ordeal.

Norwich was a sly, astute man. He'd deal with Elizabeth carefully, so there was no chance she'd ever find out about the agreement they'd signed. Briefly, she'd be upset, she'd fume and fuss over how they'd been detected, or over why Gabriel had left with no word of *arrivederci*. But her vexation would inevitably pass, and their liaison would be terminated as had always been the predicted outcome.

So where was the harm?

He'd endeavored to explain as much to John, but John wouldn't listen, and Gabriel was tired of attempting to clarify his decision. So he was leaving—and he didn't know when he'd be back. Perhaps never.

With a heavy heart, and a huge amount of temper motivating him, he dropped his bag onto the tiled floor, then went to the stand next to the door and retrieved his coat.

Just as he would have donned it, Mary slipped out of the parlor down the hall.

He groaned. While he liked her very much, and John had picked well, he really didn't know her, and he wasn't comfortable discussing what had happened. They weren't in a position where confidences could be bandied. Besides, she was Elizabeth's friend! No doubt, John had provided her with the shameful particulars as to Gabriel's wretched conduct.

What could he possibly add in his own defense that wouldn't sound appalling?

Up until now, she'd judiciously avoided butting into the mess, apparently feeling that—as a newcomer in the house—her opinions wouldn't be appreciated, and he wasn't thrilled to have her tendering them at this late juncture. In his present mood, he hadn't the necessary composure to be civil, to sugarcoat or minimize, in order not to offend her feminine sensibilities. He was mad as hell, and wasn't about to blithely chat as though naught was amiss.

"Were you going to say good-bye?"

"No."

"Not even to John?"

"Especially not to him."

She chuckled. "I suppose it wouldn't hurt for the two of you to cool off."

He shrugged, unwilling to furnish his thoughts on the subject.

"Do you have any idea of when you'll return?"

She was so confident that he would! "I'm not sure."

"Where are you headed?"

"It's springtime, and I enjoy the beach. So maybe Brighton; I haven't decided."

"You can paint seascapes, then sell them to wealthy travelers who are there on holiday." She tipped her head side to side, musing. "Not a bad plan."

How curious that she'd deduced his intentions, when he hadn't yet settled on a strategy himself! All he knew was that he had to be away. The details were up in the air. And she was so assured that he'd be painting once he selected his destination. In periods of trouble or distress, he painted more rabidly than ever, his creativity an outlet that afforded solace and contentment.

"I might do that," he said vaguely. "I might not."

"While you're gone, I'd like to show some of your work to an acquaintance of mine. I'm positive he could help us find a patron for you."

The woman was a ceaseless whirlwind of activity and, in spite of his ill-humor, he grinned. "Whatever makes you happy, Mary. I have no objection."

"Marvelous."

Surprisingly, she reached for his outerwear and aided him in putting it on, and the kind gesture was immensely touching. Strangely, it seemed as if his mother was helping him, and the silly notion induced him to suffer the old loss in a painful fashion, making him speculate as to how much he'd forfeited by being denied Selena's company.

Would he have been a different man, a better man, had she lived?

"Look after John for me."

"I will."

She was smiling at him so sweetly that he felt eight years old again, and in drastic need of a mother's love and understanding. He didn't want to go! He yearned to stay at home with Mary, to become friends with her, to mend his quarrel with John, to achieve a swift reconciliation.

Get a grip on yourself! he silently chastised.

He forced evenness into his tone. "I'm glad you're here for him."

"I'm glad he's here for me!" She rose up and kissed him on the cheek. "Send us a note when you have a chance. Just so we know where you are and that you're all right."

He studied her, pondering how lucky John was to have crossed paths with her, then, like an impulsive lummox, he blurted out, "I was certain you intended to scold me."

"For what?"

"Well—" He blushed, incapable of verbalizing his sins.

"Would a thorough upbraiding have done any good?"

"No."

"I didn't think so." A prudent, sensible person, she laughed pleasantly. "I love Elizabeth like a daughter, and I only want what's best for her, but I don't imagine it's you. If it was, you wouldn't be running away."

"I'm not running."

"Aren't you?"

Frantically, he craved the opportunity to account and exonerate himself to this woman who he suspected would comprehend at least some of his confusion and anguish. He longed to tell her about Elizabeth, how it had been between them, to confess that he loved her, how he'd cut off his right arm before he'd maltreat her, but there was no valid reason to expound.

Justifications were a waste of breath. He'd given Elizabeth a chance to cast her lot with him, and she'd declined to seize it. She'd often dallied prospects in front of him, implying that she was envisioning a future, but her insinuations had been nothing but capricious daydreams.

On that one dismal occasion, when he'd grown weary of her artifice, he'd pointed out the obstacles that she'd have to confront if she truly fancied him for a husband. He'd enumerated every hurdle she'd be required to jump, and in response, he'd received a quick and sobering dose of reality: Not only had she shied away from the impediments, she'd never again mentioned marriage.

Elizabeth would never debase herself so completely. He'd adjusted to the harsh facts. He didn't like them, but there wasn't anything he could do to alter them.

"I want what's best for Elizabeth, too," he asserted. "She'll be around, looking for me."

"Yes, she will."

"It's *best* if I'm not here."

"I agree," she said, and she opened the door. "Go directly to the bank to obtain your money." She patted his pocket where Norwich's offending bank draft irritatingly rested in a secure envelope. "I know Findley Harcourt exceptionally well. Don't trust him."

"I don't."

"A wise man."

"Good-bye, Mary."

"Not 'good-bye,' " she declared. "How about: See you soon?"

"How about?"

His carriage was ready and waiting, his belongings loaded, and he ambled out into the sunny afternoon. It hadn't shined in weeks. How could it dare to brighten the sky on this horrid day?

He was just about to toss his portmanteau in the boot when charging horses' hooves clopped down their lane. To his dismay, he recognized one of the Norwich vehicles, and he bristled with frustration. Not two hours had passed since Norwich's departure, and Gabriel had packed as rapidly as he could, but it obviously hadn't been fast enough.

What was the matter with the earl? Couldn't he harness his daughter's impetuosity for even a few minutes? How had the man bungled this so hideously? What was Gabriel supposed to do now?

He couldn't speak with her! Couldn't exculpate or rationalize! Nor could he bear to witness her agony! Gad, what if she begged him to change his mind? He couldn't ignore her entreaties. In light of her torment, how could he remain firm?

After all that had transpired so far, he simply couldn't tolerate another emotional scene. His well of patience had run dry, and an unaccustomed fury raged through him. At Elizabeth. At her father. At his own. At himself. His sole motivation had been to do what was right, to make the appropriate moves. For her. So that she would be protected and shielded from the earl's undue wrath. But how could he accomplish his goals when she wrongly inflicted herself into the resolution?

Where was her blasted father? Wasn't any of this fiasco his burden to shoulder? Why should Gabriel be the one to dash her hopes? By everyone's reckoning, he'd already done more than enough!

The conveyance rattled to a halt behind his own, and he was enormously relieved to see Norwich, an outrider at his flank, far down the street and pursuing her on horseback. He'd exited his house in such haste that he hadn't even donned a hat.

Gabriel braced, praying there would be some delay before Elizabeth was handed down, and that her father would arrive to handle the mess before her dainty little foot settled upon the walk, but Elizabeth was too distraught to await the coachman. The second the latch was turned, she was out and through, and the retainer had to catch her, lest she fall to the ground. The servant steadied her, then stepped away, overtly aware of his mistress's disturbance and wanting no part of whatever altercation was pending.

She was wearing the pink dress, and his mother's locket hung between her pretty breasts. The skirts floated and swirled around her legs, her hair was down. Evidently, she'd been attired for their appointment, just when Norwich would have told her she couldn't attend.

She'd been crying, her nose was red, and tears splotched her cheeks. His heart lurched at the sight, but he hardened his stance.

He would get through this!

"Elizabeth!" her father shouted from down the block, but she paid him no heed. Her sharp gaze was on Gabriel, on the tote sitting at his feet, on the open boot and the other bags within.

"You're really leaving," she said.

"*Sì.*"

"I didn't believe him." She swallowed. "How could you go like this?"

"Is there some reason I should have tarried?" The question was harsh, and brutally posed, but he didn't know how else to comport himself.

The earl reined in his horse and alighted, just as Mary noted the brewing tempest and chose to intervene. She and the earl both approached Elizabeth, and Norwich clasped her arm.

"Come with me, Elizabeth," her father said rigidly but compassionately.

Shaking off his grasp, she stubbornly refused to budge. Staring Gabriel down, she demanded, "Tell me one thing."

"If I'm able." Gabriel pressed his hands behind his back, clamping his fingers together so that he could not reach out to her or push Norwich away.

"Did you ever feel anything for me besides lust?"

His ire peaked. How could she dispute his affection? Especially in front of her father! He couldn't abide the prig!

"You're a fine woman."

"That's the best you can do?"

Resentment swamped him. "What do you want from me?"

"The truth."

Ah . . . the truth. An interesting, fluid concept. "What *truth* would that be?"

"My father admits that he propositioned you. That he insisted you break off with me."

"We discussed it."

"He maintains that he offered to pay you."

"Yes, he did."

"But he swears that *you* negotiated the price. That you were eager."

Clearly, she'd embraced whatever story the earl had woven, and he wasn't about to dissuade her. "I was."

"He contends that your affair with me was nothing but a swindle to the very end. That you never cared a whit for me."

He raised a brow, but provided no rejoinder. She had

so little faith in him! In his level of fondness or devotion! Her lack of confidence galled.

Mary interceded, sidling nearer, and indicating, "People on the street are watching. Let's go inside, shall we?"

Elizabeth didn't so much as glance in her direction. "Father wasn't lying, was he?"

"No."

"It was all feigned on your part. Every bit of it." Derisively, she shook her head, her chagrin profound. "What a fool you must think me to be."

No, no, he yearned to shout. But he said nothing. He did nothing.

"And your *widow* . . . Were you searching for her while you were seducing me?" When he didn't reply, she added, "Of course you were. How stupid of me to inquire."

Her scorn jabbed like a knife, at his vulnerabilities, at his pride, and he couldn't stop himself from saying, "A fellow has to earn a living."

"Bastard!" she cursed, wounding him with the epithet and the vehemence with which it was uttered.

"Elizabeth!" Mary and the earl both hissed, as shocked as Gabriel by her fervor.

Though he recognized that her temper was simmering as fiercely as his own, and she meant it in the general—not literal—sense, it was not a designation he casually indulged. If she'd been a man, he'd have beaten her to a pulp, then and there, or perhaps called her out. As it was, he couldn't see how he would ever forgive her for expressing the sentiment.

"Some of us were born to base tendencies," he said impassively, declining to let her perceive how terribly the slur had cut. "We can't help ourselves."

"Out of all the women in the world, why did you pick me?"

Petty as it was, he wanted to hurt her as much as she'd just hurt him. To belittle and offend and desolate. He shrugged and said, "Because you were lonely. And you were easy."

Mary gasped at the ugly remark. Elizabeth's reaction was a tad more vicious. She slapped him as hard as she could, her palm ringing with the ferocious contact. His head whipped to the side, but other than that involuntary bodily recoil, he didn't move, permitting her the opportunity to vent her indignity.

Snatching at the delicate chain that held his mother's locket, she yanked it from her neck and threw it at him. He didn't grab for it, and it bounced off his chest and slithered to the sidewalk.

Then, she whirled around and stormed to her coach. The footman who'd observed from a polite distance lifted her in, slammed the door, and the driver whisked her away.

An odd tableau, he lingered with Mary and the earl, a paralyzed trio that didn't stir until her carriage disappeared around the corner. Norwich jolted them to consciousness, turning to Gabriel.

"My apologies," he said, clearing his throat and adjusting his skewed cravat. "That was unpleasant."

Gabriel wasn't about to converse with the ass whom he held responsible for the entire, sordid incident. "In the future, sir, I would suggest that you exercise some control over your daughter. See to it that I am not bothered again—by her or by you."

He spun away, but Norwich clenched at his arm, impeding retreat. Gabriel frowned at the spot where Norwich touched him, then impaled him with such a virulent look that the earl immediately dropped his hand.

"You'll stick to our agreement, won't you?" Norwich asked. "You'll take the money and go. Despite this . . . this unfortunate circumstance?"

"Findley!" Mary chided. "For pity's sake!"

"He can't back out now," Norwich complained. "I won't let him."

"Don't worry about our precious *agreement*," Gabriel

assured him, sickened by the whole bloody affair. "I'm on my way to your banker even as we speak. Now"—he stepped away, needing to put ample space between himself and the despicable swine—"get the hell out of my yard."

Norwich harrumphed. Embarrassed and disconcerted, he awkwardly bowed to Mary, stomped to his horse, and rode off.

As he faded from view, Gabriel deflated as if the air had left his body. His limbs were liquid, his legs powerless to support his weight. The detestable spectacle had been inordinately trying. He was overwrought, weary, spent, his cheek smarting from Elizabeth's blow, his self-esteem and confidence shattered.

In his tenuous condition, he craved solitude while he recovered some of his aplomb and poise, but Mary dawdled, studying him, her shrewd regard absorbing every nuance of his distressed disposition. He abhorred that she could discern so much, that she could perceive how his heart was breaking.

There was no viable interpretation he could give for Elizabeth's hate-filled statements or his own. The lone explication was that he loved her, his ardor so intense that it pushed him beyond reason or sense.

Without a word, he stooped and picked up the damaged pendant, then hurled his bag into the carriage. Clutching at the strap, he was ready to hoist himself in, when she advanced from behind. Comfortingly, she rested her hand on the small of his back and stroked in soothing circles, and he flinched, lest he relax into her gentle caress.

"Come into the house."

"No, thank you."

"You can't leave when you're in such a state. I won't allow it."

"Did you forget?" He stared straight ahead, not wanting to look at her over his shoulder. "I have to visit Norwich's banker so I can retrieve my damned money."

"Blast the money! You don't care about it."

"No, I don't."

He sighed, fatigued, worn down and out by the abominable events. If only he could set the clock forward so that he could leap beyond this loathsome day, this vile experience! After an extensive period, his rancor and bitterness over the foul disaster would wane, but for now, he could only ruminate, chafe—and flee.

"Please don't go," she tried again. "Not like this."

"Let it be, Mary." Spurning her sympathy, he climbed inside, shutting the door in her face so that he was cloistered alone in the dark, and he quietly repeated, "Just let it be."

The carriage rocked and jingled, and he was finally away. He leaned against the squab and stared out at the busy street, seeing nothing as he passed.

CHAPTER TWENTY-TWO

ELIZABETH strolled along the winding path, blindly staring at the extensive gardens. The month of June was always beautiful at Norwich, the flowers in full bloom, the hedges and shrubbery meticulously trimmed, but in light of her persisting melancholia, she failed to notice.

She rounded the corner, and before she had opportunity to reflect, she was standing next to the gazebo, which vividly reminded her of why she never strolled in the yard at the rear of the manor. For lengthy periods, she could forget that it was situated as the focal point of the garden's design, then she'd go walking, as now, and stumble upon it. On each occasion, its presence sneaked up on her, taking her unawares.

For once, she didn't scurry away. She faced it, studying it dispassionately, and her ability to do so was comforting, for it implied that her condition was improving.

Since that dreadful March afternoon in London, when she'd confronted Gabriel, she'd been in a state. Any retrospection had produced such despondency that she hadn't been able to review the event, but for the past week or two, she'd mended to where she could recall the episode without the exhaustive despair that typically accompanied any reminiscence.

As a result, she'd thoroughly analyzed the incident, and she was consistently surprised that every nuance was so distinct.

She'd said some absolutely horrid things to Gabriel,

comments she wished she could retract, so of course, he'd
expressed some perfectly hideous remarks, too.

Time and distance made her grasp that he couldn't
have meant any of them. He'd simply been as distressed
and angry as she. She knew her father, and she was forced
to admit that, before her precipitous arrival, Gabriel had
likely received some fairly abominable treatment from Findley Harcourt, then she'd come charging in, demonstrating
some abundantly offensive conduct of her own.

Try as she might to justify her actions, there was no
defense she could make. She'd been so hurt by what he'd
done—and hadn't done. Her sense of outrage and betrayal
seemed to have driven her to temporary lunacy.

Why . . . she'd been so distraught that she'd actually
struck him! Gabriel! Whom she'd loved beyond imagining!
As she'd never previously lashed out physically at another,
she'd had no idea that she harbored such passionate, violent
tendencies.

Lamentably, she could recollect every aspect of that
appalling instant when her hand had connected with his
cheek, when his head had snapped to the side. She'd been
so furious that if she'd been holding a pistol, she might
have shot the knave right in the middle of his black heart.

Even now, all these months later, she could feel the
sensation as though she'd just delivered the blow. Her fingers would tingle and sting, and she had to resist the urge
to massage her palm.

What a monstrous deed!

Sporadically, she wondered if he had any concept of
how sorry she was, of the guilt and remorse that weighed
her down. Though perhaps he never thought of her, that
she'd been such an irritating, irksome detail in an otherwise
full life that he could no longer conjure her name or bring
her identity into clear focus.

The pavilion loomed menacingly, and she neared, refusing to take the path that skirted around the decorative
building.

Braver recently, she boldly walked up to it and steadied a foot on the bottom step. An inanimate object, wood and paint, it had no power to cause permanent emotional injury, but it definitely had the ability to stir memories.

Of a pink party dress. A pretty straw hat with a curling ribbon. A winsome, happy woman who'd been smiling and laughing as an artist had portrayed her beside a rose trellis.

Sometimes, when she was being exceptionally morbid, she speculated as to what had ever happened to that painting. Had Gabriel finished it? Or rather, after her ignominious scene, had he stomped to the cottage and burned it—piece by tiny piece—in the stove?

If she was really bent on torturing herself, she'd postulate how, in the distant future, she might blunder across it hanging in a gallery. He'd be famous, the old portrait displayed as a sample of his early style.

What would be its title? *Woman in a Pink Dress. Woman in the Garden.* Or perchance *The Gazebo,* with no reference to herself as being in the picture.

More often, she ruminated about the dozens and dozens of sketches he'd completed, some innocuous, some suggestive, and some blatantly erotic.

Her sensual adventure had been tantalizing, and she'd relished being reckless enough to engage in such rash behavior, but now that her carnal escapade had been exposed and terminated, she couldn't help obsessing over those drawings.

What had Gabriel done with them? She didn't believe he'd ever show them to anybody or—heaven forbid!—sell them, but she'd rest easier if she knew where they were. They weren't the sort of thing one would want floating about.

Disdainfully, she thought of her father. Wouldn't he die of mortification if he was apprised of their existence!

She'd never discussed them with him, just as she'd never talked about Gabriel. Gabriel had been too dear, and her father too despicable. He didn't deserve explanations, and she remained so vexed over his conduct that she was tempted to divulge the sketches just so she could witness how intense his affront would grow to be.

Humored and haunted by her fractious musings, she turned away and rambled to the verandah, when it struck her that she was bored with the country. Her elevated ennui was a valuable indication that she was vastly recovered, though recuperation wasn't necessarily a blessing.

If she began to feel more like her old self, what would she do? The notion of traveling to London, of sharing a house with Charlotte and her father, was so abhorrent that she couldn't contemplate it.

So far, she'd been spared the indignity of having to contend with either one of them. When she'd returned from the pitiful exhibition at Gabriel's, Charlotte had been markedly absent—perhaps the earl had locked her in her room—but they'd all been fortunate the shrew hadn't been waiting to gloat and criticize.

If she had been, Elizabeth was quite sure she'd now be on trial for murder. After having hit Gabriel, her vicious propensities were firmly established, so she'd have had no qualms about strangling Charlotte. In view of Elizabeth's mental plight during those fateful hours, she wouldn't have suffered any guilt over the crime, convinced that she was doing the world a favor.

As to her father, she was still so irate over his duplicity that civil conversation was inconceivable. Although they'd eventually reach a juncture at which they could courteously parley, she wasn't anywhere close.

Fortuitously, since she'd left town, she hadn't had to speak with him again. He hadn't had the nerve to visit Norwich, though he'd written a few letters. His invasive inquests were answered with terse notes that insinuated she was fine, which was a lie.

Once it had been verified that there was no babe, his insincere correspondence had thankfully dwindled to zero.

Apparently, with scandal averted, he couldn't be bothered with asking after her health.

The staff had been the only method by which such furtive information could have been transmitted to him, so a servant had to have been passing on intimate reports, but Elizabeth hadn't cared how he learned the news. Her agitation had been such that nothing had troubled her, nothing had mattered, not even the certitude that retainers whom she'd known since childhood had been spying on her, eavesdropping, or opening her mail.

The sole eventuality that induced a stir was the fact that pregnancy had not occurred. The loss had disturbed her immensely.

Her maid had clarified the situation on a quiet afternoon when she had brought clean pads for Elizabeth's monthly use. After their private chat, Elizabeth had been uncommonly, inexplicably morose.

If she had been increasing, she'd have been gifted with a part of Gabriel that could have always been hers! A babe. A little girl with his blue eyes and artistic talent. Or a little boy with his flamboyant, charismatic personality. When she shut her eyes, she could see a child so clearly.

She had nothing of Gabriel's to call her own. Not a baby, and certainly nothing less remarkable. No special mementos, no tokens of his affection. In the midst of their affair, she'd been too timid to carry anything home, lest any trinket be discovered and give her away. So she'd kept no souvenirs. Not even the locket containing the portrait of his mother.

It had been the lone object of his in her custody, yet in her fit of pique, she'd ripped it off and thrown it away. Oh, but to have it back! A keepsake of that magic time!

As it was, she had only her recollections, and they were fading. What would she recall in six months? In a year? In ten?

She looked down the road and was terrified that she might start to question whether any of it had really transpired. That there might be a day when she wasn't positive. If she'd had the foresight to retain some concrete trinket as proof, she'd never have any doubts.

On a sigh, she wandered into the house. It was stuffy inside, the atmosphere oppressive—she hadn't previously noticed—and she tarried at the entrance. Should she exit again so that she could persist with her aimless strolling? Or should she proceed to her bedchamber where she would lounge in the window seat while she rued and moped?

What dismal choices!

Was this to be how the rest of her life was to play out? Would she forever roam about at Norwich, a mere shadow of her former self? She couldn't return to her father's residence. She had no funds whereby she could purchase her own accommodation. Her only other viable recourse was to request that her father find her a husband, which she would never do.

What was left to her, then?

Was she to loiter in the country, to laze and idle away until she was aged and senile?

She could hear it now, the tsking of the neighbors. *How sad,* they would say. *How tragic.*

A laughingstock, a topic of gossip in London drawing rooms, she'd be whispered about, and incessantly slandered, as Norwich's demented, barely functional adult daughter, who'd been sent down and never permitted out in society again.

Mad as a hatter, people would claim. *Unstable, heedless, temperamental.*

She wanted so much more for herself than to be denounced as the earl's slightly delirious daughter. Where once, a subdued, peaceful existence had suited her, now the prospect of abiding as a forlorn old maid was the most dreary, discouraging contingency she could conjure.

Churlishly, she sauntered down the hall, just as the butler hurried up with the unexpected announcement that she had a visitor. The message set her heart to pounding. Who could it be?

Gabriel! The caprice rattled through her mind before she could stop it. *He'd finally come!* Had he forgiven her? Did he love her after all? Would he give her another chance?

The frantic thoughts raged, making her dizzy, so that when the retainer proffered her guest's card, she had to scan the inscription over and over before she could decipher the ornate printing.

"Dudley Thumberton." The name was unfamiliar, and she pronounced it aloud as if—verbalized—his identity would be clear. "Attorney-at-law and . . . Solicitor of the High Court of Chancery?"

She cited his impressive mode of employment as a question, and the butler shrugged; his concession that he had no clue as to why the illustrious man had arrived.

Why would a solicitor call on her? She couldn't think of a single reason. What could he want? Surely nothing good!

Wary, she struggled for composure as she thanked the butler and hastened down the hall. In spite of his dismissal, she couldn't shake him, though, and he dogged her heels, then butted in front of her so he could make a grand proclamation of her entrance into the salon.

Mr. Thumberton rose and bowed graciously over her hand. He was a stout, older fellow, in his sixties, with a rotund belly, balding pate, huge sideburns, and incredibly kind eyes.

"Sit, sir, please," she urged. On meeting him, she wasn't nearly as nervous as she'd deemed she would be. He looked harmless, more like a jolly elf than a stern officer of the court.

While she was terribly intrigued and without patience, she hid her restlessness, assuming her role as hostess, but he declined her offers of refreshment—for which she was extremely grateful. She couldn't bear to dally over inanities when such an odd dialogue was about to ensue. After all, how many times would she have the opportunity to secretly palaver with a solicitor?

"I'm sure you're curious as to why I'm here," he commenced and, with his straightforward introduction, she almost collapsed with relief.

"To put it mildly."

"I've been retained by a gentleman in London. I believe you're acquainted with him." In a dreadful state of anticipation, she held her breath as he retrieved some papers from a portfolio and laid them on the table. "My client is Mr. Gabriel Cristofore Preston."

"Gabriel—" she murmured audibly, relishing the sound. Since she'd fled town in disgrace, she hadn't uttered his name to another soul. It was beginning to seem as if he wasn't a genuine human being, but someone she'd created in an absurd flight of fancy.

Peculiarly, he queried, "So you know to whom I refer?"

Gabriel had thought that she would deny their association! As if she would! He must have mentioned that it was likely, and the realization pained her. How could he presume that she was still so incensed? The scoundrel knew her better than that!

"At one time," she acknowledged, "he was my best friend."

"How lucky for you," the solicitor broached. "He seems like a fine man."

"He is," she concurred. "I always thought he was remarkable."

"I'm glad to hear you admit as much. Mr. Cristofore had voiced some skepticism as to your opinion on the subject. I take it the two of you had a falling-out?"

"It was hideous," she caught herself confirming. "It was all my fault. I was upset, and I said some appalling things."

"Funny," Mr. Thumberton chuckled, "but Mr. Cristofore made exactly the same comment when I conferred with him in London."

"We're both hardheaded."

"He said that, too."

"What are you to tell me?" She couldn't dawdle over the niceties. Her hopes were spiraling, her confidence soaring. Did Gabriel wish to make amends? Why else would he have sent Mr. Thumberton if not for a reconciliation?

"Mr. Cristofore has charged me with delivering several items that belong to you."

"What?" She was confused. She hadn't left any possessions at the cottage.

He motioned behind the sofa, to the corner, where she hadn't noticed a large package, covered with brown paper, that was balanced against a chair.

"You commissioned Mr. Cristofore to paint your portrait."

"Yes."

That's all this was? A business transaction?

Her spirits plummeted. She felt as if a hole had been rent in her core, and her reserve of energy was flowing out across the floor. She'd been so positive that his message would be of atonement and absolution! This cold, indifferent contact was too agonizing to be believed.

"Many thanks to you," she managed to mumble.

"He apologizes for taking so long, but he was detained by personal events. He hopes you will excuse the delay."

"Certainly."

She was hardly able to focus on what he was saying and, a considerate man, he pretended he hadn't observed her misery. He continued on, searching through his satchel for another package. This was also cloaked in brown paper, with string and several intricate knots as a precaution against anyone peeking.

"My client made many preparatory sketches of you. Normally, he keeps them when the contract is finished, but in this instance, he felt that you would like to have them."

He pushed the packet toward her, and she glanced at him, wondering if he had any inkling of what was shielded behind the innocuous wrapping, but he innocently matched her stare. If he had any intimation, he was too experienced, and too well bred, to show it.

"Thank you, again."

"You're welcome. Now then"—he leafed through his papers as though doing a last check for errors—"I have a proposal to present to you."

"A proposal?"

"Well, *proposal* might not be the most applicable term. You see, Mr. Cristofore has recently come into a substantial amount of money."

"He has?"

How could Gabriel have stumbled upon a fortune? If he'd secured a patron as Mary had suggested, a benefactor wouldn't have showered him with unearned cash. By what other method could he have garnered any? She fervently prayed that he hadn't stolen or swindled it!

"From what source?" she hesitantly inquired.

"He did not choose to apprise me of the . . . ah . . ." —he cleared his throat—"particulars surrounding the acquisition of the funds, but he advises me that you are cognizant of the derivation, so therefore no accounting is necessary."

The way he vacillated and enunciated *particulars* made her suppose that he was totally sentient from whence it emanated, or that he recognized it was of dubious origin and, due to his confidential post, he could never acknowledge it.

"*I* am aware of the source?"

"So he claims. Purportedly, the two of you discussed it thoroughly during your final quarrel."

Every aspect of that decisive, grotesque argument flitted past, but the only financial topic they'd addressed was the bribe her father had tendered for him to . . .

She froze.

Mr. Thumberton studied her. "You *do* recall that to which he alludes."

"I do." She trod cautiously, feeling as though she was tiptoeing across a murky bog where the slightest misstep could send her tumbling into the muddy ooze lurking below.

"Mr. Cristofore has transferred his fortune to you."

"To me?"

"Yes."

"How much?"

"All of it."

"I don't want it!"

Disgusted, afflicted, she fumed. Wasn't this precisely the sort of high-handed maneuver on which the bounder thrived! At which he excelled! Well, she'd show the presumptuous villain a thing or two about pride! About contempt and self-respect! "I won't accept so much as a farthing, and you can hie yourself back to London and tell him I said so."

"Mr. Cristofore mentioned that a refusal might be your response," he calmly clarified, ignoring her outburst.

"Oh, he did, did he?" she asked hotly.

"But the cash is already yours."

"What? How could that be?"

"It's been placed into a trust."

"Well, I don't agree to it!"

He spun the papers around so that she could see the legal heading, and there it was, bold as brass: *Trust Document.*

"Mr. Cristofore wanted the matter accomplished as fast as possible, so I've taken the liberty of having an associate of mine at the Bank of London named as trustee."

She frowned at the document, while she rapped her nails on the arm of the chair. "Would you mind explaining what this trust means?"

"It *means* that you have suddenly become a very wealthy woman."

She eyed him incredulously. "How wealthy?"

He indicated an offensively large number at the bottom of the page, and she gasped.

"You now have a substantial income, with the resources to go where you want and to do what you want. You won't have access to the capital, but you'll be provided with a steady income, and your trustee will assuredly allow sufficient extras for permissible expenses. A modest house, certainly. Clothing. Food. A few servants. Nothing as illustrious as all this"—he gestured around the elegant parlor—"but definitely naught to sneeze at. If you are deliberate with your spending, you'll have more than enough to support yourself through a long and comfortable life."

A home of her own! A stipend! With no worries about the future and how she'd survive it! Everything she'd ever craved was being dangled before her.

Drat that Gabriel! He knew her secret dreams, and thus, he comprehended how difficult it would be for her to rebuff his generosity. She need only murmur the word *yes,* and she would be free. Free from her father. From Charlotte. From the confines of her monotony and tedium.

Apparently, Mr. Thumberton was adept at reading minds, or perhaps Gabriel had versed him on her weakest points, because he went in for the kill. "Lady Elizabeth," he gently prodded, "may I be frank?"

"Aye."

"I haven't been informed of what transpired between you and Mr. Cristofore to cause your . . . your rift, but it appears that hurt feelings remain. Perchance, some pride is involved. Some lingering hostility, as well. Am I correct?"

"I might concede that you are," she griped petulantly.

"Well, milady, I'm an old man who's seen much." He sat back and sighed. "Over the years, I've found it advantageous not to interfere in one's personal affairs, and I typically let others fumble toward their own resolutions, but in this case, I feel it's inherent that I speak my piece."

Crossly, she probed, "What is it you would say?"

"Don't be a fool."

Insulted, she stiffened. "I'm not being foolish. I just don't want anything from him." Which was false. If only she could discern that he forgave her, that this wasn't merely some bit of callous commerce, his tidying up of his studio! "Did he send me a letter? Anything at all as to why he's doing this?"

"No, he didn't." She was crushed, and he reached out and patted her hand in a fatherly fashion. "But his stepmother, Mrs. Preston, slipped a note into my bag for you."

He gave it to her, and its presence made her realize how isolated she'd been since leaving London, how inconsolable and detached.

A note from Mary! Oddly, she felt as if she'd been stranded on a desert island and the tantalizing missive had floated up in a bottle! She was starved for news, but she kept her eagerness at bay, laying the letter on her lap, saving it for later enjoyment.

"How kind of her," she politely said. "What did she think of Mr. Cristofore's decision?"

"She and I didn't talk about it."

"Does she know what he intends?"

"I have no idea."

"She'd probably tell him he's daft."

"No doubt," Mr. Thumberton acceded with a laugh. "I have to confess that, when he unveiled his plans to me, I wasn't overly enthused, myself."

"Really?"

"To be blunt, milady, I tried to dissuade him. It's such an enormous sum, and I felt his own circumstances could have benefited." He gesticulated dramatically. " 'At least'— I counseled him—'keep part of it.' "

"What was his reply?"

"He told me—and I'm quoting—'Lady Elizabeth needs it much more than I ever would.' "

"I see."

Her musings were so conflicted. What was best? Should she acquiesce in Gabriel's scheme? To vainly repel his largess would be downright silly.

Her confusion must have been obvious, because Mr. Thumberton interjected, "You need to separate him, and whatever sin he's committed, from the overture he's making and the result that will entail."

"But why is he making it? That's what I can't figure out."

"Does it matter why?"

Did it? In the grand design of things, did it signify if his gift was an obdurate termination of their contract? After all, their *amour* had been over for months. What had she expected? That absence would cause him to decide he loved her? That he might miss her so much he'd rush to Norwich and beg her pardon?

Ludicrous! Comical! She blushed at her wild fantasies.

"Milady, this is a fortune," he said fervently. "Don't let arrogance or temper keep you from grabbing for it. The bequest will change your life forever."

"But do I want it to be changed in this way? That's the question."

"Only you can answer it," he asserted, "but if I might pose one last suggestion?"

"What?"

"If you were my daughter"—conspiratorially, he bent nearer—"I'd tell you to take it and run. Fast as you can!"

She chuckled. "You would, would you?"

"Absolutely. You'd be crazy not to."

"I suppose I would."

With no further rumination or debate, she signed her name on the bottom line. He reviewed some of the important contractual language, the oddest being that she couldn't ever reveal to anyone the source of the funds. That prohibition was to be the only crucial stipulation. Other than that, and the fact that her trustee would oversee disbursement, the boon was hers.

With satchel tucked under his arm, he departed a short while later, though she'd encouraged him to spend the night in the rambling mansion. She'd have welcomed a guest at supper, for she'd have had the excuse to grill him for details about Gabriel. Where was he? What was he doing with himself? Was there any news about Mary and John Preston?

Citing a pressing schedule, the solicitor hadn't given her an opening to delve into concerns he likely wouldn't or couldn't divulge, and he'd chosen to avoid any unpleasantness by returning to town.

After he'd gone, the parlor seemed awfully quiet.

She perused the trust documents, then tossed them on the table, surprised to discover that they furnished none of the exultation or excitement she might have inferred would come with such an inheritance. If anything, she was more dolorous than ever.

An independent woman! Who possessed the wherewithal to live in any self-reliant manner she chose.

The notion was so depressing!

Her every wish had been granted. Her every dream fulfilled. What more could she possibly desire? What would it take to truly make her happy?

Gabriel, a soft voice whispered.

What good was excessive wealth if all it rendered was an empty house, where she would rattle around the vacuous halls? Was her destiny naught more than that of a lonely, eccentric spinster?

How gloomy! How discouraging!

Needing to occupy herself, she went to the portrait and ripped away the paper. On viewing the finished product, her rush of sentiment was so staggering that her legs were shaky and, requiring support, she fell into a chair.

The painting was magnificent. From the petals on the roses, to the individual blades of grass, to the horses grazing off in the distance, each precise stroke of his brush had been exhaustively applied, the combined effect so charming she could scarcely bear to gaze upon it.

Positioned in the center, she was at the stairs of the gazebo, leaning against the rail. Smiling gaily, she peered off to the side as if someone she liked very much had just called to her from a location outside the picture.

She'd known how he'd depict her—what she'd be wearing, how her hair would be arranged—but still, she was humbled and astonished upon witnessing how Gabriel perceived her: fetching, vibrant, and so very pretty. There were no other words to describe his portrayal, and she couldn't tear herself away.

Before she'd met him, she'd been so boring and conventional, yet he'd seen something in her, something of the real woman who'd been lurking beneath the layers, and he'd succeeded in transforming her.

Despite the damage his presence had wrought, she'd liked how confident she'd grown to be under his tutelage, and she wouldn't have modified a minute of her experience—except mayhap the conclusion. If only she could bring that dynamic, interesting woman back to the surface!

Turning, she chanced to catch her reflection in the mirror. For the first time in weeks, she took a full assessment. She was pale and washed out, her skin wan, her hair dull and lifeless. And she'd lost so much weight! When had that happened? Her gown sagged where it had been designed to fit tight and snug.

Grieving . . . one of the maids had once whispered when the girl had wrongly assumed Elizabeth to be napping. The servant had uttered the term as a mode of explicating what ailed Elizabeth, and the appraisal was valid.

For so long, Elizabeth hadn't been able to eat or sleep. Some mornings, she'd been too traumatized to rise from her bed, too heartbroken to face the day, and she was finally forced to accept that she'd been in mourning, despairing over her loss of Gabriel.

Well, the man wasn't dead! She needn't pine away as

though she'd never see him again! At this very moment, were she brave enough, she could pack a bag and journey to London.

"And what would you do once you arrived?" she queried of the silent room.

Such whimsy! Such idiocy! Would she never learn from her mistakes? Gabriel couldn't want her after all that had occurred. Hadn't he just dropped his leftover mementos into her lap like so much discarded rubbish?

She moved to sit on the sofa, and her thoughts were chaotic. The packet of his sketches beckoned to her, and she couldn't resist tearing at the wrapping. She peeled it away and gaped at the topmost drawing in the stack, then the next, and the next.

About halfway through the pile, she blundered upon one of Gabriel, and she was stunned. She'd forgotten that he'd placed himself in some of the pictures. He was standing behind her, mostly hidden, and she could just make out a cheek, a shoulder, an arm. Rapidly, she searched through the rest, hunting for the ones in which he was included, and she spread them on the table so that she could examine them.

The most erotic drawings were absent, and he'd only transmitted those where he was in the background. Still, he looked so extraordinary!

Distractedly, she traced across a sketch, while she tried to deduce why he'd sent them. Had he wanted her to have them as a keepsake? Did he *not* want them himself? If so, why had he kept some and not others?

Off to the side, Mary's letter lay unopened, and she picked it up and flicked across the seal. While she'd hoped for a lengthy communication filled with gossip and pithy chatter, it was extremely concise, as if she'd drafted it in a hurry.

I miss you, and I've been so worried. Please write to let me know how you are. In case your situation with your father has deteriorated, you're welcome to stay with me. For as long as you like.

The kind tidings, the extension of a haven, were her undoing. Of late, she'd been so tormented, so self-centered, that she hadn't conjectured as to how Mary had weathered the loathsome ordeal, or how she'd emerged from it. She'd been with them on the sidewalk, watching all, then Elizabeth had virtually disappeared, so she was probably imagining all sorts of dire scenarios.

There was a postscript under her signature.

Gabriel is well. He's come home after an extended holiday at the shore. John is relieved.

How sneaky of her! To blithely hint at Gabriel! How dangerous of her to clarify his whereabouts!

The perilous report leapt up off the page, producing a surge of inexplicable, absurd longing for the knave. Oh, to see him again! To hear his beautiful voice! What enchantment he'd brought to her. What mystery and joy.

How she missed it. How she missed him!

Giddy over her rekindled prospects, she was suffused with more animation than she'd felt in weeks—nay months! She jumped up and commenced pacing.

While she might have just become rich, might have the world by the tail, without Gabriel, she had nothing. Formerly, she'd risked everything, had gambled for a future she craved, but she'd let it slide through her fingers.

Where had that intrepid woman gone? She was still about, wasn't she?

Once, she'd brazenly grabbed for her heart's desire. Could she dare so much again?

CHAPTER TWENTY-THREE

FINDLEY glared across at his wife and mother-in-law. A more dour, disagreeable pair he never hoped to encounter.

How was it that he'd so quickly progressed from sharing a table with pleasant-natured, interesting Elizabeth, to this?

Charlotte's mother had taken up residence. Although he wasn't sure when the horrid woman had arrived, he suspected she'd been on the premises for an extended period. However, he would never lower himself to ask Charlotte for clarification, because he wouldn't want to give the impression that he was overly curious as to her affairs.

He and Charlotte rarely spoke. Since the day she'd gleefully apprised him of Elizabeth's shame, he'd made it a point to absent himself as much as he could, coming home late at night solely to effect the unpalatable task of seeing to his matrimonial duty.

Who could have ever predicted that having sexual relations with such a stunning beauty could be unappetizing? The notion of mating with her had become so distasteful that he could barely maintain a cockstand long enough to do the deed! Himself! When he'd always had the stamina of a bull!

Her mother was too ensconced in her chair for his liking, lording it over the salon as though she owned the bloody place. She was eyeing the furnishings in a manner he didn't care for, either, checking out various items as though assessing their value.

Two footmen were serving the meal, and she barked at their every move until they were trembling, nervous wrecks. Whenever one of them approached, he shifted out of range, positive that her incessant harping would eventually cause one of them to drop a ladle of gravy or spill the wine into his lap.

A man's digestive system couldn't function properly with such constant sniping, and he was just ready to make that clear when the disagreeable woman broke the tense silence.

"Milord, if I might request a word with you after supper."

"I can't think of a single topic about which we need to converse."

"It involves your daughter."

He set his spoon beside his plate and peered at her so malevolently that she shrank back, not as assured as she had been moments earlier. "What about her?"

"Charlotte has heard a rumor among the staff that she might be planning to return to London."

The information was accurate. He'd received a note from the butler at Norwich that very afternoon citing the possibility. While he was encouraged that Elizabeth had recovered sufficiently to resume her former life, he still hadn't figured out how to reinstate her in their London town house.

Furious that Charlotte—or her mother—would feel the matter was open to discussion, he nastily inquired, "What has that to do with you? Or my wife?"

"Well, we . . . that is, I . . . well . . . it's downright barbarous to subject Charlotte to Lady Elizabeth's wicked influence."

"The two of you have the gall to mention Elizabeth to me?" He threw his napkin, then stood so rapidly that his chair tipped, and one of the footmen jumped for it before it crashed to the floor. Both women scrutinized him apprehensively. "Charlotte, proceed to your room."

"I don't wish to be excused," she petulantly replied.

Where did she come by that disrespectful mouth?

"Did I ask your opinion?" He walked over to her, grabbed her arm, and lifted her to her feet. "Don't make me tell you again. Go upstairs and arrange yourself. I'll be up shortly."

"What do you intend to say to Mother?"

"None of your damned business!" he hissed, his ire spiking to a new height.

Grasping the back of her neck, he physically shoved her toward the door, as her mother gasped. Good! Let her witness the horrid scene! Let her see what an impertinent, insolent daughter she'd raised! They were fortunate he didn't take a whip to Charlotte, then and there.

Charlotte glowered at him, that mulish expression he hated marring her pretty features, then she stomped off. He waited until her steps had faded, then he whirled to face his present nemesis. She boldly stared him down with a mutinous sneer that was an exact replica of her daughter's.

"Madam," he started, for he couldn't recall her name, "I assume you are here because your daughter invited you. But your welcome has been revoked. By me."

"What? I'm not to be allowed to visit with Charlotte?"

"You'll depart in the morning. If you're not gone by ten o'clock, I'll have your bags packed and tossed out on the stoop. Do we understand one another?"

She hesitated, a hundred insults fermenting on the tip of her tongue, but wisely, she chose not to voice them.

"Well, I never!" she huffed and stormed out.

He tarried until he was satisfied that he wouldn't chance upon her in the hall, then he went to the stairs, climbing slowly, his legs like lead ballast, thoughts of Elizabeth weighing him down.

His worries about her, and her melancholia, perpetually vexed him. Had he done the right thing? Made the correct decisions?

Considering how badly it had ended, he wasn't convinced that he'd handled it well.

Where was Mary when he was desperate for her counsel and advice? She'd abandoned him to his fate, not caring a whit for the fact that he'd always needed her. He still did.

Since she'd left him for John Preston, he'd only seen her on that lone occasion when he'd chased after Elizabeth as she'd run off to question Cristofore. The resulting spectacle had been so dreadful, Elizabeth so disturbed, that there'd been no opportunity for so much as a hello. Afterward, he'd been too proud to contact her, so he couldn't be confident as to her condition in her new situation.

He brooded over her sometimes, wondered about her life with Preston. Was she happy with the bed she'd made for herself? Did she ever regret that she'd forsaken him for another?

If only she'd been available to soothe him during the persisting trauma, to persuade him that he'd behaved appropriately!

Because of her defection, he'd been compelled to take a mistress, but he'd stuck to the modern trend, picking out a girl who was attractive and vivacious, who would look fetching on his arm at social events, so it had turned out that she wasn't much older than Charlotte.

It was increasingly evident that she possessed his wife's penchant for inane chatter and frivolity. Though he would call upon her later, after he'd finished with the chore of copulating with Charlotte, the pending appointment brought none of the relief or joy he'd perpetually found with Mary. There was no consolation to be had in his youthful paramour's arms.

He entered his bedchamber and closed the door. In the adjacent dressing room, he could hear Charlotte rummaging about, and he grimaced. He abhorred being near her, yet he couldn't avoid copulation. Her impregnation was paramount.

Pouring himself a bracing drink, he swigged it down,

then went to join her. Knocking once, he intruded into her feminine enclave, and he was immediately and vastly irritated to discover that she was fully clothed and primping in the mirror at her vanity. As he insisted on executing the unsavory fornications as swiftly as possible, he mandated that she disrobe in advance, that she array herself naked on her bed, so there'd be no time wasted in pursuing the act to its natural conclusion.

"Why aren't you ready?"

She scowled at him over her shoulder. "For what?"

"To perform your marital obligation."

"You can't be serious! It's hardly past eight."

"I'm going out, and I'll be detained for many hours, so I'll have you now."

"Well, I'm not in the mood."

Effectively dismissing him, she stuck her pert little nose up in the air and studied herself in the mirror, crunching and fluffing at her blond curls. While she'd habitually shown scant deference for his authority, recently she'd grown more incorrigible, and it was imperative that she be reminded of her subordinate position.

"You will accommodate me."

"How dare you barge in here and command me about!" Enraged, she rose and spun toward him. "After the way you treated my mother! Compelling me to reside under the same roof with your whore of a daughter!"

He slapped her as viciously as he could, shutting her up with a single blow. She fell to her knees, and he experienced a thrilling, manly rush at having her so indisposed. His phallus filled, and he was elated that—for once—he'd be able to accomplish his climax with limited effort.

"Undo my trousers."

"I won't!" she said, prolonging her rebellion.

He slapped her again, inducing her to sniffle and weep. Ignoring her whimpering, he worked at the buttons himself, until his cock was indecently exposed. Her distress was such that she hadn't noticed what he was about, so he easily clasped her by the neck and, in mid-wail, impaled himself in her mouth.

She struggled and fought, endeavoring to push him away, but he refused to grant her any quarter. He thrust, harshly, propelling her against the wall, and her head banged with each flex of his hips. Her exertions excited him, her resistance sharpening his arousal, so he delayed longer than he normally would have then, in a hot torrent, he orgasmed in her throat.

He held her until she swallowed, then he retreated, and she collapsed onto the floor, gulping for air, huge tears coursing down her mottled cheeks.

She detested giving him the French kiss, but after how he'd brooked her endless attitudes, his dislike of her was so intense that he declined to show her any courtesy. There was no more offensive deed he could commit against her, and in his current state of elevated disapproval, he reveled in the insult.

"Whenever you sass me from now on"—he languidly reassembled his privates and fixed his pants—"you will service me in this fashion. With your obstinate disposition, I imagine it will only take a few dozen times for you to learn to curb your impudent tongue."

She grumbled a remark that sounded like, "Bastard—"

Incensed, he leaned over her, and gripped a fistful of her hair, shaking her as one might a recalcitrant dog. "If you haven't conceived in six more months, I'm filing for divorce on the grounds of your infertility. In light of my rigorous attempts, and your blatant barrenness, I'm sure my peers will be most sympathetic. I'll have our sham of a marriage dissolved like that!"

With a crude snap of his fingers, he strutted out, pleased with how he'd reasserted himself as lord of the manor.

As he washed up and prepared to depart for a rendez-vous with his mistress, he heard Charlotte vomiting up his seed. She was forbidden from voiding her stomach after sex, so he thought about confronting her and beating her for her effrontery, but with his cock having been sated, his anger had waned, and he couldn't locate the necessary mettle to discipline her further.

Feeling smug, and in control of his domain, he exited into the corridor and marched down the stairs.

Charlotte huddled on the floor, sweating and crying, while exhaustively reviewing every curse word in her vocabulary.

"Bastard!" she repeated viciously, and a perverse smile crossed her lips. She'd muttered the very same in his presence, and she was exceptionally proud of herself that she'd had the nerve.

How could he deign to mistreat her! To abuse her so crudely and roughly. She hated him for it!

With her mother's arrival, believing she'd found a commiserating ear, she'd confessed some of the horrid acts her husband forced her to perform. Instead of empathy, the older woman had declared that Charlotte had to put up with whatever he desired, that once he'd slipped the ring on her finger, she'd agreed to comply with any of his demands—in spite of how loathsome they might be.

Well, her mother's opinion be damned. He didn't have the right!

She shuddered and, using the chair for balance, she faltered to her feet and stumbled to the mirror where she could appraise her appearance. Her hair was mussed, her eyes red, and her cheek swollen from where he'd struck her. It throbbed painfully. He'd slapped her before, even sporadically hitting her with his belt, but never had there been such vehemence behind the blow.

All that outrage had been directed at her merely because she'd risked referring to his precious Elizabeth! His perfect, well-bred, affable, jezebel of a daughter! Charlotte would never forget the foul, sordid things she'd observed Elizabeth doing with her repugnant, common lover.

Why, Elizabeth had fled London in shame! Her reputation sullied beyond repair! Her disgrace had been a potential monumental humiliation for Charlotte, yet the earl pranced about as if Elizabeth had done nothing wrong. How he carried on! He was deluding himself and others, pretending that Elizabeth had contracted a grave illness and was gradually recovering. He couldn't bear to admit that his impeccable dove had been irrevocably soiled!

To think that he held Charlotte in such contempt that he would require her to fraternize with the fallen woman! When Charlotte had unveiled his wretched scheme, her mother had been in a high dudgeon, but not even the intimidating matron could dissuade him from permitting Elizabeth's return.

So far, Charlotte had told no one about Elizabeth's ignominy, abiding by the earl's dictate that she remain silent. His affection for Elizabeth was so strong that Charlotte had been afraid of what he might do if she tattled. If word of Elizabeth's carnal escapade was leaked, he would promptly deduce that the divulgence had come from Charlotte, so she'd been reticent, but perhaps she should reevaluate her prior decision. The entire world ought to be informed of Elizabeth's tainted nature.

"Harlot!" She uttered the term aloud then, because it felt so grand to denigrate the unrepentant strumpet, she spat it out again.

If she spread rumors about Elizabeth's downfall, the earl would be angry, but then, he was always angry, so she was no longer concerned as to any backlash. Besides, she would derive such gratification from driving him into a tizzy, and if she could incite the elderly blackguard to an acute rage, perhaps he'd suffer an apoplexy and drop dead.

Dramatically, she pressed a hand to her brow. She would be a magnificent, grieving widow. She'd be so credible; she'd generate such compassion.

"Divorce me, will you, you despicable swine?"

The fool didn't know her very well. She'd murder him

in his bed before she'd let him instigate such a heinous process!

Carelessly, she wet her lips with her tongue, and the taste and smell of him was so potent that she was deluged by his repulsive essence. Lurching for her wineglass, she gulped down the red liquid, but it couldn't allay her queasiness.

The wine swirled in her bloated stomach, mixing with the greasy mutton that she'd eaten at supper. Pacing, she tried to ignore her mounting discomfort, striving to disregard what he'd done, what he'd said, but she couldn't control the conflagration in her mind—or her belly.

She covered her mouth, then reeled to the chamber pot where she retched over and over, emptying herself of the libation, the meal, and him.

"Quit moping. Go out and talk to him."

Mary's voice had John swinging around. "I have no wish to speak with him."

"Liar. You're dying to."

Despite his insistence that he had nothing to say to Gabriel, he was loitering at the window and gazing down on the cottage in the backyard, eager for a glimpse of the wayward scoundrel. As it was a warm July day, no smoke curled from the chimney to denote occupancy, but his link with Gabriel was powerful as ever, and he sensed the boy tucked away inside.

Since his unannounced arrival a fortnight earlier, when John had been out of the house, Gabriel had isolated himself in his lair. The maid who delivered his food and drink reported that the door was locked, that he did not answer the few times she'd knocked, and that when she peeked through the curtain, he was in a painting frenzy.

When he would surface was anybody's guess, which was fine with John.

Inevitably, they had to adapt to what had happened on that long-ago, horrid day, but he hadn't determined how to make amends, how to atone, or to mollify his intractable son so that they could reestablish their former, amiable relationship. Especially now that Mary had reported Gabriel's having transferred the money to Elizabeth—how she'd ascertained the news was a mystery—John felt honor-bound to mend things between them.

How could he have impugned Gabriel's motives? He knew his son, recognized what a good lad he was deep down. He should have been supportive in Gabriel's scam against Findley Harcourt. He should have helped, instead of automatically condemning. From the outset, John should have realized that Gabriel would do what was best in the end.

And the money! To have duped such a large amount from an ass like Findley! What an incredible, fantastic denouement!

John was so proud he could barely stand it, and sometimes, he felt that if he didn't have the chance to recount every detail of the marvelous ruse, he just might burst. Gabriel was the only person with whom he could savor the particulars, but as they were fighting, there had been no one with whom John could crow and laugh over the plot's results.

Mary walked over and kissed him, and as he snuggled her close, she asked, "Any sign of Elizabeth yet?"

"You're awfully sure that she'll show up."

"Just watch," she said. "We'll have ourselves a daughter—and some sweet, precocious grandchildren—before this is all through."

He'd learned not to doubt Mary. The woman was a shrewd judge of human behavior, and a virtual miracle worker. As he peered outside again, he almost hoped that he would behold Elizabeth Harcourt. Her appearance might provide the boost of courage he needed to approach Gabriel.

"I'm so glad he's home safe and sound."

"I know you are."

"We've never been separated before."

"It's been difficult for you."

"Yes." To his amazement, tears flooded his eyes, but he didn't hide them. Mary was the rock upon which his life was steadfastly anchored. "Do you think he'll ever forgive me?"

"Oh, you silly man. How could you presume he wouldn't?" Chuckling at his absurdity, she spun him toward the hallway and conferred a gentle nudge. "You have to untangle this asinine feud sooner or later. It might as well be sooner."

She was correct, and he gave her a self-deprecating smile as he headed out to chat with his beloved son for the first time in nearly four months. Judiciously, though, he made a swing through the front parlor where he retrieved a bottle of their premium Scotch whisky and two glasses.

On the cottage stoop, he tucked the decanter of liquor under his arm, braced himself, then briskly knocked. As he'd anticipated, there was no response, so he tried again— and again—before Gabriel's irritated footsteps pounded toward the door. In a temper at being interrupted, he yanked it open.

"What?" he barked, looming into the gap.

"Hello," John said, inspecting him, relishing the view after such a protracted absence. He looked thin. And weary.

"John?" Disbelieving, Gabriel blinked, his vision adjusting in the bright afternoon sunlight.

"Of course it's John." He blustered his way inside. "Who were you expecting? The chimney sweep?"

Gabriel hovered on the threshold, staring at John as if he was a chimera, and John was exhilarated that he'd had the resolve to breach their rift.

"You don't mind if I come in, do you?"

"No, no." He was hesitant, obviously wondering if he was in for another dressing-down.

During their final conversation before Gabriel had left London, John had pulled no punches, so the lad likely had fortified himself to endure more acrimony. Gad, he might even be worrying that John would toss him out. From his very own house!

If that was his thinking, how brave he'd been to come home! And how ashamed John was for having made him feel unwelcome!

Ultimately, Gabriel's curiosity got the better of him, so he followed John in, analyzing him. Tentatively, he inquired, "What did you want?" .

"I'm here for our celebratory drink."

"What drink?"

"You haven't been gone that long that you'd have forgotten."

"I haven't forgotten. I just didn't suppose you'd care to—"

He couldn't finish the sentence, but John could surmise the rest: With their differences unsettled, why would John go to the trouble?

John plunked the whisky and the glasses down on Gabriel's workbench, then he filled them to the rim and passed one to his son. Raising his, he proclaimed, "To Findley Harcourt—for being such an idiot."

The frivolous ritual was one they'd engaged in often over the years, toasting a mark for his gullibility, saluting their success, congratulating themselves on a job well done.

Gabriel examined him, clearly unable to trust that John would initiate such a gesture. He searched for equivocation, for lack of sincerity, but detected only genuine fondness.

A slow grin curved his lips, and he lifted his own glass. "To Findley Harcourt. For being such an uncompromising nitwit."

"To his arrogance."

"To his stupidity."

"To all his lovely money."

"Aye. To all his lovely, lovely money."

"*Fai il bravo!*" John beamed. "Good for you!"

"*Grazie.*"

"Alla tua salute."

"Salute!"

"Come nuovo"—good as new—John murmured, smiling at his son, and just like that, it was as though they'd never been parted.

Elizabeth sucked in a deep breath, mustered her lagging fortitude, then banged the knocker to Gabriel's home. A pretty maid in a gray dress answered.

Elizabeth extended her card and explained, "I am Lady Elizabeth Harcourt. Might I call on Mr. Cristofore?"

The girl curtsied attentively but, on hearing Elizabeth's identity, her smile wavered, and she shifted nervously. "Beggin' your pardon, milady, but Mr. Cristofore isn't taking guests."

"He's painting, is he?"

"Why, yes, ma'am," she replied a tad too heartily. "That's exactly it. He's much too busy for socializing."

"When might he be available?"

"I can't rightly say. Perhaps in a few weeks?"

"I could pen a note," Elizabeth suggested acerbically, "requesting an audience with his exalted self."

The girl didn't catch Elizabeth's sarcasm. "That might work," she said helpfully.

Elizabeth stared her down, and the maid flushed a brilliant red. "You're a horrid liar, miss."

"Yes, I know."

"You have orders not to let me in, don't you?"

The servant gaped at the floor and fiddled with her skirt. "I'm sorry."

Elizabeth had never been more embarrassed, and she blushed worse than the pitiable maid.

Well, what had she expected? She'd never imagined this would be easy. Pride was a difficult tonic to swallow, and she'd never enjoyed its bitter taste.

"Are Mr. and Mrs. Preston in?"

"They've gone out for the day."

She sighed. "When they return, tell them that I've arrived in town."

"I will."

"Advise them that I'm staying at the Carlysle Hotel. Can you remember?"

"Absolutely, milady."

Elizabeth had nothing to add, and no reason to tarry, so she'd turned to go, just as Gabriel waltzed into the corridor. Their eyes met, and she couldn't decide who was more astonished, him or her—or the maid.

"Why, look, milady," the servant sheepishly pointed out, "it seems that Mr. Cristofore has completed his painting early."

"It certainly does."

The three of them froze, the silence awkward.

Elizabeth had replayed this moment a thousand times, and the reality was totally divergent from her fantasies.

In each of those—some tame, some not—he would sweep her into his arms, would administer a handful of passionate kisses, her sins against him would be forgiven, and they'd begin again.

Oh, how wrong she'd been!

Urbane, charming, he coolly assessed her. Apparently, he was about to rush off to an engagement, so he was poised and polished to impress, his verve and animated charisma shielded behind his elegant clothes. He wasn't happy to see her in the slightest. If anything, he was irked that he would now be delayed to deal with the unpleasantness created by her unannounced visit.

Drawing nigh, he dismissed the retainer, and she fleetly disappeared down the hall. They were alone, and he was so close that she could smell the starch in his shirt, the soap with which he'd bathed.

"Hello, Gabriel."

"Lady Elizabeth," he said, killing her with formality.

"It's been a long time," she offered lamely, nervous about breaking the ice, but he made no rejoinder, which only served to make the encounter more degrading.

Puzzled, he focused in on her. "What are you doing here?"

"I came to see you."

"Are you with child?" he baldly probed, analyzing her stomach.

"No."

"Then why?"

With his sentiments scrupulously masked, it was hard to infer his thoughts or feelings, but from how he was glaring at her, she plainly had about two seconds to speak her piece. The situation was much more dire than she had counted upon!

"I wanted to thank you for the money."

"You're welcome."

"And I'm sorry about . . . that last day. I was angry and I—"

"Apology accepted," he interjected before she could expound.

Off balance from his abruptness, she hastily regrouped. "When my father discovered our affair, he must have pressured you unmercifully, so I apologize for his conduct, as well."

He didn't affirm this subsequent expression of regret. Absolution for Findley Harcourt—if it was ever bestowed— would be a long way off.

Finally, he posited, "Will there be anything else?"

She yearned to confess some of the wrought-up emotion that her receipt of his beautiful painting had unleashed, but his demeanor evinced no display of affection, so there was naught she could mention that would pierce his imperturbable facade. Any admission of mawkishness would be totally misplaced, and she would feel as if she was explicating confidential secrets to a stranger.

Downhearted, she muttered, "I guess not."

"Well, then"—he motioned outside, politely indicating

that her time was up—"I'm late for an appointment, so I won't keep you."

Crestfallen at the rebuff, she stepped over the threshold. What could she say? What could she do? She'd irrationally convinced herself that, in the period they'd been separated, he'd missed her as much as she'd missed him but, as usual, she'd thoroughly misconstrued the circumstances.

She gazed into his exquisite face, and inanely posed the question she'd previously attempted to raise, but which she'd been too timid to pursue. "Do you ever wish—"

Because of the lump in her throat, she couldn't conclude her query, and after a portentous pause, he asked, "Wish what?"

"That things had ended differently between us?"

"No, I don't. Good-bye."

Well, he'd certainly told her, hadn't he?

He shut the door, the lock clicking loudly as though to vividly inform her that she'd abominably transgressed on his privacy.

She sniffed, hurt, and for a moment or two, she forlornly loafed on his stoop, then she trudged down the street toward her carriage. The coachman assisted her, but she didn't give the signal to drive on.

Pensive, discouraged, she leaned against the squab and peeked out the curtain, absently watching his house as she methodically strove to concoct a wiser strategy, one more likely to guarantee success. She must have hurt him so desperately! His level of pique was much worse than she'd assumed.

"How can I fix this?" she murmured to herself.

A few minutes later, to her surprise, his door opened, and Gabriel emerged. She'd been so wrapped up in her misery that she'd forgotten he was going out, and she straightened so that she could better spy on him.

Luckily, his vehicle was parked in the direction opposite from her own, and he was so intent on his destination that he walked down the block and climbed inside without so much as glancing to where she dawdled and mooned over him.

Long after he'd departed, she chafed and fumed, pondering how to proceed. Currently, he denied any lingering partiality, but his regard had once been authentic, his devotion cogent and abiding. It couldn't have vanished completely. What could she do to revive their connection, to burst through his wall of reserve, so that they could love again?

Eventually, a plan began to form. It was rash, underhanded—she'd even go so far as to call it ill-advised—but in light of her predicament, a bit of deviousness couldn't hurt.

"Poor Gabriel," she fondly remarked. He regularly failed to recollect how determined she could be when she set herself on a goal, but he was about to be reminded.

CHAPTER TWENTY-FOUR

GABRIEL closed his eyes, attempting to shut out the noise of London gliding by outside his carriage.

The interview Attorney Thumberton had set up with the Marchioness of Belmont had progressed just as Mary had predicted. He was now a *kept* man, but not in the sense he'd ever been before. The wealthy, influential noblewoman had been enchanted by his paintings, so he'd procured every artist's fantasy: a benefactor.

He'd never wanted a meddling, intrusive patron, had never wanted to become embroiled with those capricious aristocrats who had caused so much havoc for himself and John over the years. Why, next he knew, he'd be taking tea with his uncles! A loathsome idea all around!

Yet Mary had been so insistent, and his decision to honor her request had left her so cheerful, that he hadn't had the heart to disappoint her. She'd initiated the contact, and he'd acquiesced merely to please her, never presuming that her efforts would be so damned successful.

The agreement would bring him a substantial income that was much more than he would ever require to care for John and Mary. Of greater significance was his position to the marchioness and how it would convey infinite extended benefits in the future as he was introduced to the prominent lady's acquaintances. Considering the fickleness of the members of high society, they would all wish to possess some of his work for their own.

With his distinction established by her grant of sponsorship, the value of his paintings would increase, his reputation enhance, and his profits soar, so that he would never again have to deceive or dupe—or defraud—in order to keep food on the table and a roof over John's and Mary's heads.

He was about to be paid, handsomely and regularly, for doing what he loved, so why wasn't he happier? Why wasn't he shouting for joy and dancing in the street?

The coach turned down the lane toward their house, and he peered at the familiar neighborhood, glad he was in London, for he'd hated being away and at odds with his father.

The vehicle rumbled to a halt, but he didn't exit. Tarrying, he stared at the bright blossoms in the window boxes, the vines crawling up the facade. It looked tasteful, unique, picture-perfect. And lonely.

He couldn't tolerate the notion of going in, of sitting by himself in the parlor, sipping on a drink and faking elation.

John and Mary weren't home and wouldn't arrive till late, so there wasn't a soul with whom he could celebrate his good fortune. No one to whom he could brag or boast. No one who would pat him on the back or lift a glass in observance of his windfall.

At loose ends, he wandered out, maneuvered the stairs, and climbed to the front entrance, only to recognize that if he went inside, he'd be standing in the very spot where he had confronted Elizabeth a few hours earlier.

Who could have guessed that she would show up, mere minutes before he was to attend the most important engagement of his life?

He was still rattled.

If he'd had any clue that she'd be audacious enough to stop by after so much time had passed, he would have ensured that he was well hidden. But how was he to know what she would do? The woman was a mystery, and he was frightfully relieved he'd had the fortitude to repulse her preposterous hello. By calling on him, she'd been making a conciliatory gesture, but he couldn't begin to surmise why she would bother.

The past few months, he'd convinced himself that she had meant every word she'd uttered during their hideous controversy. While he'd wallowed in a maelstrom of self-pity and lamentation in Brighton, healing and salving his wounds in the refreshing sea air, her accusations and epithets had whirled repeatedly, and he hadn't discounted them. He'd permitted them to take root and grow.

When he'd returned to town, his studio had been littered with sketches of her, and the sight had been painful. He'd contemplated destroying the pictures, tossing them in the fireplace and adding some tinder, but the artist in him couldn't ravage what he'd created.

Some of it was just too bloody brilliant to be obliterated by a ball of flames, especially the portrait. But other than Elizabeth, he couldn't conceive of a single person who would want any of it, so he'd conveyed it to her, retaining a few favorites for himself. He'd been positive that she'd interpret the delivery as a curt statement as to his opinion of her. Foolishly, he'd assumed she would infer he'd dispatched the items because he couldn't care less about them, that he longed to be shed of them, and that he was merely fulfilling his end of a disastrous, unpalatable business arrangement.

The money had been an afterthought. Initially, when Findley Harcourt had presented him with the marvelous prospect for enrichment, he'd scammed the cash with the intent of handing it over to her, but after her hateful comments, he'd pettily decided to keep it. The hell with her! But as his anger had faded, so had his misguided determination to punish her.

Though he was furious enough at her to spit nails, she desperately needed the funds. He made no excuses for ruining her, and he had no regrets that he had, but she was no longer virginal, could never marry, and therefore could never escape her father's clutches.

Gabriel had heard—from her stories and John's—that the earl was an unmitigated brute, and after meeting him, Gabriel heartily concurred. If Gabriel hadn't intervened, Elizabeth would have been forever trapped in his orbit, unable to protect herself or flee. Despite how enraged Gabriel was, he'd never willingly consign her to such a fate.

Still, her appearance left him so perplexed. Why had she come? What did she want? She'd pleaded so prettily as she'd asked if he ever rued their quarrel. For a brief instant, it had seemed as if she was sincerely sorry, that she wished they could make amends and start over, and his misreading of the moment was pathetic.

They had nothing in common, nothing to say to one another. The best day of his life was the day he'd sent her packing! He wouldn't bemoan his resolution. Not when it had been so accursedly correct.

Nevertheless, he couldn't enter the foyer for he'd end up reliving the entire, odious encounter. He descended from the stoop, and followed the garden path to his cottage where he could find solitude and privacy. Perhaps after he calmed a bit, he might even paint or draw or . . .

Sleep. That's what he really needed. A good night's sleep. Nowadays, he never relaxed enough to truly rest. His nights were eternal, his dreams erratic and unpredictable— about his mother, Elizabeth, and Mary. They were in danger, and their identities melded until he couldn't discern one from the other. He'd awaken, sweating and miserable, so he'd begun avoiding his bed.

Yes, multitudinous hours of uninterrupted slumber would be a boon for which he'd kill.

Up ahead, his cottage beckoned, and he dawdled in the yard. The place was always magical, but in the summer, with the flowers in bloom, it was particularly delightful. He relished the view, then proceeded in, but the second he spun the knob, he could tell something wasn't right.

An intruder was on the premises.

It wasn't the maid; she'd have sneaked in and effectuated her tasks the minute he'd departed for his appointment.

So who? Who would have had the nerve?

Angry, he forcefully pushed the door so that it opened all the way and smacked against the wall.

On the fainting couch, in the middle of the room, Elizabeth Harcourt reclined.

He couldn't believe his eyes. Thinking her a hallucination, he blinked, then blinked again, but she was still there.

Shockingly, she was barely dressed, as though she was prepared to bask in an afternoon of pleasure such as the ones they'd enjoyed on numerous prior occasions. Her ensemble was inviting, designed to arouse: a flimsy robe, mules, lacy stockings tied at the knee with frilly garters. She sipped on a glass of wine and, as she spun toward him, their gazes locked, and she impishly licked across her bottom lip.

"Hello, Gabriel. I'd about given up on you."

"What are you doing in here?"

Disconcerted, he stomped over to her, which was a mistake. He could smell the heat and musk of her skin, could almost see her breasts and pussy, but her most enticing areas were temptingly concealed as though she'd carefully planned her pose with seducement in mind.

In a reflexive, defensive move, he took two steps back.

"I've missed you," she said.

"Well, I haven't missed you."

"Nonsense," she pouted. Stretching and purring like a contented cat, her torrid attention dropped, settling on his loins where an embarrassing bulge had formed. "You won't deny me a chance to . . . apologize, will you?"

"I no longer dabble in frivolous affairs," he loftily intoned, and he sounded like a self-righteous prig.

"Really?" Her brow furrowed. "What about your widow?"

"My widow?"

"Surely you remember your *widow*. You claimed that you had to be free of me so you could swindle her out of her money."

"*Swindle* her?" He nearly choked. How was it that she'd ceaselessly had such astute insights into his wicked character? And if she harbored such a low—but accurate—estimation of his disposition, why had she returned?

"You couldn't wait to commence with your seduction of the poor woman. Your farewell letter said so."

"Oh, *that* widow."

That dratted good-bye note! Norwich had been in such a godawful hurry that Gabriel hadn't had sufficient latitude to write the blasted thing with any amount of circumspection. What exactly had he said? He could scarcely recall. "She is . . . I was . . ." Too frustrated to make up a clever prevarication, he marched to the door and held it wide. "You're not welcome here. Please go."

She ignored him as readily as if he'd pronounced the command in a foreign language. "Well, I don't care about your widow friend," she mused. "Do you?"

"Absolutely," he lied.

"Madly?"

"Yes."

"Passionately?"

"Without question."

"Pity." She shrugged and stretched again. "I guess there's no purpose in continuing."

"In continuing what?"

"I'm trying to proposition you, but I'm not sure how a lady makes such an overture to a man."

"A *lady* doesn't."

"And here I was so certain you'd oblige me." She arched her back, thrusting her magnificent breasts up and out. "You wouldn't force me to humiliate myself by asking someone else, would you? Obviously, I'm terrible at this."

Was she now bold enough to approach another? He saw red!

These past months, his worst torture had been conjecturing as to what sort of gentleman would next tickle her fancy. She had a recklessly erotic nature and, as she'd been exposed to the sins of the flesh, she'd never remain celibate.

So . . . she was contemplating carnal indiscretion, was she? Other lovers and promiscuity? How dare she flaunt her licentious propensities! With each beat of his heart, he grieved for what might have been. How could she so idly discount what had happened between them!

He slammed the door, then huffed to her side once more. "You'll not go pandering yourself about town like an experienced harlot!"

"I won't?" She winked impertinently. "Who's to say I can't?"

"What's come over you?" He motioned up and down across her flagrantly exhibited torso. "You're acting like a whore!"

"I am not. I'm merely indulging my lustful whims, as you so diligently taught me." Like the most skilled coquette, she stroked a hand across her breast, her stomach, to where it lay, languid and arresting, on her lap. "I learned from the master, and now—when I'd like to use my skills to personal advantage—you almost seem . . . jealous. Are you?"

"No," he jeered, refusing to let her witness a hint of his true attitude.

"Well, good, because I can't imagine why you would be."

She was rubbing in small circles across her abdomen, and he tracked the tantalizing trail. He couldn't look away, her conduct making him vividly recollect when they'd made love at their last rendezvous.

How sweet it had been!

His body had no trouble reliving every detail of that

glorious episode of sensual bliss. It had been so spectacular that he hadn't since allowed himself to luxuriate in a woman's physical company. Not that he hadn't had abundant opportunity.

Women constantly offered themselves—perhaps it was his being part-Italian or that he was an artist—and his trip to the shore had been no exception. He'd generated plenty of female curiosity, but he hadn't reciprocated any sexual interest. Whenever he'd pondered a dalliance, Elizabeth Harcourt's image had irritatingly imposed itself, leaving him with the absurd feeling that he would be cuckolding her if he'd acceded.

Her hand dipped lower still, her fingers lingering over the section of robe that covered her pussy, and with a sudden need for her that bordered on madness, he grew hard as stone, the placard of his trousers swelling further. Lest she discern the effect she had on him, he whirled away, but too slowly. She'd noticed and, relishing the powerful hold she managed to wield, she chuckled at his discomfort.

Blast his unruly cravings! He pushed at his pants, striving to find some ease, but none was to be had. The bewitching enchantress had incessantly inspired uncontrollable appetites, and apparently, separation had not dimmed her prurient abilities.

Naughty, and all too eager, she queried from behind him, "Would you like me to tend that for you?"

Why was she doing this? Didn't she realize that he couldn't start up with her again? There was nothing he would love more than to revel in the type of luscious, delectable, and raucous couplings they'd engaged in before they'd been discovered. Yet he couldn't let down his guard, even for a second, because she would work her way into his life when he'd worked so laboriously to insure she was gone.

She was not only a noblewoman, but one of independent means, so—more than ever before—they had no future. For her to dangle herself before him as a kind of sensual prize was cruel and callous. He honestly could not survive a similar tragic interlude, couldn't abide another spiral to ecstasy that would invariably end in adversity and strife.

"Elizabeth, stop it," he said, staring out the window at the verdant colors in the garden.

"Stop what?"

"Desist with these games."

After a subtle pause, she said, "I'm not playing games."

"Don't pretend; it doesn't become you." He whipped around then, his regard hot and turbulent. Once, he'd been idiotic enough to embark on an affair with her, but he'd suffered severely because of it. How much trauma should he be expected to endure? There was only so much agony and torment one man could bear, and assuredly, he was far past those limits.

"I did everything for you," he bleakly proclaimed.

"I understand that now."

"Yet you toy with me, displaying yourself and taunting me with bits and pieces of what can never be."

"That's not why I'm here."

"Isn't it?" Scathingly, he evaluated her. "Look at you! Sitting there, mocking and teasing me, practically begging me to compromise you, when you know how it will conclude. How many times will you insist that I go through this with you?"

"As many times as it takes."

"Takes to what?" he inquired in a near shout.

"For you to get it through your thick head why I'm here."

"And why is that? To thank me for the money? You already did. To plead with me to have sex with you? I won't." Thoroughly exasperated, he threw his arms up in the air. "What other reason could possibly make you debase yourself so completely?"

"Because . . . I love you."

"Love! Right!" He waved away her declaration as though it was a noxious odor. "There's no such thing."

"I used to think the same . . . until I met you."

Then deliberately . . . cautiously . . . she extended her hand, beseeching him to grasp it, and it hovered there like a lifeline. She was urging him to save himself, to grab hold and obtain all he'd ever wanted, but he couldn't seize the extraordinary destiny that beckoned at the tips of her fingers.

He was too afraid that her proposal was an illusion, that if he attempted to reach for contentment, her overture would vanish like smoke. He didn't believe in fantasies. Strong emotion never lasted. It was naught but a substitute that masked other, genuine sentiments. Lust or avarice, perhaps. Love was a chimera, espoused by poets to dazzle and mystify the romantically inclined.

Her entreaty was a ruse intended to lure him back into the untenable situation in which they'd been previously enmeshed. How could it be more?

She'd had ample chances to cast her lot with his and hadn't risked it. Her upbringing guaranteed that she would perpetually lack the volition for commitment, so he would not brave all, could not open his heart only to have his hopes dashed.

"Take my hand, Gabriel." She was peering up at him with affection and empathy, as if she could distinguish the conflicting introspection that had paralyzed him.

"I can't."

"You can," she contended, so damned sure of herself. "I know what you need. No one else does. Only me."

"And what would that be?" he disdainfully asked.

"You need a family of your own. A houseful of children."

Gad, children! How could she be so merciless as to mention the prospect? The concept was so appealing that he felt he could hear their happy chatter, the patter of their tiny feet, that he could see the little blighters wrestling and roughhousing on the floor.

"Children!" he scoffed. "As if I'd have any idea of what to do with them."

"You be a wonderful father. I have no doubt."

"Anything else, Elizabeth?" He was more testy by the second.

"Yes, as a matter of fact."

She tarried—purposely, he was positive—until she had him chafing as to her next comment. Her ploy succeeded.

"What?" he barked.

"You need a wife who loves you. Who will support you in your career and care for you all your days." She shifted up off the pillows so that she could stretch her hand even nearer. "Let me be your wife, Gabriel."

"You want to marry me?" His astonishment was so great that his knees collapsed, and he snatched at a chair, stabilizing himself and sliding into it.

"Of course I do, you ridiculous man. Don't look so surprised."

Totally confused, he struggled to steady his breathing and calm his thundering pulse.

"You don't mean it," he ultimately muttered.

"Do you think I'm in the habit of degrading myself in this fashion? That I enjoy proposing to an obstinate lout who will never get off his duff and proffer marriage on his own?" Himself, obviously. "It recently occurred to me that if I was idiotic enough to pine away, hoping you would eventually pop the question, I was going to have a very lengthy wait. Probably into my old age and beyond!"

His ruminations were in such a jumble that he couldn't reply, and she grew tired of the delay. "This is where you're supposed to chime in, Gabriel. Feel free."

He massaged his palms over his face, fretting, vexed. Was she sincere?

She waited, then waited some more, for some small gesture or affirmation that would indicate he was of like mind, but he couldn't provide reassurance. His reflections were too disordered, his puzzlement too ripe.

Finally, she drew her hand away, and her ebullience faded.

"Unless I was wrong," she said quietly. "Perhaps you're not jumping in because you don't have anything to say." Her sense of expectation had been acute, and now that it had been snuffed out, it seemed like a tangible object he'd crushed in his fist, but maddeningly, he stayed silent. Her disappointment flowed across the distance dividing them, washing over him and making him ashamed.

What a coward he was!

"I had thought that—" She halted, exhaled a heavy sigh. "I guess it doesn't matter."

She started to rise, and the fear that she might walk out and never come back smothered the misgivings that had kept him immobilized.

Frantically, he reached out, groping blindly, and found her hand, squeezing till he worried that he might snap bone. There was one way to learn if her solicitation was bona fide, one way to box her into a corner from which she couldn't retreat. If she wasn't serious, he'd have his answer momentarily.

"Will you marry me, Elizabeth Harcourt?"

"Yes, I will."

Just like that! She'd agreed! No vacillation. No timidity. No indecision.

"Tomorrow?" he pressed.

"Or the next day, if we can't arrange the special license by morning."

Delighted, wary, he dared a tentative smile.

"I'm not an easy man," he pointed out, his voice rough with pent-up emotion.

She chortled. "So I've gathered!"

"You'll have trouble putting up with me."

"I will." She leaned closer and gibed, "Daily."

"I'm driven, passionate about my work. You might not

see me for days—or nights—on end. I rant and rave. I'm spoiled and set in my routines."

"You're absolutely correct: You can be a beast."

He had the distinct impression that she was laughing at him. "I'm not joking, *bella*. I'm not like anyone you've ever met. In the best of circumstances, I'm difficult to tolerate. When I'm painting, or in a mood, well—"

"I'll try not to forget your eccentricities."

"What about your father?"

"What about him?"

"He won't be happy."

"I don't imagine he will." She gave an unreadable chuckle.

"He doesn't like me."

"Well, he's not the one marrying you, is he?"

"He'll cut you off. Personally and financially. He might never speak to you again."

"His loss," she airily remarked, then she laid her wrist to her brow and wailed sarcastically, "I'll never see Charlotte, either. Oh, woe is me!"

"You say that now but—"

She swung around and planted her feet on the floor, jabbing a finger at his chest. "If you're endeavoring to scare me off, Gabriel Cristofore, you can't. So stop trying."

He studied her appraisingly, then nodded. "I love you."

"Of course you do."

"I always have."

"If I'd ever believed otherwise, I wouldn't be here."

She was so confident, and her optimism was contagious. Perhaps he was a fool, and he'd end up crushed, brokenhearted, and alone, but her sanguinity conferred hope. He simply wanted what she was offering too much to toss it away.

Abashed, rueful, he grumbled, "I'm not much of a catch."

Her ravishing smile lit up the room. "Well, I am."

"I know."

"I have many redeeming qualities."

"You certainly do."

"They complement yours."

"Aye."

"I'm placid while you're gregarious, serene while you're charismatic, unruffled while you're obsessive."

"Composed to strident."

"Tranquil to tempestuous."

"Don't forget beautiful," he added. "And sexy."

"I'm filthy rich, too."

"Exactly my type!" He assessed her fantastic anatomy, her exquisite countenance, and she glowed under his ardent examination. "You're everything I've ever wanted. And so much more."

"Lucky. You."

She opened her arms and welcomed him home.

Love Lessons
CHERYL HOLT

A resolute spinster at twenty-five, Abigail Weston is nonetheless determined to see her cherished younger sister wed to a man of Quality. But Abigail's lack of experience with the opposite sex means that she cannot allay her sister's fears about the marriage bed—unless she takes bold steps to learn what the intimacy between a man and a woman entails. Yet the one man in London qualified to teach her awakens temptation Abigail never anticipated—to experience each whispered pleasure for herself...

"Ms. Holt's fine tale is carefully woven and crafted, rich in every detail and reminiscent of the genre's masters...this book is a must!"
—*Romantic Times* ON MY ONLY LOVE

"Vibrant characters and eventful plotting kept me involved from page one. Cheryl Holt is a fresh new voice in historical romance that is truly delightful. Bravo!"
—*Affaire de Coeur* ON MY ONLY LOVE

*Available wherever books are sold
from St. Martin's Paperbacks*

TEMPT ME
TWICE

BARBARA
DAWSON
SMITH

New York Times Bestselling Author of
ROMANCING THE ROGUE

A rogue shrouded in mystery, Lord Gabriel Kenyon returns from abroad to find himself guardian of Kate Talisford, the girl he had betrayed four years earlier. Now sworn to protect her, he fights his attraction to the spirited young woman. Although Kate wants nothing to do with the scoundrel who had once scorned her, Gabriel is the only man who can help her recover a priceless artifact stolen from her late father. On a quest to outwit a murderous villain, she soon discovers her true adventure lies with Gabriel himself, a seducer whose tempting embrace offers an irresistible challenge—to uncover his secrets and claim his heart forever...

"Barbara Dawson Smith is wonderful!"
— *Affaire de Coeur*

"Barbara Dawson Smith makes magic."
— *Romantic Times*

*Available wherever books are sold
from St. Martin's Paperbacks*